Frontline

DR HILARY JONES

Frontline

WELBECK

Published in 2021 by Welbeck Fiction Limited, part of Welbeck Publishing Group
20 Mortimer Street London W1T 3JW

Copyright © Hilary Jones, 2021

The moral right of the author has been asserted.

A CIP catalogue record for this book is available from the British Library

Hardback ISBN: 978-1-78739-752-1

Trade paperback ISBN: 978-1-78739-753-8

Ebook ISBN: 978-1-78739-626-5

Printed and bound by CPI Group (UK) Ltd, Croydon, CR0 4YY

10 9 8 7 6 5 4 3 2 1

To all those who save lives on the frontline during pandemics and wars.
We owe you.

IN ARDUIS FIDELIS

Motto of the Royal Army Medical Corps

Never for them the awful joy
  That sets the soldier's breast afire,
The lust to conquer and destroy,
  The blazing passion, mad desire;
Spurred by no glory to be won,
  Not warmed by battle's heated breath,
Only a sad task to be done,
  They do their duty — true till death.

Denied the pomp and pride of war,
  The peril alone is theirs to share;
Yet, self and safety flung afar,
  They do what mortal men may dare.
Steadfast in their Christ-given faith,
  All for others, if need, they give;
Faithful in danger, true till death,
  They die that fellow-men may live.

'C. S. B.', *June 1916*

PART ONE

FEVER AND FOES

1914–1915

Prologue

Chiswick, 1910

Dr Bradstock took one look at Evie in that dark, dismal bedroom and knew without doubt that the next person to attend her would be the priest to administer the last rites.

It had all been so perfect three days earlier.

The baby was anticipated with such excitement and joy. Evie and Robbie were buoyant and happy, and a new baby brother or sister was all their boys were able to talk about. Once Evie went into labour, the boys were kept well out of the way. Time, for the boys, passed slowly.

Ten-year-old William Burnett was both bored and on edge at the same time. In truth, he did not really know how to feel. There was a tension about the house that was strange and heavy. He was used to his older brother, Jack, poking fun at him or trying to wrestle with him when he was least expecting it. More disturbing to Will was his dad, who had been pacing the floor for hours without saying a word.

His mum was still upstairs with Mrs Collier and to Will it seemed like an age since she had been excitedly summoned from the other side of Turnham Green to come and help deliver the baby. There are only so many battles you can fight with a box of tin soldiers and Jack kept knocking them

3

down as soon as Will had them standing in position, about to launch an attack.

A few days earlier Evie and Robbie had walked the boys out to Strand-on-the-Green, slowly because of Evie's condition. Will had been entranced by the bustling activity on the river: the barges with their cargoes of coal and limestone; the skiffs and rowboats with elegantly dressed ladies reclining on cushions at the back; and last, but certainly not least, the magnificent paddleboat *Corinthe*, packed from bow to stern with all sorts of handsome people enjoying a party in the sun.

They'd ambled lazily along the towpath, passing the City Barge pub where loud groups of revellers were swilling beer from large pewter mugs. When Evie began to feel uncomfortable, they sat down on a wooden bench by the side of the river and fed the ducks with the dried crusts of bread she had thoughtfully brought with her.

Will was always keen for every duck to receive its fair share. He went to great lengths to ensure an even division of the contents of his paper bag. Sympathising with the smallest ducklings, constantly shoved out of the way and pushed under the water by the others, he hurled the crusts this way and that — feinting and dodging to throw the bigger, fatter ones off the scent. Only when he was sure that each little mallard had been fed did he sit back down. Evie gently took his hand in hers.

'Look at that brother of yours, Will,' she said. 'My attention is diverted for a few seconds and there he is, trousers rolled up with his shoes and socks off, paddling in the river in all that mud.'

'Can I go down there too, Dad?' Will asked, but Robbie was not at all keen and pulled a face.

'That water, young Will, is toxic. I should know from working at the docks. I wouldn't let a dog go in there.'

'But Jack is in there and he's not a dog!'

'That's very true. He's not even as obedient as a dog. But he'll smell like one soon enough.' Robbie shook his head. 'If I'd seen him slipping away I'd have tied him to that willow tree over there and slapped his face with a wet fish.'

This made Will giggle.

'Jack!' Robbie shouted. 'Come back up here now, it's time to make a move!'

Robbie shouted again, but this time Jack did not have to pretend not to hear him because the sound of the London and South Western Railway train coming across Kew Railway Bridge drowned everything else out. Will watched in awe as the carriages rattled over the five-latticed girder structure. He idly wondered what would happen if the bridge collapsed and fell on the little ferryboat that was taking a group of people from the Richmond side of the river to the opposite bank. As the sound of the train finally disappeared into the distance and the ferryboat safely reached the shore, Robbie stood and suggested again that it was time to get back. But as Evie started to stand up, she cried out in surprise.

'Oh goodness!' she yelped. 'I think my waters have broken.'

Will didn't realise what she meant at first. When he heard the word 'waters' he thought it must be something to do with the river, but he knew that waters couldn't break. What he didn't know, however, was why his mum's skirt was suddenly soaking wet when she had not been anywhere near the river.

'The baby is telling me it wants to come out soon, Will, don't worry.' His dad added that they would have to get back home smartish and take the quieter route through the alleyway rather than the towpath, to spare Evie's blushes. Jack took a while to catch up and Robbie had had to threaten to put him to bed early with no supper unless he hurried up, which did the trick.

'Dad said you're a dirty dog,' teased Will, laughing. 'Get away from me with your stinky clothes.'

'Little Mr Goody Two-Shoes. Mustn't get his clothes dirty, must he, Mummy?' shot back Jack.

Their father had to pull them apart and walk between them all the way home after that.

Despite Evie's self-consciousness about her wet skirt, they got home an hour and a half later without further trouble. Evie went straight upstairs to the cramped little bedroom at the back of the house. By now, the cramping discomfort in her lower belly was getting stronger and occurring more frequently.

'You better call Mrs Collier,' she told Robbie. 'The baby is coming.'

Mrs Janet Collier, a birth attendant with no formal quali-fications but plenty of experience, duly arrived at 368 Chiswick High Road forty-five minutes later with her precious little bag of obstetric tricks.

*

That was eighteen hours ago and now the fun of the previous day's excursion was well and truly forgotten. The boys finally fell asleep around ten o'clock, Jack with the family cat curled at the foot of his bed and Will with his toy bear tucked tightly under his pillow.

Robbie would not allow himself to relax and only snatched an hour or two's fitful sleep in his favourite saggy old armchair in the sitting room.

Why was it taking so long? he wondered. Evie's previous

two deliveries had been relatively straightforward. Although, he reminded himself, it was easy for him to say that. He would never know what childbirth felt like.

Mrs Collier had come downstairs a couple of times to utter the usual platitudes designed to calm a fretful husband, but Robbie felt anything but calm.

'The contractions are good and strong, that's for sure,' did not settle his mounting anxiety. Then, at four a.m., 'It's just taking a little longer than usual,' was delivered in a noticeably less certain tone, which magnified his increasing worries. Surely, thought Robbie, a third baby is delivered more quickly than previous ones? He was no midwife but by the age of thirty he knew that labour was usually shorter, not longer, with each subsequent pregnancy. He could not help thinking that all might not be well.

By seven a.m. no further progress had been made and both boys were up having some breakfast and were back to their normal bickering. Mrs Collier came down the stairs looking unaccustomedly concerned and hesitant.

'Robbie,' she said, touching his forearm, 'I don't want you to be alarmed but it's taking longer than I thought and I'm going to need some help with this one.'

'We can't afford a doctor, Mrs Collier, you know that.'

'I know that. I'm thinking of Kirsty Albright in Chesterfield Road. I'm not a beginner by any means in this line of work but she is a member of the Midwives Institute and has had all the compulsory professional training a midwife is encouraged to have these days. She'll know what to do next.'

'I'm not sure . . .'

'You don't have a choice, Robbie,' she said more firmly. 'Evie needs urgent help now. I've worked with Kirsty before. The powers that be frown on her associating with the likes of a mere mortal like me, unqualified as they consider I am, but apart from being a bit la-di-da and from a more well-to-do part of Chiswick, she knows that not everyone can afford medical help and she is always supportive of the local community.'

Soon, Robbie was out of the door, sprinting to Chesterfield Road on the other side of the village, clutching a scrap of paper torn hastily from the Middlesex *Independent* newspaper with the vital address on it.

Mrs Collier was flummoxed. Evie was not a high-risk patient. The contractions were frequent and strong. The baby's head was engaged within the pelvis. Yet each time she examined Evie her cervix was not yet fully dilated and now Evie was exhausted and becoming desperate.

Downstairs, fed up and frustrated at having to occupy themselves for so long, the two boys had begun to bicker and squabble, a situation only briefly interrupted when their father fled without explanation. Mrs Collier, despite being a stranger to them, put a stop to the bickering, and while Jack tried to see how many spinning tops he could keep going at any one time, Will took his treasured Meccano set out of the dresser and attempted to build his own version of Kew Railway Bridge.

Half an hour later, Robbie burst in followed by a breathless and flushed Kirsty Albright who immediately rushed upstairs to be brought up to date by Mrs Collier. The midwife listened carefully to all she was told and then spent a few minutes patiently talking to Evie and getting to know and reassure her as best she could.

'Thank you so much for coming, Miss Albright,' Evie managed to say between contractions. 'I don't know how we will manage to reward you —'

She was cut short by the midwife as she palpated the contours of Evie's baby and said, 'You don't need to worry about that. All that's important right now is that this wee thing in here is delivered safely and soon.'

'Oh, I couldn't agree more. I'm so tired, I don't mind telling you.'

'Well, if I have anything to do with it, Evie, we will have your baby out before too long.'

Struggle as they might, however, the two birth assistants, each with their own considerable level of expertise, failed to accelerate the delivery. They recorded the strength and duration of the uterine contractions. They listened carefully to the baby's heartbeat through the aluminium foetal stethoscope that looked like a smaller version of an ear trumpet. They checked the degree of cervical dilatation at the neck of Evie's womb and carried out a manual sweep of the amniotic membranes to encourage the next stage of labour. Yet by four p.m., after twenty-four hours of natural labour, Kirsty Albright made the decision to apply forceps to the baby's head and help things along. She was one of the few midwives in the whole of London who had any experience with them, and if ever a case warranted their judicious application, it was this one.

She succeeded, with a little difficulty initially, and with a whoosh of fluid a beautifully healthy and pink baby girl was delivered. Almost inevitably, there were a few lacerations to the vaginal walls and lip of the cervix. Kirsty Albright clamped the umbilical cord and cut it. She then handed the wriggling and crying little mite to Mrs Collier at the other end of the bed, who gently wiped away the soft coating of vernix from the baby's skin and happily announced to Evie that she now had the daughter for which she had been hoping and praying.

By now, Evie was crying with happiness and relief, all the pain and anguish of the previous day for the moment forgotten. Even the baby's increasingly vigorous crying was beautiful to behold. Within seconds of hearing that welcome sound, Robbie was bounding up the stairs, kissing Evie's forehead, gripping her hand and grabbing the baby from Mrs Collier's arms and blinking down in awe at this wonderful creation before him.

'She's gorgeous, Evie. The most beautiful baby girl I've ever seen. Here, take her.'

'She's just what we'd hoped for, Robbie.'

'All our dreams come true.'

As tears fell all around, Jack, swiftly followed by Will and the family cat, piled into the room and jostled to find as close a position as possible to the newborn treasure, making the little bedroom very cramped.

'She's perfect,' said Miss Albright, checking the baby over thoroughly and feeling relieved that her earlier, delicate work was now done. The forceps had barely made a mark on the newborn's head. 'Any name in mind?'

'Kitty,' answered Evie without hesitation. 'She's Kitty, isn't she, Robbie? Named after my grandmother.'

'Her or the cat that's just followed the boys in,' joked Robbie, 'whichever you think is most important.'

'So, it's Kitty either way then,' said Mrs Collier, smiling, 'though this is no place for animals. We also need to finish off and tidy up a bit here, gentlemen, so if you wouldn't mind . . .?'

Robbie took the boys downstairs again and Evie could hear them squealing with excitement in the living room.

In the bedroom, the placenta took an age to come free and Miss Albright noticed with concern it looked fragmentary and torn in places. The bleeding also took an hour or two to settle down to a trickle. Everything about this birth had been complicated, she thought.

*

Mrs Collier was already waiting with the front door open when Miss Albright arrived again three days later.

'I'm so sorry to call upon you again,' she said.

'I know you wouldn't have done unless you were worried.'

'Come upstairs.'

As the qualified midwife walked through the living room the boys were reading comics and had a large half-completed jigsaw puzzle spread out across the floor. Robbie, however, looked dead on his feet.

'She's not right, Miss Albright,' he said. 'She is so weak and tired. She sleeps a lot, which is understandable, but sometimes when she's talking she doesn't make much sense. I pray you can help.'

The midwife could see that this man was worried sick about his beloved wife.

In the bedroom, Kitty lay peacefully in her wooden rocker cot which Robbie had lovingly made in advance. She was fast asleep and content. Evie, on the other hand, looked like a ghost, pale and still, with her face turned towards the door as the midwives came in. Her sunken eyes, once bright blue and sparkling, were now glazed over and unfocused.

Kirsty Albright knew what she was dealing with. Puerperal sepsis. The scourge of so many new mothers. A high proportion of those who experienced it would die, especially in families from poorer backgrounds like this one.

'Hello, Evie,' she whispered as she drew up a chair.

Recognition was delayed but it came to Evie eventually.

'Miss Albright. It's good of you to come.' She added, earnestly, 'Do you know what's wrong with me? I have no energy. And I can't stay awake to feed Kitty properly. I'm so worried. And the pain . . .'

Miss Albright held Evie's hand and mopped her brow with a cool flannel.

'You have an infection, Evie, but we will do everything in our power to help you get over it.'

Miss Albright asked Mrs Collier about how Evie had been since she was last at the house. The older woman gave information methodically and chronologically without referring to notes of any kind. Evie had slept initially after the birth but woke up with abdominal pain a few hours later. Despite that, she had put the baby to her breast and made sure that Kitty correctly latched on. Then she had dozed, but after the second feed she could not shake off a splitting headache and had felt hot and cold all over. She had tried putting Kitty to her breast once again but had felt weak and had no appetite. That's when Robbie had called Mrs Collier back again.

Once she arrived, she had taken every hygiene precaution she could, applying poultices and changing dressings. She had carried out all the normal nursing procedures but had eventually realised she was losing the battle.

The younger midwife listened attentively and considered the circumstances as she knew them. This had been a prolonged, partly obstructed labour. There had been difficulties applying forceps and some tears to the genital tract. There had been a ragged, possibly incomplete placenta and a greater than normal amount of bleeding postpartum.

Opening her case, she withdrew her tools of the trade and

checked Evie's temperature. 103°. The mercury never lied. Her patient's eyes had dark shadows beneath them and her skin was parched and wrinkled, both signs of dehydration. The conjunctiva was abnormally pale beneath the lower eyelids, too, a reliable sign of anaemia. Her pulse rate was rapid and thready; the midwife counted it out at 120 beats per minute on her trusty Elgin fob watch. Finally, she turned back the sheets to examine Evie thoroughly.

She was ill-prepared for what she saw.

She had certainly seen a number of cases of childbed fever before but none at this advanced stage and none so visibly evident. Evie's lower abdomen was swollen and bloated and far too tender to be touched. Lower down, there was the unmistakable odour of infection and her feet were swollen and dusky blue. On her chest and arms, and also on her back when she was turned, there were scattered purple-red bruises under the skin that did not blanch when pressed as allergic spots do.

How had this horrific condition marched on so quickly? the midwife wondered. Once she had confirmed the diagnosis and the dismal prognosis she persuaded Robbie that attendance by a doctor was now imperative. By this time, however, Robbie himself was almost out of his mind with worry. Aunt Clara had collected Jack and Will to take them out for a walk, along with the baby and a supply of milk from the breast bank, so that had been one less thing to worry about for the time being. But paying for a doctor at a full sixpence for a visit was financially impossible.

'There is a community fund available for this very purpose, Robbie,' Miss Albright insisted, 'and a local almoner to administer it appropriately.'

Any remaining worries about the money were quashed.

Evie was the love of his life and he was utterly devoted to her. Whatever needed to be done had to be done.

The doctor was summoned at once and arrived within the hour.

Evie now knew the worst was coming, too. Despite the doctor's gentle manner and best attempts at optimism, she understood the awful truth that the two boys she loved with all her heart and the baby girl she had finally brought into the world were going to grow up without her. It was too much to bear. Then there was Robbie. The man she adored. A wonderful father. A doting husband. At this realisation, her spirit broke and she struggled to stay conscious.

She lay there with Robbie's handsome face close to hers, his brow knotted with concern and tears streaming down his cheeks.

'Look after them all for me, Robbie,' she whispered. 'Love them forever, as much as I will love you forever.'

Then, somehow, as if all her remaining energy was summoned for one last act, she raised her hand to his face and ran her fingers softly across his lips as he tenderly kissed them.

When he finally placed her hand back down on the bed by her side, he knew she was gone.

In his agony, he didn't notice the small figure standing in the doorway, blinking and looking on uncomprehendingly. His youngest son. Will had just witnessed his dear and beloved mother die in her bed, because she had had a baby and developed an infection. This moment would stay with Will forever.

1

Bishop's Cleeve, Cheltenham, August 1914

Arthur Tustin-Pennington gazed through the tall sash windows of the master bedroom on the first floor of Woodmancote House. At the back of the house, on the far side of the manicured lawns and landscaped garden, backlit by the bright sunshine of a perfect August day, stood the majestic coastal redwood that Grace had climbed to the top of at the age of seven. Sequoia sempervirens was one of the tallest species of tree on Earth and his youngest daughter had scaled it effortlessly and fearlessly, sparing no thought whatsoever for the dangers or possible consequences.

He remembered hearing her before he saw her, her whoop of delight. 'What's she up to now?' he'd said to Dorothy, his wife, before he strode out into the garden on his crutches. She had asked if she could spend the morning with Clive, the head gardener, and taking an interest in nature was a reasonable enough pursuit for a girl, even in her mother's eyes, who frequently despaired of her boyishness. 'Grace?' he shouted. 'Grace?' but there was no sign of her, just the sound of a giggle being suppressed, and then not being suppressed anymore, becoming the joyous laughter he recognised so well. He let his eyes follow the sound of it, up the gnarled trunk in golden red, where, high among the branches, in one of the summer dresses that Dorothy insisted she wear, Grace was waving down at him.

Dorothy had been apoplectic. What was Grace thinking? She could have fallen and been killed. Where was Clive? How could Arthur be so cavalier a father as to allow a seven-year-old girl to expose herself to such peril? The row that had ensued was the latest in a catalogue of similar parental arguments about Grace's impulsive and impetuous behaviour.

Arthur smiled now at the recollection of it. Grace had been perplexed at the scale of her mother's reaction. What was all the fuss about? It was just a tree. She had climbed most of the others on the estate and her mother didn't even know. Besides, it was a relatively easy one. Lateral boughs every few feet and fronds and needles reaching out like cupped hands to catch her and cushion her fall if she slipped. But she would not. She never had. Sure of foot, strong and lithe, she found it almost as easy as climbing the grand oak staircase inside.

As Dorothy had tutted and cursed about the hazards and repercussions of this apparently daredevil feat, Grace had blinked back and absorbed the tirade.

Her mother was forever fretting and worrying about such little things. She worried about the children going out in the rain, lest they catch pneumonia. She worried about them wearing insufficient clothes in the winter, swimming unattended in the lake at the bottom of the hill, not getting enough sleep, having dirty fingernails or greasy hair. She had forbidden them from riding the horses without the grooms present and tried to limit the time they spent playing tennis on the lawn or playing football in the paddock for fear of injury. Dorothy was a born worrier, a woman full of anxieties and complexes, who found things to agonise over even when no risk was apparent. Arthur had once confided in Grace after yet another stern telling off that if Dorothy was not worrying about something, she would more than likely become agitated and fretful about that in itself. She would convince herself that there might be something that she had missed and imagine some impending doom about to befall the entire family. There were seven children and that was a lot to worry about.

The boys had become accustomed to their mother's foibles and fussy ways and generally did whatever they wanted while pretending to be cautious and careful in her presence. The activities they confessed to enjoying were certainly at odds with the truth. But boys would be boys of course and as far as Dorothy was concerned they were, within reason, much more able than the girls to fend for themselves.

Girls were the gentler, weaker sex. Their behaviour, comportment and roles in life were expected to be poles apart from that of the boys. Dorothy had been brought up in a manner completely separate to that of her brothers. She had not been permitted to play sport, to wear casual clothes, to consort or compete with members of the opposite sex. This mindset was ingrained in her, this unshakeable conviction about how her daughters could conduct their lives.

As far as her eldest daughter Amy was concerned, it was not an issue. Three years older than Grace, Amy was happiest wearing her pretty frocks, experimenting with different hairstyles and playing with her dolls. But from the moment Grace could stand and totter, she was adventurous and restless, on one occasion having to be rescued from falling into the roaring log fire in the living room when the grown-ups had taken their eyes off her for just an instant. Not interested in the usual girls' things, she dressed like a boy, played like a boy, and in most sports either competed on equal terms with her brothers or surpassed them in athletic ability.

Her mother simply could not understand why Grace would harangue Douglas the gamekeeper into letting her drive the car around the grounds and tinker with the mechanics of its engine.

While Dorothy worried about her difficult and disobedient daughter, Arthur watched her development and accomplishments with growing interest and admiration. Grace was an explorer, a risk-taker, an intriguing and enchanting gamine. She was bright and intelligent, curious and determined. She was not brash and loud, full of swaggering bravado like her brothers, but quietly efficient, confident and capable. She was also, her father noted, very feminine at the same time. She moved as her name suggested, light on her feet, supple yet strong. Her smile lit up a room and she giggled and laughed easily with the boys. Tease her though they might, she was more than an intellectual match for any of them.

Now, as Arthur looked at the giant redwood, he could still picture her waving her red silk neckerchief at the house from her precarious perch 120 feet up.

Grace was simply extraordinary. Unstoppable, uninhibited, charismatic Grace. Grace the rebel.

Arthur would never openly admit that she was his favourite of the seven children. And now she was leaving him, doing what he had hoped none of his children would ever do.

*

He had known war himself. The Boer War, cruel and bloody, and all for the greedy pursuit of gold and diamonds. He had held his friend Alfred's hand, while a field doctor did his best to wrap a bandage around his bullet-shattered shoulder. There had been very few nurses around and so he'd stayed there himself, listening to the screams, knowing for the first time what a bullet did to a man, what an awful thing it was to pull a trigger. Alfred had had his arm amputated, but it had made no difference. The rot had set in. The conditions weren't sanitary and there were not enough doctors and nurses. He died in agony. Arthur was sure that could have been avoided.

Months later, how relieved he had been to head back home. The voyage from Eastern Transvaal was long and uncomfortable and he couldn't wait to get back to his beloved estate in rural Gloucestershire where he could concentrate once again on running the farm, the mill and his new and exciting industrial enterprises. It had been months since he'd seen the children and he had missed the comfort, care and homely domesticity of his loving wife.

On the troopship which had brought him from the Cape the news of Queen Victoria's passing had been announced. It was the end of an era.

It was also the end of his service in the British Army. And that of his family's. No son of his would ever go to Sandhurst, join the military and fight as an officer for the British Army like him. That was his solemn promise.

He had nearly suffered the same fate as Alfred. The lancinating pain he felt in his phantom limb as the vessel pitched and rolled did nothing to lift his spirits, the result of a Boer marksman's bullet fired at Stormberg one year earlier, where the British were defeated. The missile had shattered his femur, and the tissue damage and resulting infection had left the surgeon with no alternative but to amputate. The convalescence had been stormy and he owed a debt of gratitude to the army blacksmith who'd fashioned an excellent copy of Dubois L Parmalee's original prosthetic limb creation of 1863. The New York inventor's socket had been devised to attach to the residual limb by atmospheric pressure and he had used India rubber to make the connection of limb to prothesis more comfortable and adjustable. It was by no means perfect, but it was a significant improvement on any previous type of artificial leg and at least it allowed the major to get about independently and attend to the administrative duties the Army still expected him to fulfil before his discharge. He refused to use a wheelchair, and got around with crutches. His triceps were thicker than they had ever been.

The whole campaign in South Africa had upset and disturbed him. So much so that it had forced him to confront his entire philosophy on life. He saw now how immoral the initial annexation of Witwatersrand had been, the British grasping for the lucrative gold and diamond mines recently discovered there. The British Army, almost unchanged since the days of Wellington half a century before, proved itself overconfident, under-prepared and unable to adapt to the dry and barren terrains of Natal and the Transvaal. It had been no place for cumbersome artillery units nor the complacent upper-class officers who'd spent far too long mixing in social circles and far too little time in military training.

Had any of the generals been prepared to adopt the mounted infantry tactics advocated by enlightened soldiers such as Canadian Lieutenant Colonel George Denison, whom Arthur much admired, the Army might well have had more success, but entrenched personal interests had prevented any meaningful or major reforms.

And so 22,000 men, regulars and volunteers alike from

Britain, New Zealand, Canada and India, had died; 75,000 men incapacitated by disease had been repatriated; and 23,000 like Arthur himself had returned home wounded or crippled.

He was a soldier and a military man at heart, but he passionately believed in fighting for peace, justice and preservation of the land and its people above all else. That is why he had vehemently opposed the scorched-earth policy to which the Army had resorted. The mistreatment and death of 26,000 women and children in concentration camps sickened him to the stomach. The mental images of the men under his command who had been unnecessarily killed or maimed would be forever seared on his memory.

As Portsmouth Harbour finally came into view and his new life in the bosom of his family beckoned, he reiterated the pact that he had formally made with himself.

He would never allow any son of his to go to war.

*

So far, he had managed that. No son of his had enlisted. As he thought about Grace now, he turned away from the window and dabbed at the tears running down his cheeks with his sleeve. He could not afford to let Dorothy know he was wrestling with contrasting emotions. It had been hard enough dealing with his wife's distress and despair at Grace's departure and he did not want to make matters worse.

She was barely sixteen. Mature beyond her years and every bit a woman, she was still his precious headstrong daughter. His paternal love screamed at him to protect her. But Arthur knew that love meant many different things, and that it also included giving the people you loved their freedom. While

Grace was just a little bird, vulnerable and dainty, her feathers were simply too bright, her spirit too wild and her song too sweet to be caged any longer.

Dorothy had broken down when they saw her off at the railway station in Cheltenham. 'Please don't go, Grace. I forbid you. I'm your mother, you must—' Arthur had put his free arm around her and said, 'Now, now, let her go. She'll do good work and come back home afterwards.'

'Yes, Mummy,' said Grace, kindly, though Arthur could hear her impatience. 'Please listen to Daddy. I'll be back before you know it.'

Wearing her bright-red military-style tunic top and long khaki skirt she had looked every part the proud nursing professional. Her silky chestnut hair cascaded down her back and across her shoulders, and she clutched the leather valise they had purchased for her as if she would never let it out of her sight. That one precious case held all her essential nursing equipment together with a few personal items she had carefully selected for her adventure. Arthur privately cursed the First Aid Nursing Yeomanry group for tempting her away from him. At the same time, he was immensely proud of her convictions and sheer gutsiness. It had never even crossed his mind that it would be a daughter, not a son, who would steadfastly defy his wishes.

He and Dorothy had tried hard enough to talk her out of the caper. But Grace had been utterly determined. Despite the many accolades she'd won both academically and other-wise at Cheltenham Ladies' College, she had left school as soon as she'd felt it had nothing further to offer her. She'd obtained her Nursing Association qualifications one year later. Then, making full use of her considerable horse-riding skills, she had joined the FANY and was now heading somewhere on the border of France and Belgium where the British Expeditionary Force had been sent to repel the invasion by the German aggressors.

The First Aid Nursing Yeomanry had been founded seven years ago as a first-aid link between field hospitals and wherever any fighting was and, as a Yeomanry regiment, its members were mounted on horseback. This aspect had appealed to Grace just as much as being able to rescue the wounded and giving first-aid treatment on the spot.

The lecture she had attended given by the two formidable women who ran the organisation, Grace McDougall and Lillian Franklin, had inspired her. After all, a single rider could reach a wounded soldier much faster than any horse-drawn ambulance. This was exactly the kind of adventure she craved.

Arthur would never forget his last sighting of her. He was proud, and he knew how vital her work would be. She would save lives — she would save limbs, he thought, as his left leg twinged. But, selfishly, he wanted her to stay. As the train had pulled slowly away from the platform her innocent heart-shaped face with its beautiful, wide cheekbones appeared at an open carriage window to blow them a kiss goodbye. Those sparkling green eyes and that sweet button nose. That broad generous smile and that flash of perfectly white teeth. It pulled on his heartstrings.

Though he was apprehensive, he didn't seriously consider that his beloved daughter could be in any great danger. According to his peers in the local community and in Westminster most people imagined the skirmish in Europe would be over by Christmas anyway.

2

Chiswick

Clara had rarely felt so low and conflicted, not since her husband Harold had died from pulmonary tuberculosis two years before Evie passed away. She knew what it was like to feel impotent against diseases like that and to witness the weight loss, the increasing breathlessness and the exhaustion in someone who was loved and who had once been so strong and vibrant. That had been devastating, but she had built a new life, going back to work in the school she had left upon getting married, and in her free time working hard to support her brother and the children. Here was an opportunity to become a surrogate mother to Kitty, still a babe-in-arms, and to Jack and Will, who needed her just as badly. She gave up her house nearby and moved in with them, sharing a bedroom with young Kitty in her cot.

Yet now, after she'd done her best to coax her brother from the depths of despair and the terrible possibility of him taking his own life, he had enlisted in the Army and seemed to be willing to offer up his life to the aggressive enemies in France.

*

Even as Evie's body lost its warmth, Robbie had been unable to accept her death, pleading with Dr Bradstock to do more to intervene, begging the vicar to summon help from God and the midwives to find some trick or device to revive her.

Eventually, they'd had to lead him downstairs on weak legs, his arms around their shoulders, where he had sat for days with neither food, drink or sleep to sustain him.

He became oblivious to the boys, incapable of talking to them, and so focused on his grief that the world around him had effectively ceased to exist. In the days and weeks that followed neither his mood nor his capacity to carry on with his life improved.

Clara knew all too well that such feelings could endure for weeks, months, even years. The initial disbelief, denial and anger are common, as is the longing and searching for the person who has gone. The pain is always there, especially on special occasions and on anniversaries, but, in most cases, it fades and is gradually dissipated with the passing of time. Those left behind slowly adjust and come to terms with the vacuum that remains inside their heart.

But Robbie was stuck fast with his grief. For him, the agony had never gone away, none of its acuteness assuaged by the support and love he had received from those around him – from his sister, his workmates or members of his church. Even his beloved boys and his beautiful newborn daughter had been unable to lift his gloom and melancholy.

Robbie had, to all intents and purposes, died along with his wife. And it seemed as if nothing and nobody could change that.

*

Previously a reliable and hard-working dockhand, a willing member of any team, Robbie returned to work a different man after three weeks. Surly and uncommunicative, sullen and absent-minded, he failed to complete the simplest of tasks and frequently made basic mistakes, including one time when he let a crate slip out of his hands to smash down onto the ground below him. The foreman, standing a metre away from where the wooden crate split open, screamed up at him that he had nearly killed him, that he would dock every penny of the damaged goods from his salary. Robbie nearly took another crate and slung it down towards him, but he bit his tongue and shouted down an apology.

'An apology wouldn't bring me back to life if you'd taken my head off with that thing, you useless piece of sh—'

Robbie walked back to the hold and continued offloading. The men around him considered him carefully. He was becoming a liability.

The dockyard had always been a rough place in which to work and fights were common. Robbie was formerly a natural peacemaker and a calming influence in inflammatory situations. Now he sought out disagreements.

So, it came as no surprise that after a third brawl in the warehouse started by Robbie he found himself in the foreman's office.

'It pains me to be the one to tell you this, Robbie,' Doug the foreman said. 'You've been a good worker here at Thames Ironworks and Ship Building for fourteen years. You've been reliable and popular with the lads.' He paused. 'I can't imagine what you've been through.'

Robbie looked at the floor, scuffing his feet, knowing full well what was coming.

'But it's been over three years. The bosses have had enough. I can't keep making excuses for you.'

He looked at him. But Robbie remained impassive and silent. A man whose spirit had deserted him.

'Your timekeeping. The mistakes. The disappearances and the fighting.'

Robbie looked up then, calm, defeated. 'You've done your best, Doug,' he said. 'I don't blame you.'

'These are the wages you're owed. You're paid up until today.'

Robbie took the thin brown envelope and tucked it into the pocket of his oily overalls. How far would that go to feed his children and buy them clothes?

The silence between them was only broken by the mechanical ticking of the clock on the wall.

'Get yourself some help, Robbie. You can't go on like this.'

'I don't want to go on like this either, Doug,' Robbie snapped, and then in a more subdued tone he added, 'To tell you the truth I don't really want to go on at all.'

Doug knew that this was not a turn of phrase but instead a matter-of-fact statement of desperation. But what could he do? He had 250 other men to look after and supervise. He could not be there for them all.

And so, leaving the foreman struggling to find any more words, Robbie slowly got up and left the room.

*

Clara, back permanently at the house in Chiswick and juggling the needs of a four-year-old girl and two teenage boys, only discovered the truth about Robbie's redundancy when he failed to leave home for work the next day.

'Are you not going to the docks today then, Robbie?' she quietly asked. When she received no reply, she went and sat next to him and asked him the same question again.

'Not today or any day,' he replied. 'They're finished with me, Clara. And I'm finished with them.'

She looked at him, inviting further explanation.

'Maybe I've just finished full stop.'

'Oh, Robbie, come on now, don't talk like that. The children need you; I need you. They need you to be their dad again. They love you. I can't do the things they would want their daddy to do.'

As he listened, he started to weep. Hunched over with his head in his hands, his shoulders shook with heavy sobs as the tears spilled down his cheeks. Clara drew near and put a comforting arm around him.

How often had he talked about the pointlessness of life? How often had she worried that she might hear that he had jumped from a bridge or fallen under a train? Worse still, that she would come home to find him pale and lifeless in his chair, a knife or razor on the stone floor by his side?

*

When Robbie found another way to flirt with death, when he enlisted in the Army and went off to war, he neither mentioned it nor discussed it. He left only a hastily scrawled handwritten note.

Clara took it from the envelope behind the clock on the mantlepiece and read it again.

Clara, war is upon us and men will need to fight and die.

I owe you everything for all the time and love you have heaped on Kitty and the boys and I know that you will look after them. You have been everything I could not be. I have lived with pain, it seems, forever. If God should send a bullet my way to end my existence, perhaps that would be best for everyone. Tell the children I love them so dearly anyway and that I am sorry. Far better for me to risk my life in conflict than some more deserving fellow with everything to live for. If I can do something for the common good, then perhaps I will feel peace.

Your loving brother, Robbie.

*

Since then, she had heard little from him. A brief note in December to say he was fighting with his Company somewhere called Neuve Chapelle and then a more official letter written by an officer called Drake to say he had been wounded but was recuperating in a field hospital behind the lines at Amiens.

Clara didn't know much about army life and war, only what she gleaned from the newspapers she read assiduously at the public library in Dukes Avenue. But she could only imagine how a man already so mentally traumatised and damaged could cope with the carnage and brutality of war.

She worried that almost certainly he could not.

3

Givry, 1914

Grace walked out of the front door of the Hotel Dauphin in Givry and onto the steps. She leaned back against the cold granite brickwork, closed her eyes and took a deep breath. She had never felt so tired. True, she had craved adventure and excitement, but she had never imagined it would turn out to be like this. From the moment she had arrived in Belgium, a country she knew little about, it had been a baptism of fire, and she had entered a physical and spiritual challenge that had tested every sinew and shred of resilience in her body. And so far, she hoped, she had risen to it.

Only three weeks ago her small group of nurses had travelled by train to Folkestone, happily sharing their carriage with a boisterous and buoyant cohort of men from the 1st Battalion of the Royal Berkshire Regiment.

On departure from Victoria Station, she had walked through the train to find her seat and in front of her she spotted another nurse in the FANY uniform being harangued by a bunch of leering, overexcited soldiers making loud and suggestive comments.

'How about sitting on this?' yelled one of them, pointing to his lap.

'How about sitting on this?' the nurse replied, holding

30

up her middle finger, whereupon all the other men fell about laughing.

Grace found herself laughing, too. She now had to run the same gauntlet, however, to get to her own carriage and as she followed the feisty nurse in front of her and approached the same group of men, she readied herself for similar treatment.

'Bet you've not seen a bayonet as big as mine!' said the same idiot, swigging from his hip flask.

'Penknife more like, I should think,' answered Grace, holding up her pinky and then swiftly tipping up his hip flask to spill liquor all down the man's shirt.

'What the hell!' he squawked, jumping up from his seat as the other fellows around him laughed uproariously.

'Calm down,' said the other nurse to the fool, winking at Grace as she did so. 'I'm sure it won't be the first time you've wet yourself.'

And with that, the two girls left the commotion behind them and moved two carriages further along where the atmosphere was altogether more relaxed.

They found their seats next to each other and made themselves comfortable.

'My name is Jenny. Jenny Jenks.'

'I'm Grace. And that was a masterclass in control. You're a girl after my own heart.'

'You weren't so bad yourself. Pouring a man's liquor down his front takes guts.'

'Yes, well. He deserved it.' She smiled.

As the two chatted, several more FANY nurses arrived, stowed their bags in the luggage racks above and took their seats.

A whistle blew outside, the steam engine chuffed and the train slowly moved forward before gathering speed.

Grace liked Jenny immediately. They discovered they had

a lot in common. Horses, of course, which is why they had both joined the Yeomanry nurses' group, but they also came from large families with agricultural and commercial interests. And, as seemed to be apparent, they both possessed looks and figures that attracted interest from members of the opposite sex.

Jenny explained that she was from Kent, near Canterbury, and Grace told her she was from Gloucestershire, near Cheltenham. 'My parents have a farm and a sawmill there on a big estate,' she said.

'Oh! My dad is a horse breeder,' said Jenny. 'He's been working flat out for the last few years, convinced the Army will need every horse they can get their hands on. He is obsessed with it.'

'How many horses does he have?'

'Around 700 at the last count. Hot bloods for speed and endurance for the cavalry and cold bloods for slow heavy work like pulling field guns and the like. Mules and donkeys as well.'

'We've got horses too,' said Grace, 'but nothing like as many as you. Sixty-two, to be precise, and I love every single one of them. From what you say it sounds like we should breed more.'

'You should. Dad just had to sell most of his stock through the compulsory horse mobilisation scheme. But I think he did all right out of it. He thinks we will need thousands. Tens of thousands. He's even got me trained up as a farrier.'

'A farrier?'

'You should see me with my hammer and anvil at the forge, nippers and clinchers in my hands.'

Grace giggled at the image. 'I'd like to! You must teach me. Do you ride yourself?'

'Since I was four, though it feels like I was born on a horse. I used to do dressage competitions and a bit of racing, but nothing lately. I got a bit side-tracked.'

'By what?'

Jenny paused, then smiled. 'I joined the circus.'

Grace laughed out loud. 'What were you doing in the circus?'

'Standing on a horse's back in a skin-tight glittery costume, riding around the ring and juggling ninepins at the same time.'

'That's amazing!'

'Well, it was for a while. But living out of a gypsy caravan wasn't much fun and my parents really didn't approve. Thought it was frivolous.'

'Nothing wrong with a bit of frivolity, surely?'

'Well, they wouldn't agree! So, I trained as a nurse in Tunbridge Wells. And here I am.'

As Grace filled Jenny in on her own enrolment in the profession, they paused to take stock of their surroundings and the army personnel sharing their carriage.

Neither young woman had ever seen such a fine body of men. Lean and tanned chaps in their twenties, each confidently believing he was equal to at least four Germans. 'How lucky are we?' one of them boasted. 'We'll be among the first there. Home for Christmas if we're lucky with medals on our chests.' Their eagerness and excitement was contagious and soon, despite the matron-in-chief's disapproval, the entire carriage was sharing stories, playing cards, laughing and joking.

'Another thing you should know about me,' said Jenny, watching the men.

'Yes?' said Grace.

'I've already got one of those waiting for me at home,' she smiled. 'Reggie. Though I'm not sure he'll be staying at home, with all this going on.'

'Tell me about him,' Grace said.

The time passed so quickly with their easy conversation that they found themselves arriving in Folkestone before they knew it. Later, when night fell, Grace and Jenny hunkered down on cushions on the deck of the ship taking them to France. There they compared notes on their nursing training and shared their apprehensions about the adventure they were both embarking upon.

*

The FANY had boarded three other trains before arriving in the early morning at a main dressing station about a mile from where the fighting was taking place in Givry.

Much to her surprise, Grace discovered that a small but elegant hotel long since vacated by its staff and guests had been requisitioned for the purpose of a hospital, and inside over one hundred sick and wounded soldiers lay on beds or floors awaiting treatment. Lengthy though the journey had been, there was no time to rest, and Grace was put straight to work. Upon arrival on the first morning of duty the matron quickly apprised the FANY of what was required. They'd relied until now on the services of a motley crew of Belgian doctors from both civilian and military backgrounds, local nurses, and volunteers and nuns from a nearby convent. Matron seemed more than relieved to be able to welcome a number of trained British nurses into the fold. She explained as best she could in the crowded canvas mess tent erected outside the hotel the nature and scale of the task they would be facing. Yet nothing she said adequately prepared them for what they witnessed in the next few days of their work.

It started on the first day with duties in the former hotel restaurant area. Grace, along with her colleagues, stripped off the mud-caked khaki uniforms of the injured men, cleaned them up thoroughly and made them comfortable. Most of these men's wounds were largely superficial. There were ankle sprains and back strains, torn muscles, septic fingers and sore blistered feet. Some strapping here, a suture there, and ice traction compression or a poultice were the order of the day. It was a never-ending task, but most of Grace's patients were subsequently examined by a doctor and sent straight back to their units. Grace was tired after her fifteen-hour shift but felt satisfied with her efforts and slept reasonably well.

During her training, Grace had been tutored to carry out all the routine duties of a general nurse on a dormitory-style hospital ward, such as tending to a patient's personal hygiene, renewing dressings, changing bedlinen, observing and making notes on the patient's vital signs and fluid balance, organising tests, taking blood pressure and administering medicines. The majority of the patients had been ill with infections such as gastroenteritis that caused diarrhoea and vomiting; pneumonia, with fever, coughing and breathlessness; and skin infections with redness, blisters and ulceration. Sprains, dislocations and fractures were the usual bread-and-butter: everyday challenges caused by mundane incidents such as falls or collisions. Serious and catastrophic trauma was irregular.

The second day started innocuously enough with Grace performing a routine ward round dishing out the pain relief (such as alcohol, morphine, cocaine and acetylsalicylic acid as directed by the doctors), reassuring the anxious, sympathising with the aggrieved and mobilising the incapacitated. Straight after lunch, however, she was urgently summoned into the ballroom to attend to an influx of soldiers all horribly injured and maimed. Casualties were being brought in while the shells still whizzed through the air and exploded ever nearer to the camp. Her matron had tried to warn them all about what to expect, but nothing could have prepared any of the women for the sheer noise of the bombardment, for the maelstrom of death and destruction that would whirl around them. Quickly assigned to a doctor, Grace was instructed to stick to his side like glue and carry out his orders to the letter. She was more than happy to do that. She had never seen such wounds, such grievously hurt men. All the initiative would have to come from him.

She learned fast. This soldier would need a compression bandage to stem further bleeding. That one a surgical debridement to remove macerated muscle tissue and prevent infection. The one over here with a piece of artillery shell in his stomach would need to be prepped for surgery. And the man next to him for an above-knee amputation. The one over here she was just to make comfortable. He could not be saved.

As she followed Dr Christian Williams around the room, a gentle man of about fifty, greying at the temples, with a weary and haggard-looking face, she felt a sense of hopelessness and inadequacy. Just one of these difficult cases would have kept the entire staff busy back at the infirmary in Bristol, but in front of them were countless numbers of brutalised men and a mere handful of experienced medical personnel to care for them. They worked fast but methodically, triaging and categorising patients in order of priority for treatment and dispensing doses of morphine wherever appropriate.

They worked through the night, only pausing for an hour or two's much-needed sleep when relieved by the nuns or volunteer local civilians.

On the morning of the third day, Grace was asked to assist in theatre and get scrubbed up. It was a day she would never forget. Fourteen amputations were performed that morning alone, the severed limbs thrown unceremoniously into a large wooden crate lined with a tarpaulin in the corner. Grace tried to avert her eyes from it. Pink and disarticulated, they resembled a collection of accessories you might expect to see in a doll-maker's spare parts cupboard. The surgical guillotine used for the amputations was employed for speed, as anaesthesia was not always reliable, and had been carefully cleansed of its blood and sterilised fourteen times by Grace. She would never entirely forget the sound of its descent in its track and the sharp crack of the bone through which it was slicing. Back home in Bristol, she'd had the regular theatre nurse's discipline of counting swabs and tidying instruments drummed into her. That day in Givry, her main priority was mopping up gallons of coagulated blood and sweeping up the spicules of bone strewn over the theatre floor.

Some of the seriously injured were just too sick to be moved. Any attempt to transfer them in their current state would be catastrophic. Most would die anyway from blood loss, shock or sepsis. Grace had been working flat out for thirty-six hours and was exhausted. She had been instructed to go and rest, but how could she desert these poor men with their terrible injuries and their wounds, so many of them disfiguring and life-threatening? She could not bring herself to walk away. Not while she had an ounce of energy and reserve still left in her body.

As she worked, she learned more about what had caused the damage to these men. The retreat from Mons, which had begun a fortnight earlier, had been a hasty and dramatic affair. Since then, it had been one headlong rush to flee before a ruthless and advancing enemy. Trench after trench was evacuated and many of the severely injured had to be left behind. What became of them, Grace could only imagine. Whether they would fare better as prisoners of war or be abandoned and neglected to die, she could only guess. It pained her deeply.

*

Grace was redeployed from one casualty clearing station to the next, sometimes only spending a few days in each at a time. The nurses did their best to make up for what they lacked in basic equipment with compassion and skill, but providing medical treatment on the hoof was proving to be increasingly inadequate. Grace and her colleagues were forever arriving, setting up, working, packing up and moving on. It was tiring and demoralising, and her colleagues would frequently burst into tears the moment they were away from their patients and could drop their guard. But they never questioned that there was a better way to be operating, and never contemplated throwing in the towel. If anything, the terrible state of the men they were caring for drove them to even greater efforts.

Now, standing there on the steps of the hastily adapted hotel, she found it impossible to stop dreadful images of the scenes she had already witnessed from flashing through her mind. It was pitiful to see so many broken, tired, hungry, unshaven, filthy men staggering in or brought in on stretchers. Many had walked endlessly for miles, their uncomfortable boots falling apart and their feet bruised and bleeding from the effort. Many had discarded their boots altogether and had wrapped puttees around their feet or were simply walking barefoot or in their socks. Several had thrown away their greatcoats in the melee or were shirtless. They were asleep on their feet, abjectly miserable and barely able to talk.

The roads and thoroughfares were a mess, too. The heat was stifling and there was no semblance of order or organisation anywhere. Refugees wandered about, having run from the advancing German Army with whatever meagre possessions they could muster, carried in all kinds of contraptions: wheelbarrows, prams, handcarts and even wooden trailers drawn by cattle or dogs. They often begged for food, which was not often available, and Grace feared for the dishevelled and starving children and the elderly as they silently ghosted by. Soldiers who had not been able to march any further arrived on horses' lumbers and handcarts and often had to be helped to the ground they had so little strength. And yet those soldiers were expected to move on after the briefest of respites. Grace was shocked at how quickly a tough, highly trained body of fighting men had been so reduced. Their injuries were awful enough, but the general poor state of the troops was striking.

Grace's reverie was interrupted by a scream from a first-floor window. Another limb amputation being performed.

How many had she seen or assisted with? Hundreds, now. And with no letting up. Half the problem appeared to be the delay in getting the wounded to the hospital in time. The horse-drawn ambulances did their best to ferry the men, and every minute counted, but so many lives had been lost to the blue pus infection that seemed to contaminate and complicate the majority of deep wounds. No matter how hard Grace toiled away at cleaning the macerated and torn tissues with Lysol antiseptic, infection was forever a threat. Gas gangrene was a hideous and ghastly condition. At least twenty of the soldiers in the hotel in which she stood were showing the classic signs. First, a deep penetrating wound with widespread destruction of muscle tissue or bone by shrapnel or bullets. Then clostridium, the common soil-borne bacteria, would get into the wound, where it thrived in the oxygen-starved necrotic flesh. Poisonous toxins produced by the germs would gather and invade the body, producing gas in the muscle planes and fascia which could be clearly felt with light pressure from an examining hand. The sound and sensation was akin to a dense sodden sponge being squeezed dry. Crepitus, it was called. And it crept. Unless the limb or infected tissue was urgently removed, with all organisms eradicated, it was only a matter of time before septic shock and death would inevitably follow. Grace shivered at the thought of it.

Since arriving, she had used every bit of nursing knowledge at her disposal and although she herself would never be satisfied with her efforts she had undoubtedly saved many lives. But no matter what she did, many men could not be saved, and this tormented her. Maybe if she had changed the dressings a little more often? If she had nursed the patient in a different position? If she had insisted on a blood transfusion for this man rather than another? Could she have saved more? Could she have plucked this one or that one from the jaws of death? Could she even have given more in the way of succour and comfort to the younger ones who, petrified and alone, were crying for their mothers? She could not shake off the questions but nor could she waste her concentration on them. There was too much to do.

Thankfully, there were plenty of injuries that didn't go this way. Bullets that had passed clean through a wrist, elbow or shoulder. Cautery, anti-sepsis and splinting would often suffice. Flesh wounds and other superficial lacerations frequently mended themselves. Among the worst casualties, however, were the abdominal injuries, head wounds and facial impacts. Projectiles through the gut posed a particular problem. There was no alternative but to operate. It had to be done to prevent the inevitable peritonitis that would result from the coliform bacteria and waste inside the intestine poisoning the rest of the body. And with chloroform in short supply for anaesthesia it was a logistical nightmare. How can one console a man with his manhood shot away? The patient she saw in that state could not be restrained or pacified even with morphine. He just kept pulling his bedcovers away and looking at the gaping hole and the missing parts. It was pitiful. He saw no purpose in staying alive and had begged to be left to die. The men in adjacent beds considered themselves lucky in comparison.

*

At one of the advanced dressing stations behind the lines at Givry she attended a French cavalry officer who had been mortally wounded in a mounted attack in the German lines near Maroilles. The mounted Uhlans of the Austro-Hungarian Army had charged the British trench previously and been beaten back. Viscount Xavier Moreau had ridden up shortly after at the head of his cavalry squadron and with a huge grin on his face had boasted to the soldiers of the South Staffordshire Regiment hunkered down in their trenches that his fine men would soon ride over the hill and show the enemy what a troop of properly trained horsemen could do. In their bright red trousers and electric-blue tunics, they certainly looked the part. But their tactics had been woefully naïve and as they came together to squeeze through a beckoning gap in the hedge at the crest of the hill, they were decimated by enemy machine-gun fire. Some of the horses had galloped back riderless but were terribly maimed and had to be put down. Grace shed a tear when she heard that. Men could wage war voluntarily, but these poor creatures were innocent.

Grace nursed her patient for four days before he died. Viscount Xavier Moreau was aristocratic and debonair in manner. She had never before seen such a handsome man and his looks were only matched by his chivalry and charm. He had been struck by five bullets in all. He might have recovered from the effects of three of them, but one had passed through his liver and another the left side of his chest. Both injuries were life-threatening and inoperable. He was triaged and categorised as an SI or 'serious injury' and put into a bed on his own in a side room on the top floor. Grace was assigned as his personal nurse.

'I know I am dying,' he said, 'but I could not imagine a more *belle femme* with whom to spend my last hours on earth.'

He grinned at her then: a beautiful, beaming smile exposing a row of gleaming white teeth. His long, jet-black hair was gathered in a ponytail behind his neck with an expensive-looking gold band featuring some sort of family coat of arms. He was uniformly tanned with a dense bristle of stubble on his handsome face and his eyes were as blue as the azure sky of August. His lips were soft and full, and his cheekbones were wide and prominent, much like her own. Grace had come top of her class in French at Cheltenham Ladies' College so knew the meaning of his words exactly.

'Severely injured but still fit enough to flirt?' she teased.

'I am stating just a simple fact.'

'*Vraiment*?'

'I look at you and my pain goes away . . .'

Grace smiled and cocked her head sideways. It was flattering and a much more sophisticated form of flirtation than anything to which she had previously been accustomed.

Nevertheless, she had heard of it occurring.

'The other nurses told me to be careful of you brave *Français*.'

Now it was Xavier's turn to smile, albeit ruefully. Grace returned to the job at hand and reverted to her professional duties.

'Can I bring you anything?' she continued.

'Champagne! One small vintage bottle of Veuve Clicquot. That's all I need.' He laughed softly. Then flashed that utterly disarming grin again.

'What is your name, mademoiselle?'

'Grace.'

'Oh, *mon dieu*. It's a beautiful name. The name of an angel who can take me to heaven.'

'*Oui*,' replied Grace playfully. 'But if I am an angel, sir, you are a little devil.' Again, a gentle chuckle from the bed.

'Champagne is the drink of choice for the devil.'

'And your liver?' chided Grace.

Xavier looked down at the dressing around his torso, soaked in his own blood and bile.

'My liver is already broken. Finished. What harm can it do?'

Clean drinking water was hard enough to come by, let alone champagne. Even if the man was serious.

'Why don't you begin by making yourself comfortable,' said Grace as she plumped up his cushions. She went to the door, paused and turned. 'I'll be back in a moment with relief for your pain.' That was what he needed, not champagne.

'And two glasses!' she heard as she left.

Jenny was hurrying along the corridor with a wad of clean dressings when she found Grace weeping quietly with her face to the wall outside the linen cupboard.

'Grace?' she asked, lightly touching her shoulder. 'Are you all right?'

'Oh, I'm so sorry, I'm just having a moment.' She sniffed.

'It's fine, dear, I understand. It gets to us all. I've shed many a quiet tear these last few days too.'

'But we're not meant to let our feelings get in the way of our duty, are we?'

'Sometimes it's impossible not to. We can't always be rigidly distant. Nor should we be. We are human beings after all.'

She thought if she kept talking, Grace would have longer to compose herself. Grace still looked distressed however, so Jenny tried to lighten the tone.

'Nothing to do with that Adonis you have been asked to special by any chance?' she said, smiling.

Grace turned around and smiled back, wiping a tear from her eye with her sleeve.

'He's so brave and gallant. So alive even as he is dying.'

Jenny took a handkerchief from her breast pocket and dabbed more tears away from Grace's cheeks and lips. 'He is very handsome. I suspect no woman's heart would be quite safe in his company. Would you . . . prefer to be reassigned?'

'No, it's all right, Jenny, I just need to be strong and stay focused. Not get too close to the patient.'

'Principal Sisters' rule number one.'

'Yes, I know,' said Grace, sniffing back another tear and flashing a lightning-quick smile. 'I'll be OK. Thanks, Jenny.'

Thirty minutes later, Grace returned to Xavier's room and saw his motionless body. Her heart missed a beat. She felt faint and dizzy and had to hold on to the heavy cast-iron radiator beside her. His skin was grey and ashen, his eyes sunken deeper into their sockets under that noble brow. His eyelids were closed. How could she have left him to die alone? she thought. It was unforgivable. But then, just as she was beginning to recover herself, he opened his eyes and looked steadily at her. He was still alive, still breathing, and so too was Grace once more. After taking a furtive look along the corridor, she shut the door behind her and came and sat next to Xavier on the bed. She withdrew a small bottle of Napoleon brandy from the side pocket of her gown and opened it. She extricated two small shot glasses from the pocket on the other side and Xavier's face lit up.

'Where on earth did you get it?'

'Better you don't know.'

She had not been able to locate any champagne, but she had finally found a passable alternative deep in the bowels of the hotel's wine cellar.

Xavier grinned his devastating grin. 'I think perhaps you are the devil.'

'Not at all, monsieur. Always an angel.'

45

She poured two fingers of the tawny liquid into each glass, set them on the bedside table and helped her patient up into a better sitting position. He grimaced only slightly and put his left hand over his abdominal dressing.

'*À votre santé*,' she said as she placed one of the glasses in his right hand, and then in English: 'To your health.'

'Ironic,' he said, smiling. 'But amusing all the same.'

She clinked her own glass with his and they downed the tipple in one.

'That's halfway to paradise,' he said, laughing.

Grace smiled back. Her cheeks flushed crimson with the effect of the brandy.

No, he thought, he would not mind dying so much if he could take this gorgeous virginal young lady with him.

'I wish you could accompany me on my next trip.'

And then, as he spoke, a massive shell exploded on the roof of the building, filling the room with red dust and causing plaster and paintwork to fall from the ceiling. People were screaming and shouting in the corridor and in the foyer.

'With all this bombardment I could very well accompany you,' she called over the noise. 'Monsieur, I must go. I will see you soon.'

'Go, of course. Take care.'

She opened the door and hurried off to join the commotion, not knowing these would be the last words she would hear him utter.

Xavier reached over for the bottle of brandy, put it to his lips and threw back his head.

4

In the two years Robbie had been at war he had sent no more
than a handful of letters. Will had tried to approach them
as optimistically as possible, but they made for gloomy
reading, and it wasn't just the accounts of lice, or the
mentions of the dead; it was the tone of them — as if all the
death and destruction was as unremarkable as what he had
eaten for breakfast that day.

Clara, a strong advocate of reading, had enrolled him in
the public library and kept him supplied with the books he
liked to read, about biology, and the natural world. This
interest had led him to apply to apprentice as a hospital porter,
where he soon proved himself a reliable and more than capable
member of the staff. His strong build and natural athleticism
made light work of the tougher duties such as wheeling patients
in their heavy cast-iron beds from one part of the hospital to
another or lugging bulky medical equipment up and down
flights of stairs. His even greater asset was the keen interest
he took in the patients themselves, a fact that did not pass
unnoticed by several of the ward sisters and doctors. Unlike
some of the older porters, who had been doing the job grudg-
ingly for years and felt they were underappreciated and
underpaid, Will would chat away happily to the patients he
came across, enquiring tactfully about their ailments, sympathising and taking the trouble to return to the bedside from
time to time to ask about their treatment and progress.

On delivering surgical patients to the operating theatre he

would steal glances through the windows in the doors, to watch the surgeons work, and ask the nurses in the post-op area about the various tubes and pipes emanating from the patient's airways or veins. He was curious. In fact, he was transfixed. As he toured the hospital on his rounds he would spend any spare time he had with sick children, telling them stories and making them laugh. He was kind and attentive to the elderly. He also became known by the patients as a dependable purveyor of goods from the local corner shop. Slip him the necessary coins, and a small tin of McVitie's or a bottle of stout would quickly be delivered.

Some of the portering team not privy to his sensitive, caring side considered him rather eccentric and odd. In their eyes, he spent rather too long in the mortuary watching the post-mortems and asking too many questions. What the hell did he want to look inside the chest cavity of a heavy smoker for? Or desire to know how much the knobbly shrunken liver of a dead alcoholic weighed? They thought it bizarre. Sawing off the top of the skull and removing the brain of a fellow human being made most of the chaps in the porters' department feel distinctly sick. Not Will. He seemed to relish it. Just like he did the anatomist teasing out the path of a delicate nerve under layers of muscle in a cadaver in the dissecting room. Just like he did the work of Mr Robson who took blood samples from the living patients. Mr Robson had even got him putting on the tourniquets and passing across the appropriate sample tubes. Weird they thought he was, with an all too macabre fascination with disease.

Sometimes, when Will was hoisting a patient onto their trolley or wheelchair, he would be captivated by the words of the doctor talking to the patient behind the curtains just next to him. Apoplexy. Cyanosis. Strangury. What did these words all mean? The patient turned out to have something called pericarditis. Will looked it up in the medical dictionary and found it meant something to do with inflammation around the heart. That was why he was breathless.

He would pick up a stethoscope left on the sisters' desk and listen to his own heart. He'd take up the auriscope and press it to his colleague Tom's ear. He was amazed to see the shiny reflection of his eardrum.

He played with the veins on the back of his own hands, running a finger down them to empty them and seeing how they never filled up from above because of the venous one-way system. For Will the portering was just a job which paid him a few pennies each week. What mattered was the opportunity it gave him to learn about the human body and how it reacted to things like exercise or disease. Often he was so distracted and mesmerised he was accused of sleeping on the job and shirking.

'Come on, you lazy young sod,' they would shout. 'Show a little interest, would you?'

But Will was showing plenty of interest. It was just not in the area they expected.

Jack worked in construction and enjoyed aspects of the job, like the banter with the other young lads, though the foreman had taken against him. Just for being cheerful and handsome, thought Jack.

'Enough bleeding talking already, pretty boy,' he'd shout at regular intervals, and recently he'd threatened to throw him off the scaffolding.

Every day, the foreman's wife would walk by to give him his sandwiches. She was a good-looking woman, far too good-looking for the foreman, thought Jack.

'I think she's gorgeous,' he whispered to his friend Billy as they looked down at her handing him a paper bag.

'She's old enough to be your mum!' said Billy.

'Shut your gob,' Jack said angrily.

'What?' he said. 'What did I say?'

'Never mind,' said Jack.

Today, the foreman had been called away to deal with some-one's fall on another site, and Jack was swinging himself down to the ground to eat his lunch when she appeared with her usual paper bag.

'Hello, Mrs Ogden,' he called.

'Hello, young man. Have you seen my husband?'

'I'm afraid he left ten minutes ago with another lady.'

'A lady?'

'Yeah, another lady. A good-looking woman, though if I may say so, not nearly so handsome as yourself.'

'You cheeky thing. Is he expected back soon?'

'I'm not sure. Why don't I walk you in the direction they went? Perhaps we'll come across them.'

'That's very kind of you. My Fred must be glad to have a nice young man like you on his team.'

'He says so all the time, Mrs Ogden.'

'What's your name?'

'Will.'

'Nice to meet you, Will.'

'Pleasure's all mine, Mrs Ogden.'

He didn't know where he was leading her, was just enjoying the chance to stand next to her, and then they found them-selves standing in an alley between the finished houses and those still going up.

'You saw him going here?'

'I must have been mistaken. I am sorry.'

There was no one else around.

'Quiet here, isn't it?' she said.

'Very quiet. I hadn't noticed before. You could get up to anything here.'

He looked at her and smiled. She frowned.

'Did you lead me here on purpose?'

Jack began to worry now about what she'd say to his boss.

'No, honestly, let's get back, shall we?'

'What was your name again?'

'William, Will for short. Would you like me to take those sandwiches? I'll give them to him when he's back.'

Before she handed them over and walked away she gave Jack a hard stare, which he told himself was a look of smouldering sexual intrigue.

He realised he couldn't give the sandwiches to Mr Ogden without acknowledging it had been he who'd been chatting up his wife, so he sat down against a wall and ate them himself. Cheese and chutney, very nice.

Later that evening, when tea was on the table — potatoes, cabbage and pork chops — Clara took out the latest letter from Robbie. She read it herself first, frowning a little, then put a hand to the corner of her eye and sighed.

'Would you like to read it out for us all, Will?' she asked.

Dear Jack, Will and Kitty

I am sorry I am not writing so regular. It is hard to find peace here with all the noise of the shells and the guns. Hard even when it goes quiet, which it often does. I am still in France, close to Ypres. I had a good chum for a while, George Jackson, but he died to a sniper's bullet, and I have been missing him. The privates are mostly decent blokes, the

*officers too. There is danger every day and if you don't work together
you die. We die frequently, in any case. Behind the trenches, there are
wild flowers, but in front, everything is blasted and churned up. I am
sorry I am not with you. I hope you are happy with work and school. I
will not say when I will next see you, if it is in this life, or the next, with
your mother, but I hope it is soon.*

Yours, your loving father.

The table was quiet after Will had read the letter.

'Poor Father,' said Will.

'He's all right,' said Jack. 'He was never much of a one
for words, was he?'

Not for many years. Though Will remembered the man
he had been before his wife died — the joker, the singer, the
man who loved his walks by the river.

'We should get out there and give him a hand!' said Jack.

'Yes,' said Will.

'You're both too young, thank goodness,' said Clara.

'Bertie from my school year is already there,' said Jack.
'They don't check your age if you look old enough.'

'Don't even think about it. You need to finish your
apprenticeship. You're almost done now.'

'But they need every man they can get, Aunt Clara,' said
Will. 'That's what I've been reading.'

'Every man, maybe; they don't mean fourteen- and
sixteen-year-old lads barely out of school.'

'Big Willy could pass for older than that, don't you think?'
said Jack, reaching out and squeezing Will's arm. 'He's got
arms nearly as strong as mine. God knows how, pushing
trolleys around a hospital while I'm hauling bricks all day.'

'Please don't go,' said Kitty quietly.

'We're only joking,' said Jack, quickly. 'Don't you worry.'

5

Gheluvelt

No wonder the men were dead on their feet. They had marched hundreds of miles over the last few weeks, often back and forth over the same ground, sometimes retreating and at other times on the attack. Grace was shattered too but at least she had had the luxury of a horse-drawn carriage or a charger of her own to get from one place to another. She had now served in twelve different casualty clearing stations, eight separate advanced dressing stations and two general base hospitals and had never remained in the same place for more than twelve days. She was a nursing nomad with no fixed abode. The war seemed to ebb and flow like the ocean tide with each side having failed to outflank the other. It was a race to the sea that had involved the digging of 450 miles of parallel trenches stretched all the way from Switzerland to the North Sea. It was a stalemate. Yet it had not stopped the terrible slaughter.

The initial German onslaught had been halted eventually by the British and French at of the Battle of the Marne. Then, when the Allied troops had pushed the enemy back again at the Battle of the Aisne, the Germans had dug in on the high ground above the river and massively reinforced their position. Maybe the war would end sooner if there weren't so many damned rivers, mused Grace. She knew the form by now. It was one of the favourite topics of conversation in those rare moments around the work. Like everyone else, they wanted the war to be over as soon as possible. If no one was winning, what was the point in carrying on? Why not sue for peace? But, as far as Grace was informed, the Army generals in their wisdom seemed convinced the next big push would achieve glorious victory. Now Grace was stationed at a hastily erected casualty clearing station behind two square miles of twisted metal and concrete rubble which had once been a village called Gheluvelt.

It had been bitterly cold lately. A chill October wind blew in from the east and the ground was rutted but hard as rock. She pitied the poor soldiers hacking away at it all night in an attempt to improve the latest line of defensive trenches a few miles away at Ypres. The word was out that they were currently outnumbered seven to one and taking heavy casualties. That certainly seemed credible judging by the number of injured men constantly being brought in. The walking wounded had been immediately sent back to the frontline and anyone else who could hold a rifle had been sent to join them.

Grace was kneeling at the bedside of a man who had been shot in the stomach, the bullet perforating both his small intestine and pancreas. She knew the digestive enzymes now leaking from that deeply buried organ together with the blood loss would inevitably kill him but she kept that knowledge to herself. She held tightly to his hand.

'Nurse Tustin,' said a curt voice behind her.

She looked up. There stood Principal Sister MacCailein of Queen Alexandra's Imperial Military Nursing Service, who ran things in this sector. Grace gently let go of her patient's hand, stood up and smoothed down her apron and gown with her hands.

Sister MacCailein was a staunch disciplinarian and a formidable woman in her own right. It was well known that she was not a person with whom one would want to fall out. The first time Grace had been introduced she'd made the easy mistake of mispronouncing her name and had had a strip torn off for it. 'It's pronounced McCallen,' she had said. 'McAllen is from the Western Isles of Scotland. Please get it right.'

Now, she glared at Grace furiously. 'Yes, Sister?' said Grace.

'Would you come with me, please.' It sounded more like a command then a request. No doubt a prelude to another dressing down. Lately the woman had been chiding Grace for the smallest of things. She followed her superior into a more private corner of the tent which served as her office. This fearsome and intimidating woman had a bizarre technique of delivering her rebukes in a whisper. Grace had to strain hard to hear what she was saying. Her strong Scottish accent added to the problem. Anyone listening was forced to crane their neck forward and turn their head slightly to the side so as not to miss exactly what was being said. And what was said was usually stinging and quite malicious. The dramatic effect of the professional assassination was all the greater for its near-subliminal rendering. Grace braced herself for another inaudible tirade from the whispering witch, as she was known.

'Where in your training did it tell you to kneel at the bedside and hold the patient's hand?'

'The poor man is dying, Sister. He is frightened. I thought some kindness was in order.'

'Kindness,' she said through pursed lips. 'Never confuse kindness with care. What these men need is first-class nursing care founded on basic principles.'

Grace was stunned. She had done everything she had been instructed to do for the man in question and more. Why was Sister once again questioning her ability?

'You're a member of the FANY, are you not?'

'Yes, Sister.'

'Under our auspices and wearing our uniform.'

'Yes.'

'I always thought that ghastly military-style dress you Yeomanry nurses used to wear was ridiculous anyway. Most inappropriate. But now you have dispensation to wear the Queen Alexandra's uniform you are expected to conform to our high standards.'

She looked disdainfully down her aquiline nose at the slip of a girl in front of her.

'Unlike the FANY or the VAD nurses who mean well but who quite frankly are sometimes not up to it, the Queen Alexandra's nurses train for a full three years. Furthermore, we do it in highly reputable hospitals designed for the purpose.'

It was true that several of the nurses who had signed up to help with the war effort and who had been recruited and trained by the Red Cross and St John Ambulance association had found the horrors of trench warfare too much to take and had been repatriated to work in hospitals at home. But tens of thousands of them were still serving on the Western Front and doing an admirable job. So were nurses from the Territorial Force Nursing Service and several other organisations. Without them, the QAIMNS would be utterly unable to cope, with only around three hundred nurses who

56

had reached the gold standards that Sister MacCailein expected them all to attain. But, of course, Grace thought, there was also the element of their esteemed social standing and provenance, probably the most important requisites to satisfy the registration approval standards of the Nursing Board. The principal sister in her eyes was just a professional snob.

'Perhaps your time would have been better served if you'd remained in the saddle rather than on the wards, Nurse Tustin?'

Constructive criticism was one thing, expected from a superior. Grace could handle that. But this verbal assault was a complete surprise.

'It's Tustin-Pennington in fact, Sister. And we do still ride, by the way. Sometimes it is by far the quickest way to deliver essential medicines and equipment to the clearing stations, the advanced dressing stations or the regimental aid posts. I don't know if you've ever been exposed to that danger yourself?'

MacCailein raised an eyebrow.

Grace continued. She was more than irritated. 'This was especially true earlier on when we were supporting the British Expeditionary Force. Partly because the FANY — with or without three years' training at the Edinburgh Royal Infirmary like you, or at St Thomas's Hospital — were the first to arrive in Europe. Before even the QAIMNS, I believe.'

'You are being impertinent and missing the point.' Her whispering was almost imperceptible now, but the meaning was deafening. 'When you take a man's hand in yours, young lady, you are giving him permission to proceed to all kinds of liberties. They are lusty young men a long way from home and are likely to try it on at the drop of a hat.'

'Yet that has never happened to me in all my time serving here.'

'Then it's only a matter of time, child, before it does. But it doesn't mean you should encourage it.'

Grace could hardly believe what she was hearing. It suddenly occurred to her that despite her relative youth she was already far more worldly wise than this bitter spinster would ever be when it came to understanding men. Her brothers' peer groups had effectively seen to that long ago. Parts of her felt a kind of pity for this woman whose undoubted nursing experience and professional abilities clearly did not extend to understanding the character of the opposite sex.

'I apply all the official protocols as regards the correct nursing methods. As far as I know the RMO is satisfied with my work,' she said, as the regimental medical officer had made that clear, 'and sometimes I feel that little bit of extra caring can make a big difference. The men are sick or dying. Exhausted, hungry and ready to collapse. I find them without fail to be grateful, polite and respectful. I believe they're incapable of misinterpreting the tenderness we administer.'

'Nevertheless, it is not acceptable to lead the men on in such a fashion.'

'As I say, Sister, it has never happened.'

Sister MacCailein folded her arms and stared at Grace. Grace felt uncomfortable. 'But that's not quite true, is it, Nurse?'

'What do you mean?'

'I'm talking about a certain French cavalryman put into your individual care at the Hotel Dauphin in Givry. A viscount, no less, I'm told.'

'What about him?' Grace was flabbergasted. She had no idea where this was headed.

'Although you didn't know it, I was the principal sister in that clearing station at the time.'

It was quite possible she had been, Grace thought, but if it was true, she had never seen her on the wards there.

'After the hotel was heavily shelled, and in the ensuing chaos, attempts were made to rescue and evacuate as many casualties as possible.'

'I remember. I was ordered to pack up as much equipment as I could and get all the patients out of the ballroom and away in the ambulances.'

'And Viscount Moreau died in the meantime.'

Grace felt a stab of regret on hearing his name.

'He was mortally wounded. He lived longer than anyone had expected. But there was no question of any impropriety. That's absurd.'

'Yet an empty bottle of brandy was found in his hand when he was pronounced dead. I wonder how he might have come by that. You were the only one responsible for him.'

It was a direct challenge and an obvious accusation. She wanted and expected Grace to squirm.

'I'm sure I don't have to tell you, Nurse Tustin, that alcohol of any kind is contra-indicated in anyone taking analgesics or facing possible surgery. Brandy, I believe, is around forty per cent proof. And you were there by his bedside?'

Grace had to think on her feet. Rum was routinely dished out to the soldiers on the frontline at the dawn stand-to and the stand-down at dusk. Two ounces of overproof rum to each man. Regulations ordered it should be drunk in the presence of an officer or non-commissioned officer or poured away to prevent hoarding but Grace knew that did not always happen and that none was ever wasted. It was a combat motivator, a medicine often given by the medics to men in pain or dying and was also part of the soldiers' reward system. Others took it to calm nerves. They all took it. They took it when wounded, pending transfer from the aid posts to the hospitals. The doctors prescribed it, too. Grace knew without a shadow of a doubt that she had granted Xavier Moreau his last wish by providing the comfort he found in draining the last of the bottle.

'Not at the end, Sister. He was very much alive when I left him. I imagine whoever furnished him with the liquor must have been totally at odds with your nursing protocols. Is there anything else?'

Sister MacCailein was livid. Much as though she would love to throw the book at this cocky young girl, she needed every nurse she could get. And although Grace would never know it, underneath her cold and aloof veneer the woman regarded her as one of her most capable nurses.

'Off you go, and heed what I've said. I'll be watching you.'

As Grace returned to the general ward, she reflected on what the principal sister had inadvertently told her. Xavier had finished off his Napoleon brandy, the one she had dug out from the far corner of the hotel's wine cellar. He had requested it and craved it. And she had given it to him. Despite not being able to share his last moments with her, the nurse with whom he'd harmlessly flirted, he would have died with that mesmerising smile still on his face. Grace had not a shred of regret. Her own wish, as she resumed her duties, was that she would never have to lay eyes on Sister MacCailein again.

6

It had been months since Jack had lost his job.

'A letter of reference? I've a good mind to report you to the police!' Mr Ogden had shouted at him as he left the building site.

Mrs Ogden had mentioned her meeting with a charming but strange young man, and enquired about the woman with whom he'd been consorting, and it hadn't taken Mr Ogden long to work out who 'Will' was. Mr Ogden was unsure about which outrage was the greatest, but he kept returning to the eating of the sandwiches, the straw that broke the camel's back.

All that fuss when Jack had only been trying to be helpful! At the time he had not been so sad. Freed from the duties of a wage slave by a cheese and chutney sandwich. Prepared by the delicate hands of a beautiful woman. Who had betrayed him. That was disappointing. But there were plenty more fish in the sea.

Now he was earning some money as a bookie's runner, avoiding the attention of the local bobbies. They would turn a blind eye to it, but you were expected to scarper quickly when you saw them. It was only polite to act like you were scared of them.

Clara was worried. 'It's not legal, Jack!'

'It's fine, it's tolerated. Everyone likes a gamble. It suits me.'

* * *

But Will was worried too. He knew Jack was impressionable, and when you did something a little bit outside the law, you met men who operated further outside of the law. He didn't like Jack's new friend, Trevor, a sallow-faced man of small stature who was not much older than Jack but who had the flashy clothes and leering smile of someone much older.

He ran into Jack and Trevor all over the place – they lived outside, darting around, taking bets, darting off again.

'What's your brother got in the satchel he's always carrying round?' Trevor asked Jack one day in front of Will. 'You selling stuff on the black market?'

'Books, Trevor, books. He's a regular brain box, our Will.'

'Books! I thought it was going to be something interesting. What books? Are they worth anything? Come on, let's have a butcher's.'

Will hurried away, but from then on whenever he saw Trevor he was greeted with a cry of, 'Professor! Hello, Professor!'

There had been no letter from Robbie for a long time now and though Will felt distant from his dad, he also longed to see him. He had joined the Army Cadets and was keeping himself strong with the rigorous programme of calisthenics and press-ups they advised. He ran long distances with other cadets along the river, and learned map reading, along with other fieldcraft skills.

Jack had come with him at first, but grew frustrated. 'I thought we were going to learn how to fire weapons. This is hard bloody work, all this running. I'm on my feet all day as it is.'

*

Will was on the way back from the hospital one night when he heard the familiar call.

'Professor!'

Trevor was leaning against a wall, smoking with Jack.

'Want to buy a packet of cigarettes, Professor? Half what they cost in the newsagent's. In fact, you could help us sell them. Fill your satchel with them, offer them to the patients and nurses. What do you say?'

'Where did you get them from?' asked Will.

'From the getting place. Right, Jack?'

Jack looked unusually uncomfortable. 'Don't involve Will, Trevor. He's got enough on his plate with the hospital and the school and all his cadet training.'

'The professor's a regular goody two-shoes.'

Will stepped forward and looked at Trevor. He was scared of him, of his worldliness, of his attitude, but when he sized him up, compared Trevor's body with his own, he was not so intimidated.

'I best be getting off,' he said.

Jack was out somewhere with Trevor that evening when the policeman came knocking.

'I'd like to speak to Jack Burnett. Is he in?'

'I'm afraid he's out with his friend,' said Clara. 'What's this about? He's not in trouble, is he?'

'We've been watching him for a while, miss. He keeps some bad company. There are things we can turn a blind eye to but not stealing.'

'Stealing!'

'Or selling stolen goods. Cigarettes. Do you know anything about that?'

'Jack wouldn't steal anything, officer. He's lippy, and he's feckless, and he's a pain in the bloody backside, but he's not a thief!'

'Are you sure?'

'Quite sure!'

'Well, I'd like a word with him when he's back. Can you ask him to come and see me at the station. PC Arkwright.'

'I'll march him straight down myself.'

Clara took Jack to the station first thing in the morning. He denied all knowledge of any stolen goods. He said he was offered a carton by a guy outside a pub and thought he'd make a bit by selling individual packets.

PC Arkwright didn't believe him. 'I'll be keeping my eye on you, lad. If you keep behaving the way you do, you'll end up behind bars.'

Outside the station, Clara was tight-lipped. 'What am I going to do with you, Jack? I know I'm not your mother and I know you're missing her – and your pa – but I love you and I can't bear to see you setting off on the wrong path.'

'Come on, Aunt Clara. Relax. It was only a few packets of fags.'

'I don't want you seeing that friend of yours anymore. That's it with him. All right?'

'I'm seventeen years old – you don't get to treat me like a kid.'

Jack began to walk off.

'Where are you going?' Clara said, exasperated.

'See you later, Clara. Give Kitty a kiss goodnight from me and tell her I'll be along to see her soon.'

7

Neuve Chapelle

Grace, for all her boundless energy and unbridled spirit, had never felt so utterly exhausted. She had slept no more than four hours a night for as long as she could remember. There had been two days of relative respite at the beginning of April when she had taken a long relaxing walk in the countryside with her friend Jenny. They had strolled through a magnificent pine forest and shared biscuits and chocolate in a glorious poppy field on the other side. The vibrancy of the scarlet petals, the greenery and the scent of pines wafting in the breeze contrasted vividly with the blasted stumps and the foul-smelling mud slop of the battlefields. For a few peaceful hours, they had been able to forget everything else and revel in the beauty of the natural world around them. Grace regaled her friend with her knowledge of trees and Jenny responded in kind with what she knew about the various insects they found beneath each fallen log. It was one of the quietest times they had experienced in recent weeks and, while all too brief, it gave them the chance to take a breather and regain some strength.

It was made all the more pleasurable by the fortuitous discovery of a litter of four abandoned kittens in the ruins of a bombed-out farmhouse they passed on the return journey. Their mother lay bloodied and dead, trapped amid the rubble. With light golden fur on their backs and pure white fluff on their undersides they looked identical in colour and size, yet three ran off as soon as they were discovered. The last, the cutest little creature Grace thought she had ever laid eyes on, meowed earnestly and headed straight over to her. Grace squatted down and held out an arm, and the kitten nuzzled her hand and looked straight at her, as if asking desperately to be loved.

'Oh, she's such a sweet little thing,' laughed Jenny. 'What a shame about the mother. What will become of them?'

'They have no home here, that's for sure,' said Grace.

They looked for the others, but they were nowhere to be seen. They had scampered off across the fields into the forest probably, leaving this tiny one even more abandoned.

Grace stood up, cupping the little feline in her hands. Much to Jenny's surprise, she undid the top button of her blouse and popped the cat inside.

'What on earth are you doing?' she said.

'Giving her a home, of course.'

'In your blouse.'

'Well, only for the time being. I'm sure I'll find a more suitable berth for her when we get back.'

So, laughing and flushed with the child-like joy of it, they set off for their lodgings.

'You'd better give her a name then,' said Jenny.

'I already have one.'

'And . . .'

'Omelette.'

Jenny burst out laughing as she took another look at the gold-and-white kitten peeping out from her friend's collar. 'What kind of name is that for a pussycat?'

'Well, she's gold on top and white all around and under-neath just like a fried egg.'

Jenny looked at Grace sideways with a puzzled expression.

'Only I don't like fried eggs. I prefer omelettes.'

'Fair enough, then. Who am I to quibble? At least she keeps her national identity. But Grace, have you considered the fact that this is a French kitten?'

'So?'

'What's the French for Omelette?'

Grace looked momentarily puzzled before slapping her friend on the shoulder and giggling uncontrollably.

'You're a fool, Jenny. But you do make me laugh. And thank God for that. I don't know what I'd do without you.'

'I think you'd manage just fine, Grace. Give me a hug.'

They clung to each other tightly and laughed some more while Omelette's furry little face peeped out from Grace's clothing.

8

Jack had been spending so much time with Trevor that he ended up moving in with him. He soon hated staying with Trevor and his alcoholic father, who was cruel and abusive to Trevor when he arrived back late at night, reeking of beer. But he was too proud to admit it. Instead, he'd appear back at the family house frequently around the time Clara was putting out the dinner and pretend he hadn't realised what time it was. 'I was supposed to be having tea back at Trevor's, but he won't mind if I stay, if you're sure that's OK, that is?'

Though Clara was always tempted to send him off, to teach him the lesson he needed to learn, she was not the sort to let a young man go hungry, particularly one whose little sister loved him so much.

She had a terrible vision of Jack later in life, with yellow teeth, stinking of tobacco and beer, his optimistic soul having gone rotten somehow.

It had been months since they had heard from Robbie.

Meanwhile, Will was continuing with cadets and enjoyed telling Jack that he had missed out on firing Lee-Enfield rifles.

'No way!'

'At a firing range in Hammersmith.'

'I bet you didn't hit anything.'

'Not at first.'

'I knew it.'

'And what, you'd be a natural, would you? How do you know?'

'You're the brain box, Will; I'm the practical one.'

'Will listens to instructions,' said Clara. 'I imagine that's useful in the Army.'

Jack frowned. 'I've been thinking about joining up, actually. Getting some real experience while Will plays around in the cadets.'

'Oi!' said Will.

'The Royal Engineers, I was thinking – that's the place for me. Better pay, building things and blowing things up. My construction experience would come in handy with them.'

'Your limited construction experience,' said Will.

'I did bloody years with that fool Ogden.'

'Language, Jack,' said Clara. 'And you're still too young to sign up.'

*

But as much as she wanted to, she could not be as fiercely against the idea of the boys signing up to fight as when the war had begun. There was no doubt now that Britain needed men – 'Your Country Needs You', pointed Lord Kitchener from the posters – and that the soldiers were fighting a battle that could go either way. It had to be about more than keeping those you loved safe now; there was a duty to defend everyone.

Jim Wilson, who lived next door with his wife Sally, had recently returned from the front. He was twenty-four years old, now declared unfit for service. He was without any obvious injury, that was the strange thing, though perhaps there was a hidden one beneath his clothes. His wife Sally did her best to cheer him up by throwing a party. Jim sat in the corner, not saying anything. Will had sat next to him. He'd always enjoyed Jim's company, such as when he'd take him and Jack fishing on the river.

'Have you been out fishing yet?' he asked.

'No, no. I'm, er. I'm not so into that anymore.'

'Was it very hard out there?' he asked.

'Very hard,' Jim nodded.

'You didn't see my father.'

'No. There's a lot of us out there. So many of us.'

As he said that, something in him broke. He twitched, and looked like he wanted to hurl himself to the floor, and as he noticed what he had done, a tear rolled down one cheek. 'Don't mind me,' he said. 'I had some friends out there, you know. Some of them are still there. Hard to think of them. Hard to think of the ones who aren't.'

Will kept up his visits after that, and would sit with Jim, who wouldn't say much.

'Are you sure you don't want a trip to the river?' he said.

'I spent a lot of time fighting by a river,' Jim said eventually. 'There was a jetty where the bodies would wash up. I have dreams, now. Of reeling in the line and pulling out one of those big doughy bodies, the eyes eaten by the fishes.'

'Wow,' said Will.

'I'm sorry. It can't be fun talking to me.'

'Who cares about fun?' said Will. 'I want to know what it was like.'

And, haltingly, over those weekly visits, Jim described his war to him. The noise of the shells when you were at the front. The terrible feeling of waiting for something to happen, for something to land near you. The smell, of other men, of decaying corpses, of the latrines. These details frightened Will, of course, but not enough to stop him from imagining signing up. A big lad, he could easily pass for eighteen now, even if they were strict about checking. He knew this from an incident yesterday on the bus home from the hospital. He'd been tapped on the back, and behind him, a woman not much older than him was waving a white feather at him. 'For you,' she said, mockingly. He didn't understand, for a second, before the man sitting across from him called over, 'You leave him alone. He's probably not old enough to fight. And what do you know about it anyway?'

'Enough to know you're both cowards,' she said, sitting back, pleased with herself. 'Here, perhaps you would like it instead.'

'Thank you,' he said, getting up and taking it from her and throwing it on the floor. 'Or do you want me to take it back to the lads at Ypres? I'm in my civvies while my uniform gets deloused, actually. But if I had it on, I wouldn't be half as lousy as you.'

Will wanted to talk to him, ask him questions about what it was like, but the man had walked to the back of the bus and got off, shaking his head. The woman behind him was quieter now, watching the man as he walked away, not so confident in her righteousness.

'I'm fifteen,' Will said to her.

'So what?' she said.

And Will thought about that. He knew how to fire a gun. He knew about other people's pain and how to help them. He was desperate to track down his father. Why shouldn't he go?

*

But Jack beat him to it.

'Now, Aunt Clara,' he said that night. 'I want to ask you to take a deep breath after I tell you what I've got to tell you.'

'No! Not prison!'

'Will you give it a rest?' he said. 'Prison! I've done nothing wrong at all.'

'What is it then?'

'Promise you'll take a deep breath.'

'What is it?'

'Promise?'

'OK, I promise.'

'I've enlisted. With the Royal Engineers.'

'Oh, Jack! You're not old enough.'

'I'm going to be trained first, don't worry. I was right, you know. They need builders. Lads who can help dig in, lads who are used to hard labour. It's better paid than the Army. The sergeant convinced me it would be a good opportunity for me.'

'A good opportunity,' said Clara, doubtfully. 'Oh, Jack. You're a brave lad. I hope you're right.'

'When will you go?' asked Will.

'You'll come back?' said Kitty.

'Before you know it,' said Jack. 'Before you know it.'

9

Ablain-Saint-Nazaire

Grace was woken in the early hours by the noisy clatter of a heavily laden lumber wagon passing behind her tent. The sound of the horses' hooves and their loud snorting reminded her of happier days back home in the stables at Bishop's Cleeve.

Leaving Omelette curled up at the foot of her bed, she popped her head out of the tent to look at the horses and was surprised to see a Zeppelin high in the distant night sky drifting over the hill to the north. Within moments, a huge flash of fire erupted into the darkness where the airship had obviously dropped an incendiary bomb on its target below. Only yesterday two Taubes had overflown the camp, one being pursued by a friendly aeroplane and the other clearly on the attack. The battle in the air seemed to be becoming as attritional as the one on the ground.

She found it difficult to go back to sleep after that, her thoughts turning first to the ever-present threat of a shell falling through the roof of the tent, and secondly to the welfare of her beloved parents in Gloucestershire. She wondered how they were managing on their own on the estate with four of her brothers gone to war and most of the farm workers and mill staff enlisted as well. She had heard that Zeppelins were now flying over parts of England.

Climbing back into bed and taking care not to disturb the kitten she turned onto her side, praying these worries would fade and that she would rediscover the restorative properties of the sleep she so desperately needed. She dozed fitfully for a while but in a ghastly dream she saw the image of a man blown into several separate pieces, all neatly arranged in correct anatomical position like parts of a macabre puzzle. His face was one she recognised. It was that of Private Frank Perkins, a man who had both his legs blown off and who Grace treated before his life finally ebbed away. She turned over but then another frightful vision, of a patient with the top of his head missing and empty eye sockets, made her cry out and sit up. Sleep was becoming an elusive luxury. Yet it was so badly needed. She thought back to her favourite Shakespearean quote, which she had committed to memory for her classes at Cheltenham Ladies' College.

> *Innocent sleep.*
> *Sleep that knits up the ravelled sleeve of care,*
> *The death of each day's life, sore labour's bath,*
> *Balm of hurt minds, great nature's second course,*
> *Chief nourisher in life's feast.*

She recited it silently in her head.

She had awoken several times in recent nights from similar nightmares, unable to breathe. Her eyes were open, she could see and think clearly, but she could not move her arms or legs, and nor could she inhale or exhale. She had to arch her back and force her rib cage upwards to try to passively fill her lungs. Then, just as she thought her pounding heart would leap from her chest from suffocation, the vice-like muscles in her throat gradually relaxed and she was able to gasp and take in some oxygen. The first time it'd happened she was convinced she was going to die. She had deliberately avoided going back to sleep in case she did. The second time, she realised it was not a fatal phenomenon, and by the third time it occurred, she had become resigned to it. The RMO who overheard her telling an orderly about it told her it was a well-known condition called sleep paralysis.

'It sounds bloody terrifying,' he said. 'Glad I've never had it!'

But at least it was not serious, he added. Something to do with the twilight stage of sleep — the transition between deep sleep, when the muscles are paralysed, and light sleep, when the brain is still semi-conscious. Stress-related, he explained. Well, that was no surprise to hear. On this morning, her busy mind and the noise of the cockerels crowing half a mile away at the little farm in the valley combined to keep her awake, so she gave up trying and rolled out of bed.

After a cursory wash in cold water from a rusty metal drum she donned her grey dress, scarlet cape and white cuffs and glanced in her hand-mirror to make sure her white muslin cap was symmetrically deployed across her shoulders. Finally, she pinned her bronze service badge on the right side of her cape, then made her way to the hospital ward. Tea and breakfast would not yet be ready in the mess tent, but she arrived in good time for the overnight report and handover. The ward was full of soldiers whose wounds needed dressing and changing and it seemed all of them were demanding drinks every few minutes.

Grace rolled up her sleeves and proceeded as fast and efficiently as she could to perform these routine tasks, keeping in mind that her time and skills were better reserved for the seriously wounded. Sister MacCailein hovered all the while, making Grace feel more pressure than she needed.

Private Martin Dewberry had been shot clean through the spine and was paralysed from the waist down, was doubly incontinent and his breathing was rapid and shallow. He could still move his head and both arms, however, and Grace, once she had cleaned him up from the mess he had been lying in all night, helped him sit up so he could write a letter home to his family. She even helped him compose it. He chose not to go into any detail about his injuries. It was extraordinary, she thought, how little curiosity some patients seemed to have about their plight. Would you not want to know as much information about your condition as possible? 'What is the extent of the damage?' 'What does it mean?' 'How will it be treated?' 'What will be the outcome?' Would you not want to be told the truth?

Martin had never asked a single question. Maybe he did not want to know. Maybe he already knew. Grace helped him fold the letter into an envelope and, sharing his hopes that it would not be censored by the authorities, posted it in the out tray in the sisters' office.

Corporal Ronald Seymour was propped up on his pillow. His shattered right leg was bound up in one of the new Thomas splints which had made such a difference to the treatment of soldiers with compound fractures of the femur. When Grace had first been engaged in nursing the wounded in Belgium, eight out of ten men whose bones were so badly shattered that they were sticking out through the flesh would perish. If the initial torrential blood loss did not kill them immediately, infection would several days later. Now with this splint the majority were surviving with impressively little misalignment of the bones when they healed. Advances in medical techniques were having a significant effect on survival and recovery rates but they still lagged hopelessly behind the development of ever more sophisticated weapons that could maim and kill hundreds of the military or civilian population in one fell swoop.

At that moment, someone cried out from behind her.

'Nurse.' It was the subaltern from the Royal Field Artillery whose leg had been amputated several days previously.

'Nurse. I can't stand this pain in my missing leg. It's like a bayonet sticking in and being twisted. It never goes away. Never.'

'I'll fetch something for it straight away,' said Grace, hurrying off to find morphine. It was tragic how many of these amputees suffered from such severe agonies long after their operation. The medications seemed so ineffective. Some men begged to be left to die. Morphine could help for a short while, but the men could not be given it indefinitely. Too many had already suffered an even worse agony. The agony of opiate addiction, from which recovery and the prospect of normal civilian life was nearly impossible.

Grace gave the poor man the injection he needed and, having finished her rounds of the ward, met up at her rendezvous with two duty RMOs and scrubbed up for surgery in the theatre.

James Duffy was a corporal in the 1st Australian Tunnelling Company who had been struck a powerful blow on the side of the head about two hours previously by a buttress that had collapsed in his dugout. He had been dazed and unsteady on his feet at first but had swiftly recovered and apparently seemed all right. An hour or so later, however, his mates had noticed him slurring his speech and that he seemed confused. Then he had started vomiting, before lapsing into unconsciousness.

He lay now completely insensible, his breathing deep and

irregular. The two RMOs — Dr Bernard Morgan and Dr Leonard Marks — were familiar with one another's work and made a great team. Unlike the military personnel Grace dealt with, they respected her work highly and were delighted to have her on board. Grace was equally proud to work with them. She had already learned so much and was ready to assist them in theatre whenever necessary. It also got her temporarily away from Sister MacCailein's scrutinising eye. The three of them now stood either side of the patient in their scrubs and gloves, ready to operate.

'Blood pressure and pulse?' asked the more senior doctor, Bernard Morgan.

'190/130 and thirty-two,' Grace replied.

'Mountain high, valley deep,' said the surgeon.

'What we have here is an extradural then,' replied his colleague.

'Yes, we do. So, we'd better hurry up.'

As they prepared the injured Australian sapper for surgery Grace carried out a final last-minute sterilisation of the instruments, taking particular care with the trephining drill.

'He's deeply unconscious now, Nurse, but if this goes to plan we will shortly need some chloroform on the sponge.'

'Drill, please.'

The doctors worked methodically in tandem while talking through each step of the procedure. Grace wondered if this was a routine practice or whether it was for her benefit. It was a little like the theatre training she had received in Bristol.

'It's a classic extradural hemorrhage, Nurse TP.'

This is how they affectionately referred to her now, as Tustin-Pennington seemed too formal.

'The blow to the side of the head around the temple area fractures the skull and tears the artery beneath.'

His colleague picked up the conversation from there.

'The bleeding continues steadily between the inner surface of the skull and the meninges that lie on the surface of the outer layer of the brain.'

'The enlarging pool of blood compresses the soft under-lying brain, displacing its vital midline structures and forcing the brainstem downwards.'

'Unless the pressure is quickly relieved the patient is done for. That's what we're trying to do now.'

The doctors delivered one statement in turn almost as if they were rehearsing a stage play. Grace could not help but be amused by the way they spoke almost as one and like an old married couple finishing each other's sentences.

'That's when the lucid period comes to an end.'

'The speech begins to slur. The headache becomes intense, confusion kicks in and . . .'

'And then they collapse.'

Grace looked from one to the other and waited for the next line.

'That's why we call it . . .'

'Talk and die syndrome.'

'Exactly. Hopefully, though,' said the more senior man, 'we can bring him back from the brink.'

He marked a point on his patient's head one inch in front of the ear and one inch above it. He made a small incision in the skin and then carefully started to drill.

Grace flinched at the brutality of the surgery.

'Doesn't he need anaesthetic now?' she asked incredu-lously.

'He will. But not yet. He is deeply unconscious right now and can't feel a thing. But that might change.'

The drill looked like the type of tool Grace had seen handymen use to put screws in walls and erect shelving back home, twisting with one arm as the bit rotated into the surface. Here, the drill bit bored straight into the patient's head. Dr Morgan began drilling more slowly then and addressed Dr Marks airily.

'Can you ready the osteotome.'

Grace passed the chisel-like instrument over from the trolley.

'Got it.'

Then, as the rotating drill broke through the full thickness of the skull, bright red blood spurted out and dribbled down the side of the patient's head.

Grace was transfixed. Nibbling away with the osteotome at the edges of the hole he had created, Dr Morgan enlarged the opening and swabbed away as much blood as he could.

But the patient was stirring now that the pressure was relieved and his consciousness was returning, and was clearly experiencing pain.

'Chloroform! Now!' said Dr Morgan. His voice conveyed urgency but absolute control.

Grace poured the colourless sweet-smelling liquid onto the pre-prepared sponge and held it gently over the patient's mouth and nose. The medics paused for a few seconds and when the patient was lying still again continued their work.

It took them around another five minutes, because the spurting blood kept obscuring their vision through the tiny hole, but eventually they found the ruptured artery inside and tied it off. A few further dabs with the swab and the wound was dry.

'Good job,' said the principal surgeon with a sigh, looking over his mask at his colleagues. 'Here's one who will live to fight another day.'

'He'd probably prefer not to fight another day, though,' said Dr Marks, laconically.

'I suppose not. But as you know, he's got a fifty-fifty chance now of having some permanent residual disability anyway, and possible epileptic seizures. So, if he's lucky he'll be a bit mentally slower, walk with a limp, be honourably discharged and sent back to Australia to lie on the beach for the rest of his life.'

'I imagine that would be infinitely preferable.'

Grace enjoyed the dark wry humour of the medics she worked with and these two in particular had no equal.

'I can think of worse outcomes,' she said as they de-gloved and left her to suture the skin incision.

10

Robbie was in the hole. There were lots of holes in no man's land, but he was the only man in his hole, so he thought. No one had answered him anyway, when he whispered. It was dark now and he was wet through and freezing and could hear the cries of other men in other holes, or who were lying on the ground with holes in their bodies where bullets had passed through, or got stuck, or far worse. One minute Robbie had been leading the charge and the next he was in the hole. He supposed people might see leading the charge as courageous, but he figured that if you went first, you wouldn't see the people in front of you getting torn to pieces by the machine-gun fire, or the rifle fire, or the shells, or whatever it was the Germans sent their way. They knew what they were doing, the Germans, with their artillery. The shells would blast down and the lads would cower beneath the lip of the parapet, hearing the shrapnel flinging itself into the walls behind them. It was when the shelling stopped and seemed to fly beyond them that they really had to worry, because that's when the Germans would hurl themselves forward over no man's land, bayonets fixed, heading for them, and they'd have to leap up and aim rifles and the machine gunners would set to work to keep them at bay. They had just held on in the face of the Germans' last attack – the stretcher bearers had been busy at the frontline trenches, carrying away those wounded or killed by shrapnel or picked off by snipers as they cut the Germans down. Now, wounded English voices were calling out for help.

When the order had come for a counter-attack, the officer who was leading the charge looked white as a ghost. So did most of the men. Robbie was almost relieved. Better to get it over with, to face things head on, than to cower like an animal. He knew he was probably about to die, but when the order came he threw himself up the ladder and advanced as quickly as he could, pounding through the slop and around the craters filled with water.

Then, a bang on the head and he woke up in a wet hole in the ground with a terrible headache but no other injury he could feel. There was a dent in his helmet but no other damage he could find. He was merely wet and cold. Which was dangerous in itself. It was dark now and he would have to get up. He would make it back to the trenches, if they were still there, still occupied by Tommies. He couldn't find his rifle and then, when he pulled himself up out of the hole and looked around, he saw the shape of it on the ground. Why was God rewarding him with so much luck now, when he had taken so much from him before? Men were making terrible noises around him. The stretcher bearers would be out soon, if they still had access to the trenches, if they hadn't been overrun by Germans. He would go and help however he could. He would try to get back to his men. He didn't care about his life so much but if he could do something useful with it perhaps he might learn to care about it again. He was alive. Incredibly, he was still alive.

11

Though Will was fascinated and rewarded by his work at the hospital, he was not immune to the pull of adventure, or the desire to help out his country. Outside the newsagent that morning was a big placard advertising a set of speeches on Saturday afternoon in Trafalgar Square about life in the trenches, and a chance to join up with your friends in a 'pals battalion'.

So, on that Saturday, after Will had finished his morning shift at the hospital, he set off on foot. It was a crisp November day, and Will was happy for the walk along the Thames and into Hyde Park where, deep in its green and orange depths, it was possible to forget for a few minutes about his father and the danger he must be in. Coming down the Mall from the park he noticed Buckingham Palace was covered in scaffolding for renovations. Will watched the lads up there tossing poles to each other, shouting, and considered that some of them would be fighting soon. He wondered where Jack was now and how long it would be before he reached the front. Perhaps he was already there.

There was a big sign resting against the stone lion at the foot of the square: 'The Need for More Fighting Men is Urgent'. A troop of boys no older than ten marched in dress uniform, holding bright swords against their left shoulders. Behind them, in the crowd, a military band beat the drum and sounded their bugles. Men in civvies, in suits and bowler hats, looked on. The children saluted, and a sergeant stood up on the stage and began to speak about duty and honour.

'Professor,' Will heard. 'Professor!'

Not now, he thought, and turned around to Trevor's smirk.

'What are you doing here?' Will said.

'What do you mean? I'm as patriotic as the next man.'

'You enlisting, then?'

'I might. I just might. Why, are you?'

'I'm only fifteen.'

'I'm only eighteen,' said Trevor. 'You're taller than me, what difference does it make?'

'Keep it quiet, you two — this is important,' said a man, turning around.

When he had turned back Trevor made an obscene gesture behind him.

'You heard from Jack?' he whispered.

'Not yet. He's not really one for writing.'

'You know where he is?'

'No. Sorry.'

Will looked more closely at Trevor. His suit was shabby and dirty and he wore no overcoat. He looked . . . yellowish, underfed. Trevor stared down at his boots, suddenly quiet, listening to the sergeant's speech.

He looked up at Will. 'It doesn't sound too bad, does it? Food, a roof over your head. A gang to chum around with.'

'No,' said Will, 'it doesn't.'

The line to the desks was long and he and Trevor queued for about an hour to reach the front of it, listening to the military drums, the rattle of sabres, and the brass band playing 'Rule, Britannia!' and 'Land of Hope and Glory'.

'I'm not signing up,' he told Trevor, 'I just want to ask questions.'

'You should just do it. You'd pass for eighteen easily.'

'Isn't it nineteen?'

'You hear different. But I don't think they ask to see your birth certificate. I don't even know if I have a birth certificate.'

'Perhaps you weren't born of woman.'

'You what?'

'Perhaps you came out of an egg. Perhaps you're just a very developed chicken.'

'You calling me a chicken? That's fighting talk, that is.'

Trevor was saved from having to pretend further to be outraged by them reaching the end of the line.

'You two together?' asked a sergeant.

'Sort of,' they both said.

'Are you or aren't you?'

'We are,' said Will, noticing Trevor's grateful look at that. Trevor was not so full of himself without Jack to back him up.

'Stand up straight,' the sergeant said, looking at Trevor. He looked them over, frowning when he turned to Trevor. 'Here to enlist, are we?'

'I'm only fifteen,' said Will. 'But I can fire a Lee-Enfield. Do you think I might be able to enlist soon? I would like to help out. My father's there, you see, and my brother.'

'That's the attitude. Though . . . fifteen? That's too young. What a shame, strapping lad like you. Just what we need to fight the Hun. And you, are you fifteen too?'

'Eighteen!' said Trevor, indignantly.

'Really?'

'Really!'

He frowned again. 'Come with me. Let's look at the both of you properly, get you weighed and your eyes tested.'

Both of them paused to take in the billboard on the way in to the tent: a soldier lying wounded, and a man with a bandage on his head standing over him, looking out into the distance. 'Will they *never* come?' said the caption, which Will heard in his father's voice.

'What do you eat, son?' he asked Trevor, as he stepped off the scales.

'Whatever I can,' said Trevor.

'It's not enough, whatever it is.'

'No point weighing you, is there?' he said to Will. 'Do you want to go to war?'

'Erm . . .'

'He doesn't,' said Trevor.

'Yes, I do!' said Will.

'Well, get on the scales here in any case, will you? Might as well have your measurements.'

Trevor caught the bus back west after signing up. He looked slightly shocked by what he had done, and Will thought he probably needed some company, but he wasn't ready to leave yet. He told Trevor he was going to walk, and lingered by the recruitment tent.

'It's a shame,' the sergeant had said to him as they were walking out. 'You seem like just the kind of man we need, unlike your mate, who, to be honest, we wouldn't take under usual circumstances. Do you think he can become a good soldier?'

'I don't know, sir. I think he might.'

'It's a shame you won't be there to help look after him.'

'You could say that, sir.'

'I think I see your meaning, lad. Do you want to know something? A little trick.'

'What's that?'

'Every time you do a circuit of Trafalgar Square, you get a year older.'

'What?'

'*Pardon, sir.*'

'Pardon, sir.'

'I said, every time you do a circuit of Trafalgar Square, you get a year older.'

'I'm not sure I understand.'

'That's a shame. You didn't seem dense at first.'

Will thought. 'If what you were saying was true, I could walk round the square three times, then walk back in here and tell you honestly I was eighteen.'

'You could, son. That you could.'

Now Will began to walk around the square, thinking about his life at home; thinking about his father, somewhere in Belgium, he imagined; and his brother, perhaps crossing the channel right now; even Trevor, on his way next week to be trained as a private in the New Army.

Once around the square he went, twice around the square, and thrice. The queues had died down and they were about to take the tent down and leave. Will took a deep breath and walked back towards the sergeant, who smiled when he saw him and said, 'Hello, young man. I don't believe we've met.'

12

Chapelle Blanchette

Second Lieutenant Charles Tustin-Pennington of the Royal Flying Corps adjusted his belt and checked the camera next to him: a mahogany box with a leather concertina pull-out containing a whopping great lens, and a little handle he had to use to change the plates. Not only did a pilot have to train to master the BE2c plane but he had to learn how to be a photographer, too. The camera was strapped to the side of the cockpit and he would have to lean out to look through the sight — at eight thousand feet in the air — in order to make sure he'd got the photos the general had asked for, of the enemy trench lines and their artillery batteries, their machine-gun posts, trench mortars and any signs of their headquarters behind the lines. Once identified, the British artillery would have something to aim for.

In front of him, under the double wings of the plane, was his observer, Corporal Bill Hurst, wedged in between struts of wood and canvas, which obscured his vision of the ground, and in front of him a machine gun was fixed on a swivel. Charles and Bill both hoped they would not have to use it, for it would be easy to hit one of the propellers in front of them. It was a terrible place to fire a machine gun from but it was the only place, and Charles would rather have had a machine gun in a terrible place than no place at all. Both men had rifles wedged in next to their seats.

It was a beautiful morning for a flight, the skies clear blue and the sun just up in the east. Safer to go out at night, of course, but then the camera would be useless.

He'd received a letter from Grace yesterday and had replied to it immediately. He was proud of his little sister, the first of all of them on the ground. The things she said she'd seen, and all of it narrated without any melodrama. She was a tough little thing. He did worry about how she would ever find a husband, and how he would cope with such a spirited woman. But there were worse things to worry about. Much worse.

The engine had started and the propeller was going and the ground was rushing under their feet. The nose of the plane began to lift off, with that alarming swing. It was incredible to him every time, that this vehicle of wooden struts and canvas and wire was nosing through the air and climbing higher and higher.

Height was their friend, now — this was one of the most dangerous moments, when they became visible to the enemy's artillery and machine guns and were still in firing range. Charles moved the plane from side to side, to prevent any snipers from following the line of where he would be going. So far, so good. In front of him Bill looked left to right, right to left — fat lot of good he was going to be, but he was necessary for the balance and the handling, and Charles was glad he was there, really, glad he wasn't having to sit squashed in front of someone doing the flying.

Down below, he could see the sprawl of their own trenches, the supply lines reaching back, and the villages, seemingly untouched by the war from this height, though there would be soldiers billeted inside all of them now.

In front was the salient of no man's land, a startling contrast, with its smashed trees and great water-filled craters, and rotting corpses of horses lying unburied. What a shameful thing. He thought of his old steed, Marmaduke, whom Grace had liked to ride long before she was big enough for a horse of his size. His father had given him up to the war effort: for all Charles knew he could have been one of the corpses he saw below.

No time to dwell on that. Here were the German trenches, similar in style to the British; there were the artillery batteries — keep away from them! Higher and higher he took the plane, his stomach clenching as he heard the rattle of a machine gun beneath him. Now was the time to lean out and operate the camera with his right hand, while his left hand steered the plane — a tricky business. Click. There was the photo. He leaned back in and looked around. Back out to change the plate with his right hand, cranking the little handle.

'How's it going?' shouted Bill. 'I can't see a bloody thing.'

Charles ignored him and focused on keeping them alive.

For the next ten minutes they flew up and down the line, listening to the rattle of the guns beneath, and loud bangs as the artillery took aim at them. At this altitude, they were pretty safe.

But then there came a different sound, of another engine coming near. Perhaps they had a fight on their hands. He had the shots he came for; it was safer and better to retreat, perhaps.

'Coming in from the left!' shouted Bill.

A single German plane was heading for them. Charles registered the machine gun pointed straight at its own propellers. He dipped the nose of the plane and veered in a circle back to base.

And then the bullets hit. They tore through the fuselage and knocked the plane off its trajectory.

Bill was swinging the gun but the German plane was behind their own. Charles turned around. Somehow, it was firing through its propellers. It was heading straight for them. Bill tried to swing the gun around but was hit three times in the chest and flopped face down against it.

Charles knew he had no chance in a fight now, and dipped further, swinging the plane around and heading back to his side of the trenches. If he could point it in the right direction, even if he was hit, the camera might make it back unscathed.

He dodged and rolled, but the German kept coming, the gun kept firing. He was nearly there. But the gun was blasting at him, and that was the last thing he heard before something hit him hard in between the shoulder blades and he blacked out.

13

Ypres

Something terrible was going on. To have every available nurse and medical officer summoned to the frontline was unprecedented. The horse-drawn ambulances had already departed and as soon as the last motorised vehicle had been loaded with extra equipment, two orderlies and a medical officer jumped in the back behind Grace. A flustered sergeant from the Queen Victoria's Rifles squeezed in the front with Grace and another nurse, meaning Grace now found herself in the driver's seat. The sergeant now loudly ordered her to 'step on it'. She pushed down hard on the accelerator and slung the ambulance around.

'Steady on,' said one of the orderlies, 'or we will be back in the hospital for all the wrong reasons.'

The town of Ypres, the hub of so much of the continual recent fighting, was about six kilometres ahead of them. The road was becoming increasingly jammed with traffic and the walking wounded who were fleeing the besieged town. To her left, Grace passed open fields of ripened crops that she knew would never be harvested and further on, to her right, a small stone outhouse where a middle-aged woman was hanging out washing on a clothesline as if it were a regular day. A young boy was enjoying an elongated swing suspended below the sturdy branch of an oak tree which must have been at least 200 years old. Twenty feet in girth and with an impressive spread of branches, it had deep fissures in its bark which looked large enough to put a man's fist in. Its knobbles and bumps reminded Grace of a rucked-up cardigan that her mother might wear on a winter's evening. She still experienced that childhood itch to climb it right to the top.

'Eyes on the road,' said the same nervous orderly, a good and reliable man but clearly a classic back-seat driver at the same time.

She drove furiously along the Poperinghe—Ypres road, weaving around all sorts of obstructions, the usual evidence of rapid evacuation from towns and villages under attack. In the first mile they travelled they saw bedsteads, mattresses, furniture and clothes, a discarded motorbike and a rusting tractor, and as they approached the outskirts of Ypres itself she was horrified to see a dead mule in the ditch beside the road, its belly ripped open by shell-fire and its hind leg hanging off. A continuous stream of people trudged past with their heads down, defeated and bloody, while in the distance massive explosions could be heard from every direction. Small groups of German prisoners of war were also being shepherded along, not looking frightened or contrite, more relaxed and relieved. They must have believed their future to be relatively safe. Weary and demoralised though they must have been, they still looked up as the ambulance hurtled towards them, perhaps hoping it had come for them.

Several hundred yards away in the failing light Grace saw flashes of shrapnel and the occasional light of rockets. Driving on, the cacophony of the bombardment grew ever louder, and men were stretched out on both sides of the road, some writhing in pain and others lying ominously still.

Suddenly galloping towards them from the Yser canal was a group of horses, their riders frantically urging them on. They were soon followed by dozens more. For a moment the swirl of dust they created almost obscured Grace's vision. Whatever was happening on the frontline it was terrifying the men and creating panic. Amid a mass of stricken soldiers, the ambulance was waved down by an agitated officer and they were exhorted to start work.

Grace parked, switched off the engine and jumped down onto the grass. Officers and staff officers were straining their eyes, gazing off into the distance. They looked bewildered and dumbfounded. What on earth was going on? Grace wondered. Had a huge German offensive been initiated? Men were running this way and that like headless chickens. And then she saw it. Coming from the north-west a breeze was slowly bringing a pale-green mist that seemed to hug the ground, spilling down into the hollows and filling bomb craters in its path. Soldiers were doing their utmost to flee the eerie cloud, some stumbling and falling, but others were apparently unaware of their surroundings and groped with their arms outstretched for something familiar with which they could orientate themselves. Then she noticed a strange kind of smell. What was it, exactly? An odd mixture of pine-apple and pepper, she thought. Faint at first, but then the odour became stronger and unpleasantly pungent. Her eyes smarted and she began to cough.

'Get this ambulance loaded and get the hell out of here,' yelled the sergeant. It was an order Grace and the orderlies were only too happy to obey.

They retraced their journey back with a total of thirteen poor victims packed like sardines into the rear of a vehicle intended to carry no more than eight. The soldiers' coughing and spluttering was harrowing. Whatever the foul green substance was, it was wreaking an awful toll. When they reached the clearing station, chaos reigned. Every bunk was taken, and men lay sprawled outside on the grass, in the garden, and even on the sanded area usually reserved for games of boules in quieter times. The station was equipped to deal with around eighty men but today there must have been around 250 waiting to be treated with more arriving all the time.

The worst of the cases were pitiful. Their eyes, streaming with tears, were puffy and swollen to the extent they could see nothing at all in front of them. They entered in long lines, blindfolds around their heads and one arm clutching the shoulder of the man in front. Their coughing was violent and continuous, their faces were puce with effort and their lips and noses blue through lack of oxygen. Gasping for breath, they were asphyxiating before Grace's very eyes. Both doctors and nurses felt equally powerless to help them. The awful scene continued all night, with incoming soldiers given beds as soon as vacant ones became available. The turnover was frantic, as hundreds of men died like flies throughout the night.

Another group of men in the Royal Marines Light Infantry had been attacked in a similar way somewhere on Hill 60 and they started to find their way to the hospital the next day. Their symptoms were different, however. Their exposed skin was horribly burned and blistered with widespread vesicles oozing copious amounts of yellow fluid. They were coughing severely, their lungs affected in the same way as the other soldiers.

It was one of the ghastliest episodes Grace had experienced

throughout the war so far. The thought of either side using poisonous gas to achieve their ends was anathema to her.

She later discovered that it was chlorine gas and mustard gas that had been used. Some of her patients' uniforms still exuded a strange smell, reminiscent of garlic or horseradish.

Many soldiers had come to the hospital that night but others who suffered delayed reactions drifted in gradually over the next three days. It was a fraught time, and Grace was glad when it was over.

Several days later, in the aftermath of the emergency, the nurses were treated to a tutorial on the subject from an officer sent down from further up the frontline who was apparently a biochemist in civilian life. He was a pale, slight-looking fellow with thick spectacles and a badly repaired harelip. Grace wondered how he had ever been certified fit for active duty.

'My name's Fletcher,' he said. 'I'm here to apprise you of the cause of the singularly unique injuries you have recently been dealing with.

'Chlorine gas,' he told them, 'is a diatomic gas about two and a half times denser than air. It comes in liquid form and is put into glass containers inside artillery shells. The glass breaks on contact and the liquid evaporates, forming a dense cloud.'

The nurses listened, spellbound.

'When it is inhaled it reacts with water in the lungs to produce hydrochloric acid.'

'Good God,' mumbled Jenny, sitting next to Grace.

Sister MacCailein stood very still with a hand around her own throat. This was as new to this experienced nurse as it was to the rest of them.

'Indeed,' he continued. 'This quickly destroys the delicate

air sacs in the lungs and the lining membranes of the major airways. Even in moderate concentrations it can prove fatal.'

The room was silent.

'At lower concentrations, if it doesn't reach deep into the lungs, it will still cause coughing, vomiting and eye irritation.'

Grace knew this already, having suffered two of the symptoms mildly herself.

'In higher concentrations, in unprotected soldiers, it will kill fast.'

The nurses looked at one another, aghast.

'You said in unprotected soldiers, sir,' said Grace. 'What kind of protection is useful?'

'Water,' replied the chemist. 'Chlorine is water-soluble. So, wrapping a water-soaked rag or sock, indeed any piece of clothing, over the nose and mouth can mitigate the effects of the gas. To some extent, anyway.'

'But what if there is no water to be had when the men are attacked?' asked Jenny. 'Should the men carry extra water bottles with them as well as all their gear?'

'No need,' smiled the expert on poison gas, obviously quite pleased with himself. 'Urine is just as effective. And most of the men will have a ready supply of that.'

If it was intended to be funny nobody laughed, and the tutorial continued.

'Other forms of protection are being developed as we speak. John Scott Haldane, my mentor, with whom I worked in Edinburgh, is a renowned biochemist working day and night back home to design a breathing apparatus similar to the ones he manufactured for use in the mining industry following explosions. He's hoping to come up with some kind of veil or box respirator. A gas mask, you might call it. The Germans already have them.'

'I can't imagine fighting hand-to-hand while wearing breathing apparatus will make life easier,' piped up one of the staff nurses.

'Well, John is a great self-experimenter, Nurse,' he said eagerly. 'He is famous for it. His view is this. Why experiment on monkeys, dogs or guinea pigs? They can't speak, so they can't tell you anything. But experimenting on yourself . . . You can report precisely what you're feeling.'

'A bit dangerous, isn't it? How many of his nine lives has he used up?'

A ripple of laughter lifted the mood.

'Well, he is a bit of a character I can tell you. As soon as he heard that chemical warfare was being waged, he accelerated his research programme and expanded his lab into his home. You wouldn't believe it, but he proceeded to expose himself to much higher concentrations of gas then he would have done in peacetime. Word has it that he even got his eighteen-year-old daughter Naomi to wait outside the door, which had a window in it with instructions on what to do if he suffered an untoward reaction.'

'I've got a crazy father like that as well,' said Jenny, and this time even the biochemist laughed.

'The men with the blisters were poisoned with a different gas. Mustard gas. Bis two-chloroethyl sulphide.'

Jenny glanced at Grace and rolled her eyes up to the heavens.

'It's nasty stuff and can cause long hospitalisations. But the one we really need to be wary of is phosgene gas. Unfortunately, it is proving more effective and more deadly by far than chlorine gas. It's colourless, so unlike chlorine gas you don't see it coming. The Germans prefer it for that reason. Our troops have less time to escape. In high concentrations it smells like musty hay. It's highly toxic, however. It reacts with proteins inside the alveoli in your lungs and this stops oxygen being transferred into the blood from the air we breathe. It can also take up to forty-eight hours for the symptoms to manifest themselves, which is why you continued to see men coming into the hospital several hours after the first gas attack. Fluid builds up in the lungs, which you all recognise as pulmonary oedema, and this is responsible for the vast majority of the fatal cases you've been seeing.'

The nurses were then given instruction about what was referred to as the optimum management and treatment of gas poisoning. It was brief, simply because other than giving oxygen, which was in short supply, no effective treatment existed.

The whole episode of the gas attack and the sheer numbers of men incapacitated by permanent blindness or breathing difficulties had deeply upset Grace. It was one thing running towards enemy machine guns dodging shells, or fighting hand-to-hand with a pistol or fixed bayonet – you might not be completely in command of your own destiny, and injury or death was still very random, but at least you had a chance. A cloud of poison gas enveloping you, however, would give you no hope at all.

Interesting though the talk had been, and useful in terms of how best to treat these poor victims of chemical warfare, Grace felt depressed and despondent about this latest noxious twist in the course of the war. She got up from her seat, leaving Jenny still chatting to the woman on the other side of her, and walked towards the exit. There, right in her path, stood Sister MacCailein. The woman seemed to follow her around like a bad smell. That was all she needed, Grace thought, another dressing down. What had she done this time?

'Nurse Tustin-Pennington,' she said curtly, her face pinched. 'A telegram for you.'

Grace was taken aback. She had never received a telegram before in her life. And delivered by the principal sister herself no less. She took the small brown envelope from the sister's outstretched hand and watched as she turned and walked away.

Grace put her thumb under the flap and tore open the envelope as she left the tent.

14

'Will, no, please no,' his aunt Clara said, holding her hands to her head as if to keep it from falling off her shoulders and onto the floor.

'I thought about writing you a letter and leaving secretly. But we've had enough of that in the family.'

'I'm going to go straight down there and tell them how old you are.'

'You could do that, I know,' said Will, keeping his voice calm. 'But then I'd go and join up somewhere else, and I wouldn't be able to come back and say goodbye to you and Kitty because I'd know what you were going to do next.'

'Will, you're only fifteen!'

'I know, but I think I might be more useful than some people a bit older than me. I have experience helping injured people. I know how to march and shoot. I'm fit and healthy. I know what it's like to see people die.'

And as he said this, he realised that he did possess a certain strength, because of the pain the family had been through. He had strength because of the role he'd had to play as the sensible one, the strong one, so that Clara could devote her energies to young Kitty and keeping Jack on the straight and narrow. He'd been no fuss, and now he thought he had the qualities to get through hardship.

'They're crying out for reinforcements, Clara. Useful reinforcements. Father and Jack, that is! They're crying out for help.'

'We hear so little from your dad. You wonder if we'd even hear if he were dead.' And then she looked stricken, as if she'd revealed a cruel world to Will he'd been unaware of. But he had been aware of it, he had thought about that most nights before he fell asleep; had dreamed about his father, his body stranded in between the trenches, slipping under the mud, pecked at by crows.

'I have considered that,' he said firmly.

They argued into the night. 'What about Kitty?' she said.

'Kitty has you.'

'She'll miss you awfully.'

'Do you not think I'll miss her? And you?'

'You're such a boy. You think there's only one way to be heroic. There are other, quieter ways than firing guns and getting yourself killed.'

'I know that,' he said. 'But I'm not getting killed.'

Clara didn't go to the recruitment office and tell them about him. 'It's your choice,' she said eventually. 'You have two weeks to change your mind.'

But he didn't change his mind, tortured though he was by the idea of leaving Kitty an orphan with two dead brothers. Don't be gloomy, he told himself, it doesn't help.

He was heading away from the war first, up north to Staffordshire, where two Army training camps had been built in Cannock Chase. That was all he knew — there had been reports of having to sleep in tents. How cold was a tent in winter, he wondered. He might be about to find out.

He would not admit his worries to Clara when she asked him.

'They have huts, Clara, with coal fires to heat them.'

'How do you know?'

'I was told when they recruited me.'

Another white lie.

On the day it was time to leave, he shouldered his canvas bag and looked around the room he and Jack used to share. It was tidier than it used to be. A neat stack of *Boy's Own* newspapers sat next to the books he had borrowed from Clara. It was a boys' room, without any boys left in it, and there would be no boys left to return to it after war. They would be men, or they would be . . .

Down the stairs he went.

Clara and Kitty were waiting in the hallway.

'You've got your gloves and your scarf packed, and those jumpers I knitted for you.'

'I have, Aunt Clara, thank you.'

'Will you say hello to Jack for me when you see him?' asked Kitty.

'It's quite a big war. I might not see him for a while.'

'And tell him Tilly the cat had kittens, two boys, two girls.'

'Of course, I'll tell him.'

'And Father?'

'And Father. Of course.'

'Keep safe,' said Clara. 'Keep your wits about you. You've got plenty of them, in spite of this foolishness; it's what's making me hopeful.'

*

At Euston he found Trevor, with a much smaller bag than him, shivering in the same suit he normally wore without an overcoat.

'I've never been north of London,' he said.

'Me neither,' admitted Will.

'Well, I'm sure they're no more savage than the savages my dad knocks about with.'

'You'll eat them alive, Trev.'

'I am quite hungry. Think there'll be decent grub there?'

Will shared his sandwiches with him on the train up. Strange how things had changed between them already. There was no more talk of 'the professor', even when Will took out the book he'd brought along with him. And Will realised what he'd disdained in Trevor had been related to circumstances. He'd been trying to make a living, just like Jack. He hadn't had a steady influence on him, like Will had with Clara. Poor Clara. She had given up so much for Evie's men, and now all three of them had deserted her.

*

When they arrived at the training camp, they were relieved to see rows of long wooden huts stretched across the land, with flat chalk roads between them.

A sergeant greeted them. 'You're lucky lads, arriving now. Would have been tents for you a year ago.'

They slept in bunks, with thirty soldiers to each hut. Trevor had been assigned to a different hut and seemed to be making friends there.

There were no uniforms for them yet, and the first days were spent tediously on the parade ground, learning how to march (something Will already knew), how to obey orders, how to follow drill instructions.

Discipline was tough and no backchat was tolerated. Will wondered how Jack was finding that. They marched and marched and marched till their feet were numb and their bodies shattered. Will fell asleep almost instantly every night when he hit the bunk.

One week on, they were presented with their uniform: a thick woollen tunic with breast pockets (one to keep your pay book) and an internal pocket where soldiers kept their emergency field dressing, plus two shirts, trousers, boots, and puttees to wear around the ankles and calves. A peaked cap, too, 'though you'll be wearing a helmet when you're in the line,' admonished the sergeant as he gave it to Will, as though Will had just suggested otherwise. That was this sergeant's style. He must have learned it by copying all the other sergeants' styles. What was more exciting than the uniform was that they were given their Lee-Enfield Mk III rifles to practise with, and taught how to affix the vicious eighteen-inch bayonet to them.

Drill Sergeant McAllister was a tough Glaswegian, five foot six, with a ferocious moustache. He led bayonet training.

'The bayonet is grooved,' he shouted, standing by the sandbag. 'If you pull it straight out it doesn't leave much of a hole in the Jerry.' He plunged it into the prop. Will thought that would leave quite a big hole in anyone. 'You thrust and twist on the way out. Like this.' He demonstrated. Will imagined pushing sharp steel into another man's body and twisting it while it was still inside him, imagined how that would feel. Whenever he had imagined killing it had been with a rifle, at a distance, clean, shots to the chest and the head. This was something else.

'Are you all right?' said Trevor next to him. 'You've gone a bit green.'

'I'm fine. Dodgy stomach from something.'

When it was his turn, he charged and shouted and thrust the blade deep into the bag, wrenching it with his hands to twist its innards, then pulled it out.

'That's the spirit,' shouted the sergeant. But Will knew the difference between a sandbag and a man, and he could not for the life of him imagine doing this to a man. Perhaps he was a coward; perhaps he was too young for this.

But he was here now. He was going to have to find out for himself.

15

'Darling Grace,' began the telegram. 'It is with the heaviest of hearts that we are informing you of the tragic loss of your brother, Charles. Killed in action on a reconnaissance flight over Verdun on 15 April. We pray that you are safe and for your swift return whenever possible. With love always, your devoted parents, Dorothy and Arthur.'

Grace felt weak on her legs. And instantly nauseated. Charles had been killed and she did not want to believe it. Of course, she'd known it could happen. It could happen to any of her brothers. James or Henry serving on the Western Front, or Rupert in the Navy. It was always a possibility. But it was only a theoretical possibility. Was that not how everyone in her position rationalised it? Nobody really wants to believe such a loss could happen to them. But it had. Charles! Oh no, not Charles. She re-read the harrowing words, crumpled the paper in her fist and let it drop to the ground. Omelette nudged it with her paw but then jumped quietly up onto Grace's bed and curled up, seeming to sense her companion's emotions.

A fury welled up inside Grace. A wild rage that she could not control. The feeling of weakness was immediately replaced by an irrepressible surge of energy which jangled her nerves and tightened her muscles as she strode off along the path between the rows of tents, heading for the horse line. When she arrived, she walked along the row of tethered animals until she came to the one she was looking for. An officer's horse, a powerful bay gelding with its saddle and bridle already in place, who was eyeing her warily as she approached. She untied him and led him over to an old tree stump a few yards away. She stepped smoothly onto the stump, put her foot in the stirrup and launched herself into the saddle, her long skirt flying around her and draping across the horse's back. Taking the reins, she jabbed her heels hard into the flank of the beast, and took off along the track. A shrill cry came from somewhere behind her, a surprised subaltern in the cavalry no doubt, whose duty it was to supervise the horses, but Grace was disappearing into the distance already, leaving a swirl of dust behind her. So what if she had borrowed one of their precious horses? What could they do about it now? They could discipline her; they could chastise her. Right now, she did not give a damn.

Charles! How could he die? How could he leave her? Why didn't he take more care? The gelding charged eagerly, happy to be spurred on by its determined rider. He sensed that this particular outing was something exceptional.

Grace, angry and numb at the same time, stood in the stirrups leaning over the animal's strong neck, urging him on as fast as she could. She could feel his mighty muscles bunch and release as he galloped and was aware of a similar tension in her own shoulders, back and thighs. They flew across the ground like an express train, the gelding's ears pinned back and his hooves pounding beneath them as they ate up the miles. Faster and faster she drove him, following the hypnotic nodding motion of his noble head with her hands tightly on the reins. They rode at a frenzied pace for what seemed like an age, the horse breathing hard and snorting while Grace, herself breathless and aching, pressed him on to ever greater efforts.

Her eyes smarted from the wind and made the tears she was shedding in her grief tumble faster.

There was a rickety wooden gate at the end of the track ahead of them, but she was in no mood to stop her mad, headlong rush. She gathered the horse, readied it, accelerated and flew over the gate with yards to spare. The coarse hair from the gelding's long mane whipped at her lips and mouth and she was reminded of similar experiences she had enjoyed on rides with Charles during their childhood. She pictured the two of them on the estate, laughing and playing together, galloping across the fields down by the lake, racing each other to see who could reach the folly at the top of the hill first. Grace had always won, but only because Charles had usually allowed her to. The memory of it made her slow to a canter. She could see his face so clearly in her mind's eye. His dazzling smile. His cheeky laugh. His twinkly eyes. She sobbed.

She tugged on the reins, brought the horse to a halt and dismounted. The animal was bathed in sweat and panting hard. She put her face against his handsome head and patted him. She stood silent for a few moments without moving.

She looked into the animal's huge dark eyes and in them saw her own sad reflection, her hair matted with her own sweat and tears. Standing still and statuesque, the horse seemed to be looking deep into her soul.

'My brother died,' she whispered in his ear. 'My lovely brother. And I loved him so much.' The horse dropped his head slightly in commiseration, as if it could somehow sense her despair.

She led the gelding over to the side of the path, dropped the reins and flopped to the ground with her back to a tall silver birch tree, one of a row. The horse pawed at the ground and whinnied quietly.

Behind her, a thick carpet of bluebells swarmed over an ancient woodland floor, the deep violet-blue petals drooping mournfully to one side of their stems as if bowing their heads in prayer. At Bishop's Cleeve she and Charles would often sit together at this time of year in the bluebell woods by the sawmill.

'Some people call them cuckoo's boots,' he had told her. 'Mother calls them fairy flowers.'

She could still remember his exact words. 'Imagine, a cuckoo wearing boots! According to her, if you pick one, you'll be led astray and end up wandering aimlessly, totally lost for evermore.'

Grace sobbed again, able to hear his voice so clearly in her head. She reached over and picked one, knowing that her mother's prophecy had been right and that she would indeed now be lost for evermore. She rested her head against the silver bark of the birch tree and looked up through its branches at the blue sky above. It looked infinite and vast with no beginning nor end, peaceful and majestic at the same time. It held a few fluffy clouds in its thrall, yet the sky was empty and cold, and it had not safeguarded Charles as it should have done.

Charles had longed to fly for as long as she could remember. He had always wanted to touch the sky. He said that if he could come back in another life as a different living thing it would be a bird. So that he could flit and soar over the hills, fields and forests. Maybe he would, she thought. She would look at every bird she saw differently from now on; maybe it would be a reincarnation of her brother. When she was six and he was nine he had turned his attention to kites and built up an impressive collection. He had box kites, delta kites, rainbow kites and bat kites. He flew them, he crashed them, and he even constructed novel ones himself. Whenever the wind blew at Bishop's Cleeve her brother would be out there at the top of the hill, his little arms tugging the strings violently this way and that to make the kite lift and dip, dart and turn at his command.

Grace sat there for a long time. She had no idea how long. The horse was patient, seeming to realise that Grace needed some time alone.

Hours later, as darkness was beginning to fall, she heard the familiar sound of horses' hooves coming her way. She dried her eyes and stood to get a better look. The horse and rider drew nearer. They saw her and trotted towards her. It was Jenny.

'Grace, I have been so worried,' she said, dismounting.

'I don't know how you managed to find me, Jenny,' said Grace. 'I could have been anywhere.'

'But I did. I'm a good scout.' Jenny smiled and took her in her arms.

They tethered the horses, made their excuses to the relieved but irritated subaltern who felt he had failed in his duty to guard them and hugged each other tightly again. Once apprised of the circumstances, the grumpy subaltern promised to keep quiet about the 'borrowing' of the two officers' horses on condition that one of the nurses unsaddled the horses and washed them down. Jenny took her cue and agreed to meet Grace later in their tent.

Grace went inside to her bunk, and found Sister MacCailein waiting for her on a stool beside the bed. This is the last thing I need right now, Grace thought.

'Sit down, please,' said the senior nurse, in her customary unfriendly tone.

'I found this.' She held out the crumpled telegram Grace had discarded before her fugue. 'I'm so very sorry.'

Grace looked up at her, but the sister was fixated on the telegram in her lap and her lips and hands were trembling.

'I'm not very good at this, Nurse Tustin, as I think you know, but I realise I haven't been very kind to you, and I know what it's like to lose a brother in wartime.'

Grace studied her face. She could see she was distressed and struggling as always to express her feelings. The sister had acted horribly towards her in the past, but at that moment she felt quite sorry for her.

'The loss of your brother must be a terrible blow.' She closed her eyes as if doing it would protect her from being caught showing emotion. 'You are a skilled and dedicated member of my staff, an excellent nurse admired and respected by all. You are also blessed with the gift of empathy and compassion, which you show to all your patients so easily. It's a gift not all of us possess.'

Grace knew to whom she was referring but was more than surprised to hear this thinly veiled confession. What was it about some people, she wondered, that made it so hard for them to open their heart to others? The sister clearly had one, and a decent one at that; she had to, to be in the job she was in and to be here now fighting her better instincts.

'I will struggle to find anyone to carry out your duties as well as you and to adequately fill your shoes. But you have toiled without any leave for far too long and I know you must be exhausted.'

'But Sister, I—' Grace got no further before she was interrupted.

'Your family will also need you at this time. I have arranged for you to take some immediate leave, effective from tomorrow.'

Grace was both stunned and bewildered. She had never thought this cold and emotionally bankrupt woman capable of such consideration, but obviously she had been wrong. She was also stirred by the prospect of getting home to see her parents, who she knew would be united in their terrible grief.

'Pack your bags and get some sleep if you can. A driver will take you to the train at six o'clock tomorrow morning.' She reached out as if to take Grace's hand, then hesitated and thought better of it. She stood and left the tent.

Grace put her head in her hands and cried quietly.

16

Munich

Jürgen Altmann had never had the slightest desire to visit England, but after the incident with Freya, the factory foreman's teenage daughter, his father had to take him aside.

'What did you do to her?' he hissed.

'Nothing she didn't want me to,' said Jürgen.

His father slapped him across the face. 'What have you become? The foreman, one of my best workers, wants to go to the police! You can no longer be here.'

As a chance to redeem himself, he would travel to Birmingham and study engineering at the university there, while spending a day a week in a factory, which his father owned a small stake in and which manufactured the parts he imported to make the engines Altmann's was famous for.

'This is your last chance, Jürgen!'

'Just because of some *schlampe*—'

His father slapped him again. 'Get out of my sight.'

*

Jürgen ended up spending three years there, studying engineering and haltingly picking up the language. For a while he

had one friend, Lukas, an Austrian studying English liter-
ature. They would drink foul-tasting flat beer in the English
pubs and talk about the women they saw around them, and
how they might introduce themselves. Jürgen had tried
several times, but was always laughed at. Sometimes he would
try to rope Lukas in.

'This is my friend, Lukas — he studies English — a girls'
subject! Perhaps you have things to talk about to each other,
yes?'

This tactic met with little success, and gradually Jürgen
noticed that Lukas was ignoring him. He would knock on
the door of his guesthouse and be turned away by the aggressive landlady — 'don't you foreigners know we can't have
visitors at all hours!' — though he could see that there was a
lamp burning in Lukas's room.

Jürgen was desperately lonely. He wrote letters to his
father, telling him what a foul country this was; how the
food, people and beer were horrible. The men in the factory
laughed at him and mimicked his accent.

As he exaggerated the treatment he received there in his
letters, it became true to him, and he became angrier and
angrier.

His father wrote back every time. Stay there. Finish the
degree. Learn the language. You will be more useful to me.
You will learn how to be an adult.

Jürgen kept himself to himself, spending the nights on
his own, drinking the disgusting flat beer. Sometimes he
would be drawn into an argument with other students about
the Kaiser's aggressive militarisation. Jürgen thought this
was a marvellous thing. It was self-evident that the German
culture towered over the rest of Europe's: the over-passionate
Latins, the sentimental English. Power and steel were what

was needed. They would be laughing on the other side of their faces one day.

In the final year of his degree, in early 1914, he received a telegram. 'Father very ill. Come home. Mother.'

He arrived too late to say goodbye to his father. The first stroke had paralysed him; the second, four days later, killed him outright. Now, as the eldest son, he was in charge of the estate and the family business.

His father had been too incapacitated to leave instructions, and so everything passed to Jürgen.

The first thing he did was call the factory manager into his office, the one whose slut daughter had caused him so much trouble, and asked him who the most capable man below him would be to run the factory, in case anything ever happened to him.

The foreman informed him, then Jürgen fired him without delay and appointed the man he had named in his stead.

The next thing he did was enlist. Someone like Jürgen, of prestigious stock, of an engineering education, who knew the English and all their weaknesses, a natural commander of men (so he thought) — surely such a man could go far in the Kaiser's Army.

17

The train pulled into Cheltenham in the middle of the afternoon. It had been a long journey — several trains in France, then the ferry — though Grace had barely registered it. It had been raining as she'd stood out on the deck, staring at the grey sea, at the frothing wake the boat left, which reminded her of the clouds in the sky her brother had flown so close to. She had never asked him what that was like. There were lots of things she had never asked him.

Jenny had offered to come with her, but Grace was adamant she would travel alone. 'They can't afford to lose the both of us at once. I really shouldn't be going at all.' Though she was glad Jenny had been able to go home briefly a few months before, to see her fiancé Reggie before he'd gone to join the fight himself. 'Plus, I need you to keep an eye on Omelette.'

Jenny had hugged her and looked her in the eye. 'Of course. Now, Grace, I'm going to tell you something you won't like hearing.'

Grace had looked at her, hoping for something curt, some-thing like, 'Snap out of it,' or, 'Get back to work.'

'You on your own — you can do good work, you can make a little difference, but that's all it is, a little difference. And there are new nurses arriving every day who can make the same little difference you can. You're not so special that this place will fall apart without you.'

Grace felt the truth of this while also bridling at it. She realised she did think she had become a particularly exceptional nurse. But it was proud and foolish of her to think she was vital to the operation. And even working as hard as she could, she could not attach those missing limbs, or rebuild those shattered faces. They would die and die and die whether she was there or not.

Often in vain, though not always. Charles's plane had crashed on the British side of the Western Front and though it had burst into flames, the soldiers on the scene had the common sense to grab the camera, after they had ascertained that Charles and Bill were dead. On her way back she planned to visit, to see that he was properly buried and to mark it somehow.

Since her moment of fleeing with the horse, she had been in control of her emotions — everything seemed to be happening at a distance, to somebody else. As the train stopped and she picked up her case she realised she would have liked the journey to carry on for longer. She was not looking forward to seeing her mother.

But it was only her father waiting for her, swaying awkwardly as he shifted his weight from his good leg to his prosthetic.

'Grace, my darling, I am so glad you've made it back,' he said, holding her shoulders and looking into her eyes.

'Who's here?' she said, looking around her.

'Your mother's at home with Amy and Fitzwilliam. She's taken to her bed. Probably for the best. Your brothers, of course, are all still out there, fighting.' His face fell. 'We've heard nothing to the contrary. Just this awful news about Charles.'

'Oh, Father . . .'

'In any other circumstances to see you would be such a celebration. All the stories you must have to tell.'

'There are stories I shouldn't tell in front of Mother.'

'Yes. I wonder if you should tell them in front of me.'

'Oh, Daddy, I have to tell them to someone.'

'Come on, then. You can talk while Douglas drives us home.'

*

Dorothy rarely left her room, and Grace and Amy took turns visiting her there.

'Why me?' she'd say, and Grace tried to stay patient, as she knew it was not just her that this was happening to, but mothers and fathers across the land, thousands and thousands and thousands of them, and that the men were suffering awful privations, and that not all those who did make it back would be recognisable as the same people. She could not talk about this, because she intended to get back to France as soon as she could, because she needed to be useful, because — selfishly, she supposed — she needed to be with people who understood what it was like there.

The atmosphere in the house was heavy, and she felt like her brother Fitzwilliam was avoiding her. She tracked him down one afternoon in the library. There was a pile of open books spread out on the desk but she interrupted him doing physical exercises. He hated the handicap that his heart defect imposed on him and clearly he was still trying to compensate for it when nobody was looking. He started when he saw her and leaned breathlessly against the desk.

'Don't stop for me, Fitzy. Carry on!'

'That's what you call the Germans, isn't it? Fitz? I've got the same name as a German.'

'Fritz, Fitzy, not Fitz. Oh, there are lots of names for them: Jerry, the Hun, the Boche.'

'What do you think makes them such bad people? Why can't they just behave decently?'

'Oh, Fitzy. I think their average soldier is the same as our average soldier. Not entirely sure what he's doing there, scared, fighting for his life. I've treated a few of them.'

'Then what's it all for?'

'Good question. You're the one reading the books. You tell me.'

'The more one reads the more one realises how stupid one is.'

'Well, I suspect I shall never know how stupid I am, then.'

'You needn't rub it in.'

'What?'

'I would be there fighting too, if I could.'

'Oh, Fitzy, of course. No one doubts this.'

'My damned heart condition.'

'It is hell there, Fitzy. So you know. It is hell.'

'Why should I be allowed to avoid hell? As if the heart wasn't bad enough, this feeling of uselessness compounds everything. I'm scarcely a man at all.'

'I've seen soldiers unmanned in much more awful ways than you could imagine.'

'You mean . . .'

He looked down at his lap.

'Yes,' she said.

'My God.'

'Yes.'

'Tell me more about what it's like there, Grace. I know you protect Mother's feelings, but I'd like to hear. There's no pretending there's no danger now, in any case, is there?'

She told Fitzwilliam more than she had told her father, not feeling like she owed him the same duty of staying unmarked by her experiences, not feeling like she had to be the fearless and rebellious young girl she had once been.

*

Later that day she was by her mother's bedside.

'Promise me you won't go back, Grace,' Dorothy said, squeezing her hand. 'It would be better if you didn't.'

'But wouldn't you rather have someone like me there to patch up Henry if he falls over and stabs himself in the foot with his bayonet?'

'But darling, there are plenty of women like you there, with mothers who have not lost their firstborn.'

There would be plenty of women there whose mothers *had* lost their firstborn, thought Grace, but she tried a different tack.

'I'm working behind the frontline, Mother. It's perfectly safe.'

'How can it be? If the Germans penetrate the frontline don't they come straight through and meet you, with their shells and their gas and goodness only knows what vileness they're capable of?'

Her mother wasn't an idiot. It was good for Grace to be reminded of that sometimes.

'Promise me you won't go.'

'I won't, I'm sorry, I won't.'

'Oh, Grace. I'm being selfish, I know. I just want to know you're all safe.'

'I know. I'm safe here now with you. I'm glad I'm here now with you.'

She held her mother's hand until she fell asleep.

* * *

In the weeks that followed, Grace realised how tired she had been, falling asleep immediately each night as soon as her head hit the pillow.

There were nightmares. Of course there were nightmares. But sometimes she could sleep straight through for ten hours at a time.

Her mother began to get up, to take walks around the garden with Grace and Amy and Fitzwilliam. The family began to eat dinner together again. It was not only the soldiers who had to recover from the effects of the war. Grace saw that it was affecting those at home too.

Out in the garden she looked at the giant redwood and imagined it stripped of its leaves, blasted by shells, but she blinked and it was still there, still glorious. She would go back to the front and it would be hard. She would go back and it would be hard for her parents. She would go back and she would struggle to cope with what she saw, but she would, and later she would return, and the tree would still be there, having grown another ring or two below the surface of the bark. That was how to think of it. She would be there, changed a little below the surface, but ready to endure.

18

Cannock Chase, Staffordshire

It was April, and Will and Trevor were both sick of the routine by now. There was the bugle call at 5.30 — time to sweep their quarters and make their beds and brew a cup of tea — and then an hour and a half of parading before breakfast at eight, laden down with their gear.

Will was more comfortable with rifle training. The regular Army prided themselves on being able to fire fifteen rounds per minute, reloading their rifles speedily with the bold-action mechanism, and this was the aim for the new recruits.

Will was nowhere near that yet. Though he'd fired the rifle before, he was still new to the mechanisms; he would have to know his weapon and ammunition by feel alone before he could reload and fire it at that speed.

But he was accurate, hitting the target most times; not always in the bull, but usually in the inner or outer ring at least. It was easier to pretend this was a contest only with yourself, easier to disassociate the bullets and the paper targets from the men he'd be firing at when he reached the front.

And then there were the Mills bombs. For throwing down into the Germans' trenches. Will was taught to pull the pin and hold the handle carefully. Once you let go there were five seconds before it exploded.

'Throw it like a fast bowler,' the sergeant said. They practised manoeuvres with a trench dug for the purpose. They'd
line up in a team, with riflemen and bombers. After the
bombers had thrown the grenade, the riflemen would leap
down into the trench from either side and head towards each
other.

'And what are the Germans doing while we're standing in
front of their trenches?' asked Trevor.

'I guess we have to hope they're being kept busy by the rest
of our boys,' said Will.

*

On Saturday, after dinner, they would walk down into town,
proudly wearing their khakis, smiling at every woman they
passed.

Will felt a spring in his step then, pride at being a man
and doing what a man was supposed to do — which allowed
him to forget Clara and Kitty for a little while.

'Hello, darling,' called Trevor to a blonde pushing a pram.

She smiled politely and put her head down.

'Your brother Jack would like it here,' Trevor said. 'He'd
know what to say to her to make her more friendly.'

'She's a young mother!'

'So what?'

'Her husband's probably around somewhere, or fighting
at the front.'

'Yeah. Or dead.'

'Trevor!'

'It's true. We're dying out there. If we can be of some
comfort to grieving widows . . .'

'I can't believe I'm hearing this.'

'You're still such an innocent, young Will. Come on, I'll buy you a pint.'

There wasn't much Will could say to counter that. He was an innocent. Trevor was older than him, and had grown up without the protective influence of Clara. He did know more about the world. Will had never even drunk beer before arriving at the camp. Their pay wouldn't stretch to much of it, but he would feel lightheaded on the way back up to the barracks from the two pints he'd drunk with Trevor.

'This isn't so bad, is it?' he said to Trevor.

'This is the life, mate,' said Trevor. 'Fresh air, good food, exercise. I'm healthier than I've ever been.'

And it was true. Trevor, still slight, was more wiry now than skin and bones, and he had lost his sallow complexion.

'You're becoming a soldier,' said Will, looking at him.

'You too,' said Trevor.

'I don't know if I can do it,' Will admitted. 'Stick a bayonet in a man and twist it around.'

'I think you might feel differently if Fritz is charging towards you with a bayonet attached to his own rifle.'

Will looked around him, at the trees swaying in the breeze, the factories in the distance. It was best not to think about that.

'What did you think of the barmaid?' he asked.

*

Just as the first shoots of spring were coming, the crocuses and daffodils unfurling, it was time to go. Will looked up for the last time from his bunk through the window at the ashes and sycamores, whose branches were beginning to bud.

The barracks were busy with the news of the conscription act: that all able-bodied single men between nineteen and forty-one were now required to report to duty.

'Where in the hell will we put them?' Will had heard the drill sergeant asking an officer.

'I suppose we'll just have to move them through here more quickly,' he'd said. 'We need the men, don't we?'

Now the battalion was assembling to march out and board trains to Southampton.

The young officer who had known so little about how to direct the company through their movements was now very confident, and once they were assembled, wearing their packs, with their rifles gleaming, they were off, marching down through the town on their way to the station.

People came out of houses and shops to cheer them on, and men too old to fight walked alongside them, offering to carry their packs, their rifles.

'Left, right, left, right!' shouted the young officer but their rigid formation was soon impossible to keep under control because of the attention the men were receiving from the townfolk, many of whom were saying goodbye to their friends and husbands.

'Thank you! Thank you! We'll see you soon.'

Will looked over at Trevor.

'Think we'll be back here again?'

'Shouldn't think so? What for? Nah, we'll be back in Turnham Green, where we belong.'

'You want to go back?'

'One day. Not yet. I want to see France. A bit of the action.'

'That's where we're heading.'

The action. The bullets and the bayonets and the hand

bombs. The trenches and the shelling and the Germans – to kill them.

'Left, right, left, right, left, right, left.'

Will and Trevor marched on.

PART TWO

SURGERY AND THE SOMME

1916

19

In France, there was much more of the same in store for Trevor and Will. The marches with the equipment pulling at your shoulders, making your back ache. Left, right, left, right. About turn. Right dress. All the men were tired of the parade ground, and the hard boots that tore up their feet — which a lot of men would urinate into in the hope it would soften the leather before the ten-mile marches with their full packs on, a pick or a shovel attached, and belts of bombs and ammunition, besides all of one's standard-issue belongings.

They had arrived in Le Havre from Southampton two months ago. It had been the first time either Will or Trevor or indeed most of the men had ever crossed the channel, and both of them had kept to the deck, pressed in with hundreds of other men, staring out at the horizon while the boat pitched up and down with the waves.

'Feeling seasick?' asked Trevor.

'No, you?'

'Not a bit.'

Both young men had a little greenish colour to them, but they were proud, semi-trained soldiers now, and queasiness had not been something worth mentioning.

The British Expeditionary Force was arriving in France in ever-increasing numbers now, with France having lost hundreds of thousands of men in 1915 and in desperate need of support.

There was news of Jack, which Will had received by writing back to Clara. He was in France too, stationed near ——— with Welsh miners in a company of the Royal Engineers waiting for ———. The censor had blacked out two sections. Top-secret stuff that Jack evidently wasn't supposed to write about.

No news of Robbie, but this, Will knew, was good news. If he was confirmed dead, or missing presumed dead, the telegram would have made its way to Clara.

*

It was April and Will and Trevor were heading to the Somme, where British forces were needed in droves while the French were tied down in heavy fighting further south in Verdun. The Somme was to be the first time that the British Expeditionary Force really took control of a large area of fighting in France. There was talk about leading a huge offensive in the summer.

'It's about time we saw some action, don't you think, Will?' said Trevor.

'Definitely,' said Will. He was as bored as Trevor was with the menial tasks. The carrying and the digging, the endless parade-ground square-bashing.

'Sharp shooters like you and me are wasting our talents lugging boxes,' Trevor complained.

Shooting practice was still the best bit of the week but had become more disconcerting the closer they were to using their skills at the front. There was such satisfaction in hitting the target, the motions now so practised that the rifle would be reloaded almost before he had thought to do it. Will could no longer hold off imagining what it must be like to look through the sight of his rifle and send a bullet towards another person. What that bullet would do once it entered flesh and penetrated organs or struck bones. How the body would react to that. His body, Trevor's body, anyone's body. The harmonious system of the body intruded on with lead, and then an inevitable infection. Will knew that fixing the damage the bullets had made was only part of the problem, and how easily wounds could suppurate even if they themselves weren't fatal. He could not help thinking of his mother's death at times like this, which Clara had told him was down to infection, not blood loss. There must be a way of preventing such deaths.

A good soldier should not get bogged down thinking about things like that, Will told himself. But it was easy to tell yourself something and harder to obey your own orders.

They were stationed twenty miles away from the frontline, and occupied every day with the carrying and unloading of supplies: food and shells, medicine, horse fodder. They slept in tents and Will was glad they had not arrived earlier, in the winter. It was cold enough as it was.

They had a couple of hours to themselves every day at four. Will liked to slip away on his own, when he could, and walk in the countryside. At other times he'd join Trevor and the lads for a glass of *van blonk*, as Trevor liked to pronounce it with some relish — sharp white wine — at one of the cafés in the village they were stationed beside. One or two of the officers could speak French to the waitress, and Will thought that later he might politely ask them to help him memorise a phrase or two.

Letters came weekly from Clara: she was keeping busy with Kitty and the school, was scared as news began to filter through of soldiers killed, and said she'd heard of soldiers with terrible injuries being kept out of sight by their loved ones. *I can't understand what they think there is to be ashamed of. Surely we can all stomach seeing war wounds!* Will wondered to himself how far her imagination extended. He had heard stories of men with great holes in their faces, with shoulders taken clean off with machine-gun fire.

And now he was about to see some action, if the news was to be believed. The roads were busy with trucks pulling guns and howitzers. Will and the men were set to work digging huge holes in which to mount the guns, ten feet deep and much longer wide.

One day, after they'd just finished digging such a hole and were taking a five-minute break, they heard an awful crash and a furious mooing. A famer's cow had got loose and stumbled into the hole. It was funny at first, but it took two hours and twelve men to come up with a way of lifting her out.

At night, his shoulders ached. Everything ached. He wrapped himself as tightly as he could and slept.

20

The Somme

Jack was making his own contribution to the offensive at the Somme. He had recently become a member of the 183rd Tunnelling Company of the Royal Engineers, a unit that had been formed in France at the end of 1915 to dig short underground tunnels, or 'saps', into no man's land. They were also tasked to create more ambitious and dangerous tunnelling: deep underground, below the enemy fortifications, to make surprise attacks on them with explosives. The enemy were doing the same to them too, and part of the company's job was to detect them and stop them from what they were doing. The company was filled with large numbers of recruits from the mining industry, and it was the miners who knew most about what they were doing.

'Remind me what use you are here, boyo?' asked his new friend Rhys, when Jack asked him another question about how the shafts would be dug and kept supported, and how they would have air to breathe, and what were the right sort of explosives they would need to use. 'You ask a lot of questions, but what do you actually do?'

'Well, at least I'm something nice to look at,' said Jack.

Rhys looked over at Jack, his face streaked in oil and dirt.

'You are, are you? Maybe English standards of taste are different to Welsh ones.'

'No one's doubting that. What do your Welsh women like in a man, then?'

'Strength, a sense of humour and a massive—'

'Corporal Evans, I forbid you to reveal our secrets to cocky young English lads,' interrupted their commanding officer. 'We don't want him with an unfair advantage around our women if he ever makes it up to Swansea. Stick to educating him in the important skills, please.'

And Jack was learning all the time. The shafts were dug carefully and as quietly as possible, supported with timber. The men wore felt slippers or worked barefoot on top of sandbags. They listened out with stethoscopes against the walls, pricking their ears for the sound of German tunnellers. There was often water down there, too, which needed to be pumped out. They worked by candlelight and at points there was so little air in the tunnels that the flame would wane and the darkness would press down and Jack, bringing down the tools and doing whatever he was told, would feel the fear of being left there, in the dark, struggling to breathe. There were collapses all the time, and men were crushed and suffocated, though sometimes men were found alive, sheltered in a shaft that was ventilated from above. He imagined that; how you'd wonder if your men believed you were still alive, wonder if they'd give up on you and leave you there to starve. They took canaries with them, little caged birds who would die quickly if there was anything poisonous in the air, giving warning to the men to back up and work out what they could do to ventilate the shaft from above or below or the side. Jack didn't pretend to understand everything they were doing; he was most interested in how the explosives worked, how running a current through nitroglycerine would turn inert material into something that could punch through the earth like the fist of an angry god and destroy whole buildings.

The French had started the mines they were currently working on and the Royal Engineers had been brought in to help. The idea was to detonate a huge charge under the enemy trenches when the British assault began. The BEF would occupy the crater and override any remaining, dismayed troops who hadn't perished.

But the Germans knew the Allies were trying to do this. In February, they had found one of the tunnels and detonated a camouflet just under it, filling the British shaft with carbon monoxide and killing two officers and sixteen sappers. Jack had helped to dig them out, working late into the night. Not one of them was left alive.

*

Jack was also learning about women. A Royal Engineer's salary was better than a standard infantryman's, and so he had more money to spend in town when he was on rotation back behind the lines.

There, he and Rhys would treat themselves to a night in the local café, and their willingness to spend a few francs had been noticed by the proprietress.

'You are very handsome,' said Madame Giroud. 'There are many women in the town who would like to show you a good time.'

'Don't tell him that,' said Rhys.

'You are very handsome too.'

'I'm a married man,' he said.

'What difference does that make? You are men, this is war — any good wife would understand.'

'A French wife, maybe.'

'Ah, yes, you English. You have a reputation. For being, what's the word?'

'Constipated,' said Rhys.

'Is that the right word?'

'He means courageous,' said Jack. 'Brave. We're known for not being afraid of anything.' He was grinning at her.

'Perhaps I will send a girl to see you,' she said. 'If you're not afraid.'

'Oh, I'm not afraid. Not at all.'

When she was gone, he whispered to Rhys, 'Do you think I might stand a chance with her?'

'Madame Giroud? She's married. She's old enough to be your mother.'

'Zees is war,' said Jack in a French accent. 'Any good husband would understand.'

But it was not Madame Giroud who sat down next to him on their next visit. It was a younger woman who looked rather like her, the same nut-brown hair, mahogany eyes, sharp cheekbones and full lips — was it her daughter?

'*Je m'appelle* Sylvie,' she said. 'How do you do?'

'*Je m'appelle* Jack,' he replied. 'I do what I choose to, mostly.'

'Do you? Oh, that is *très* romantique. Would you like to buy us a bottle of wine?'

'I very much would. What do you need?' he asked, pulling out his money.

She told him.

'How much? That's daylight robbery.'

'Daylight? It's night-time, *Jacques*. A much nicer time than day-time. We will drink the bottle in my room upstairs. I think you will find the price very reasonable.'

Jack handed her the money immediately. She stood up and walked away. Jack looked at Rhys. Rhys was looking at Sylvie. 'She's taking you for a fool,' he warned.

Sylvie turned and beckoned him with her finger.

'Funny,' said Jack. 'I don't feel like a fool.'

He stood and followed her up the stairs.

21

Chapelle Blanchette

It had taken her an hour or so, but thanks to her Swiss Army model 1890 penknife, the initials *C T-P* were now clearly visible, carved into the bark of the imposing oak tree. Grace was back in France. After the weeks she had spent home in Gloucestershire, she felt restored and invigorated, but she was determined to rejoin the struggle. She was desperate to ensure that the loss of her brother would not be in vain. She would stand side by side with him in resisting this implacable enemy.

Now, having taken a short diversion to Chapelle Blanchette near Verdun, she knelt in front of her brother's grave, a simple mound of earth marked at one end by a flimsy white wooden cross. Engraved across the horizontal slat with a crude knife of some kind were the words:

'Charles Tustin-Pennington. Pilot of the Royal Flying Corps. Killed in Action. Verdun, 1915.'

She bowed her head and closed her eyes.

'My darling Charles,' she said to herself. 'I will love you forever, my wonderful big brother; and I shall never, ever forget you. You were the bravest and the best. Mother and Father are still in pieces and they wanted to be here with me, but of course that is not possible right now. Perhaps it will be in time to come. I will be back, I promise, but until then I want to give you this.'

She took a small pot from her pocket and pushed the tiny seedling with the compost still around it firmly into the ground at the foot of the grave where she knelt.

'I took this seedling from one of Father's greenhouses,' she said. 'It has grown from an acorn over the last two years and has been regularly re-potted as it slowly developed. I've brought it for you so you can watch over it as it matures. It is my hope that I will be able to find you and return to you. I will look for the sentinel oak tree beside a little wooden cross just outside the village of Chapelle Blanchette, then find the growing sapling that you are nourishing in body and in spirit. So one day, you might be at the very top of another majestic oak, with a breath-taking view of a glorious countryside. You will be floating in the wind, as free as a bird and soaring into the heavens, as I know has always been your dream. I will find this tree, Charles, and I will find you. Goodbye for now.'

She stood on shaky legs, glanced once more at the white wooden cross, and turned and climbed on to her horse.

22

It was late May and Will had been at the front for a month now. The battalions rotated between the frontline trenches, second trenches and the supplies area behind, and Will and Trevor were currently in a support trench, waiting to go forward to the frontline in a few days. The discipline and routine and drudgery continued. He'd be woken at four a.m. to stand to, until it was light enough at five to clean his rifle. At six o'clock an officer would inspect the rifles, and at half past he and Trevor would carry breakfast up to the company at the frontline. Some three or four hours after he'd been woken, Will would finally get his own breakfast of bacon and bread, before he would turn out for whatever fatigue he'd been assigned, such as filling sandbags and carrying them where needed for whatever was being built or repaired.

After lunch, with any luck, he would get some rest, falling back into his tent to lie there, stunned, listening to the birdsong, imagining life back home in Turnham Green: Kitty sitting at the back of the class, perhaps, while Clara put her pupils through their paces.

In the afternoon, he would clean his rifle again, have it inspected again, then some clot moving through the lines might knock it over from where it was standing and he'd have to do the same all over again. He still had not fired at a living man.

Hundreds of artillery cannons were moving up the line,

drawn by horses, and who was carrying all the ammunition? The men were, at least to the wagons. It took two men to lift one of the shells — in between, you had to roll them.

After dinner, he might join another working party, carrying ammunition between the artillery posts, filling more sandbags, always more sandbags. So much of his work was maintaining the existence of this world carved out of the earth, propped up with sand and rough timber, always in the process of turning back to mud, of rejecting the men's unnatural presence there.

His commanding officer was Captain Jacob Daniels, and Will was grateful for that. He was a jovial man, who the soldiers obeyed willingly with no need for threats and abuse. He had won medals for his bravery. He stood a few inches shorter than Will and the first time he had addressed him he had leaned back exaggeratedly and looked up into the sky.

'You're a big lad, aren't you, Burnett? A baby face all the way up there on top of a tree top. You better crouch down when you're walking around here or some bloody Boche will blow the top of your head off.'

Will had instinctively crouched and Daniels had put his hand on his shoulder.

'Only joking, you're not that tall. Anyway, even the midgets round here crouch down when the firing's going off. And who can blame them? Take no unnecessary chances, that's what I say. Stick with me and we'll stay as safe as we can.'

Will looked up at the parapet of the frontline trench.

'Yes, I know,' Daniels said. 'As safe as we can is still a little less than ideal, here, but we have a job to do and we'll do it well.' In a quieter voice he whispered, 'How old are you, Burnett?'

'Nineteen, sir.'

'You haven't started shaving yet.'

'I, er . . .'

'No need to lie to me, Burnett. You're here and I'm grateful for that and I like to know who my men are.'

He looked so earnestly at Will that he felt himself about to tell him that he was *nearly* sixteen, but a private arrived. 'The general wants you, sir.'

A look of annoyance crossed the captain's face. 'We'll talk again, Burnett. We'll talk again. Dismissed.'

Will walked past him later that night. Daniels was smoking and staring up at the parapet of the trench. He was looking at Will but when Will smiled Daniels didn't seem to see him. He was looking through him almost, past him, and Will looked over his shoulder to see if there was something interesting behind him, but there was nothing, just the bags of sand and the wooden struts and above them all the stars. Daniels was somewhere else completely.

Now Will was on the frontline. He would be there for a week and he had a sick feeling in his stomach most of the time now. The battalion rotating back to the supply trenches to let them take over were looking at his battalion with something like awe. Because they knew — they all knew — they were about to go over the top.

Daniels was increasingly far away.

'He looks scared to me,' said Trevor one night when they were eating dinner with the rest of the privates.

'Aren't you scared?' asked Wilson, a man from Liverpool. 'You bloody should be.'

'I'm scared,' admitted Will.

'The baby-faced giant's scared,' said Wilson to his friend O'Reilly.

'Baby face is intelligent,' said O'Reilly.

'We used to call him the professor,' said Trevor. 'Always see him with a book in his hand.'

'*You* used to call me the professor,' said Will. 'No one else did.'

'You'd see Daniels reading in the past,' said O'Reilly. 'Though recently he just seems to stand around and smoke when he's not giving us orders.'

'Have you been with Captain Daniels long?' asked Will.

'Oh, yeah. Right from the winter of 1914. He's seen a lot. We've seen a lot. He saved my life!'

O'Reilly told the story, about a night mission, being caught on razor wire while a flare lit them up and bullets zinged around them. Daniels was nearly back into the trench before he noticed O'Reilly's predicament.

'He ran straight back and ripped it off me with his bare hands. They knew we were out there then so there was no running back — we were on our stomachs crawling, desperately looking for a hole to get into. And then we found one and lay there and the bullets kept coming for hours before they stopped and we managed to get back before the sun came up. His hands were bleeding awfully. "You saved my life," I said to him. "You'd do the same for me," he said. And I would, you know, I bloody would. But it's easy when someone's done it for you already. I don't know if I'd have gone back to him if he hadn't saved me first.'

Later that evening Will, on sentry, saw Daniels crouching down in the trench, smoking a cigarette, looking up at the stars. He caught his eye and Daniels called out, 'Eyes forward, Burnett.'

Will turned his gaze back.

'You're too young for this,' he heard Daniels say behind him. 'But then I suppose we're all too bloody young for this.'

And then he was gone, down the trenches, checking on the men one by one, making sure they were ready.

24

Grace was strangely pleased to be back in France. As soon as she had arrived at her billet, Omelette had come straight over to her. The busyness of her working days distracted her from her sadness and stopped it from becoming depression. The conviction that she was once more involved in the war and making some sense out of Charles's death energised her. She had not felt this alive for weeks.

She was not sure what to expect when she arrived back near the frontline but she had at least hoped there might have been signs of progress, of territory having been taken, conditions for the men improved and fewer soldiers being sacrificed. That had not proved to be the case.

It was her second day back, a clear and very cold spring morning. There had been a heavy frost on the ground at dawn which was only just thawing and many of the wounded were suffering from hypothermia. She was working at an advanced dressing station at the Hohenzollern Redoubt near Loos and had been instructed to urgently take four wounded men to the casualty clearing station six miles away. One man in particular needed immediate and expert care having been struck in the back by shrapnel. One of the younger doctors on duty had instinctively removed the foreign body, imagining that what you did with wounds elsewhere on the body was what you did with chest wounds. He meant well but it only made matters worse for his patient. Removal of the metal shard left an opening in his chest wall the size of a florin. When he breathed in or out hissing and sucking sounds could be heard and bright red foam bubbled and frothed around the hole.

The young medic was puzzled and could not understand why his patient was becoming more breathless even as he watched. His pulse was rapid and his lips were becoming a duskier shade of purple. Grace had seen a small number of injuries similar to this already on her first stint of duty seven months previously. She felt sorry for the doctor, who was obviously something of a novice. But he would learn fast, it was certain. She found out later that he had been in a quiet rural general practice near Weybridge before enlisting and was only practised in minor surgery such as routine tonsillectomies, and the simple lancing of boils and abscesses.

'It's a sucking wound, I think,' she said. 'Air is sucked into the pleural space from outside each time the lung recoils under its own elasticity. But the wound acts like a valve, preventing air getting out again. The pressure builds up around the lung, which is compressed into a small knuckle and pushed over the other side of the thorax.'

The doctor looked down at the patient and nodded. He placed a stethoscope on the injured man's chest and listened carefully on either side. All the air entry in the lungs was on the opposite side. Percussion of the injured side with his fingertips sounded like a drum. He noticed the distended veins in the man's neck and realised that venous return to the heart was being jeopardised. The doctor looked hesitant and unsure of himself. He was not accustomed to asking a mere nurse for guidance but on this occasion, he was only too grateful to receive it.

'What do you think we need to do?'

'I'm not a doctor but I have seen a thoracostomy chest

drain used to relieve the pressure and buy time. If we can get one in, we can get him to the casualty clearing station within half an hour. There is a mobile x-ray vehicle there to confirm the diagnosis and inform our treatment.'

'I've never done one.' He looked mortified. 'My RMO is at the first-aid post.'

'I can't do it myself, Doctor. I'm not permitted. I can't even be sure I am right.'

The wounded man was clearly unaware of what was happening around him and a decision had to be made immediately. The doctor knew that he had to act or lose the patient. At the same time, Grace recognised his dilemma.

'I have no choice,' he said quietly.

'I can talk you through it.'

'Please,' he said. 'I would be grateful.'

So, she did. Under her supervision he covered the wound and sutured it. Then he made another incision between the eighth and ninth ribs under the armpit and inserted a steel trocar about five millimetres in diameter. The patient, now unconscious, stirred very slightly. He was not totally unresponsive to pain. Pushing slightly harder, the point of the metal instrument pierced the intercostal muscles and pleural membrane and entered the chest cavity. There was another more distinctive hissing sound this time as air was expelled from his thorax, a little like a balloon deflating. Grace connected a flexible rubber tube attached to the trocar to two sealed bottles arranged in series to one another and the air emanating from the chest bubbled out under a few inches of sterile water in each. The weight of the water itself prevented any air from flowing back in the opposite direction. Within a matter of minutes the wounded man's lips became pinker, his blood pressure increased and his pulse rate stabilised.

He was loaded into the horse-drawn ambulance along with three other patients and another orderly to help Grace and with a tug on the reins the four horses took off.

It had been a dramatic start to the day and, as was usual for the person most involved with tending to an urgent casualty, Grace regularly looked down at her patient to observe his colour, his breathing and other vital signs. The first three miles of the journey passed uneventfully enough but halfway to their destination she heard the driver shout, 'Aye aye,' and bring the horses to a halt. In front of them stood a 1910 Wolseley motor ambulance completely blocking the road with steam pouring from its radiator and water dripping down beneath it. Grace's driver jumped down to investigate and, after a further glance at her patient, so did Grace. The driver of the vehicle was nowhere to be seen. The orderly standing by the tailgate informed them that he had set off to the CCS to summon help without even trying to identify the cause of the problem.

'Said he's just a driver in civilian life,' said the orderly. 'Knows nothing about engines.'

'That's handy,' chirped Grace. 'Maybe he and I should swap places. He'll find Dobbin over there harnessed up to his three mates much cheaper to run and infinitely more reliable.'

Grace strode to the front of the Wolseley and, pulling her sleeve down over her hand in case the casing was still hot, lifted the bonnet. She peered inside.

'Did you notice anything before this happened?' she asked.

'Well, we heard an odd kind of squeaking noise for a mile or two and then steam started spewing out. Then the engine coughed a few times and it stopped.'

Grace cautiously unscrewed the cap from the top of the

radiator and looked in behind it. 'Who do you have in the back?' she asked the orderly.

'Walking wounded. Three of them. Not too bad, luckily.'

Grace looked thoughtful for a moment.

'George,' she said to her own orderly. 'Squeeze these three men into our chariot and go on to the clearing station. I'll catch you up.'

'What?' said George. 'You mean leave you here?'

'I'll be fine. But that man with the chest drain needs urgent treatment now. Go on.'

George looked at Grace but knew her well enough to know it was not worth arguing. He moved the three soldiers over, climbed up onto the cab, took the reins and set off.

Grace glanced around and saw a large puddle in the ditch next to the road.

'Have you got anything in the back that holds water?' she said to the remaining orderly.

'There's a kidney dish and some urine bottles,' he replied, puzzled.

'Can you fill them with water from the pool down there and pour them into the radiator?'

He disappeared into the rear of the Wolseley, collected the items, and when he reached the ditch, crouched down at the bottom of it and filled them with muddy water. As he clambered back to the road, he saw Grace with one foot up on the running board with her skirt hoisted up on to her thigh. He was pleasantly surprised to see her rolling down an elegant silk stocking held up by a tantalising suspension belt of some kind from her pale but shapely leg. She noticed his interest but did not bat an eyelid.

'Get that water in!' she ordered him.

She then took another quick look into the engine bay,

threw out a stringy strip of frayed rubber and carefully ripped a roughly measured length of the hosiery she had just taken off. The orderly had one eye on what she was doing and the other on the job she had given him. As he filled the radiator, she twisted the length of silk into a thicker plaited band and with it connected an engine spindle to the cog of the cooling fan and tied it firmly. She checked the tension, screwed the radiator cap back on, closed the bonnet and jumped into the driving seat.

'What did you do?' asked the orderly, jumping in beside her.

'Replaced the fan belt,' she said matter-of-factly. 'That's why the engine overheated. Fingers crossed.'

She turned the ignition key and the engine started up on the third attempt. When she was satisfied she could hear the fan whirring she double de-clutched, put the gear lever into first and set off.

As she manoeuvred the Wolseley along the rough road she hoped her improvised fan belt would stay on long enough to see them home. The ride, bumpy though it was, was infinitely smoother than it would have been in the horse-drawn vehicle, and she was grateful to John Boyd Dunlop who had not very long ago patented his idea of putting an inner tube of compressed air inside an outer case of vulcanised rubber with a tread.

Twenty minutes later she turned off the camp's perimeter road and pulled up behind the horse-drawn vehicle she had been driving earlier. She stepped down, opened the bonnet again and inspected her handiwork. The strand of silk hosiery was still intact but looking slightly worse for wear.

A tall, ruddy-faced man in a peaked cap, khaki uniform and with stripes on his arm came over and squinted into the engine bay beside her. He was Royal Army Medical Corps.

'Bloody good job,' he said, smiling and twisting his moustache. 'I could do with a good man like you in my team.'

Grace laughed.

'Major Morris, RAMC,' he said extending his hand.

'Miss Tustin-Pennington.'

'I'm very pleased to make your acquaintance, Miss Tustin-Pennington. Where did you learn a trick like that?'

'I used to help my father around the farm. Tinkering with the tractor or harvester, and later on Douglas the gamekeeper taught me how to service and repair the Daimler.'

Major Morris examined her more closely. 'I hear you're a damn good nurse as well. And clearly you can drive.'

Grace nodded. 'It's not the first time I've driven one of the motor ambulances, sir.' She was not sure where this was going.

'How would you like to do the job permanently? Drive, I mean. You'd still be a nurse first and foremost but you would drive the motor ambulances more commonly than the horses. I need someone who understands basic machines.'

Grace was flattered and rather excited. 'I'd need to clear it with Sister MacCailein.'

'What? The whispering witch?'

Grace tittered.

'Already done. What do you say?'

She hardly had to think about it. Despite her equestrian background, five horsepower from a motor car had to be better than one horsepower from an old nag. She knew they were all different types of machines that had been donated to the war effort — such as Wolseleys, Morrises and Vauxhalls — but they had the same basic workings. And anything that got her away from Sister MacCailein's clutches even part of the time would be welcome.

'I'll say yes, then.'

'Splendid. The job is yours. Starting tomorrow. Meanwhile,' he said, looking down into the engine bay again, 'I'll get my mechanics to remove your underwear . . . from the cooling fan that is . . . while you go and see that casualty you fixed up with the chest drain.'

'How is he?'

'The x-ray confirmed your clinical diagnosis. He's doing well. And asking for you.'

23

Fricourt

Jack was beginning to tire of Rhys and the Welsh boys' jokes. He had arrived back at the café on the last night before being transferred back to the front with a bunch of flowers for Sylvie and found her sitting with her arm around another soldier, a Canadian. So, pretending he had intended them for her all along, he strode to the front of the bar and presented them to Madame Giroud. 'For the most beautiful woman in the village,' he said.

'Surely you want me to give them to Sylvie,' she said.

'Sylvie looks like she has enough on her plate.'

'Oh, she is just being friendly. You have to be friendly when you work in a café.'

'Well, these are for you,' he said. 'And you are the most beautiful woman in the village by far.'

He winked at her, turned around and walked out.

Rhys had told the story to the men at least a dozen times now. 'Oh, you should have seen the look he gave her. Oh, it broke my heart, so it did!'

'You're just jealous,' said Jack. 'What you'd have given to be a fly on the wall in lovely Sylvie's *chambre*.'

'I hope you had a bath first,' Rhys said. 'And afterwards.

Everything still in working order, is it? It's not dropped off, has it?'

'All present and correct.'

'I'm pleased to hear that. One day you might need that for Madame Giroud, the most beautiful woman in Northern France.'

'Less talking and more digging,' shouted the commanding officer, and they got back to work.

The mines were planted and the work now was to distract the Germans who were looking for them by sending out diversionary tunnels, in which they'd make more noise than usual and try to draw their fire that way, make them think they'd thwarted the Allies' plans.

The explosives under the German trenches were primed and ready to go, three charges designed to protect the advancing British infantry from Germans firing downhill from the village of Fricourt. As well as killing the Germans, the craters would provide a lip of earth to block the firing line. That was the theory.

Jack was busy digging all the time. He knew his stuff now, and was helping finish the saps, the little tunnels out into no man's land that would be opened when the attack began and allow the troops to come out much closer to the Germans' trenches. Everything was ready to go.

24

Pozières Ridge

The confirmation came that the next morning they were going over the top. Will was too numbed by the news to feel anything until he sat down to write to Clara and Kitty, and then he felt terribly guilty and couldn't complete the task. He would write to them tomorrow, once he was back safe and sound. He had to believe he would be.

Once the artillery had blasted the enemy's trenches with an unprecedented bombardment, they were due to charge.

Will had never seen anything like it. Or heard anything like it. The shells burst over their trenches and, peering over the parapet, the soldiers could see mud and sand flung through the air. The skyline was lit with flashes of different brightness and size: they came over Will's head with a roar like a freight train. There was no way the Germans could take all that on the chin and leap up and fight. Will imagined leaping into a trench of dazed Germans who were ready to surrender. He had fixed his bayonet and cleaned his rife. He had wire cutters and Mills bombs strapped to him.

'That'll shift them,' called Trevor. He was standing beside Will, holding his rifle tightly, the vicious blade gleaming at the top of it.

And suddenly the shelling stopped.

Captain Daniels was standing beside them. He looked at his watch.

'Now, men, I'm going to give the order in two minutes to charge. I'll charge with you, and be there with you when we take their trenches. I want you to spread out and keep their fire spread out. First job is to cut any barbed-wire fencing that our lads' shells haven't done for us — we can see through the periscope that it's not all clear. And then we'll need you riflemen to lie down and provide covering fire while we get through it. There is battalion after battalion doing the same down the line. This is the biggest attack we've made yet. You are brave strong lads and exceptionally trained and disciplined and you are going to come back from this as heroes. Get ready, and wait for me to call out the order.'

The world shrank to the boards in front of him, and then Daniels called the order and Will planted his feet on the ladder and they were out, free, with a clear view of no man's land. He was there, marching forward, on the ground that had been so close to them for so long and yet so far away.

And then the shooting started.

All around him men ran, aiming rifles, and Will began to see them fall, heard the rattle of machine guns from the trenches they were heading towards. Will could see him now, the German at his post on the parapet with the gun, and he took aim and fired off a round of shots, but he was too far away, and none of them found their target.

Shells began to arrive, bursting above their heads and flinging shrapnel into the mud. Will felt a sting in his left thigh but there was no time to worry about that. He flung himself forward and took up a position behind a mound of earth, firing and reloading as quickly as he could. In front of him a lad with wire cutters was hit with a volley of machine-gun fire and blasted backwards. The next man ran towards him and suffered the same fate, though managed to loosen the wire enough that the soldier following could push himself through and roll and try to find cover. The Tommies were sprinting across the land now, but so many of them were being hit, suddenly falling backwards.

He couldn't see Captain Daniels. Nor Trevor. The shells stopped and he got up and charged into the gap in the fence, where various holes had appeared, helped in some sense by the Germans' artillery. He was through. His thigh was aching. The shells had stopped, and then they started and suddenly the part of land he was charging towards disappeared and he was flung backwards. He didn't pass out, but the world went very loud and very quiet. He lay on his back and laughed. The ground began to fill with bullets. He picked himself up and ran forward more, there was Trevor, holding his rifle and keeping up a steady barrage at the machine gunner who suddenly stopped firing, just as Trevor's body spun and collapsed into the mud.

Will reached him before he knew what he was doing. There was a crater which might provide some cover and – nothing for it, though he knew you should not always move an injured man nor even go to his assistance during an all-out attack – he lifted him under the shoulders and pulled him along the ground towards it, and they fell into it just as a round of machine-gun fire struck the ground around them.

'Where did they get you?' Will asked.

'Stomach,' Trevor said, barely audible, holding on to it.

'Let me see,' said Will. He undid Trevor's jacket and looked down, to where blood was seeping through his shirt. 'You need to press down on it,' said Will. 'Compression to stop the bleeding.'

'It really hurts, Will. It really hurts.'

'They'll get you something for that, don't worry.'

He took out his emergency field dressing and bottle of iodine. This was going to be painful, he knew, for Trevor, but he soaked a bandage in it and pressed down.

Trevor screamed.

The battlefield was a vision of hell. Explosion after explosion, and the relentless noise of the machine guns. And in moments when it stopped, the cries of the men. The awful sound of a bullet hitting someone. The groan as he went down. Everyone running and dodging and falling and calling. Will raised his rifle to aim but put it back down and checked again on Trevor. He would need to get him back to the trench – he would die otherwise.

'Stay there,' he said, realising what a stupid thing it was to say as he said it. He looked back to where there was a bigger hole in the barbed wire now more men had come through, now more shells had landed and knocked over the posts holding it up. The easiest way to carry Trevor would be over his shoulder – he could do that, Trevor being smaller and skinnier than him, but he'd be sinking his shoulder straight into Trevor's wounded stomach. Perhaps that would help the wound, he thought, keep pressure on it. But it would be terribly painful.

'Trevor, this is going to hurt,' he said, and he crouched and planted his feet and slung him up and over, staggering under the weight of him. Trevor screamed. 'We'll be back over soon, don't worry.' The hardest bit would be running up out of the shell crater he had pulled them into to escape the bullets. Trevor screamed again and there was nothing for it: Will dug in his feet and drove himself up the slope, nearly falling as he hit flat land. And then he was running, as fast as he could, which wasn't fast, while bullets zinged around him and men called out and shouted in shock. He kept moving – waiting for the bullet to punch through his exposed back, or through one of his thighs – back through a section of the wire fence that had been knocked flat, his trousers snagging on a barb and ripping. Trevor was whimpering, and Will could feel his warm blood soaking through his khaki and into his shoulder. Not far, not far, he said, to Trevor, to himself. A shell burst above them and the shock of it made Will trip forward and pound Trevor into the earth. Trevor screamed, or was it Will himself? Somehow he picked him up again and moved forward, unhurt, his ears ringing, until he reached his own trenches. 'Someone help!' he called, looking for someone who could take Trevor down, but there was no one to help. So he took close hold of Trevor and jumped down. 'Stretcher bearer!' he shouted, and he was not the only one. Shouts were coming from all over no man's land, but it was too much of a maelstrom to distinguish soldiers from stretcher bearers, if the Germans had been inclined to. They would have been mown down at the same rate.

He was crouching over Trevor and looking for something to hold against the wound when finally a field medic arrived. There was work enough for the stretcher bearers inside the trenches at the moment as more and more injured dragged themselves or were dragged back over.

'I guess this is bye for now, Trevor,' Will said.

Trevor was pale, wincing with pain.

'A bit of a rest for you now,' Will said.

And then the stretcher bearers were off with him and Will had to work out what he should do now.

Injured men were calling out for help.

Will shouldered his rifle and went back over.

25

Only two of the three charges had detonated. The elation Jack felt at seeing the first two go up, the spurt of black earth flung into the sky followed by a ball of flame that turned to oily black smoke, was tempered by the failure of the third.

'Bloody water. Must have got damp,' said Rhys. 'That one was the trickiest to pump. What a bloody waste of time.'

They had opened the saps now and were on their way back to the reserve trench: their skills too valuable for them to go over the top with the others.

'Do you feel like a coward?' said Jack.

'I feel lucky,' said Rhys.

The shells were screaming in the air and smashing into the front trench and they both knew that their fellow soldiers were being minced by them, and by the firing from the village on the hill that the craters hadn't fully obscured. It was going to be a massacre, on both sides.

Jack wondered what their next job was going to be. It would have to do more good than all their work this time had achieved. It would have to, or else what was he here for, what was anyone here for?

A shell screamed overhead and burst and he grabbed his helmet and crouched as shrapnel landed dangerously close.

'You OK, Rhys?' he shouted.

Rhys was flat on his stomach, covered in mud, pulling himself up.

It wasn't the time to joke about that now though.

26

Bazentin Ridge

The British soldiers had kept pouring out into no man's land and dying in droves but they had gained ground and driven the Germans back into what turned out to be a heavily fortified reserve trench behind their first trenches. Captain Daniels killed the machine gunner who had done so much damage to their battalion but not before being wounded in the arm.

Will was with him when they made it up to the Germans' trench. He hoisted three wounded men on his shoulders and took them back to the British trench, returning again and again with his rifle aimed but each time distracted by someone who needed help.

'Use one of your bombs to make sure they're not waiting for us,' Daniels told Will, pulling the pin from a grenade. 'You do that side and I'll do this.'

He scuttled his grenade into the trench and looked back at Will.

Will was holding his grenade, looking at it. He hadn't pulled the pin. He was thinking of the things he had seen that day, men's legs blown clean off, men's arms hanging by a thread.

'Duck,' said Daniels, and they both crouched and held their steel helmets as the explosion went off.

Daniels put his hand on his arm. 'It's OK,' Daniels said to him. 'You're right. One was enough.'

Behind them, men were calling for help. They looked back. So many men, ripped apart, their bodies opened and failing.

'You go,' said Daniels. 'Go and help those who need it.'

The scream of a shell arrived behind them, bursting into the ground and sending bodies flying into the air.

Daniels put his hands over his face. 'Christ,' he said. 'Good Christ. Go and see if there's anyone you can save.' Other men were arriving and jumping down into the trench. 'Takes a brave man to look at men in that state and if you can do it, then you're a brave man.'

Now Will and Captain Daniels were at a dressing station back behind the British line, while men sent to hold the gained ground were blasted with artillery. 'It's just a scratch,' Daniels said to the nurse who was trying to bandage him, a strikingly pretty young woman. 'We should be out there.'

'You're no use to anyone if you get gangrene,' she scolded, and Will marvelled at her voice, so musical and clear. It was the voice, he couldn't help noticing, of one of his 'betters', the kind of woman who, in other circumstances, he would never get so close to.

'I doubt any of us will have time to develop gangrene,' drawled Daniels. 'I'll have the whole arm blown clean off tomorrow morning before I've even had lunch.'

'Well, as long as you keep one of them so you'll be able to use a spoon.'

'Thank you, Nurse, thank you. Always look on the bright side, yes. Oh, yes, look on the bright side, all those men—'

He went somewhere. Will watched him. It was like he was

trying to swallow something far too big for his mouth, for his throat, for his stomach, but somehow he managed, and came back from where he'd been and shook his head.

'Nurse,' he said, 'you should have seen this lad out there today. His first time out on the battlefield.'

Will had two pieces of shrapnel embedded in him, one in the thigh and one in the space between the shoulder and his neck. Little pieces, not much to write home about. He wouldn't mention what he had seen today to Clara, in any case. He could not have her thinking about the things he had seen today.

He had been bandaged up already and was waiting for Daniels. He wanted to talk to him about the incident with the grenade and apologise. He wanted to know how to pull himself out of his fear and act.

'I'm ashamed of myself, sir.'

'You're what? What on earth for?'

'I froze. I couldn't throw that Mills bomb.'

'You froze! Are you serious? You must have saved four men's lives out there today!'

'I think I might be a coward. I was too scared to fight so I decided to help others.'

'You went over the top three or four times to bring back soldiers who needed help. Did you hear that, Nurse? Burnett goes over the top four bloody times and thinks he's a coward?'

'He doesn't sound like a coward,' said the nurse. 'Doesn't look like one either.'

She winked at him and Will felt a whoosh in his stomach and wondered what he did look like. He couldn't imagine that he would look the same after all that. What he had seen had changed him so profoundly on the inside that it must have left a mark on the outside.

'What's your name?' he asked, surprising himself.

Daniels looked at him and smiled broadly.

'Miss Tustin-Pennington,' she said. 'But you can call me Grace if you like.'

*

News reports arrived back at the dressing station. New men were flooding into the frontline and over the top, trying to defend the vicious counter-attack coming through from the Germans as the British were forced back to their trench.

'I hope to God the general knows what he's doing here,' said Daniels as they walked back through to the reserve trench where they would get some sleep.

'He must do, surely,' said Will.

'Did it look like he did?'

'It didn't look like—'

'What?'

'Like a decision I could make. To send men out to do that. He must be brave.'

'Bravery again. It's easy to be brave if you lack imagination. But can you be kind? And what good is bravery without kindness? Here, I'll be kind now. Have some of this.' He rooted in his knapsack and pulled out a steel canteen flask.

'I've got my own,' said Will, patting his hip.

'No you haven't,' said Daniels.

Will held the flask to his lips and smelled the alcohol. Whisky, he imagined. He took a gulp and immediately coughed in surprise.

Daniels laughed. 'Yes, it's rough stuff, all right. The best one can get round here.'

Daniels looked at him again, at Will's watering eyes. 'If I

didn't know better, I might think that was your first ever taste of whisky.'

'Guilty as charged, sir.'

He shook his head. 'You're quite something, Burnett. Most of the infantrymen they're sending us are all skin and bones, tiny little men. And then they send us someone like you, with a baby face and the body of a flanker. How old are you, Burnett?'

'Ah, eight—, I mean, nineteen.'

'You're definitely not eight and you're definitely not nineteen. Don't worry, you can be honest with me.'

'Isn't it easier if I'm nineteen?'

'Makes no difference to me. I've had boys under me no older than fifteen.'

Will nodded.

'Oh,' said Daniels. 'I thought you were a bit older than that. What do they feed you where you come from? Where is that?'

'Chiswick.'

'Chiswick? Well, there's no accounting for anything. And what were you doing there before you enlisted?'

'I was working in the hospital, sir, as a porter.'

'Really, you were?'

'Yes.' Will told him what he did there. What he enjoyed doing there.

'Well, we can't have someone like you bunging Mills bombs at Jerry. We need you to help our men. You've got skills at this. You've got talent. Any fool can shoot a man, just look how good Jerry is at doing it; we need men who can bring our boys back and help patch them up.'

Will thought about Trevor. He was someone he'd 'brought back'. But he didn't know whether he was even still alive. It was usually impossible to find out what had happened to casualties, such was the chaos and rapidity of the triage. It had been a serious wound and whatever treatment he would have had he would have needed urgently. Will hoped to God he had made it safely back to England.

'But sir, I want to fight for my—'

'You will, Burnett, you will fight for your country every bit of the way.'

27

Grace had been struck by the humble and unassuming young soldier. He was clearly courageous, from his captain's account, having repeatedly returned to no man's land during a furious onslaught. And he was obviously very caring as his overarching motivation in doing so had been to tend to the wounded and rescue his comrades. Yet he still questioned himself and wondered if he could have done more. Apart from that, and his strong physique, he was also rather baby-faced and devilishly good-looking. With a dense head of dark hair, a broad forehead, large deep-seated hazel eyes and full fleshy lips, he seemed to be blissfully unaware of his own allure. Which made him even more alluring. She did not feel the slightest bit guilty that she had noticed his attributes; after all, she told herself, it was a nurse's sacred duty to keep her patients under close observation at all times. She smiled at the thought of it. At one stage she had been so aware of how close he was, and wondering if he might even be inspecting *her* clinical handiwork, that she had found it quite difficult to concentrate on the job at hand. And goodness, without even thinking, she had winked at him. And then he had asked her name. And she had told him her Christian name!

As she rinsed and sterilised some surgical instruments in the sluice area of the ward tent she thought back to when she was dressing Captain Daniels' arm wound. How after-wards, as Daniels was momentarily recuperating, the young soldier had sat by the bedside of some of the other men and gently talked to them. She had surreptitiously watched him as he had helped them to sip water or make them more comfortable. It was a rare propensity, particularly in military men, many of whom in her experience felt awkward and embarrassed in medical environments. They tended to avoid hospitals and clinical settings like they avoided machine-gun fire.

Jenny sidled up beside her and interrupted her thoughts. 'Is your mind fully on the job today?' she asked cheekily.

'Hmm? In what way?'

'Oh, I don't know,' Jenny teased. 'I just wondered if that particularly handsome young man who was standing next to your patient with the lacerated arm might be distracting you in some way?'

Grace smiled and blushed to her roots. How the devil had Jenny even noticed?

'I don't know what on earth you can mean,' answered Grace rather too quickly, pursing her lips to prevent a grin.

'Well, that's good then. It wouldn't do to lose objectivity in your work, would it? What would Sister MacCailein say?'

'Sister MacCailein has nothing to do with it. If your own head has been turned by anybody in particular, Jenny, surely it's you, not me, who needs to retain your professional integrity and detachment.'

'As you know, I'm already spoken for, Grace. Engaged to my beautiful beau, Reggie. But I'm not blind, either. There'd be nurses aplenty queueing up to give that young soldier a bed bath, I can tell you!'

'Jenny! Behave yourself. You're dreadful.'

'You could do a lot worse.'

'I hadn't noticed. And you should mind your own business.'

'I will, I will,' said Jenny grinning. 'But tell me one thing.'
'What?'
'Do you believe in love at first sight?'
'Oh, shut up!' said Grace, blushing again then laughing and digging Jenny hard in the ribs with her elbow. 'Some of us have work to do.'

28

Will was now a regimental stretcher bearer. Daniels had spoken to the general and to the chief medical officer, and Will had been transferred out of his battalion and into the Royal Medical Corps.

He was allowed to wear a pistol in his belt, and while he was still technically an infantryman he was not supposed to attack the enemy. At the same time, he was not covered by the Geneva Convention protocol and instead of wearing a Red Cross armband he wore one saying SB, to distinguish him among his own men, and to stop officers taking issue with him for lack of courage if he wasn't charging forward with guns blazing. He knew some men looked down on the stretcher bearers, thought it unmanly. He didn't care about that, not much. Charging out there without a rifle, and without anything the Germans would see easily to mark him out as non-combatant, was one of the most dangerous things a man might do in the Army. He would go back and forth, back and forth, and never be able to stop and hold ground. And the chaos of a battlefield was such that even if the Germans weren't firing at him specifically, he could still be mown down.

On the first day in his new assignment, Will was introduced to an Indian man, with his hair wrapped tightly in a khaki turban and a terrifically thick dark moustache. He had dark brown eyes and a boyish smile and looked like he was in his mid-thirties.

He held out his hand and Will took it.

'My name is Arup Nur. I have heard you showed great bravery on the battlefield.'

'Captain Daniels is kind. I showed nothing of the sort, just did what anyone else would do. I'm Will Burnett, nice to meet you.'

'Modest, too. This is a good quality for a man.'

Will looked into Arup's twinkling eyes and felt deeply reassured in the presence of this older man.

'I don't know what I'm doing, really,' he admitted.

'I am here to show you, my young man. You will learn from a man with much experience in the ways of war. Too much experience, in fact. A year ago, I made a vow to myself never to kill again. But I will not desert my fellow soldiers. We are here to help them, and I am glad to have you with me.'

The day was frantic. The stretcher bearers worked in pairs and Arup and Will worked closely with two others, a pair of likely lads from the East End called Frankie Bull and Ed Baker. All day they took risks, bringing back bodies from the frontline while shells exploded around them, while bullets zipped through the air. And as soon as it was dark they were over and into the salient, to pick up those bodies it had been too dangerous to retrieve while it was light. The flares would go up and they would still be targeted. Arup was always calm and Will didn't know how he did it, how he managed to focus on what needed to be done and not the constant fear of death. But with him as a guide, Will found he could focus too, could tune out the noise around him and do what needed to be done. When he got back to his billet that night, he had never felt so tired in his life.

The following morning, Will found his way to the mess

tent to grab the breakfast he had been craving since the previous day. It was a hive of activity inside, the atmosphere energetic and noisy. Once he reached the front of the food queue, he gratefully accepted his slice of bacon and bread and went over to plonk himself down next to Arup who was sitting on his own at a table in the corner.

'Want some company?' he asked.

'Company is always good, young Sahib,' Arup said, 'especially when it seems not everybody else wants your own.' Will looked around at the hostile faces staring in their direction.

'Why wouldn't they want yours?'

Arup regarded Will with an expression of utter calm and patience. It was a look an experienced teacher might give a particularly naïve and backward pupil.

'They think I'm a conchie. That's what they call me.'

'A what?'

'A conscientious objector. Someone who has claimed the right to refuse military service on the grounds of freedom of thought, conscience or religion.'

'But that doesn't make sense. You're a part of the military.'

'Yes, I am. As part of the British Raj, I signed up voluntarily to join the British Indian Army to help fight for the British Empire.'

'So, you used to fight?'

'I fought for years, Will. And I am still part of the fighting. Part of the war. Just like you, I'm helping as a soldier against the enemy.'

'And to me you seem fearless. I've seen you. You're not scared of anything. So why do they call you a conchie?'

Arup pondered the question. 'You need to understand, Will, that many of these men have seen several of their friends wounded or killed. They see them walk slowly towards the enemy lines and they see them mown down in their hundreds by the unseen enemy. They see them torn apart by the machine guns or blinded and suffocated by chlorine or mustard gas. The German soldiers are responsible for this and they hate them. But war is a two-way street, and it is easy to lose one's humanity.'

Will stopped eating his breakfast at this stage and went on listening carefully as Arup continued.

'If I stop to help a dying enemy soldier mortally wounded by our own guns, am I disloyal? Am I hindering the war effort? Am I a traitor? Am I expected to abandon the man, any man, when my role as I see it is to help the wounded?'

'Any decent man would help a dying soldier, Arup.'

'But others would, how should I say, be very keen to put them out of their misery.'

'They shoot them?' asked Will incredulously.

'I've seen it on both sides, but I won't do that.'

'And that's why they call you a conchie?'

'I would rather save lives than take them, Will.'

'I think you're brave, Arup. I've seen what you do, and I don't care what they think.'

The Sikh put his hand on Will's forearm.

'You should be careful, Will. You are young and very brave yourself, by the way, but you mustn't make enemies in your own camp by associating too closely with Arup Nur.'

'Maybe they'll come around in time,' said Will, hopefully, 'after all, you're on our side, fighting with us.'

'I'm also an alien. I'm from a far-off country that many of these men know nothing about. They have never visited or heard about it. The colour of my skin is different to theirs. I'm not generally considered an equal in status or stature. I hear what some of the men say. I'm lucky, they think, to have been given the chance to escape my impoverished backward country, take the King's shilling and enjoy the privileges afforded to me by the British Army.'

There was a silence for a moment.

'How did you come to be here in the first place?' Will asked. 'It's true, you do stand out like a sore thumb!'

Arup smiled.

'The British Indian Army is an extension of the British Raj in India,' he explained. 'My division is the Meerut. We originally arrived in Marseille and were put under the command of General Sir James Willcocks, who in turn was answerable to Herbert Kitchener — First Earl Kitchener himself.'

'When was that?'

'In 1914. A few months after that, the British Expeditionary Force had been so depleted in the first stages of the war that the British couldn't recruit and train sufficient numbers of men to stop the German advance at Ypres.'

'So, your division came to the rescue?'

'We did. Sir Douglas Haig's First Army began an artillery bombardment such as I have never seen. The shells fell from the sky like the kind of monsoons we see in my country. Then we attacked in the Artois and Champagne regions where the enemy had surged into France. But they were ready. Thousands of *jawans* like me — that's a junior soldier — fought in the trenches at Neuve Chapelle and hundreds of gallant men were killed. In the end, it was futile. We gained very little ground.'

'But you fought then in that battle as an infantryman. As a soldier?'

'Yes, all of the men in the British Indian Army are professional soldiers, never conscripts. One of the men was the first Indian soldier to be awarded the Victoria Cross, Khudadad Khan. I knew him. He was a hero, fearless and defiant. A man who leads by example.'

'It must've been a shock to the Germans when they saw all of you fellows wearing turbans coming towards them?'

Another disarming smile from Arup.

'It didn't really matter who they were shooting at, Will. We were all just moving targets. At the end of the battle, corpses littered the countryside like sheaves of harvested corn.'

Will considered this sacrifice. All these men, so far from home. 'Why would you put your lives on the line to fight for the British in France?'

'Because this is our profession, Will. We do it for pride, and also because in return for support in this war we will have the beginnings of self-rule in India when it is over. That's the promise we have been given. It is for that reason that many of us are willing to die for the cause.'

'So how come you are a stretcher bearer now? I'm glad you are one. I sort of feel safer with you around. I'm just wondering.'

'Killing many men . . . It starts to devour your soul.'

'How many men have you killed?'

'Too many, Will, too many. And that is why I now prefer to save lives rather than take them.'

'Even German ones?'

'Even German ones.'

'But in your division, you're still a soldier who has to fight?'

'I'm still a soldier but I have been reassigned to alternative duties. These duties sit better with my conscience.'

Will was aware of furtive and resentful glances coming

their way from other tables in the kitchen tent. He turned away and shifted uncomfortably on his bench.

'Why don't you tell *them* all this?'

'They have their own worries, Will. And maybe limited knowledge. They believe what they've been told. It is the Army, after all, and as our leaders say, they expect every man to do his duty.'

'I'll put them right soon enough,' vowed Will.

'Don't even think about it. I'll do my talking through my actions. In the trenches and in no man's land. Like Khudadad Khan. Now finish your breakfast and let's get going.'

29

Grace noticed the good-looking Mr Burnett coming in and out of the hospital. There was something about him that set him apart. When she had initially seen him, he was dressed in a soldier's uniform. But lately his attire indicated he was a stretcher bearer. He had a manner and energy about him that was unique. Where other men looked haggard, beaten down and stooped, he always seemed to look cheerful and strong. His affable demeanour made him popular with everyone around him and he had an easy charm and kindred connection with his fellow soldiers. He was also one of the few who appeared oblivious to class or race — he spoke politely and confidently to his supposed betters, and to his Sikh friend Arup Nur, with no trace of the resentment towards difference in background that she often witnessed among the army ranks. She wished she could find an excuse to talk to him and discover more about him. She did not even know his first name.

*

It was a quiet day, one of those rare ones when many of the wounded had been evacuated to the ambulance train, others discharged back to normal duties and with no new casualties coming in from the frontline. In the last few days, much of the action had been taking place ten miles to the north or south of them. It was a day to clear up, refresh, restock, and replenish. Watching from afar, outside the officers' mess, Will tried not to make it obvious that his eyes were locked on the attractive Queen Alexandra's nurse folding bedlinen in the hospital tent opposite. She was the one who had tended Captain Daniels. He had thought then that she was a stunner. That thought was being reinforced by the minute.

30

Flers-Courcelette
The Somme, September 1916

Will lay panting in the rim of the blood-soaked bomb crater, waiting for the smoke to clear. Heavy machine-gun crossfire was still raking the area and artillery shells were dropping in every direction. He could just make out the steel helmets of the other men pinned down in adjacent bomb pits and the plaintive cries of the wounded men he was supposed to be rescuing.

He turned his head away from the action, slipped further down the slimy walls of the crater and closed his eyes in a vain attempt to blank everything out. Through his closed lids he could still see the flashes of explosions, and he could not escape the sound of the staccato rat-a-tat of small arms fire and the dull thud of artillery shells. When he finally opened his eyes again, he wished he had not.

Below him, three men lay in a ditch of filthy water, one decapitated and the others with their chests blown wide open like figurines in a pop-up book, hearts and lungs exposed. Despite not having eaten since the previous day, Will was almost sick when he saw a large rat emerge from the chest cavity of one of the dead soldiers and scuttle towards him. Kicking it away in disgust Will frantically looked around for

Arup, hoping against hope that he was lying in a similar hellhole a matter of feet away. It was tempting to jump up and go and look, to take his chances dodging bullets as he scampered left and right, searching for his friend. But Captain Daniels' words about self-preservation still resounded in his ears. 'You don't run deliberately into danger. Don't get yourself killed by being stupid. Bravery is one thing, suicide is another. Wait for a lull in the fighting then get going. Time is of the essence to the wounded men but we also want you back in one piece.' The trouble was, Will had already been out to no man's land and back to the casualty clearing station four times today, a distance of 1000 yards or so at a time, with each journey taking four hours in all. To make matters worse, two of the men assigned for this stretcher had already been wounded so there only remained Arup and Will, one at each end, to ferry the wounded. By now, Will was exhausted. The combined weight of an injured man and the stretcher itself meant that on each step he sank at least a foot into the quagmire. This made it almost impossible to place one foot in front of another and move forward. His instinct at that moment was simply to collapse. To give up, to cry. But Will knew it would serve no purpose. He had one more lap of the relay to complete and if he could scoop up one more of his injured comrades, by hook or by crook he would.

At that instant Arup slithered into the crater beside him, having crawled the few yards from his own hiding place, dragging the stretcher behind him. Breathless and caked in mud he adjusted his bloodied turban and slapped Will firmly on the back.

'Time to go, Sahib,' he said grimly. 'We wouldn't want you to be missing tiffin in your officers' mess.'

It was a flippant bit of gallows humour, but it certainly seemed to galvanise Will. How could anyone attempt humour at a time like this, he thought. Their very lives were at stake, for goodness' sake! But he could not help admire and like this man he'd increasingly come to know and respect. Arup was unquestionably brave to a fault, hugely compassionate and always had a good word to say about everybody. Much to Will's surprise this even included the enemy themselves who Arup admitted he felt sorry for whenever General Haig ordered another one of his heavy bombardments. He seemed incapable of hatred. In no man's land or under the barbed wire Will had seen him tend to wounded soldiers from both British and German armies with equal care and profession-alism, much to the disgust sometimes of the other enlisted men. It was a quality in experienced fighting men that he had rarely seen anywhere else since his arrival in France.

And he was right. It was time to go.

Taking one short diversion as they threaded their way back to their own trenches, they picked up an infantryman screaming with a compound fracture in his right leg and a missing left foot. They then progressed as rapidly as they could back to the casualty clearing station and handed over their wounded comrade to a surly lieutenant who was taking notes and shouting orders. His last command to the two stretcher bearers was to jump in the back of the ambulance and look after the wounded on the way to the field hospital. It was not one of the usual horse-drawn ambulances this time, Will was surprised to note, it was a motorised one with the letters RAMC painted boldly across its sides.

There were two men lying on stretchers, two sitting on the floor and two more propped up against each other on a bench. None were in a good way.

The driver jumped into the cab at the front and they set off in haste. As they bumped and lurched along the rough tracks leading away from the frontline the man with the shattered femur yelled out in agony each time the vehicle's crazy movements caused the bone ends to grate together. After the jarring caused by one particularly nasty pothole in the road the poor man finally passed out with the pain. Arup tightened the man's makeshift splint as best he could in an attempt to immobilise the limb further. Now the main sounds were the roaring of the engine and the muted moans of the other traumatised soldiers.

After about twenty minutes the road surface improved, the ambulance picked up speed and the noise of battle became a more distant soundtrack. The vehicle still swayed side to side somewhat but the ride was becoming infinitely smoother and within another fifteen minutes the soldiers were being gently unloaded into the hospital tent at the dressing station. Several orderlies took care of the stretchers while Arup supported one of the walking wounded by his arm, guiding him into the dormitory.

Will stepped out of the back of the ambulance and, leaning back against it, took a quiet moment to reflect on the dreadful scenes he had witnessed that day.

He realised that he had been in considerable danger himself for quite long periods. Death seemed so random and so unpredictable. Yet somehow the fate of the men he was sent to bring back and the terrible mutilation and butchery he observed made any concerns about himself seem frivolous. He looked up at the sky and took a long deep breath. Back home, before he had enlisted, no lad his age ever considered that anything dreadful would happen to them. Taking risks was normal. Accidents and injuries only happened to other people. Yet Will knew now without any shadow of a doubt that in the blink of an eye his life could be snuffed out as well. It was a sobering thought.

He heard a few soft footsteps coming around the side of the vehicle and there, to his amazement, was the very same nurse who had attended to Captain Daniels' arm. Miss Tustin-Pennington, Grace, who he knew for certain now was the prettiest women he had ever seen. She had wide cheekbones, auburn hair, the whitest of teeth and the deepest green eyes. She looked to be only a couple of years older than him. Her military-style uniform only enhanced her attractiveness.

'Miss . . . Grace. I'm sorry,' blurted Will. 'For a minute there I thought you were the driver.'

'I am the driver,' she said.

31

Will seemed to have lost his tongue. When he recovered, he said, 'I didn't think nurses drove ambulances.'

'They don't, usually, but I do.' She coolly gazed at him to gauge his reaction and seeing only a blank look of bewilderment, she pressed on. 'I've got a kind of dual responsibility.'

Will seemed to be wondering if she was teasing him. 'It's a Rover?' he asked.

'Yes, it is. This here is a Rover Sunbeam Ambulance donated by a rich benefactor to the war effort. The Army fitted her out with the ambulance panels and painted RAMC markings on her sides. Then she was shipped out here together with the generous chap's chauffeur to drive it. A typically magnanimous gesture of the aristocracy, wouldn't you say, to do their bit for King and country? Send some of the hired help to make the ultimate sacrifice?' She raised her eyebrow, cocked her head back and laughed.

'So where is the chauffeur now?' asked Will, attempting to tease her back. 'Taking a break while his navigator fills in for him?'

'Oh, I don't navigate. I like to be behind the wheel. Besides, he was killed by a sniper three weeks ago.'

'Oh, I'm so sorry,' said Will, and he looked like he meant it. He was a kind boy. She could see it. And sweet. She liked how awkward he was, how he didn't pretend to be more manly than he was, in spite of his broad shoulders and straight back.

'Nothing to say sorry for,' said Grace. 'It happens in war and I didn't know him. Besides, it's given me the chance to drive this beast. To enjoy another new adventure.'

'Enjoying? You can't really enjoy this nightmare?'

'No, you're right. It's awful. But the whole thing was *meant* to be an adventure.'

'But surely,' he said, 'you never anticipated being on the frontline? It's brutal, it can't surely be—'

'A suitable role for a woman?'

Will looked as embarrassed as he should do.

'Look, Private Burnett, isn't it?' she said.

'Just call me Will if you like.'

'I will, Will. Look, nursing at the front results in a paradox. Women's roles as nurses have been established for decades. Forever, in fact. That role doesn't threaten men because it isn't what *they* do. But dress us up in a military uniform and suddenly the menfolk are up in arms and chuntering that we are getting too big for our boots and trying to get above our stations.'

'But it is pretty darn dangerous out there. Don't you want us to protect you?'

'Protect my arse! Why should serving on the battlefield solely be the preserve of men? It's aggressive men that are responsible for getting us into all these dreadful useless bloody wars in the first place.'

Will, surprised by her language, had to admit she had a point. 'You certainly seem to feel quite strongly about it, Grace.'

'I do. There are so many roles out here that women can do just as well as the men. Not only being cooks, bottle washers, drivers and nurses either. One of these days I wouldn't be at all surprised if women have rifles in their hands so they can fight too.'

Will wisely decided to keep his thoughts to himself.

There was a silence between them then that lasted for several moments.

After a little while she said, 'And I sense, Will,' now looking straight into his eyes, 'that a sensitive and troubled young man like you sometimes needs an understanding woman like me, to help you get through?'

Will was lost for words.

'How old are you, Will?'

'Eighteen,' he lied, looking up at her briefly, to see whether she had believed him.

'And how old are you really?'

'Sixteen.'

'Sixteen. If it wasn't for that cute earnest way you have about you, I'd have believed eighteen. Same age as me.'

After a pause and what Grace realised must have been a rather awkward line of questioning for Will, she thought it only fair to share a little more about herself and how she got there.

'The FANY — First Aid Nursing Yeomanry — were the first ever British women's voluntary organisation to come out to war,' she explained. 'First to provide nurses and ambulances for the Belgian Army, then the French, and then us. I'm proud of the job we do. The officers are not fond of us, though. They can't bear it if we answer back or tell them how much they'd miss us if we weren't there. Some of them even see us as part of the suffragette movement. To be fair, Emily Davison is my all-time heroine. I actually saw her throw herself in front of the King's horse at the Epsom Derby a few years ago when my parents took me there. Horrible. They're more than happy to order us around when we are needed though. And I'm not in fact militant in that sense. Not politically.'

'I'd give you the vote any day of the week,' said Will, smiling. That made Grace toss her head back and laugh out loud.

She studied him carefully and then took his hand, pulling him away from the Rover Sunbeam.

'Come on,' she said. 'Let's get out of here and get you cleaned up. You look absolutely done in.'

She led him to the empty bell tent where she and five other nurses had their simple stretcher beds. She sat him down and took a saucepan of warm water from the embers of the coals used to warm the sleeping quarters.

'Who's this?' Will said, grinning, when he saw the cat wake and stretch on the bed one down.

'That's Omelette,' said Grace.

Will went to stand up so he could run his fingers across the cat's furry belly.

'Uh-uh,' Grace said, sitting him back down. 'Not yet.' She took a block of carbolic soap, dipped a flannel in the water and gently wiped all traces of soil and dirt from his eyes, nose and ears, finishing off with a thorough cleansing of his neck, forearms and hands. He looked unfathomably tired, she thought, yet still he had the energy to smile back at her.

'You'd better go and get some sleep,' she said.

Wearily, he stood up. He leaned down and gave Omelette a little tickle between the ears. Then he turned and looked into Grace's eyes and leaned forward and for a second she thought he was about to kiss her, but he must have just been fainting forward a little bit, as he straightened up, appearing startled, and then turned around and left, looking back softly at her and the cat at the tent entrance before he disappeared.

32

Aunt Clara had been astonished by the week's post. There was Will's weekly letter, regular as anything. He seemed to be in the habit of writing it every Sunday, and it would usually arrive on Wednesday. She read it out as usual to Kitty over dinner.

'*The food is still fairly basic but is keeping us alive. If I never see another tin of bully beef again it will be too soon, though, as I write this, I hear my stomach rumbling and take back everything I said. We eat what we get and we eat it quickly. I have made a new friend, an ambulance driver — but you will be shocked when I tell you she is a woman.*'

Interesting, thought Clara.

'*And a nurse, too! A very good nurse. She treated my commanding officer Captain Daniels' small wounds, and mine too (nothing to worry about).*'

His wounds! thought Clara.

'*She gave me quite a ticking off when I showed surprise at her taking such an involved role in the war — she believes strongly in the capabilities of women, and in talking to her I realised that in spite of my initial shock I always have too, in no small thanks to the example you set, Aunt Clara.*'

What a good boy he is, thought Clara. I wonder if he's as charming to this nurse he mentions.

She was aware, too, of what he didn't mention in his letters. She knew his role as a stretcher bearer must involve him seeing all manner of terribly damaged men, but he never responded directly to her questions about the exact nature of the work.

'*The work is hard and there is much to do, and it is sad that often our*

*labours are in vain, though I reassure myself that we save people from death
every day, and so I am lucky to be engaged in a task with a definite and helpful
purpose.'*

His tone was careful, distant. A boy his age having to be
so mature in the face of death — she wondered what it would
do to him.

*'Please tell me more about my sister. I expect she is a better reader and
writer than me now, with your uninterrupted company at school and in the
home. I think about you both every day and hope to get back to London before
too long. I will put up my pen now and sleep. God bless you, and all my love,
Will.'*

'What will you tell him about me?' asked Kitty.

'I'll tell him you're a terribly wicked girl who never eats
her cabbage,' said Clara.

'But I do eat my cabbage!' she said, forking some of the
untouched greens into her mouth. 'I save it to the end
because I like it so much.'

'You know, I can't tell whether you take after Jack or after
Will sometimes,' Clara said, looking at Kitty's angelic face.
'You might turn out to be more trouble than the pair of
them.'

And talking of trouble, the next day — unusually — saw a letter
from Jack. Jack's letters always started with an apology for not
having written and a promise that next time it wouldn't be so
long, though the time between each letter continued to grow.

'I have some good new friends,' she read out, *'uncivilised brutes from
Wales, though I must be uncivilised too, as they make me laugh. I have learned
to appreciate fine wine, and the differences between English and French
women, as well as how to differentiate between the main types of explosive.
How is Kitty Kitten? Still miaowing all around the place? Neither of you
need to worry about me — I do my work below ground, far from the hard
stuff above. I'm grateful for the news of Will. Please tell him I admire him.*

He's always been a bit of a wet flannel, but that's a hard and decent job he's doing. Must go now. Will be back to brighten up your days soon. Love and kisses, Jack.'

'Brief as usual,' said Clara.

'He's like a mole, isn't he?' said Kitty. 'Digging tunnels everywhere. Jack the mole and Kitty the kitten!'

Even rarer than a letter from Jack, the next day saw a letter from Robbie. She read this to herself before she read it aloud to Kitty.

Dear Clara and Kitty

I am sorry you have not heard of me for a long time. The fighting has been hard and I have been injured twice, once a bullet in the shin that broke a bone, another time a piece of shrapnel through the thigh. No wounds above the legs so far so I have been lucky, and the leg has healed up quite well. That's what the nurses say. The injuries have kept me out of the firing line for some months. I was in a field hospital in France for a while. I didn't want to worry you. I have probably worried you anyway. I have been sunk deep inside myself for a long time and everything has felt like so much work. It is the right place for me here. I have no choice but to do what I am told or I am endangering the men around me, and they are good men and don't deserve that. For a long time I wished to die. That is an easy thing to achieve round here. There is a good chance I won't come back alive. It would be silly to make a promise. But now I think I will try. I would like to see you again, to put my arms around Kitty and speak to the boys about their adventures. Please tell me if you have heard from them. I worry about them all the time, as I watch boys their age throw themselves against the guns. I would like to live long enough to try to make amends. I hope I can, though I am moving to the frontline again soon. I will do my best to stay alive and come back.

Your loving brother and father,
Robbie

It was too much to read this out to Kitty, she thought, dabbing at her eye with her hanky. What a sad letter it was, but she had become used to sadness, and what it was that was bringing a tear to her eye was the glimmer of some hope she sensed in his words, of some awakening from the cold sleep he had been in for the last seven years. It had taken such time! Perhaps he was really coming back to them. If he could stay alive long enough.

*

Grace had lost count of the men she had treated whose bodies and clothing were chronically infested with lice. They would be washed along with their uniforms and sent back to fight but she knew the lice would only go to sleep for a day or two and then re-emerge from the seams in the clothing to irritate and torment their hosts all over again. Several had suffered from trench fever because of the bacteria transmitted in lice bites and were plagued by high temperatures and pains in the muscles and joints. Even more tiresome was the fact the symptoms could often relapse.

She was weary from the innumerable cases of skin infections, exposure, and frostbite, from seeing men shivering violently, blue with cold, who had developed pneumonia as a result of the terrible conditions. Pneumonia was always a serious disease and in soldiers who were malnourished, exhausted and demoralised, it was often fatal. Many new soldiers, hastily recruited back home to replace diminishing numbers of fighting men, had never been constitutionally fit or healthy enough to enlist in the first place. They soon wilted and withered in the challenging conditions and ultimately only put extra and unnecessary strain on the already stretched medical services. Most were quickly evacuated to the base hospitals on the coast for immediate recuperation and repatriation: a result many had secretly been hoping for from the beginning. There were patients with impetigo, a blistering bacterial infection leading to oozing yellow crusts around the nose and mouth. And trench foot, a wasting disease of the skin caused by the pressure of ill-fitting boots and constant immersion in cold water — this could cripple a man or even lead to gangrene, requiring amputation. In the last few days, Grace had also attended to at least a dozen victims of rat bites. The marks from their nasty sharp teeth were obvious to the trained observer and three or four patients were wracked with the fever of typhus caused by bacteria spread by the fleas the vermin carried.

There were neglected wounds contaminated by maggots; and patients with cellulitis, a creeping infection beneath the skin that steadily migrated along tissue planes until eventually it poisoned the blood and led to fatal sepsis. Every day she had to lay out bodies in the mortuary and try to comfort the ones who would almost certainly be joining them in the next few hours or days.

She would use anti-tetanus serum routinely because wounds were so often contaminated by soil and animal waste yet still they would lose men through the action of the toxins produced by the Clostridium tetani germs. It was hard to watch: even as long as three weeks after an initial wound, lockjaw could set in, along with painful muscle spasms of the back and limbs together with a high temperature and respiratory failure.

Interventions intended to prevent disease had caused unforeseen problems of their own. A significant proportion of soldiers given typhoid vaccine had suffered quite severe side-effects like abdominal cramps and temperatures and had been out of action for days.

Widespread burns from explosions and resulting fires had become commonplace too. They were bad enough on the hand or limb, where infection thrived and where scarring produced horrific contractures robbing people of useful function. But on a face, burns were intensely painful and disfiguring and simply not amenable to skin grafting. Burns on over fifty per cent of the body's surface were invariably lethal, with the patient slowly observing the approach of their own death through fluid loss and fulminating infection.

Intravenous fluid and blood transfusions could make a difference in some cases but the sheer volume of casualties, particularly when they all came in at once, strained supplies and resources to the limit and made choices difficult and progress near impossible.

The contrast between arrangements at the distant base hospitals and the casualty clearing station was dramatic. There, the perpetual filling in of forms and the need for documentation, red tape, formality and rigid military discipline was paramount. Here, it was the opposite. The only imperative was to save as many lives as possible. Even German ones, occasionally, and it was a credit to the entire clinical staff that the enemy soldiers were generally treated with the same consideration and urgency as everyone else.

Now, the latest offensive was in full swing and the hospital was becoming completely overrun. Throughout the war so far there had been busy periods – frantic periods, sometimes – when the doctors and nurses struggled to cope with the casualties. And then there were quieter times when the fighting was occurring elsewhere or when both sides were regrouping, planning their next move, or content just to keep watch on the enemy. This onslaught, however, and the sheer number of severely wounded casualties, was unprecedented. The foul unrelenting weather had only made matters worse. Never before had Grace seen men brought in who had literally drowned in mud before they could be resuscitated.

The men exposed to nitrogen, mustard or phosgene gas would need to be stripped and thoroughly washed, their blistering eyes intensively irrigated with sterile saline and then bandaged. The men with fractures or dislocations of their arms and legs, however badly displaced or deformed, and in however much pain, would need to wait. So would those with superficial wounds or minor first- or second-degree burns. Those with severe blunt or penetrating injuries would need to take priority. The worst of them, with little or no chance of survival, and who at any rate would take up large amounts of time and resources at the expense of men more likely to survive, would not be treated at all.

Grace looked across at the chaotic entrance of the large hospital reception marquee in the forlorn hope of spying Will. She knew he was somewhere out there, either in a forward trench or in no man's land, fearlessly risking his life to bring in the wounded.

In a way, they were all risking their lives as the German artillery seemed to have found their range recently and were dropping shells increasingly closer to the camp. Just the day before, one had fallen directly onto one of the bell tents, killing all six inhabitants instantly.

She peered up at the ceiling of the tent, imagining what a shell would do here, and when she looked back down her spirits lifted as she caught sight of Will bringing in another stretcher.

'Resus tent,' she heard him shout. The medics knew him

well enough by now to trust his judgement. The resuscitation tent had heated beds and intravenous fluid lines which could warm and awaken a severely shocked patient prior to urgent surgery. It was miraculous how a blood transfusion could bring a cold, still, almost lifeless body back from the brink. On some occasions she had seen a previously moribund man sitting up, chatting and smoking a cigarette an hour or two later.

The pre-op tent was already congested, she could see, so the six tables in the main operating tent were going to be even more in demand.

She watched Will set down the injured man on his stretcher and speak confidently to the doctor as he described the circumstances of the soldier's injuries and his condition during transportation. He hadn't seen her. She watched the doctor nod and gratefully pat him on the shoulder. Will moved away. The doctor saw her watching, and came over and said to her, 'A reliable pair of hands is often welcome when we are busy, as you know. Someone who has seen it all before. Someone who won't faint at the sight of blood. That lad has often offered to assist me and other doctors when he's off duty, so he's become an unofficial surgical assistant. Knows his stuff.'

She kept watching as Will saluted a different officer and left to return to the ambulance without any apparent thought of rest or sustenance. As he turned, he finally saw her at the opening of the ward tent and smiled broadly. Lord, he was so handsome, she thought. And as he walked over towards her, her heart skipped a beat and she felt a curious sensation in her stomach.

'Good to see you again,' he said, grinning from ear to ear. 'How's it going?'

'It's mad, honestly. We'd only just evacuated most of our patients to the train or barges when the floodgates opened again. What about you?'

'It wasn't a good day. The enemy were expecting us. But there are twenty-two clearing stations now in the area and some more medical teams have recently arrived, so the worst is over.'

She looked at him, trying not to give away her feelings. 'It's good to see you again too.'

Will grinned again, blushing slightly himself this time. 'I'd better get back. I'll look out for you later, shall I?'

'Do.'

As he turned and hastened away to the ambulance she ran after him. 'Will?'

'What?'

She pressed a bar of chocolate into the palm of his hand. 'To keep your strength up. Take care of yourself and come back safe.'

He put the chocolate in the top pocket of his tunic and looked into her eyes. Then he bent down and kissed her on the cheek.

33

La Boisselle

It was a cool, cloudy summer's day with a light breeze coming from the east. The Battle of the Somme had raged for weeks, with countless dead and precious little ground gained by either side. A forward enemy trench might be overrun and taken for a few hours only to be retaken shortly after, leaving scores of lifeless bodies to show for it. Yet still the offensives and counter-offensives continued.

At dawn, the Germans hurled themselves forward at Delville Wood, overcoming and occupying the forward British trench, and now they were engaged in a holding operation, resisting counter-attacks by British and Canadian forces while holding out for reserves to reinforce and consolidate their position.

The British trenches had been constructed to facilitate firing towards the east and the Germans, firing towards the west, had no fire step on that side of the commandeered trench. They had to improvise the best they could to gain any kind of vantage point. Some stood on empty ammunition boxes, others on broken timbers or duck boards so they could look over the parapet and scrutinise the open ground ahead of them for signs of enemy activity.

Jürgen Altmann, who had seen his commandant fall with

a fatal head wound during the advance to their current position, took huge pride in taking what he considered his rightful place in the hierarchical pecking order. How impressed his late father would have been with him now. His chest swelled at the long-awaited prospect of being regarded as their general in command and he wasted no time in reinforcing his authority by leading by example.

In the trench in front of him lay the body of a Canadian soldier who had died in a sitting position just outside his dugout. He had been killed in the skirmish about three hours previously and because he had been a thick-set and well-muscled man rigor mortis had already set in. His head and neck stood ramrod straight, his limbs as stiff as boards and his torso flexed rigidly at the waist in a right angle. His eyes, wide open and staring, were equally anchored and immobile. Altmann grabbed the body under the armpits, heaved it up and dragged it to the parados on the other side of the trench where he propped it up. The back was now against the muddy wall and the legs stuck out into the walkway like a grotesque marionette at rest. Then, putting his right boot on the corpse's right shoulder, he levered himself up and steadied himself by placing the other boot on top of the opposite shoulder.

'Look, they have even left steps for us!'

He laughed loudly at his own joke. The men within earshot merely looked at him in consternation as he stood on the dead man's body. This could soon be the fate of any one of them, they were thinking. They would hate for their bodies to be so cynically desecrated. Altmann didn't seem to notice.

'There is some sort of building here in front of us,' he said, unperturbed. 'A byre by the look of what's left of it. Our comrades in the artillery have done a good job.' He took his Goerz Fago Berlin officers' field binoculars from his greatcoat and scanned the ground in front of him. At first, all he could see was a 400-yard stretch of flat, pock-marked terrain with a few broken and twisted tree stumps where once a cherry orchard or thicket may have been. He quickly scanned the far horizon from left to right for any imminent sign of a counter-attack and satisfied himself there was none. Then, as he focused the lenses on the middle distance, he smiled when he saw what he had actually been looking for. Thirty, maybe forty enemy wounded, some waving their arms in supplication, some crawling on all fours, and others on their bellies pulling themselves along by their elbows. The stricken and defeated enemy.

'Dieter! Knut! Come with me.'

The two German privates looked at each other hesitantly.

'You others protect us from covering fire.'

Altmann and the two other men heaved themselves up out of the trench and ran over in a crouch to the ruined stable as their comrades liberally sprayed bullets across the span of open ground in front of them. In response, there was some sporadic answering fire on either flank but much to their relief none of it near enough to threaten them.

It was something of a miracle that the old farm building was still standing. When Altmann reached it, he immediately saw it had been some sort of stable for horses. On one side of it the wattle and daub walls had largely been blown out by shell-fire but at the far end beyond the stalls the tack room remained almost intact. Three-quarters of the roof drooped precariously yet still somehow supported itself. Better still, in Altmann's reckoning, two small windows gave out onto the area where the British and Canadian casualties now lay and beyond it the whole of Western Europe.

He bent down on his knee at one of the windows and brought his rifle to his shoulder.

'What are you doing?' asked Knut.

'Watch.'

The rifle was a standard Gewehr 98, chambered with eight-millimetre Mauser rounds, and it was the best plaything Altmann had ever possessed. Better than his Springmesser stiletto switchblade, which he prized so highly, and better still than his serrated garrotte that he bought on the black market from a seedy Spaniard three years previously in London's East End. He looked through the scope with its four times magnification and carefully combed the ground for any evidence of movement. As his line of vision traversed the ground, he settled the centre of the crosshairs on a horizontal figure in a khaki uniform lying on his left side, his right arm and shoulder immobile and drenched in blood. Altmann could clearly see his face: the eyes screwed up in pain, the nose bloodied and the lips pulled back in a rictus grimace. He focused the rifle on the man's forehead first, then, thinking more on it, he moved the sight down to the hollow at the base of his throat. Which target to choose? he asked himself. A quick kill? Or give the man a moment or two to realise what had happened before he drowned in his own blood? He adjusted his aim slightly, squeezed the trigger and dispassionately shot the man in the stomach.

'What the hell are you doing?' yelled Knut, appalled by the actions of his superior officer. 'That's a wounded man.'

'Twice wounded now,' said Altmann as he purposefully lined up another shot.

'You can't do this,' said Dieter, equally shocked but also nervous about being seen to criticise his commanding officer. 'It's a crime. It's against all conventions of war.'

Through the scope, Altmann could see the casualty doubled up and writhing in pain, his face contorted even further, his eyes darting frantically this way and that.

'There are no conventions in war,' he said. 'In war, you need to win. At any cost. If you are soft, you embolden your enemy. If you show weakness, you are defeatist.'

'Jürgen, these men cannot defend themselves; they are suffering.'

'Not for long, Dieter. Not for long.' Returning to his scope, he coldly examined the magnified distant image of an enemy soldier shot in the shoulder and side and put the next bullet clean through the back of his head. The target slumped and lay still. Dieter and Knut looked at each other, aghast.

'Jürgen, I cannot stand by and allow you to—'

'To what?' snarled Jürgen, spinning sharply around. 'You will do as I tell you and obey orders.'

The two junior men exchanged further desperate glances for moral support. Neither had ever been in such a position. Both felt sickened and disgusted by what they had just witnessed. Altmann glared at them.

'If you let the enemy live today, they come back and kill you tomorrow. That is how the German Army will be victorious. Under Jürgen Altmann, you take no prisoners. Now keep watch on the flanks and grow some balls.' He repositioned his rifle, angrier than ever. He selected another target and mercilessly pulled the trigger. The silence that ensued between the three of them was deafening.

34

The 1st Battalion North Staffordshire Regiment that had been overcome by the German assault a few hours previously had retreated to a rearguard position and were regrouping. A charge had been mounted to reclaim the lost territory but casualties had been heavy, leaving dozens of men wounded and lying out in the open. In response, the artillery that had been hastily brought up were pounding the flank to the left of a dilapidated stable block, and stretcher bearers had been mobilised to fetch back the wounded. Will and Arup, Frankie Bull and Ed Baker were among them. The Germans seemed determined not to relinquish the hard-fought ground they now had control of and were shooting at anyone and anything that moved. Two companies led by Captain Daniels had therefore been sent out to support them. One hundred yards to the left and in front of them, firing was coming from the window of the stable and just behind it, on both sides, there was further sporadic shooting from the former British-held trench. They desperately needed to get closer to the wounded men but the whole area in front of them was being raked by relentless rifle and machine-gun fire. They were helplessly pinned down. Captain Daniels took out his field glasses and assessed the situation.

'Christ,' he cursed, 'the bastards are deliberately shooting the wounded.'

'What?' said Will. 'Are you sure?' He had seen wounded men incur further injuries before but only because they happened to be in the wrong place at the wrong time and never because they were deliberately and individually targeted. This was horrific.

'Some evil swine in that outhouse.'

'That means we are all possible targets,' said Arup gloomily.

'And that's why you will all stay here. Until my men make it safe.'

'But Captain, there is no cover. It would be suicide,' said Will.

'I'm not lying here while my men are being used as target practice. And you're not going to be their ducks in a row, either.'

'What can we do?' asked Frankie, feeling a little helpless. Like Ed and Will and the other regimental stretcher bearers he carried a Webley pistol in his belt but still felt surplus to requirements. Arup had chosen not to carry a gun months ago.

'Wait here and don't move. Our artillery is getting their range now and the enemy's right flank is hunkered down. I will take my men forward and attack their left flank. If we take back the trench we should be able to storm and capture the outhouse.'

He took his Army-issue Webley from its holster on his belt and got to his feet. 'Men,' he yelled, 'let's go.'

Daniels was a king among men as far as Will was concerned. Confident and courageous, he never seemed to hesitate. He always seemed to know instinctively what was required. But was he living on borrowed time? The Germans were well protected in the trench behind their sandbags and, by the sound of it, heavily armed. But how many were there? And why had they foregone all modicum of human decency and taken to murdering the wounded? Will felt hatred and bile rising in his throat.

Daniels rose up, pistol in hand, and leapt forward, urging his men to follow him. They scampered, zigzagging this way and that as he had taught them to do, diving flat on their bellies into any rut or bomb crater before sprinting on again to the next. At least there was no barbed wire to hinder their progress here but, even as he watched, Will saw two, three and four men thrown backwards by the force of bullets. Within moments, he lost sight of the captain and feared that he had already fallen. The smoke from the artillery shells falling to the right of the stables and wafting across on the wind obscured his vision.

'Jesus,' said Ed, 'they're getting slaughtered.'

'*Theirs not to reason why, Theirs but to do and die*,' murmured Arup to himself.

'What?' said Frankie.

'It's Tennyson,' said Will nervously. '*Into the valley of death rode the six hundred*, and all that.'

'Oh. "Charge of the Light Brigade", right?' replied Frankie.

'If only there were six hundred of them. There aren't even sixty.'

The smoke billowing across the battlefield proved fortuit-ous. Daniels had succeeded in edging his way closer to the new German line and together with fourteen remaining men had flopped into a funk-hole and were keeping the enemy occupied and mostly distracted from the place where Will and his fellow stretcher bearers lay.

Now that it was quieter, the stretcher bearers gingerly crawled their way towards the wounded men to their left, pausing every few yards to avoid the chance of their move-ment alerting the enemy to their presence. After what seemed like an age, and with their arms aching from dragging the stretcher behind them, they found themselves within twenty yards of their first casualty. Now they could clearly hear the retort of one solitary rifle firing from the window of the stable building. Will's concentration was broken when another group of four stretcher bearers ran across his field of vision to his left and set themselves down by the side of one of the wounded. Will watched as they went about their duties while continuing to crawl further forward himself. Crack! One of the stretcher bearers he had been observing tumbled forward like a felled tree. What? Crack! His comrade next to him collapsed and pitched forward across their patient's body. Crack! The casualty's body jerked and spasmed, the legs extending and the backbone arching in the rigour of spasticity. The sniper in the stable block was deliberately killing the medics as well as the wounded. Will was so incensed he tried to stand and run wildly towards where the shots were coming from but Arup saw and clasped him in a bear hug on the ground.

'Don't get yourself killed, Sahib,' he whispered in his ear. 'We must tread carefully.'

More shots came from the window and Will and his team distinctly heard the occasional dull thud of bullets hitting flesh and bone. He balled his fists, flexed every muscle in his body and tried to get his breathing under control. Arup held onto him tightly. The four of them were lying in a shallow ditch and several shots pinged so close by them they were totally unable to move. A different sound, initially difficult to identify because their heads were glued so close to the ground, made itself heard — a whining and roaring noise that rose and fell as it got louder. It was the sound of a vehicle engine straining and revving furiously as it battled to make headway over the rugged terrain.

'I don't believe it,' said Arup.

'What the hell's that doing here?' said Frankie.

They watched in amazement as the RAMC ambulance bounced and juddered towards them, its steering wild and erratic yet nevertheless holding true to its intended course. Then it stopped. It had come to a halt right in the direct line of fire between the stable window and a number of wounded men scattered in a small tragic group about seventy-five yards away.

'Oh! Oh no!' said Will, fighting to shake off Arup. 'That's Grace's ambulance. That's Grace.'

35

Grace had been kicking her heels, waiting with the RMO for the stretcher bearers to return with the wounded. She would treat them immediately and ferry them back to the casualty clearing station. The medic was occupied, performing open surgery with limited equipment, and would clearly be busy for some time. Idly, she picked up a pair of field binoculars lying nearby and scanned the barren landscape in front of her. It was rare she found herself this close to the frontline and she was shocked by what she saw.

Where were the trees she loved so much? Where were the trees which were, for her, the embodiment of nature and life itself? The only remaining sign of the ash, birch, oaks and hornbeams that would once have previously grown there was the occasional gnarled and splintered stumps just three or four feet high and totally devoid of branches or foliage.

She also saw an excuse for a tree, a hollow spy tree built by the Royal Engineers from steel and wrought iron and camouflaged to resemble the real thing. She wondered if there was a sniper inside manning it now. The Germans had been constructing them too, she had been told. *Baumbeobachtung* — wasn't that what they called them?

Who would ever have thought that even trees themselves could be recruited as deadly weapons and ranged against one another in this awful war? Would she ever be able to look at a real living tree in the same light again?

Suddenly, beyond the artificial tree, she saw the spark of

a muzzle flash in the distance. Immediately she realised what was happening — the medics and the injured were being shot down mercilessly by a lone rifleman in the farmhouse. She was appalled and incensed. Without the slightest thought of waiting for back-up, she decided to go it alone. On impulse, she jumped into the driving seat of the motor ambulance and hared off toward the killing ground, flooring the accelerator and wrestling with the steering wheel. Getting as near to the casualties as she could, she slammed on the brakes and killed the engine.

'She's crazy,' said Ed.

'She's bloody incredible,' said Will, his emotions torn between fear and pride. 'Do you see what she's doing? She's using the ambulance as a shield. The shooter can't see his targets anymore.'

'Come on, let's give her a hand.'

They could see Grace stretching across the front seat to pick up her medical bag and then, in a flash, the passenger door was torn open and a burly brute of a man hauled her out of the vehicle and dragged her roughly towards the stable with his arm around her neck. Frankie was on his feet and sprinting towards the ambulance. He got four yards before taking a bullet in the chest.

'Frankie!' cried Ed, who wriggled over to him and held him. It was too late. There was nothing he could do. Frankie was gone.

36

Captain Daniels, with only eleven of his company remaining, now had the advantage of surprise. The trenches were never built in straight lines, to prevent the enemy from firing down the length of them; they were constructed in a zigzag fashion with alternate fire bays and traverses. The soldiers had edged their way along one such traverse and were painstakingly picking off one German soldier after another as they peered cautiously around each corner.

Approaching within a hundred yards of the stable ruin they saw approximately thirty of the enemy around the next corner, all with their rifles trained on the same ground they had just crossed. They could not confront this many headlong, so Daniels diverted his men to the right along a twenty-yard saphead which soon gave them a favourable position to the rear of the Germans. It crossed the captain's mind that the positions generally assumed by the two armies had been reversed. The British soldiers firing one way towards where the Germans were now and the Germans to the west of them. The difference was that the enemy were looking the other way and had no knowledge of their presence. To the right, beyond the stable block, Jerry was being kept quiet by the allied artillery which was scoring accurate hits on the intended targets. There were no threats coming from that direction any time soon. If only they could get nearer. If only they could creep up closer to the enemy, it would even up the odds considerably.

After a swift head count of the opposing troops, he turned to his men and gave them detailed instructions with hand signals. With grim, determined faces they nodded at their captain. Then, they pulled themselves silently up and over the parapet, guns levelled in front of them, and began crawling slowly towards their objective.

37

Grace could not believe the strength of the man. Kick and punch as much as she liked, her blows were like water to this ogre of a German as he forcibly dragged her inside the building in a brutal neck hold.

'Stay by the door and watch the left flank,' he instructed Dieter and Knut. 'There's nothing coming from the front or the right.'

The two men exchanged glances again but did what they were told. Knut felt sorry for the pretty young nurse. She was being far too harshly manhandled, but by now Altmann had already manoeuvred her halfway towards the tack room.

What did this man want from her? Grace asked herself. She was a nurse, not a soldier. She didn't know any other nurses who had been treated this way or, for that matter, taken prisoner. Why did he not show her the customary courtesy and respect? She had heard of one high-ranking sister who had been shot as a spy, but she had never seen anything like it herself and had hoped she never would. Despite her predicament, and mounting fear of suffocation, she was able to take in her surroundings. She recognised the broken partitioned areas that once would have been horse stalls — with their water troughs, blanket racks and open-grilled feed boxes. It was a stable, she realised, the kind of building she would normally feel so relaxed and at home in. But now her life was in danger and this particular stable might be her final resting place, her personal mausoleum. In the tack room, Altmann pushed her into the corner and released her head from his arm lock. He pulled off her QAIMNS nurses' cap and leered at her.

38

Ah, but she's especially attractive, this one, he thought as he examined her more closely. A lovely face and one hell of a figure to go with it. Nothing like the hags that passed for nurses in the German military hospital.

The fear in her eyes and her defiant attitude only excited him more.

'I always wanted to screw an English girl,' he said, 'but they were all too bloody frigid.'

Grace was taken aback, both by what he said and that he could say it in half-decent English.

'But the heat of battle will have warmed you up enough I am sure.'

Grace was petrified, but refused to show it. 'Don't even think about it. Have some respect.'

'That's the thing about war,' he said, grinning at her, 'you can take what you want. What is the saying? To the victor the spoils?'

'You will never be the victors. And one day you will be made to pay for this war, too.'

Altmann's attention was distracted by Dieter shouting from the other end of the building. 'There's shooting in the trench behind us.'

'Of course, you fool!' he yelled back impatiently. 'Our men are strafing the fields like I told them to. Stay alert.'

He turned back to Grace with a mad look in his eye. 'You

talk of us paying for it. Let me tell you who is going to pay for it.'

He grabbed her hair at the back of her neck and pulled her towards him. He stared wildly into her eyes. Grace stared defiantly back and Altmann smirked. His breath was foul. He looked over his shoulder furtively to ensure they were alone and in one swift action hurled Grace down to the floor onto a thin scattering of mouldy hay that proved no use whatsoever in breaking her fall. She landed with a thump on her hip and shoulder. It hurt like hell but there was no way she was going to give this brute the satisfaction of knowing it. She got onto all fours and went to stand up. Altmann grabbed her by the throat and threw her back down. Grace gasped and scrambled away from him, her back to the wall, but he was quick for a man of his size. He dropped to his knees in front of her and grinned. Shells were dropping close to the stable now and the noise and clamour were deafening. But Grace was focused entirely on the immediate threat in front of her. She was strong for a young woman and she wriggled and struggled, kicked and lashed out as much as she could, but the more she fought the more the big German seemed to enjoy it. He had forced her thighs apart and was now kneeling between them; her gown was gathered around her waist and this bastard of a man was undoing his belt and fly buttons. She knew about men, she thought; she was worldly wise and skilled at avoiding unwelcome attention or dangerous situations. She was not naïve. She understood that in a time of war terrible things could happen, but never in her worst nightmares had she considered she might be raped.

He had one huge hand on her left breast, squeezing it

painfully and pinning her down firmly, and the other hand was busy starting to extricate himself from his trousers. Tears filled her eyes as she fought and strained against the sheer power of him. She waited for the inevitable.

39

Will, Arup and Ed had reached the ambulance and were tentatively edging around the side of it. Strangely, no further shots had come from the stable for a few minutes. A frontal assault, however, was fraught with danger. Was the position now abandoned and unmanned? Or was the sniper just biding his time, lulling them into a false sense of security and a fatal trap? It was a horrible dilemma, but Will's determination to come to Grace's rescue prevailed. He broke cover and sprinted towards the building.

Reckless young fool, thought Arup, but a bloody brave fool and one that had, in recent days and weeks, become almost a son to him.

Without a second thought, and totally unarmed, he followed his protégé. Twenty yards, ten yards, five yards away from the building and still no muzzle flashes from the window. They threw themselves flat against the outside wall and caught their breath. Shots were coming more frequently from their right in the trench in front of them where Captain Daniels had been heading, but as far as they knew Grace was being held here inside the stable by the enemy. Keeping their backs to the wall they inched their way to the side of the building, and as they did so Arup saw something black and metallic lying on the ground in front of him. He stooped and picked it up.

Inside the tack room, Altmann was interrupted by the arrival of Dieter.

'Leave her alone,' he said. 'You bring shame on us all.'

Altmann buttoned his fly, brought himself upright and turned, his pleasure curtailed before it had even begun.

'Dieter Meier, you will pay for your subordination. I will personally—'

His words were cut short by Knut screaming from the far doorway. He had stepped out and seen the figure of Will coming towards him. He yelled and raised his gun, pointing it directly at Will. He could not miss.

A shot rang out and Knut fell dead with a bullet lodged in his heart. Will stopped on the spot. He turned and saw Arup, his face inscrutable, lowering his arm, the German Luger still smoking slightly from the round he had fired in order to save Will's life. The gun slipped from his fingers and fell to the ground not far from where he had found it.

40

'Careful, lads,' said Ed just behind them, 'there may be more of them inside.'

As they tiptoed in their heavy boots down the walkway past the smashed stable stalls, Altmann and Dieter Meier drew their pistols and readied themselves for a shootout. As far as they knew, there could be scores of enemy soldiers armed to the teeth coming towards them. Grace, still shaking in the far corner, hoped there were. Will, with Arup and Ed just behind him, was within two yards of the tack room doorway when a shell burst directly onto the rear of the stable, punching a huge hole in the wall and demolishing much of the remaining roof and supporting rafters.

Altmann was thrown violently forward onto the ground, something sharp slicing across his face and plaster dust and wooden shards showering him. He was dazed and shaken but alive. Dieter's limp and contorted body was slumped next to him, the eyes wide open and staring vacantly. He glanced over to where Grace had been but could see nothing through the dense miasma of swirling dust. A few steps away, on the other side of the shattered wall, the three stretcher bearers were also picking themselves up off the floor.

Grace, thought Will. Where was Grace? If she was still being held here, could she possibly have survived that? The shell had struck much nearer to the far end of the building yet it had still knocked the three of them sideways. Dust and flying debris still billowed towards them and it was impossible to see through it. But he had to know. He staggered to his feet and crept toward the doorway.

Altmann's men were depleted in number now, but still in the trench and ever watchful. There, they had witnessed three khaki-clad figures with the symbolic red cross on their sleeves sidle around the stable block and shoot one of their men. Furthermore, they seemed to be taking fire from all sides now for some reason. The picture was increasingly confused and chaotic. The British artillery had also landed a huge shell in the corner of the building and three of their men, including their commanding officer, were still in there. The German soldiers climbed up their makeshift parados and began their advance towards the building. Not far behind them, Jacob Daniels and his men could not believe their luck. There, outlined in stark silhouette against the pale blue sky, were at least a dozen German infantrymen.

Will burst into the tack room, stumbling over chunks of plaster and rubble on the way. He looked around frantically, hoping against hope that Grace would be there, alive and well and running into his arms. And at first his hopes were dashed. But then there was an almost imperceptible move-ment and a quiet scraping sound coming from the far corner. He picked his way through the dust and saw her. Grace. Impetuous, foolhardy, adventurous, lovely Grace. She managed a small smile, sat herself up and reached out to Will. He ran to her, gingerly helped her up and took her in his arms, not quite able to believe she had somehow survived.

Over his shoulder, she had a sudden realisation and

scanned the room. There was Arup and Ed, both covered in plaster. She also saw the dead body of the German soldier who'd had the decency and courage to stand up to his superior officer and attempt to come to her rescue. But there was no sign whatsoever of that butcher Altmann.

41

Altmann slid down into the funk-hole and put his hand to his bloodied face. He had been lucky to escape; whoever was advancing through the stable would have killed him. He harboured no doubt that they would not have hesitated. The left side of his mouth was a painful mess.

'*Scheisse*,' he cursed. '*Diese Bastarde!*'

He had survived the explosion but whatever had sliced through his lip and cheek had taken out three molars simultaneously. His torn lower lip hung down over his chin, grossly everted and still bleeding, the remaining teeth under the jowls exposed and visible like those of a rabid hyena baring his fangs to protect his prey.

'That whore,' he lisped. Why was it that women were at the heart of every bloody catastrophe in his life?

There was furious fighting going on now to his left along the adjacent traverse trench and his own men were clearly coming off much worse. He checked to see that his Mauser was still in its holster and rapidly set off in the opposite direction.

42

Will and his friends were enraged to hear of Grace's ordeal. It was yet another disgusting and bestial dimension to this terrible war. Grace was badly shaken but was recovering herself.

Her deliverance had arrived in the nick of time, but the perpetrator had escaped. The man who had tried to protect her lay dead. There was no justice in this world. Not a shred.

Will was just relieved that Grace was alive and in one piece but the four of them were certainly not out of the woods yet.

'We need to get out of here fast,' said Ed. 'All hell is breaking loose outside.'

They made their way cautiously back past the stalls and peeked out of the entrance to where the Germans were. About a dozen or so were walking slowly towards them with bayonets fixed, looking menacing.

'Let's get to the ambulance while we have a chance,' said Ed, taking the lead. 'Go and get it started and I will follow.'

They ran, Will holding Grace firmly by the hand and Arup one step behind them. It was the Rover ambulance with its hard dark-green top and big red cross. It stood there beckoning them like a waiting omnibus at a public bus stop. It was only a few yards away but with all the bullets whizzing past their heads it felt like a mile.

Will intuitively pushed Grace in first to keep her out of harm's way and the two men threw themselves in behind her.

They turned to look for Ed, but he was nowhere to be seen. They waited. An eerie stillness had descended and all they saw were bodies lying on the ground and behind them Captain Daniels frantically waving them away.

His men had succeeded in outflanking the enemy, surprising them from behind. However they had achieved it, they had saved the lives of the three of them, at least. Will hoped that held true for Ed as well but somehow that did not look likely.

The captain motioned. They understood his gesticulations as meaning he and his troops would try to hold the trench. That they should get going.

But Grace had other ideas. With no more shooting for the moment she jumped down from the other side of the Rover and marched off.

'Where the hell are you going, Grace?' asked Will, incredulously.

'There are casualties,' said Grace. 'That's what we came for.'

In his desire to rescue her, Will had almost forgotten about that. He could not believe it. He quickly composed himself and chased after her, much to the ire of the captain, who kept furiously gesticulating. But even he eventually realised Grace would not be persuaded to desist, and so the group of them scouted about for survivors. Three were found still alive, cold, dehydrated and frightened, and soon they were made as comfortable as they could be in the back of the vehicle on stretchers. Ed had made it just one step outside the stable. They were too late for him. Once the survivors were loaded, Grace heaved the battered ambulance into gear and set off.

Grace drove with Will beside her and Arup did his best

to tend to the wounded in the rear. As they bounced and jolted over the rutted ground they each reflected on their recent ordeal. Grace had had a very narrow escape. From the shell and from that monster. Will had stared point blank down the barrel of a gun. Arup had broken a solemn vow he had made to himself but at the same time saved his precious friend's life.

Grace was familiar with this ambulance and she knew exactly what it was capable of. In theory, its four-cylinder water-cooled engine could reach forty-five miles per hour on a smooth straight road. Grace was somehow coaxing forty-eight out of it over a ploughed field.

Will reached across and put his muddy, bloodied hand on top of her own.

PART THREE

SHELL SHOCK

1917

43

Home on Leave

'It's a different world, Grace,' said Will as he sipped his beer at the Café Royal in Regent Street and cast his eyes about the elegant splendour of the place. Every dining table was taken, with men and women enjoying lunch surrounded by bulging bags of Christmas gifts for their families at their feet. 'No one would think there was a war on.'

'But look at the reception we've been getting. Ushered to the front of the queue for the bus. No charge for the taxi. And here, your beer and my coffee are on the house.'

'Maybe there is a benevolent God looking down on us after all,' said Will.

They looked into each other's eyes. Since the terror they'd endured at the stable, they had allowed their feelings for each other to flourish, had snatched small moments here and there when they were able. Now, being in London together and away from the front — they could barely believe it.

'I can't wait for you to meet my little sister, Kitty, and Aunt Clara,' he said.

'You'll meet Mother and Father, my lovely little brother, Fitzwilliam, and my useless layabout sister, Amy,' said Grace.

'And I appreciate that. I also appreciate you sharing this

place with me,' said Will, placing his knife and fork together on the plate. 'The poshest nosh I've had up till now was in Joe Lyons in Oxford Street. Did a nice vanilla ice cream, they did.'

'It's Christmas, Will, and I want to spoil you. Where shall we go next?'

It was a difficult question. Where hadn't they been? The train in France had taken them to Le Tréport where Grace had been offered a room for the night at the British-Canadian base hospital and Will had found a simple billet nearby. The next morning was grey and cold and a biting westerly wind flew in their faces as they walked along the seafront with its ramshackle houses of all shapes, sizes and colours. They watched a number of well-off people with their neatly dressed children, who, unlike children of the same age back home, were clearly not allowed to paddle in the sea or make sandcastles.

They had boarded a ship at nine a.m. and, because of the ever-present danger of mines, it steamed slowly and cautiously towards Folkestone, finally arriving about three p.m. On the train to Waterloo the carriage was full of weary-looking men, many still caked in mud with ragged uniforms and matted hair, some slumbering while they could and others animatedly sharing plans for Christmas with their comrades. In the next carriage a group of men from the same regiment had been sharing some French wine and brandy and were singing heartily. *'Take me back to dear old Blighty, put me on the train for London Town, Take me over there, drop me anywhere ... Tiddley-iddley-ighty ...'*

On the trip they discussed the recent events of the war and their good fortune in being granted this leave together.

'I heard there was no such thing as leave in the first year of the war,' said Will. 'They all thought it would be over within a few months, so letting soldiers take off wasn't an option.'

'It's not much better now,' she said wistfully. 'Not for the ordinary men, anyway. Once every fifteen months for them. Every three months for officers. It's all dependent on rank. How can that be right?'

Will loved Grace's principled outlook on life. He knew she came from landed gentry, yet she seemed devoid of any sense of privilege or entitlement.

Now here they were at 6.30 p.m. in the heart of Piccadilly. Everywhere they went there were decorations and baubles, lights and exhibitions, elaborate displays of toys and gifts in all the shop windows. Advertisements everywhere exhorting customers to enter the stores and purchase the goods. At Sainsbury's Will and Grace stopped to look in the window. If it was true that food was scarce there was no sign of it here. An impressive queue was waiting patiently outside the door, but few young men formed part of it.

There must have been 300 plucked turkeys hanging upside down from metal hooks across the facade and the junior staff, still plucking more at the back of the store, were replacing them as fast as they were being sold. The public, Will thought, had been encouraged to consume less and never hoard. But he had never seen grub this expensive flying off the shelves so fast. It was a far cry from the meagre fare on offer in the trenches. There was freshly shot wild game, rabbit, pheasants and even something called glazed ox tongue. Give me bully beef any day over that, Will thought, but according to the written signs, the shop had attempted to restrict their produce to goods from local farms and food that boasted it had exclusively been prepared in house at their own factory in Blackfriars. Hen turkeys, one and nine per pound, prime-quality cock turkeys, one and six per pound. Then capons, geese, ducks and hams. Stilton and cheddar cheeses.

'Don't know about you, Grace, but I'm done in. And Aunt Clara will be expecting us back soon before it's too late.'

'I bet Kitty is excited to see her big brother.'

'She will be. Come on, let's get a cab.'

*

Clara opened the door but was almost knocked over by Kitty rushing out. She threw her arms around Will who lifted her up. She clung tightly to his neck as if she would never let go.

'Hello, Kitty, my lovely,' he said, carrying her inside. 'And hello, Clara, it's wonderful to see you. This is Grace.'

Clara closed the door behind them and looked warmly at Grace.

'I read a lot about you in Will's letters.'

'Not all bad I hope.'

'Quite the opposite.'

Grace blushed. 'And I've heard so much about you too, Mrs—'

'Call me Clara,' she laughed. 'People call me all sorts of things, especially Jack. But Clara is just fine.'

'She hasn't met Jack yet, Aunt Clara, but I've warned her.'

'Good job,' she said. 'Forewarned is forearmed. But you'll have to wait till your next visit to see him. He's still out there.'

They sat down in the little lounge, Clara and Grace on the settee and Will on the same dilapidated armchair his father used to sit in with Kitty jumping up and down on his lap. It made him think of Robbie, but he knew from Clara's letters that there was no good news so he let the moment pass. Kitty looked so grown-up. Her hair had gone a darker brown and was down below her shoulders, her eyebrows were darker too, her eyes bluer than ever, and when she smiled there were a couple of gaps from where she had recently lost her milk teeth. Her irrepressible energy and enthusiasm had also intensified.

'We brought you a present for Christmas, Kitty,' he said. 'Grace chose it herself.'

'Can I open it now, Aunt Clara? Can I? Can I?'

'Shouldn't you wait until Christmas Day?' said Clara, looking at Will for guidance.

'We only have a few days' leave, Auntie. Tomorrow we should go and see Grace's parents. They're still in a terrible state.'

Will felt bad he didn't also have time to check in on Trevor. It had taken a while for the news to filter through but he knew that, while Trevor was weakened and would forever have digestion issues, he was at least safe and well – permanently discharged.

'Of course. I'm sure they are. I feel so sorry for them. And you, Grace. How awful. And you have other brothers serving too?'

'I do. Three of them. Thank you, Clara. I know it will mean a lot for me to be there. And for them to meet Will as well.'

'Open your present, Kitty,' said Will, changing the subject. 'And this little one is for you, Aunt Clara.'

Kitty tore off the wrapping and squealed in delight at the intricate doll's house with its different compartments and figurines. She jumped down off Will's lap and started to organise its various components. Clara carefully unfolded the wrapping paper from her own small gift and, typically, made sure it did not tear so it would be reusable. She extricated two small bottles of French perfume, one labelled Bouquet Jeanice and the other Les Roses d'Orsay. She sprayed some of each onto her wrists and inhaled deeply.

'Beautiful,' she said, smiling. She gave them both a hug. 'But the best present of all would be to have both of you returning home safely once this dreadful conflagration in France is over.'

'That's our plan,' said Grace and Will almost simultaneously. Then, they gratefully accepted her gifts to them. For Grace, a necklace and locket, and a hardback copy of Pye's *Surgical Handicraft* for Will. 'A manual,' Will read, 'of surgical manipulations, minor surgery, and other matters connected with the work of house surgeons and surgical dressers.' It had over 200 illustrations.

'Aunt Clara, this is a wonderful present.'

'I know this is something you're fascinated with and hopefully it will help you with your work over there.'

'You shouldn't have bought us anything, Auntie,' protested Will. 'You've already done everything for us as a family with next to nothing in return.'

'With everything in return,' she said. 'And by these tokens I'd like you to remember us waiting for you here at home.'

'We will, we promise.'

*

Despite Grace's reassurances, Will felt nervous about meeting her parents for the first time. The gulf in social standing between the two families could hardly be greater and he was conscious that he might be regarded as an unworthy or an inadequate suitor for a Tustin-Pennington. Might they think he was too young for her? Some working-class oik out to take advantage of her or after her wealth?

Grace had fitted in easily at his own family's house in Chiswick and showed no sign of surprise at how tiny and humble it was, or must have seemed to her. She had got along famously with his aunt and in particular Kitty, who'd had to be physically prised off them to allow them to leave. Aunt Clara had prepared Will and Jack's room for Grace to sleep in and Will had had to make do with the settee downstairs. Any romantic ideas he may have harboured about spending a night in Grace's company would have been doused anyway as Kitty had insisted on spending the entire night in Grace's bed herself.

Will suspected Grace's parents would prove even more strict on that score than Clara. He realised that having a more physical relationship with Grace in their unmarried state would generally be considered immoral and unscrupulous but he loved her and his unconsummated longing for her was becoming unbearable. He only hoped she felt similarly. If the passionate kisses and physical caresses they had been increasingly enjoying for the past couple of days of the trip were anything to go by it seemed likely. Perhaps she was simply more relaxed and able to openly show her affection away from the front. As the train from Paddington pulled into Gloucester station, he forced himself to think about something else.

They stepped off the train with their little leather holdalls and Grace took Will by the arm to walk along the platform. Over the heads in front of them Will saw a tallish man of about fifty-five with a full head of greying hair and a handlebar moustache. He wore a professionally tailored three-piece tweed suit. Next to him hovered a nervous-looking lady of about the same age in an elegant navy-blue dress under a woollen ankle-length overcoat. Around her neck was a handsome string of pearls and on her head a Bella-style leather cloche hat with a fur frontispiece. He did not need Grace to point out who they were.

Dorothy ran to Grace, hugged her and smothered her in kisses. Arthur steadied himself on his good leg, stepped forward and took Will firmly by the hand. Then he, too, took Grace in his arms and held her for what seemed like an eternity.

The four of them exchanged news in the Daimler on the way to Bishop's Cleeve but the conversation didn't open out fully until after dinner when they retired to the drawing room with Fitzwilliam and Amy. Rupert had been involved with a number of other Navy ships in chasing off German vessels after their second naval raid on Lowestoft, and James had been part of the Allied landings at Piraeus in Greece on the thirtieth of November. Henry was stationed somewhere near Arras. Fitzwilliam told Will this, and was intrigued by any titbit of information he could extract from Will about action on the battlefield.

Will was more than impressed with Fitz's shrewd and prag-matic interpretation of what was going on over in Flanders. He must be scanning all the news reports, he thought, because he knew for example that in November at the Battle of the Ancre Heights the Canadians had finally captured the last of the Regina Trench north of Le Sars, albeit at the dreadful cost of at least a quarter of the entire Canadian Corps. Fitz was excited to say that he understood it had paved the way for the recently formed British Fifth Army to capture Hawthorn Ridge in the final offensive of the Battle of the Somme. What he did not know, Will thought bitterly, was that they'd failed to take the very same objective on the first day of the battle over four months previously. When he thought of the lives lost, he felt sick. He had no intention of enlightening Fitz on this. Fitz was keen to learn more, but Will was grateful for Amy's interruption. She was more interested in what they had got up to in London than anything else.

Arthur told them that the estate was in pretty poor shape at the moment, with so many of the young men on their staff having gone off to war themselves. The older chaps had struggled with the physical demands of the workload without the younger men to help. Arthur had taken the advice that Grace had passed on to him from Jenny, and they now had around 350 horses ready to be taken by the Army and shipped over to France.

Arthur had been worried about the difference in background that Grace had alluded to in her letters, but he liked Will immediately. The feeling was mutual. Both were generous and caring in nature, inquisitive, intelligent and unassuming. Grace noticed that her mother had lost a little weight and looked as anxious and edgy as ever. But as usual she was putting on a brave face and was clearly pleased to have Grace home. Dorothy indeed could only concentrate on what she had planned for them over the next few days.

The wine over dinner had been excellent, a special vintage bottle of Petrus from the cellar, and the brandy in the drawing room was finishing them all off. Later, Will was shown his room at the end of the luxurious first-floor corridor and to the right of the grand staircase, and Grace retired to hers at the other end of the corridor to the left of the staircase.

Whether by chance or by design the distance between the two rooms was considerable. Once again, any ideas that either Will or Grace might have had about a nocturnal liaison went out of the window.

*

On Christmas morning, they exchanged presents under the beautifully decorated Norwegian spruce in the lounge. Grace gave Will a beer jug made from a British 18-pounder Mark 2 shell case emblazoned with an RAMC badge and with a handle made of two 7.92 German rifle rounds. 'So you can drink to the German defeat,' she said. Will loved it and was pleased his present to her could match what she gave him. 'What's this?' asked Grace, unwrapping a silver ring made out of a two-shilling coin with a motif on its outer surface of galloping horses, and an oak tree with a cat at its base. 'It's Omelette!' she said.

'Yes,' he said, and he told her about his fellow infantryman who had made it to his instructions.

'I love it!' she said. 'It's the best present I've ever had.'

Now, after putting on warm clothes, Will, Grace, Arthur and Dorothy rode out to the top of the hill where Charles as a youngster would regularly fly his kites. Grace and Dorothy rode two abreast in front and Arthur and Will chatted away behind them. Dorothy was delighted to have Grace to herself and it crossed her mind that for the first time in her life she seemed to have lost most of her overprotective maternal concern about her daughter's safety on the back of a horse. She was, after all, a much more skilled and competent horse-woman than she herself had ever been.

'The work you are doing over there on the Western Front

is quite remarkable,' Arthur was saying to Will. 'It's hellishly dangerous and takes considerable guts. You're only a young man, but I can tell you have a wise head on your shoulders. I take my hat off to you.'

'Thank you, sir. That's a huge compliment, coming from you.'

Will was aware of Major Tustin-Pennington's military credentials, reputation and experience. He also seemed more composed, and more realistic, than many of the senior officers he had encountered over in France.

'When this bloody war is over what do you think you'd like to do?' asked the major.

'Well, you'll probably laugh,' said Will. 'But as I've told Grace, who by the way thinks it's a good idea, what I would like to do is study to become a doctor.'

'Why would I laugh? That's a very noble ambition to have.'

'I've always been interested in medicine, sir. I worked in a hospital as a porter before I enlisted. To tell you the truth, I was always getting into trouble for paying more attention to what the surgeons were doing than carrying out my duties.'

'Sounds like you're cut out for a medical career then.'

'But it's a foolish notion, I realise that. I'll have to settle for something more lowly.'

'Why would you do that?'

'Sir, I'm just a young man from a humble background, as Grace may have told you. All the doctors at the front are officers from well-to-do families with means. It's a bit like a gentlemen's club really, with an exclusive membership. Many of the doctors are sons of doctors. They've all been to medical schools in hospitals or universities and those cost money. As one doctor put it when I asked him, it's a bit above my station.'

'The Army is a little like that,' said the major, pensively. 'And that's why it's still stuck in the Middle Ages. Don't give up on the idea, lad. Times are changing and it's my conviction that when this war finally ends, which it will, opportunities for gifted and ambitious chaps like yourself will present themselves.'

They rode on in silence for a while then until they crested the hill and came to the folly. The Cotswold stone tower stood thirty feet high. It had arched windows at different levels at each point of the compass, and a cantilevered wooden staircase spiralling around the outside from the ground to the turrets. Between the stairs and the wall was a smooth polished slide. They all stopped to admire it.

'Who lives here?' asked Will.

'No one, silly,' answered Grace. 'It's a folly. It has no functional use whatsoever. It's one of my father's whimsical ideas. Architecturally, it's just a bit of fun.'

'I got the idea from a funfair in Hull about twenty years ago. They called it a helter-skelter and I thought one might look good here.'

Will could make out something metallic at the very top glinting in the light. 'What's that at the top?'

'That was Mother's idea.' She turned to look at Dorothy, who was grinning.

'It's a sundial.'

'Forgive my ignorance, Mrs Tustin-Pennington, but why would you put a sundial right up there?'

Dorothy looked at her husband and appeared rather pleased with herself. 'So that the children who spent so many hours playing up there would know when it was time for tea.'

Will laughed. 'Fair enough.'

They rode on again past an enormous copper beech and

between two gigantic cedars of Lebanon and then down through a lane with a row of ancient yew trees on either side. As they emerged from it, ahead of them stood a majestic coastal redwood at least 120 feet tall.

'Guess who climbed that when she was seven?' asked the major.

'I can quite believe that it was Grace,' said Will. 'She can do pretty much anything she puts her mind to.'

'And I prayed that none of my children would ever go to war, you know. I meant my sons at the time. But then Grace took up the gauntlet and there was nothing I could do about it. I think "stubborn" is the word.'

Will looked over at Grace and did not contradict him.

'I'm proud of her, though, Will. Incredibly proud. The medical treatment of my men in the Boer war was appalling. More or less non-existent. If they didn't die of dysentery or cholera, they died of their wounds. Or of simple neglect. What she is doing – like you, lad – is ground-breaking. And may very well help determine the course of the war.'

They contemplated the redwood for a few more minutes and marvelled at its ridged bark, its perfect shape and over-whelming size. It dominated the entire landscape and as they watched its branches swaying in the breeze, flurries of snow-flakes began to settle on its needles.

Arthur was beginning to feel the cold now. The pain in the stump of his leg was becoming quite acute.

'Come on, everyone. Time to be getting back.'

44

Château des Rosiers, Querrieu

Captain Jacob Daniels lay on the threadbare mattress covering the slatted wooden pallet in the locked and guarded room that was his prison. He was chilled to the bone and his body ached through but he was oblivious to it. He had not slept for two solid days and, although awake, was generally insensible.

The previous day he had attended his own court martial, uncomprehending, unaccompanied and legally unrepresented. His former exemplary military career and achievements were ignored, his two military service medals never mentioned. The details of his alleged crime — disobeying a direct order for the second time, and desertion — were read out and unanimously accepted by the hastily arranged tribunal. The accused was invited to speak and give evidence in his defence. He did not. He could not. His usually sharp and astute mind was elsewhere, scrambled and disassembled by his recent near-death experience, the latest in a series of similar, dramatic episodes.

The three senior military personnel overseeing the court martial had each spent considerable time in Army service — in strategic, organisational or administrative roles. As such, they had earned recognition and regular promotion. They had never seen action on the Western Front themselves or served anywhere else in combat. Nevertheless, they felt more than competent and entitled to make a fair judgement in this particular case. The first man was irritated by Captain Daniels' silence and apparent refusal to even look at him. He was obviously truculent and insubordinate, he thought.

'I would encourage you to acknowledge your superior officers in this courtroom and give us the courtesy of replying to these charges.'

The second took his failure to respond as a clear admission of guilt.

'I will ask you again, Captain Daniels, do you have anything to say in your defence? Can you attempt even a modicum of justification for your actions, witnessed as they were by Major Napier and Colonel Farquharson?'

The third man, who was in control of the proceedings, felt similarly and was under increasing pressure from above to make an example of deserters in order to dissuade other serving officers from following suit. Nor would he resist an opportunity to give the accused a further punitive dressing down. Good grief, he thought. Men had been summarily shot before now just for being asleep on a sentry's night watch! A desertion offence was by far the most serious offence of all.

'A military court martial is a serious disciplinary convention organised in special circumstances reserved only for cases involving the most significant and intolerable examples of military misconduct or cowardice in the face of the enemy. I have observed nothing in your demeanour throughout this tribunal other than disinterest, disregard and blatant disrespect. You give me no alternative in considering my verdict.'

Captain Daniels, at this moment, was oblivious to his

surroundings and his predicament. The explosion of the German artillery shell that had buried him alive beneath the blood-soaked clay of Flanders, surrounded by the body parts of his men, had broken the balance of his mind. With the weight of two feet of loose earth crushing his chest he had scratched and torn at the soil in his nostrils and mouth with his bare fingernails until at last, gasping for air and with a racing heart, he had crawled out into the open trench. It was a miracle he had survived. Many around him had not. The infantrymen who helped pull him out were dumbfounded. He looked like a man who had risen from the dead. He was covered head to foot in a dark brown sludge so thick it was impossible to discern where his skin ended and his uniform began. It matted his hair, filled his eye sockets and ears and dribbled from his mouth and nose. When he coughed, he brought up muddy slime. They set him down but he was restless and could not stay still. He refused tea or rum and seemed unresponsive. Every time a shot rang out or a shell burst he jumped and looked about in terror. This was not the Captain Daniels they recognised.

In his cell, as he lay staring at the brick ceiling, he would utter an occasional cry as if rousing from a horrible nightmare. But he wasn't rousing from a nightmare. He was wide awake and living one.

The corporal on guard outside his cell peered through the bars of the square window in the door and scratched his head.

'He's a strange one, this one,' he said to his confrere. 'A bit loopy if you ask me, by the way he's behaving.'

'As long as he doesn't start screaming and hollering or hammering on the door like I've heard other condemned men do. I fancy a quiet night and a bit of shut-eye.'

'You and me both. The last thing I want is to have to go in there with my baton and sort him out, that's for sure.'

'Shame, though. I heard on the grapevine that this fellow had been a good soldier. Considerate and protective towards his men, even earning a medal for it. Pity he went and deserted, really. Stupid thing to do.'

'And now it's us who have to shoot him.'

Well, he did not fancy that much. Tomorrow morning, they were to be joined by four other men selected to be part of the firing squad. He had not joined the Army to shoot soldiers on his own side, for God's sake. But he had been given orders and he would have to follow them. Looking through the rusty metal bars of the window again he watched the man twitch and tense, sit up and rock forward and back. He wrung his hands while his eyes cast about left and right.

The corporal could not help feeling sorry for Captain Daniels, despite him being a deserter. If anything, he looked like he needed a sedative and a strait jacket rather than six bullets through the heart. The corporal wondered if he would actually be able to pull the trigger. When it came to it, how would he feel, seeing the man tied to a post, blindfolded and defenceless and facing him front on? Putting a bullet through another man's chest might be a natural instinct in the heat of battle with your enemy – kill or be killed – but doing it to one of your own in cold blood was something else. Still, he thought, at least there are six of us and no one would ever know which one of them had actually killed him. He had heard of other men selected for firing squads who'd deliberately aimed away from the heart at the shoulder or clavicle. That way they felt they would not have so much on their conscience. But the officer in charge always had his pistol at the ready. To deliver the coup de grâce if necessary.

Perhaps it wouldn't even come to that. In the case of most men found guilty of desertion and sentenced to death by firing squad, the order was never carried out. It was a device calculated to give the condemned men the fright of their lives and shock them into going back and doing their duty. Maybe this man's sentence would be commuted, too. The decision was not in the corporal's hands. He sat back down on the stool provided for him in the corridor and took the opportunity to start writing the weekly letter he always sent to his wife and family back home. He would leave out this court martial thing. It left a nasty taste in his mouth. And it was gloomy. Not something the folks at home would want to read about. He idly wondered why this poor man in his cell was not furiously writing what might be his last letter right now. To send his undying love, or to confess to what he had done, to ask for understanding or forgiveness and try to explain.

But then, judging by the state of him, he either had no one significant in his life or he was incapable of putting pen to paper. The corporal considered offering to take down a message for him and posting it on. But the other man on duty might think him soft. Besides, the condemned man had not uttered a single word and was mumbling incoherently even now. Partly the corporal was afraid of him, afraid of making any kind of social contact with him, and anyway it seemed like too much trouble for what it was worth.

He went over to the cell door again to check on him. Daniels, wasn't it? By the vacant stare in his eyes, he did not seem to have a clue about what was planned for him at dawn the following day.

45

Tilloy-lès-Mofflaines

Will had been back for weeks now. The heavy bombardment that had persisted relentlessly throughout the day was finally abating and the men were rebuilding the sandbag fortifications of the forward trench walls. They had to keep their heads down as German snipers had their rifles trained on the smallest of gaps and were taking full advantage. Will had already seen one man picked out through a tiny slit in the wall, shot clean through the side of the head just under the rim of his tin hat. As the speeding bullet exited from the other side of the poor man's cranium, the ricocheting bullet then struck his neighbour in the chest but with insufficient remaining velocity to kill him outright. Will and Arup did what they could at the scene, hurrying him away on their stretcher to Grace's motor ambulance, which would ferry him onwards to the clearing station.

Now the two of them sat exhausted in the bottom of the communication trench now known as the King's Road, where they rested their aching legs and got their breath back.

'Well done, lads,' said Bill Needham, an officer that Will had come across a few times already that week. 'The Jerries have certainly kept you busy lately. How many casualties have you brought back today for Christ's sake?'

Will had lost count.

'Nine,' volunteered Arup. 'Nine good men and true. Three blown up. Four will never walk again. One peppered with shrapnel and shot through the eye, yet still alive. The other dead before we got him home.' He was shaking his head and wiping mud from his mouth as he spoke. 'Five were shelled and injured right there in the forward trench. The others had got no further than ten yards over the top.'

'Jesus,' was all the officer could say at first. 'Well, you've given some of them a fighting chance, anyway. It's all you can do, I suppose. Listen, the boys have got a brew on. It's piss-poor, to tell you the truth. But better than nothing. Fancy some?'

Both of them were dehydrated and parched. 'Tea, Sahib, would be a luxury,' said Arup. 'Especially if it's Indian.'

'You're pushing your luck there,' said Needham. 'These are just standard-issue British Army tea leaves I'm afraid. And I doubt they've ever seen a genuine tea plant either. But you're welcome anyway.'

Taking two paces to his left he leaned down into a dugout and yelled, 'Johnny? Two extra mugs of your finest *cha*, would you?'

'Sarge!'

'It's Will, isn't it'? said Needham, turning to the stretcher bearers once again. Will nodded.

'You know Captain Daniels, I think. He was a bit of a hero to you, wasn't he?'

'He is. Not was.'

'So you didn't hear the bad news about what's happened to him?'

Will's heart skipped a beat, and he froze. His first thought was that this brave man had been killed. It would be more than he could bear. Injured or wounded he could accept, provided it was a recoverable trauma. But please God not killed. He had seen too many courageous men die already.

'Don't tell me he's gone, Sergeant. Not Captain Daniels.'

'No, no, he's alive, Will. It's not that.'

Will visibly relaxed. 'What then?'

Neither Will nor Arup could understand the sergeant's meaning.

'He's been arrested for desertion and cowardice.'

'What? What do you mean? That's ridiculous!'

'I know, I know. We all know it's nonsense but that's what's happened.'

'Captain Daniels showed amazing bravery in protecting all of us and rescuing one of our field ambulance nurses in the face of the enemy. Without him we would have all been done for. It was only a few months ago. How could this happen?'

'It's perfectly true,' added Arup. 'He is a very courageous man. And I understand he is in possession of two good-conduct medals to prove it. As if proof were needed.'

'The lads are up in arms about it, I can tell you,' said Needham. 'He is one of the finest officers we have but . . .'

'But what, Sergeant?' implored Will. 'What's happened?'

'Last week, you'll remember, the Jerries launched that thunderous barrage all night and all day and several of the trenches were blown to bits. Daniels had only just returned from a sortie over the ridge and he was caught in a huge explosion which killed eleven of his men outright. There was pandemonium all around, smoke and screaming and goodness knows what. Several other fellows had limbs sheared off or head injuries. We couldn't find the captain himself at first. But then it transpired he'd been buried alive in the mud and the sand. He clawed his way to the surface, through

249

the blood, mud and body parts — exhumed himself, gasping for breath. He was in a pitiful state.'

'My God,' whispered Arup.

'But he wasn't himself afterwards. Not at all. He was real dazed he was. Dazed and confused.'

'But he was unharmed,' asked Will hopefully.

'Physically, he was, but he couldn't hear us shouting at him. He was looking into the distance as if we weren't there. He just stood there for ages. Wouldn't have any tea to warm him up, not even a tot of rum. We couldn't get through to him. We reckoned it was from being buried and maybe not getting enough air or a blow to the head or something.'

'But there was nothing to see?' asked Arup.

'No visible external injury, that's for sure. We checked him over good and proper. But then the major took him aside and spoke to him. Don't know what he said exactly but the gist of it was he wouldn't be asking him to lead the men in attack the next day. He'd just keep watch with the periscope, giving out the orders, and rest up.'

'So why has he been arrested for desertion? It doesn't make sense,' said Will.

'We reckon he didn't understand the instruction. Couldn't take it in. He wandered off, see. Like he didn't know where he was. As if he didn't recognise anything or anyone around him.'

Arup and Will were listening attentively.

'The next thing we know, the major has had him court-martialled for abandoning his post.'

'That's just plain stupid,' exclaimed Will, furious to think his hero had been so callously treated.

'It's worse than that, lad,' said the officer, softly. 'The court sentenced him to ninety days' field punishment number one.'

'What does that mean?' asked Will.

'What in their wisdom has the British Army imposed on him exactly?' enquired Arup.

'It's nothing short of a humiliation,' said the officer. 'They cuffed him to a timber at the corner of King's Road and the supply trench for two hours every day. In a cramped, kneeling position as well. It's what they call a stress position and it's bloody barbaric. There were explosions going off all around him. Taubes dropping bombs from the sky and artillery opening up relentlessly and he had nowhere to run or take cover. He didn't even have a gun to defend himself if the enemy stormed the trench.'

Will felt an anger surge up inside him that he found difficult to control. How could men fighting together in the same war for the same cause do this to each other? It was utter madness. Needham continued where he had left off.

'Anyway. The captain is resourceful, as you know. We don't know how he did it and the rest of us were distracted by several enemy attacks, but he somehow got free and went walkabout. He couldn't have known where he was going, though, or what he was doing because two of the boys had to restrain him from going over the top without his helmet or gun. Three hours later they found him wandering about in Poperinghe and he was arrested again. This time for desertion and displaying disobedience to a lawful command.'

Will shook his head.

Arup mumbled. 'There is no question of disobedience or desertion here. It is Soldier's Heart.'

'Soldiers what?' cut in Will.

'Soldier's Heart. Battle fatigue. I've also heard it called Bullet Wind. In my regiment they refer to it as operational exhaustion and the majors are good to the men who suffer from it.'

'We've all seen it, all right,' said Needham wistfully. 'It's like the explosions and the noise drive the men temporarily insane. Not responsible for what they do, like.'

'We fought with the BEF early in the war, Sahib. By the end of that first year, they say that one in every ten officers was stricken by this and half as many ordinary soldiers too. It is not uncommon.'

'I've seen lots of men just like the captain as well,' said Will. 'Out there after an attack or after artillery bombardment. Haven't we all had that ringing in our ears and dizziness when shells explode nearby? Half the men we brought back can't even remember what happened to them. And even if not too badly wounded, they are twitchy and jumpy. Their nerves are shredded.'

'One of the corporals was thrown ten feet into the air by a whizbang. When we got to him, he wanted to fight us. He was like a wild savage.'

The three men looked at each other and then down at the pools of muddy water lapping at the top of their boots.

Just then, Johnny appeared with the three mugs of tepid tea that had been promised. Taking them from him, they clunked the mugs together and heard the metal edges give off a dull tinny sound. Will drank half of his straight off.

'Johnny, you knew Captain Daniels pretty well, didn't you?' said Needham.

'I was with him at Gallipoli, sir. Bravest man I've ever seen. Two years ago it was in the Dardanelles Strait. We was rowing towards the shore – W beach, it was codenamed – and fifty yards out we got hit by machine guns firing on us from both sides. It was meant to be a simple amphibious landing. But no. Ferocious, it was. And relentless. We hadn't seen them, you see, the Turks. They were lying in wait for us.

And we were so exposed. So helpless. Half the men in that company got wiped out in seconds. Some jumped into the sea to get out of the boats. Some that did got shot to pieces in the water. Others drowned because the weight of their equipment pulled 'em down.'

Johnny paused to take a deep breath as he relived the scene.

'A few of us who got ashore were still getting massacred when we hit the beach. There were landmines tearing people's limbs off and most of us couldn't fire back because our rifles were clogged with salt water and sand.'

The other three men were listening carefully, imagining the carnage.

'Around a thousand of us set off in that first wave. And about three hundred lived to tell the tale. The captain was one of 'em. He never wavered. Never flinched. Running forward, he was rallying the men. Well, he got over the dunes and took out several of the Turks on his own. I dunno how we done it but by the end of that day the beachhead was ours. But at what price? So many of our mates shot dead, riddled with bullets or drowned. Half the officers too.'

There was a long pause as he ruminated.

'Bloody disaster, it was. Six VCs they awarded, and I reckon the captain should've got half of them an' all. They gave him a good-conduct medal but it weren't enough if you ask me. Next thing we're both posted 'ere with the 15th Battalion of Lancashire Fusiliers. And the captain? Well, he's still doing the only thing he knows best. Keeps buggering on and sticking it to the Jerries.'

'Until now, anyway,' said Bill pensively, 'until now.'

'It's just a huge cock-up,' Will chipped in. 'They'll know about his record and everyone can speak up for him. He'll be back here and back to normal before you know it. Won't he?'

'I don't know, Sahib,' said Arup. 'We all know that Captain Daniels is no coward and would fulfil any command ordinarily. But desertion and disobeying an order is considered a very serious offence.'

'And this will be his second court martial,' said Needham. 'That will go against him, and the ultimate punishment could be the firing squad.'

'This is just stupid,' said Will. 'The man's not right. Anyone will see that. What happens at a court martial anyway?'

But as the others tried to explain and discuss the various possible outcomes among themselves, Will's mind was elsewhere. A desperate plan of action was forming in his head and it meant getting back to the dressing station as soon as possible.

'Sir,' interrupted Will as Needham was still speaking. 'The more of us that stick up for the captain and tell our officers the truth, the quicker we can get him off the charges. If you can talk to your major, maybe we can get the message higher up the command chain?'

'Listen, lad, don't think I haven't tried. I did my best to stop the arrest there and then. They weren't having any of it and I was warned off.'

'But surely there is safety in numbers,' Arup jumped in. 'Johnny here and his comrades can testify together on his behalf.'

'That can't happen, mate,' said Johnny flatly.

'But why?' asked Will.

'I'm sorry, son. Apart from me and one subaltern who is currently unconscious with a head wound, everyone else who served with the captain is dead.'

Will felt winded.

'Listen, we'll try, lad, we'll try. But you don't know them like I do. It won't be as easy as that. To some of them at the top, men's lives are cheap. They like to maintain discipline. But we can do our best, at least.'

'And Arup,' said Will, 'let's go and talk to Dr Lilley at the hospital. We've got to know him quite well now and I'm sure he'll be able to help. At least, I think he'll listen.'

'OK, Will. We can give it a go.'

The four men drained the remnants of their cooling tea, shook hands and set off in their separate directions. Needham to the periscope at the forward trench and Will and Arup to the supply trenches and the base. Half an hour later, they found Dr Andrew Lilley in the canvas-covered operating theatre, having just finished an emergency appendicectomy – ably assisted by Grace. Scrubbing the blood from his hands and forearms and tired though he was, he listened attentively to what the two stretcher bearers had to tell him. It was a familiar enough tale, he thought. And a tragic one.

'Come and sit over here,' the surgeon said, pointing to some comfortably upholstered armchairs in the corner that had seen better days. The men slumped down gratefully into the soft padding and worn-out springs.

'From what you say, your man is suffering from something called shell shock. What you described, Arup, as Soldier's Heart. Shell shock was first examined in detail a year ago in a reputable medical journal called *The Lancet*. I read the article myself, written by a doctor called Charles Myers. What's interesting is that this Dr Myers attended a number of men with similar symptoms. He listed some of the typical features. Tinnitus, headaches, dizziness, tremors and hypersensitivity to noise. Panic attacks were common, along with the inability to think clearly and to reason. Sleep is fitful and interrupted. The victim can become totally mute. He also described a strange abnormality of memory which he called a fugue state.'

'Fugue?'

'It describes a condition where the sufferer wanders away from his normal surroundings for a period of hours, days or even weeks. What is interesting is that this Dr Myers attended several men with exactly the same symptoms and realised that what they were describing, if indeed they were *able* to describe it, corroborated each other's experiences to an uncannily accurate degree. They didn't know each other. Weren't in the same company or regiment. He concluded that the syndrome must be genuine and not what some of the military top brass wanted to label it, a sign of weak moral fibre or cowardice.'

'I've seen it hundreds of times, too,' said Grace. 'Men just staring straight ahead. Tortured expressions on their faces. I've seen men with terrible wounds, like fractures with the bones poking out through their uniform, but oblivious to any pain. It's difficult to know what to do for them.'

The surgeon nodded in agreement, studying the floor.

Will leapt to his feet. 'If this state of mind is a documented medical condition, surely we can explain that to Daniels' court martial and they'll be lenient? We just have to get word to the right people.'

'That will not be easy, Will,' added Arup. 'In my experience, the leaders in the British Imperial Army are not easily given to making exceptions.'

'But we can try, can't we? We must.' Will restlessly paced around the tent like a man possessed.

'I don't know the man. I'm not in charge of his case,' said

the surgeon. 'I fear any intervention from me will count for nothing. At best, it might be seen as interference with military justice.'

'And much as I would campaign for his release and fair treatment,' added Arup, 'I fear that my rank and provenance, coming from an Indian regiment as I do, might make matters worse.'

Grace was on her feet. 'Let's consider. The man has two good-conduct medals and the men in his regiment regard him highly. They can testify to his previous record and we can bring this newly described medical syndrome to the attention of the authorities. We can overturn this, can't we?'

'Stop,' insisted Dr Lilley, holding his hands up. 'Just stop for a minute. I know you mean well, but it isn't that easy. The other doctors and nurses here have talked about this. We even brought it to the attention of Sir Anthony Bowlby who is now advisor on surgery for the whole of the British area front and base. He's a damn good man, but his hands are tied. Last year, a military tribunal back home looked into what they called artillery shell concussion—'

'So, they know about it?' interrupted Grace.

'Yes, but there is a big caveat. If a victim's concussion is deemed to be caused by enemy action he is considered "wounded" and a W prefixes his medical report. He would then wear a W and a wounded stripe on the arm of his tunic. If, on the other hand, his "illness" is a breakdown, as they referred to it, and not obviously caused by a shell explosion – in other words, not by direct enemy action – it is attributed to shell shock with a capital S, denoting sickness.'

'That's ridiculous,' interjected Will. 'How can you possibly—'

'It gets worse.' The surgeon raised his hands for hush. 'A

man with a capital S on his report would be denied a wound stripe and . . .' he paused now and took a deep breath, 'denied any military pension in the future.'

'It is obvious to me what they are thinking,' said Arup. 'Unless there is a clear and visible connection of the syndrome with bravery in the line of patriotic duty, for example a courageous action witnessed by many others, the authorities don't want to admit the illness exists.'

'Precisely. I'm told efforts are being made right now to expunge the word "shell-shocked" from the military lexicon completely. They want to ban it altogether. Even from the medical journals.'

The four of them pondered these words, with only the gentle slapping of the canvas tent sides in the breeze interrupting the silence.

'I can't just stand by and do nothing,' said Will, his fists balled and with tears in his eyes. 'This man saved both our lives.'

With that, he pulled back the flaps of the hospital tent and raced out.

'I've never seen him like this,' Arup said to Grace. 'I fear for what he might do.'

Grace took off after Will.

46

Verdun

One hundred and twenty miles to the north, Robbie lay on his camp bed fully clothed in his filthy corporal's uniform, staring at the canvas roof above him. He had been awake for over eighteen hours and in the thick of fighting for fourteen of those. He was physically exhausted and mentally at the end of his limit but still he could not sleep.

He sat up and lit another Woodbine. In the darkness he could make out the occasional glow of two or three other cigarettes being quietly smoked. Otherwise, all around him were the slumbering figures of his fellow soldiers, most of whom had fallen asleep within moments of their heads hitting the pillow.

Death and injury were so random, he thought. Most of the men he had talked to thought they were indestructible at the outset. That they somehow had a charmed life. That the bullets would never touch them or if they did they would survive them. No shell or grenade would come their way. And their months of training and their hard bodies and military fitness would see them through. They could run faster than the others, they could weave and dodge when attacking. And they had their wits about them and could seek out shelter whenever it was expedient. They had all started out believing the schoolboy fantasy that all brave, strong men were survivors. That only the weak, the hesitant and above all the unlucky would fall. That was it. To begin with, they had all felt so lucky.

But now they all knew it wasn't like that. However fit and fast a man was, it made no difference. A streaming fusillade of machine-gun bullets or a blanket bombardment made no distinction between them. If you happened to be in the wrong place at the wrong time, your number was up. It was as simple as that.

How many first-rate courageous and athletic comrades had Robbie seen die without firing a shot or making it further than a few feet from his trench? How many men had been killed by indiscriminate ricochets or friendly fire? How many were caught in a poison gas cloud that arbitrarily came their way after the wind had changed?

Every man was on edge and apprehensive at the start of it all, of course. No one went over the top without a dry mouth, a pounding heart, loose bowels and a knot in the stomach. But most of them genuinely thought they would make it back. How else could they drive themselves to do it in the first place?

He had been one of the only ones who had been spared that bright, cheerful over-confidence. That blind faith. At the beginning, he had not cared. He had joined the Army feeling like a failed husband, an estranged father, an ungrateful brother and a worthless employee. His own life mattered to him not a jot.

He had dragged his sorry carcass across the battlefields of Belgium and France, obeying orders and doing whatever was asked of him for King and country. He had put his body on the line because it had not mattered to him whether he lived or died. He had done nothing heroic, nothing particularly daring or valiant. He had not had that level of energy or motivation. He had simply got on with the grim plodding relentlessness of ordinary soldiering. He had suffered injuries in doing so, a bullet through the shinbone and shrapnel in the thigh, but nothing life-threatening and nothing as bad as hundreds of other soldiers he had known and fought alongside had experienced.

What an irony, he thought. He had watched as his mates advanced across no man's land with him, diving and dodging, skipping this way and that to avoid getting hit. So often in vain. Robbie had walked steadily ahead in a determined straight line, waiting for the fatal missile that would tear through his chest or brain. But it had never come. He had put his right foot in front of his left, then again and again repeatedly while beside him, out of the corner of his eye, he had seen so many of his comrades cough, stutter and fall in motionless heaps.

Why them and not him? It was so utterly, meaninglessly random.

At the beginning, he had not minded either way. Life or death. He genuinely had not. But recently, he had begun to wonder. Why had he been spared? It made no sense.

He took another drag on his Woodbine and scanned the silhouettes of the bodies lying sleeping in their bunks.

He had seen many of them writing letters to their loved ones back home on a daily basis. Like a ritual. He himself had only managed maybe half a dozen short notes home in the entire time he'd been at war. Yet now, more and more, he felt himself wondering how his family were all faring and whether they were safe.

As he thought about the tens of thousands of men who

had lost their lives, he began to think of Evie's death in a different light as well. She was not the only person dear to him whose life had been snatched away. Was her sacrifice in vain like those fallen in battle? Or was it so that Kitty could be given life, just as the outcome of the war would determine who would remain sovereign and free? He was not religious, but he wondered, was there a divine or pre-destined purpose to it all? Was there a more profound reason as to why he had survived for so long against the odds? Could it be Evie's way of looking down on him and guarding him? Keeping him safe? If so, he should bloody well be grateful, shouldn't he?

Maybe she was willing him to stay alive so that he could return to Kitty, Will and Jack and be the father she had always thought he would be to them. In the quiet darkness, he could almost see her face and hear her voice in his head.

'Robbie, my love,' she was saying to him, smiling, '*pull yourself together now. I'm watching over you so you can get back there and be the Robbie I loved and married. They need you and you have to be the mother that I would've been to them as well as their father. You can do that. You can be the best father. You are my hero, remember?*'

'Ouch!' He was awoken from his dream by the red-hot fag-end burning his fingertips. He threw it to the ground, swung his legs over the side of the bed and stamped it out.

He reached underneath his bed for his kitbag and pulled from it a barely used notebook and pen and started to write.

Dearest Clara . . .

47

Château des Rosiers, Querrieu

Eight days after talking with Dr Lilley, Will had finally discovered where Captain Daniels was being held. He and Grace wasted no time in covering the twenty miles to get to Querrieu in the charabanc that had once served as an ambulance but was now deemed unserviceable.

'It's a ridiculous notion,' Grace insisted, still trying to change Will's mind. 'You won't get further than the front door.'

'I have to try, Grace. I can't rest until I've done *something*. It's so unfair,' he said. 'I won't be able to live with myself if I don't try.'

'You won't get past those two heavies at the top of the steps. It's the regimental headquarters, for God's sake.'

Will looked at her imploringly. 'I can bloody well try, can't I?'

Grace sighed, realising there was no talking him out of it. 'Well, you've certainly got guts. I can't imagine what they'll do to you when they apprehend you.' She moved towards him and reached up to touch his face. 'I am proud of you, Will.'

Emboldened by these words from the girl he had come to adore and, frankly, would happily die for, he jumped out of the rickety old charabanc and strode purposefully towards the building.

As he did so, he mentally rehearsed the vague plan he had

formulated in his head, knowing full well that he would be challenged by the sentries at the entrance.

'Urgent message for the major from the hospital,' he confidently told them when they stepped forward to bar his path.

This seemed reasonable as far as the sentries were concerned, since he looked so young and flustered. He had also just jumped down from the hospital wagon that had drawn up outside, so he was duly let in.

Waving an envelope at the next set of officers and giving the same explanation, he continued on. He was only halted by an officious-looking corporal sitting behind a desk outside Major Davison's office on the second floor.

'Hand that to me and I'll have it delivered,' said the man curtly. Will stretched out his arm, pretending to offer him the message, but quickly withdrew it and hurled himself towards the double doors behind him. Twisting the handle and throwing himself into the room he was swiftly followed in by the man he had just sidestepped. Major Davison was sitting at his desk with the brigadier standing beside him and both looked up, startled.

'What the hell?' said the major.

'I'm sorry, Major, there was no stopping him,' said the embarrassed officer who had gripped Will and was manfully struggling to hang on. 'I'll have him removed.'

But Will had not got this far only to be unceremoniously ejected. A man's life was at stake.

'Major, can I speak to you, please? I'm sorry, I didn't know what else to do, but there's been a terrible mistake.'

'Who the hell are you, and what do you want?' barked the major, sitting back down behind his desk again.

But Will, wriggle though he might, was losing his wrestling match with the officer and was being dragged out.

Will was in turmoil. He was breathless from running up the stairs and fighting with the brute next to him and his heart was racing to the extent he thought it would burst from his chest. His mouth was so dry he wondered if he would be able to even speak.

'I'm sorry, sir. Major Davison, I mean. But I didn't know what else to do,' he said, planting his feet down hard. 'Something's happened that's very wrong and very unfair but what I tell you will make it all right.'

'Go on,' said the major impatiently, holding up his hand for the officer to pause in dragging Will out.

'I've tried talking to my superiors almost every day for the last few days but they're not listening to me. I don't think they believe me. But my dad always used to say to tell the truth. Tell the truth, no matter what. So that's why I'm here. I'm sorry, sir, but someone has to help.'

The major looked at the brigadier and then at the man still holding Will by the collar. 'How the hell did he get in here?'

'He said he had an urgent message for you from the hospital, sir.'

'And you bluffed your way past everyone?' he said to Will. 'Yes, sir.'

The major, exasperated by this obvious lapse in security, raised his eyebrows in despair.

But both he and the brigadier were intrigued. This intrusion by such a youngster was unprecedented. 'Let him stay, Adams,' said the major, 'you can unhand him.'

Adams promptly did so and Will shrugged to rearrange his uniform.

'If you were any older, I would have you severely disciplined for this. Perhaps I still will. I should at least have you thrown out on your ear. But since you are here you can tell me what it is that you think is so important. But hurry up about it. In case you haven't noticed, there's a war on.'

Will nodded. 'I understand, Major. Thank you. There is a man called Daniels, a captain in the Lancashire Fusiliers, who has been accused of being a deserter. Worse still, he has been court-martialled and isn't able to defend himself. But there is no way this man should be punished.'

'Is that so? You consider yourself a one-man judge and jury, do you? Rather presumptuous of you, don't you think? And how exactly did you come to this judicial revelation?' The major's words dripped with cold sarcasm.

'Because the punishment is so unjust.'

'I don't even know why I'm wasting my time listening to this boy,' said the major, looking up at the brigadier. Then, turning back to Will, he added, 'A deserter, young man, is a coward. A traitor to his country. A man who runs away sets a terrible example to everyone else. Imagine if every soldier simply ran away at the first sound of gunfire. The war and the country would soon be lost.'

'But sir, Captain Daniels isn't a deserter. He's a hero.'

'Heroes don't turn turtle and run away,' interjected the brigadier, contemptuously.

'He didn't. He never would. He saved my life and many more a hundred times. He is one of the bravest men I've ever seen.'

The two men at the desk either didn't believe Will or simply were not interested. They looked bored.

'Not in fact all that brave,' said the major, clearly unmoved by Will's tirade, 'as his report, I remember, clearly stated he was apprehended as he ran away a matter of days ago. He had discarded his weapon and was fleeing. I was present at Captain Daniels' disciplinary case myself.'

'Sir, what you need to realise—' continued Will, but he was rudely interrupted.

'In Kitchener's Army, lad, you need staying power. You can't just pick your moment with a flourish here and a gesture there and then flee when things aren't going your way.'

'Sir, listen,' implored Will.

'Do not be impertinent!' yelled the brigadier.

'He wasn't running away. He didn't know what he was doing.'

'He knew he was retreating against orders,' insisted the brigadier.

'He didn't, sir. He didn't, I swear. I've seen it before. When men are in a daze. They don't know what they're doing. Captain Daniels wouldn't have known where he was, where he was going. His men said he was just walking around aimlessly. And I'm sure that given a bit of time he'll recover and be back to normal. But he's not a deserter.'

'What's your name, son?' asked the major, aiming a level gaze at Will.

'Corporal William Burnett, sir. I'm stationed at the hospital with the RAMC. Stretcher bearer and surgeon's assistant.'

As it happened, the major had been a qualified doctor himself, before he had opted for a career in the Army, but he had found the job of caring for the sick and infirm tedious and unfulfilling. He much preferred the status and prestige of his exalted position in the military.

'A stretcher bearer and a surgeon's assistant,' he sneered. 'So not in fact an orderly, as your uniform seems to suggest.'

'No, sir. I didn't know how else to get in to see you.'

'Well, full marks for initiative and guile. Maybe we should send you to spy behind enemy lines.' He laughed at his own joke and the brigadier swiftly followed suit. 'How old are you?'

'Sixteen, sir.'

The major glanced up again at the brigadier, but it was impossible for Will to read his thoughts.

'Look. We can't brook any nonsense with cowardice,' said the brigadier. 'Millions of brave men are risking and sacrificing their lives every day on the battlefields and no exceptions can be made.'

'Captain Daniels has risked his life many times before, sir. Ask any of the men and they will tell you. When he was shot in the arm and bleeding heavily, he still helped me to bring the stretcher and a wounded man back through mud deep enough to swallow a tank. He inspires the other men too, leading by example. Wherever he goes, the other men follow.'

'And that's precisely why we can't condone desertion, don't you see?' said the major, losing patience now and scoring what he considered a clever point.

Will felt like he was swimming furiously against the tide, and yet sinking faster than the *Titanic* had done five years previously.

'To me, he's a man the Army should be proud of. Instead, he's been court-martialled for something he hasn't done,' he persisted.

'Watch your mouth, soldier,' shouted the brigadier. 'How dare you force your way into the major's office, making demands and questioning his authority. Who the hell do you think you are? If you were any more than a callow youth who knows no better, you'd be clapped in irons yourself. Now, get out.'

'I'm going, sir. But will you at least consider what I've

said? If there is a God, you'll pardon the captain and allow him to get back on his feet.'

'I'll consider what you've said, Corporal Burnett,' said the major, after a long pause, 'but I don't think we'll be able to help Captain Daniels to any great extent now. He was executed, you see, by firing squad, at ten o'clock this morning.'

48

Grace saw Will emerge from the building. He looked stunned.
The two sentries on either side of the steps and three other
men in uniform closed ranks behind him, barring any
possible attempt he might make to go back in. But Will
turned and began arguing with the sentries, gesticulating
angrily.

Grace got out of the charabanc and rushed over to him.
'Come on, Will. You'll only get yourself into trouble.'

Reluctantly, and wiping a tear from his eye, Will allowed
her to take him by the arm and guide him back to the vehicle.
Only when she had closed the door on him did she go around
to the driver's side and jump in. She gunned the engine and
roared off. Two blocks later, Will still had not uttered a word
and she looked at him with concern. His jaw muscles were
clenched and his fists balled.

'Will?' she asked.

'They had him shot.' His voice broke.

Grace was incredulous. She must have misheard him.
'What? That can't be right.'

'Believe it. The bastards murdered him.'

'But— No! He was such a good and brave man.'

She thought back to the pivotal action Daniels had taken
that had saved their lives and recaptured the British trenches
only a few months ago. She and Will had both had a narrow
escape, which would never have been possible without the
incisive intervention of the captain.

'He was a hero many times over,' she said.

'I'd like to shoot those bastards myself. I'd happily put them up in front of a wall and massacre the bloody lot of them. I can't imagine anything so unjust and undeserved. Those judges or whatever they call themselves should be put on trial themselves.'

Will was seething and out of control. Grace was worried he might try to take the law into his own hands. She had never seen him like this before and worried he might do something stupid if she could not calm him down. Three streets further on she passed a hotel restaurant bustling with activity and drove on. The last thing he needed now was a crowd with witnesses to what he might do or say. At the far end of the next street, she spied a typical little French establishment with the words 'Bar Tabac Colette' emblazoned over its entrance. She parked at the kerb and dragged Will inside. Apart from an old boy in the far corner and Colette herself presumably behind the bar, it was empty. It was sparsely and simply furnished with spindly wooden chairs and tables that had seen better days, but it was clean and cheerful and just what they needed.

She looked over at the only other customer, a man in his advanced years wearing a grubby beret, a shabby three-piece woollen suit that was too big for him, and scuffed and worn black leather boots. In front of him on a red gingham-style tablecloth stood a three-quarters-full bottle of a greenish liqueur, and a shot-glass he occasionally lifted to his lips with his gnarled and rheumatic right hand. A half-smoked Gauloises cigarette hung from his lower lip. These were the cigarettes that were so popular and dished out freely to soldiers in the French Army. Grace had grown to love the rich aroma of the black caporal tobacco.

'Monsieur?' said the elderly lady in a simple black frock and white apron who had come over to take their order. Will woke from his trance and looked clueless. Grace was not sure what to order, either, but she thought Will might need something alcoholic to drown his sorrows.

'The same, please,' said Grace in French, pointing at the green beverage on the old man's table.

'Absinthe?' asked Colette in surprise. It was not the usual drink of any young English person who had made their way into the café. It was at least eighty-five per cent proof. Selling it had been banned the previous year by the French government.

'The green fairy? It will make your head fall, miss.'

'What did she say?' asked Will, by now feeling desperate for a drink.

'She calls it the green fairy and says it will knock our heads off.'

'Excellent. Let's get a bottle.'

Grace smiled for the first time in hours. '*Une bouteille, s'il vous plaît.*'

'A whole bottle?' Clearly these kids did not know what they were getting into. She should not sell it to them at all, she knew, but her other customer was drinking it and trying to explain why he could and they couldn't would be awkward. She only had a few bottles left and there would be no more forthcoming. Besides, they were over here fighting for the liberation of France and there was a war on. Who was going to come to arrest an 82-year-old widow for bootlegging?

She disappeared behind the counter, fished out one of her last three bottles, and as she poured a carafe of water and put two shot glasses on a tray she examined the young couple more closely. They were very young, she thought, for military personnel. Still teenagers, probably. The boy looked pale and upset, the girl animatedly comforting him. She was a beauty, too. An enviable figure like she herself once had, and a face that was naturally attractive with no need whatsoever of make-up. She was tenderly stroking the boy's hand and looking into his eyes. The romantic bond between them was palpable and it stirred memories of her own love life many years previously. Smiling, she brought the tray over to them, placed it on the table, opened the bottle and half-filled the two glasses. She went to dilute the liquor with water from the carafe, as was traditional, but Will placed his hand over the top of his glass and stopped her. Colette looked at him, nodded, and topped it up with the neat alcohol.

Grace, knowing she would need to keep her wits about her, gladly accepted the water. As she gently encouraged Will to open up, she had one ear on the conversation happening now on the other side of the room.

'I lost it all,' said the old man sadly and to Grace it sounded like a mantra, something he had told the café proprietor many times before. He had lost his wife just as war was declared; his house had been destroyed, his farm animals requisitioned; and his children had gone to fight. Colette sat with him, listening patiently and refilling his glass at regular intervals.

Two women at opposite ends of the age spectrum, in the same room, consoled the men in front of them.

An hour or so later, Will was heavily under the influence, and the old man shuffled over to their table, bleary-eyed and reeking of alcohol. He placed what was left of his bottle of absinthe in front of them and flicked his finger at it.

'For young lovers. Do not waste time.'

Grace smiled up at him.

'*Merci*,' she said and stood to give him a peck on the cheek. His eyes twinkled and his wrinkled face creased into a smile.

'Go, young man,' he said looking directly at Will. '*La vie est courte.*'

'Pascale!' scolded Colette from the bar.

Grace translated for a curious-looking Will. 'Life is short.'

'It is,' slurred Will, the absinthe now clearly affecting his speech and coordination. 'Too short for Captain Daniels, anyway.' He turned his head and gazed out of the window, struggling to focus on some fixed distant object that was not moving. He was feeling rather maudlin. A strong and resilient young man at the best of times, his bones now ached to the marrow and the flashbacks and torments that disrupted his sleep were taking their toll. He suspected that it was only Grace and his growing love and adoration for her that was saving him from madness. Beautiful, bright, carefree Grace. Brave, even reckless, Grace. Such fun to be with. So exciting and irrepressible. He turned back to look at her green eyes which flashed and danced as she smiled back. Since coming back to the front they had shared brief, secret trysts in the forests and meadows beyond the camp. The touch of her full lips and sweet breath on his face and her body against his filled his thoughts. They were not lovers yet in the physical sense and he was aware of his inexperience and naïveté in such matters but he adored and loved her and would wait to take any further amorous cues from her.

Grace looked at the boy's handsome face in front of her and the eyes that were fighting to stay open and her heart melted. He had proved once again this day that he was a decent, brave, resolute young man. She extended her right hand and lifted his chin.

'Come on, lover boy,' she said, laughing. 'Let's get you home.'

49

Messines

Jack and his company were now stationed in Flanders near Ypres, where they were joined by the 1st Australian Tunnelling Company. Jack had never met an Australian before, but they and the Welsh lads hit it off immediately, making jokes at the English officers' accents.

'My dear young boy, I would absolutely love a cup of *cha*, wouldn't you?' said Lieutenant Bruce Wilson, emerging from the mine shaft, his face streaked with mud and grease, his clothes dripping with grey clay.

'Very kind of you to offer, sir.'

'You cheeky little Pom. Run along and get brewing. You'll want one yourself as I'm putting you on the listen-out tonight.'

They were there to deal with the problems of the high ground the Germans had won at the Messines Ridge, which had perfect vantage over the town of Ypres, and which made it very hard for the British to approach them or dig in without suffering terrible bombardment and firepower.

General Plumer was in charge of the operation led by the British Second Army, and was gathering in artillery while the tunnelling companies made their most ambitious foray yet, feeling their way forward in multiple tunnels and trying to place explosives all the way along the German ridge. They had been doing it for months now; there was a complicated network of tunnels below the surface, and they were always scared they were about to be discovered by the Germans. The explosives had to be detonated at exactly the right moment, though days turned into weeks and every day they waited exposed them to discovery.

Listening out for the enemy was a lonely, frightening job. That night, Jack sat there with a stethoscope against the wall, listening to what could easily be the heartbeat of a German about to stab through the wall with a bayonet, but what he had to tell himself was only the sound of his own blood, beating against the earpieces of the stethoscope. And then he heard what sounded like scraping, and his blood ran cold.

Over the past months the Germans had detonated several charges into their tunnels that had buried their men alive. In spite of this, the Allies never responded. They took their casualties and did nothing, refusing to give away where they were. All of this was on the orders of the general.

They might have been setting the explosives only feet from where he was sitting. He wanted to call out to Rhys, who was stationed further up the tunnel, but he didn't dare for fear of giving himself away.

His candle guttered briefly, as if a new draught had entered the tunnel, or was that his imagination?

'Here, Burnett,' came a whisper: it was Rhys.

Jack put his finger to his lips and pointed at the wall. Rhys took the stethoscope from him and held it there, wincing when he heard what Jack had heard too.

'They're close,' he mouthed.

'Get the lieutenant,' Jack mouthed. They had become adept at lip-reading, working silently down in the mines. Rhys set off slowly on his felt slippers, heading back up the shaft to the lieutenant.

Jack listened out while he waited. There it was again. Scrape, scrape, scrape: coming straight towards him. He took out his revolver and waited.

'Put that away,' came the softest voice behind him, that of Lieutenant Wilson.

Jack did as he was told.

Wilson was busy fitting a package of explosives behind a supporting strut, and attaching wires to it.

'Stay there and listen out. Don't make a sound,' he whispered, and then he was gone, leaving Jack with a German tunnelling towards him and some wired explosives ready to blow besides him. He understood what was happening. Rather than reveal their position, if it looked like they were going to be discovered they would set a small explosive to blow up their own tunnels and then try to access the large explosives they had already planted from another route.

If the Germans burst through, they would blow the charge and hope the enemy believed it was a booby trap for them to fall into rather than a defence of the Allied tunnels.

Would they sacrifice me? Jack wondered, knowing that every soldier would be sacrificed if necessary, that for the commanding officers the military objectives always took precedence over individuals' lives. This was not fair, but war was not fair. There was a logic to it. But why did he need to be there? He could keep watch from a bit further up, even if he couldn't listen out. He should go. He was alive. He was alive and he wanted to stay alive. He didn't care about the war. He didn't hate the man tunnelling towards him. He would kill him but he didn't hate him.

He realised he hadn't heard him for a while.

Now he loved him. He wished nothing more for him than a good night's sleep, safe in a dugout, dreaming of his sweetheart back home in Munich.

He listened and listened for the next two hours, feeling his heart beat stronger and stronger, trying not to look at the explosives wired to bring down the tunnel around him and bury him alive if they didn't blow him to bits.

There was no more scraping. The German must have decided there was nothing here for him.

It was a long night before he was relieved and able to crawl back out of the tunnel and into the light.

50

It was approaching the longest day of the year. Arthur Tustin-Pennington, unable to sleep, affixed his prosthetic leg, pulled open the curtains in his bedroom and watched the sun come up, the clouds turning red. Shepherd's warning. He rarely spent the night in his wife's bed these days, and he wondered for a moment if she spent mornings like this, glad for the moment when the daylight began to seep through the curtains giving her an excuse to get on with the day. He thought about crossing over the landing and knocking on her door, but what if he woke her instead from a pleasant dream, a holiday from all the awful worry she suffered. Charles's death had only confirmed her right to suffer. Arthur could no longer tell her everything would be all right. He did not know whether it would be.

Those farmhands they'd kept hold of were out already, and the maid would be bustling around downstairs in the kitchen. It was a day in which he would have liked to take a scythe and go to work in the fields, a day to get his hands dirty — sometimes he forgot his injury, his status as the lord of the manor. Sometimes he wished he were back in the Army, where distinctions about who you could and who you couldn't be familiar with were dissolved in the common endeavour.

Anyway, he was the lucky one, he knew, making his way out into the garden and looking out across the lawn to where the trees sprang up and formed a canopy over the wilder parts of his land. He had all this for himself, this beautiful view, and it was sentimental of him to crave conversation with another person when greeted with all of God's splendour.

'Father,' came a voice from behind him. Arthur turned to see Fitzwilliam walking towards him. 'Isn't it a waste to spend such mornings in bed?'

'It is, son. It certainly is.'

'What do you think my brothers are doing now?' he asked.

'Couldn't say. You know James is out in Italy now, I believe. Henry is in Ypres. Terrible weather there, his last letter said. It's a giant mud bath. I hope he's safe and warm in a billet somewhere.'

'Yes, let's hope so.'

'Such a beautiful sky. Think there's a storm coming?'

'That's what the rhyme would have us believe.'

'Think it'll reach Rupert?'

'I wonder. Not nice to be on a ship in a storm.'

'No, not nice at all. I wonder where Grace is.'

'She'll be haring up and down the country roads in her ambulance. Poor soldiers getting bumped along by her crazy driving.'

Arthur laughed. 'She's probably learned to go carefully. She does seem to care about the men she looks after.'

'Yes, I gather that too. She seems very fond of that stretcher bearer she brought to see us.'

'Mmm. I liked him. Do you think it's right that I didn't put a stop to that? They are from such different back-grounds.'

'I, I don't know.'

'I wondered before I met him what kind of man becomes a stretcher bearer.'

'One who cares about helping wounded men?'

'Exactly. I wondered and then heard how stupid my thoughts were. I've been one of those wounded men myself crying out for a good man to come and help, and there I was being sniffy about such a man from afar! My goodness. What a fool.'

'You're not a fool, Father, you're just— You've always been very fond of Grace, very protective.'

'Protective! Tell your mother that. She thinks I should have chained her up to stop her going back.'

'You can't look after someone by keeping them prisoner. That's boxing them in, so they don't grow right.'

'When did you get so wise, Fitzwilliam? I guess it's spending all that time in the library.'

'I, er. Well, I wish I could learn about the world in other ways, but that's what's available to me now.'

'You'll have your own adventures, Fitzy, don't you worry.'

'I would like some.'

'You will. Like your brothers and your sister.'

The sky was bright red now, burning behind the branches of the great redwood that Grace had famously scaled. The storm was coming. Arthur prayed that his remaining children would weather it safely.

51

Finally, it was the night of the big bang. Rhys and Jack and two of the Australians had accompanied Lieutenant Wilson as he tested each of the leads. The Australians and Rhys worked silently while Jack kept an ear out for the scraping that had come so close to them on the long night he had spent on listen-out.

'How are the resistance tests over there?' whispered Wilson.

'Everything in order,' said Rhys.

'You two stay here and listen out,' he whispered to Rhys and Jack. Then said to Rhys, 'If he hears anything, you come straight back and tell me. And if anyone comes through the walls, kill them.'

'You'll come and get us, won't you, before you pull the switch?'

'I'll try to remember,' whispered Wilson, with a straight face. His expression shifted into a broad grin when he saw the looks on Jack and Rhys's faces. 'Don't worry, lads. We wouldn't leave you.'

The minutes passed like hours. Neither man dared speak to the other. Both were sure they would be sick.

Jack listened to the beating of his heart through the stethoscope until he felt like he could hear several other heartbeats, a troop of Germans about to claw through the walls and thrust their bayonets into his stomach.

There was a scraping again.

It wasn't as close. But it was there.

'Listen,' he said, and as he held out the stethoscope to Rhys there was a muffled bang and the earth shook above and around them. Dirt showered down from the supporting struts that propped open the mine shaft. Both men instinctively moved underneath the sturdiest of the wooden struts, helping prop up the ceiling. They looked at each other in fear.

When the ground stopped rocking, the earth was still falling from the ceiling.

'That wasn't us, was it?' asked Jack. 'That lousy Aussie piece of—'

'Shhhh! We'd be in a million bits if it was us,' said Rhys. 'Let me go back and find out what's going on. You OK here?'

'Be quick. Ask if I can come up too. I'm ready to go now.'

Rhys went and came back quickly. Too quickly.

'What are you doing?' asked Jack.

Rhys had his hand on his forehead. 'OK,' he said. 'Deep breath. We're not going to panic, but the tunnel's collapsed up there.'

Jack took a deep breath. Then he panicked. 'What the hell do we do?'

'They'll come for us,' said Rhys.

'Will they?'

'I hope so. But let's not leave it to chance.' He picked up a hand shovel and a pick. 'Let's dig.'

They went as fast as they could, throwing the earth behind them.

'They're just going to blow the thing, aren't they?' said Jack.

'Shut up and dig,' said Rhys.

Jack saw the logic in this and kept quiet. Both men knew the time to hit the switch was imminent, and the men responsible for throwing it would certainly not pause it for the lives of two men when many thousands of others were at stake, when many more thousands had died already to get to this point. So Jack and Rhys dug and they dug and they dug until they could hardly lift their hands, and just when they were ready to give up they heard a Welsh voice.

'Evans? Burnett, are you there?'

'Yes!'

'We're coming. We've got about five minutes.'

Jack found a reserve of energy he didn't know he had possessed. They dug as hard as they had ever dug. Those minutes that had seemed like hours now seemed like seconds. They were going to be too late. It was already too late—

And then a hand was reaching through. And another hand. There was enough space now for these hands to grab hold of Rhys and pull him through.

And now it was just Jack, and there were no hands. He was going to be left. He was going to die. He could feel the heat of the explosion at his back. Feel what it would be like to be evaporated.

And then the hands were back and he was being pulled through the hole in the dirt they'd made and was on the other side.

And there was Rhys and his friend Colin.

'Come on,' Rhys said. 'We're not safe yet. Let's get out of here.'

The night sky had never seemed so light as when Jack emerged into it, though it was cloudy and there was little moonlight to illuminate the ridge on the other side of the trench where, they hoped, nineteen different explosions were about to go off. The one Jack and Rhys had been responsible for was the biggest of them all.

'You're alive,' said Wilson, looking up from the detonator switch. 'Well done.'

'Has it worked?' said Rhys.

'We're about to find out.'

They stood there, watching him. Then the signal arrived. He looked around them, took a deep breath, pulled the switch and stood back.

The men looked up.

They felt it before they saw it. The whole hillside rocked like it was a ship in a storm. At the same time, the British artillery began to fire behind them. And then a burst of yellow and red flame shot up into the air above them, rising to an incredible height, a sheet of fire that burned bright red and then began to turn black, sending off waves of smoke across the sky. It was incredible. It was terrible.

'We've done it,' shouted Wilson. 'We've done it!'

And across the trenches came the sound of men going over the top, charging towards the bursts of flame that must have killed thousands of Germans.

And then came the noise of the enemy's shells shrieking towards them. They kept coming. But so did the Allies. Again and again and again. Jack felt so tired all of a sudden. But he was elated, too. What a thing they had done. He turned and slapped Rhys on the back. 'Come on,' he said. He looked down at his bleeding fingers, realising he had lost two nails in his desperate scrabble for safety. 'We should get checked out.'

* * *

They were halfway through the communication trench when Jack heard a shell coming in, that shrill whine, close and loud. He was not going to die from a shell today, he thought, as it burst directly above them, pelting that section of the trench with shrapnel. He was on the floor, his shoulder stinging, his hip numb, covered in wet mud. Where was Rhys?

Neither of us are going to die from a shell today, he thought.

And then everything went black.

PART FOUR

CONFLICT AND CONTAGION

1917–1918

52

Passchendaele

Padraig Cremin, leaning against the wall of the trench, pulled out a damp packet of Capstan full-strength cigarettes from his top pocket and lit one. He took a long drag of the thick smoke and turned to offer one to his brother Niall on his left.

'Oh, Jesus,' he cried. There, sticking out of the trench wall only six inches from his face, was a human arm bone. He recoiled from it in disgust and went to pull it out.

'Don't touch that, you eejit,' a voice from behind him shouted. 'You'll pull the whole fecking breastworks down with it!'

He was right. There were times, especially after a heavy bombardment, when holes blasted in the breastworks had to be hastily reconstructed and reinforced with whatever materials were available. Sometimes it was expedient to use body parts to shore up the defences. It was horrible work, not just because of the necessity of using human remains, but because there was always a risk of being picked off by an enemy sniper concentrating his aim on the unprotected gap. Several men had already been killed that way nearby.

The bone was a humerus, the bone of the upper arm. The head of it, which would normally fit into the shoulder joint, remained deeply buried under the sandbags above it. But the other end, pearly white, stuck out about four inches into the void.

Padraig examined it more closely with a morbid fascination. It had two semi-circular flanges with a deep groove between them where he imagined the bones of the lower arm articulated. Still firmly attached was the gristle and cartilage, which fleetingly reminded Padraig of the ends of the chicken bones he would suck clean after one of his mother's Sunday roasts. He felt like Hamlet contemplating his friend Yorick's skull. Maybe this had belonged to someone he had known and fought alongside. Someone he had shared a billet or a tin of corned beef with. Maybe he'd had an arm wrestle with him at O'Donoghue's in the Carrickbrack Road back in Dublin. It was quite possible. Whatever the case, the bone – solid and unyielding – was now an integral part of the fabric of the trench.

'I know we Irishmen think about things kind of sideways, lads, but I can't help meself thinking. Whoever this bone once belonged to, to be sure he'd be proud as punch to know that he's still putting his body on the line for King and country.'

The men around him smiled laconically at his black humour. A tall man and a good leader, they looked up to Padraig Cremin in more ways than one. His height put him at a real disadvantage in the forward fire bay because it made him a perfect target for a sniper. It reminded him to re-inforce to the men to keep their heads down if they didn't want them blown off, especially the men in the Scottish regiment who had not yet been issued with their steel helmets and were still wearing their tartan bonnets. So, crouch down they did, but even that was hardly preferable as the trench had been flooded for the last fortnight with foul-smelling muddy water. It reeked of human excrement and rotting human flesh, an evil odour that once inside a man's nostrils never seemed to leave it.

As they waded to and fro along the trench, all manner of detritus flowed past them: morsels of food that had been discarded, empty tins of meat or biscuits, the supernatant from the latrines and even pieces of burned human skin. Often, they found themselves competing with the rats for any place that was drier to sit.

Padraig took off his tin helmet and tried to use the top of it like a hammer to nail the arm bone back into the wall. It didn't budge. All it did succeed in doing was dislodging a sandbag perched precariously above it at the top of the breastworks, followed by a cascade of filthy water.

'Mary, mother of Christ,' he cursed again. 'It's like living in a feckin cemetery here.'

'A sewer, more like. You can even see some of the shite floating past. Worse still, it all seems to be coming my way.'

'It's following you around like a faithful puppy,' quipped Niall.

'It's coming down from the sap where the jacks is. We dig it five foot deep and two foot in diameter and every day hundreds of us squat over it to relieve ourselves until it's one foot from the top.'

'Then we fill it in and dig another.'

'Indeed we do. But since the water table here about is two foot below the surface and the trench itself is six foot deep what does that tell us, Connor.'

'That we're not digging it deep enough.'

At that, they all roared with laughter at the young Irishman's expense. He looked at them, genuinely perplexed.

'No, you eejit. It means you're never going to keep a lid on it. It will all just rise to the surface, especially when the trench is two foot deep in rainwater like it is now.'

'That's why the gentleman now prefers a convenient shell crater.'

Eoin, who was shorter than the others at five foot six, was standing up to his mid-thigh in the fetid slop and listening carefully to the distasteful exchange. 'You call it a cemetery. It's more like being buried at sea if you ask me,' he said.

'Niall nearly feckin drowned yesterday. I swear he was chest deep and going under. It took three of us to pull the culchie out.'

'Who are you calling a culchie, you oul jackeen, you?'

'If it's drowning you're after, don't torment yourself with shallow water. That's what's my oul wan one used to say.'

'Well, she was right enough there,' said Finn. 'The water is deep enough around here to drown the entire feckin Army. We should've sent in the bloody Navy if you ask me.'

Padraig laughed. Without the constant banter, the hell they were all living through would be even worse. If they were going to die, at least they would be dying in the company of thieves.

'I'll bet you can't even swim,' said Eoin.

'Sure, I can swim, you flaming gobshite. I just can't swim through bloody quicksand. No one can.'

Eoin just grinned. 'And you know why it's quicksand, do you, Niall?'

'Because it's been raining non-stop for the last bloody month. There's not a day gone by since it hasn't pissed down furious on our lovely parade.'

'Ah, but us boys will be used to all that. Especially you,

Eoin, coming from Clonmel. I'm sure we're all feeling right at home.'

Padraig looked at Connor again. 'Major!' he yelled to a man further up the line. 'Connor here isn't a strong swimmer and wants to know, bearing in mind it's been raining stair rods for a month, just why it's so bloody wet.'

Major Pinnock and his men from the 502 Field Company Royal Engineers had been doing their level best for the last two weeks to make any kind of headway and bring more guns and equipment nearer to the frontline. He'd lost countless pieces of artillery in the process, along with around forty pack mules and horses – all sucked under by the cloying mud.

How he missed the contrasting topography of the trenches at the other end of the front in the Vosges Mountains. Over there, instead of the snake-like meandering corridors of water in Flanders – more canal than trench – he and his men had literally cut their defensive positions out of solid rock.

'Several reasons,' he said seriously, not quite in tune with the Irishmen's sense of humour. 'Firstly, this is low-lying land reclaimed from the sea donkey's years ago. It's effectively a shallow basin, only about sixty feet above sea level. Secondly, to the east of here, where the Jerries are ensconced, is a wide series of low ridges and hills from which an array of streams and brooks usually drain into a well-constructed network of watercourses and canals. Unfortunately, constant shelling and bombardment has changed the clay soil into a sodden morass and pulverised the drainage systems completely. Several millions of shells must have peppered that ground.'

'It's like a potato that's been mashed,' added Niall, helpfully.

'On top of that, there is the incessant rain,' continued the major, undaunted. 'I've never seen anything like it. There are tens of thousands of craters out there, all filled with water.'

There was silence as the Irishmen processed this information and looked at each other.

'Well, I'm sure your British commander Sir Douglas Haig must have a very shrewd plan up his sleeve. Why else would he send so many good men out here when the enemy fortifications on the ridge are the only things still dry and not floating about?'

'Why indeed?' answered the major, wistfully. 'But weren't you chaps at Messines in June? That was a victory and a half.'

'If you can call it that. Sure, those underground mines and a million tons of TNT blew the flaming guts out of the Boche all right and made a job easier. But we still lost twenty-four thousand men, Major, and here we still are.'

'We're going to give you all the support you need. We are moving the guns further up and putting duck boards down everywhere to give you bridges over the mud. Is there anything else you need?'

'I need it to stop bucketing.'

'We all do. Amen to that.'

A whistle blew and about thirty or forty men from the 16th Irish Division and the 36th Ulster Division slid together up the muddy trench wall and trudged forward into the quagmire in front of them. They were hopeful at first, with memories of their impressive advance in the north in June firmly in their minds, but the situation they found themselves in here in Langemarck – a stone's throw from their objective, Passchendaele – was very different.

'Niall?' said Padraig.

'What?'

'May you get to the gates of heaven an hour before the devil knows you're dead.'

'I've no intention of dying, Padraig,' said Niall. 'I'm just looking forward to getting well and truly fluthered when I get home on leave.'

As they put one foot in front of the other, the trailing leg would immediately sink down one or even two feet into the deep devouring mud. Their greatcoats absorbed the water from above and below like a sponge and added yet more weight to their load. It took an age to advance just a few yards, their boots being sucked from their feet by the glutinous ground. Rain was pelting into their faces as they went. The bullets were raining down, too, and any possible shelter from tree stumps or boulders had been vaporised long ago. Why the hell had General Haig, in his infinite wisdom, waited so long to press forward his advantage over the enemy after the Messines Ridge attack? Now, three months later, the Hun had not only regrouped but dug in and reinforced. Heavy machine guns mounted in concrete were strung out all along the length of the ridge and had every inch of the terrain and every water-filled bomb crater covered. Some of Padraig's men dived into shell holes for cover but then could not clamber out. He saw them frantically slip and slide, but it was hopeless. They were weighed down and exhausted, their muscles screaming and their lungs bursting. The more they struggled the more the crater sides oozed down on top of them, burying and choking them. Padraig's men were drowning, hundreds of miles from the sea, and there was nothing at all he could do about it.

As he looked around him, it seemed everything else was sinking too. Wounded and dying men were being hauled away on carts pulled by mules and horses who also failed to find any purchase on firm ground. The animals' terror was plain to see and many, sunken to their bellies, would never be saved. He saw men helpless and weak in their wounded state roll off the stricken carts into the slime and drown. It was heart-breaking. Any mobile light artillery in sight had become anything but mobile. Stuck like glue like everything else.

Off to his left, he was surprised to see the top half of a Mark I tank, the front part of its massive rhomboid bulk totally immersed in the mud. It was only held afloat by its bulging sides with its steering tail wheel hanging uselessly in the air.

The ground through which Padraig squelched had been ploughed up and churned by shells not just once but multiple times. There was nothing whatsoever solid on which to get a purchase, just loose semi-liquid and treacherous slime. Only the circular shape of the largest and most recently made craters was identifiable. These also quickly filled with water, a swirl of cold sticky brown liquid stinking of old and rotten human flesh. To his right, he fleetingly saw a man he thought he recognised. A nervous type, a bombardier from the Royal Field Artillery. He looked terrified. Paralysed. Mad. More afraid by far of drowning in mud than the bullets and shells coming his way. Either way, it was a frightful choice. Padraig looked on in horror as the man took out his pistol and shot himself through the temple.

He searched about frantically for signs of Eoin and Niall, but without success. He put both hands under his right thigh to pull it free from the sticky grip of the mud and suddenly saw a spray of scarlet jump from the front of his chest. It splashed onto his rifle butt and into the brown puddles in front of him. Momentarily, he wondered what the hell it was. Then he felt a terrific crushing sensation in his breast-bone and all the wind was knocked out of him. What the devil was the matter with him? he wondered. Then, bewilderingly, his knees buckled, and he sank into the mud as the ground came up to meet him, hitting him full in the face. Padraig Cremin died with his face half-buried in the water with tiny crimson bubbles escaping from either side.

53

Carrying the wounded men on stretchers and manoeuvring them along the fire bay to the regimental aid post had never been so difficult. At this particular point on the frontline, the width of the trench was no more than two feet at the bottom and four feet at shoulder height. The staple-shaped traverses with their right-angled corners made it impossible to turn the corner without tilting the stretcher at head height: a procedure which briefly exposed their charges to sniper fire. If a man was in extremis with a chest or abdominal wound, they could pass him up and over the parados wall and cut and run towards the rear, but the risks to both the stretcher bearers and the patients were considerable. Will had done it several times before and he had lost three colleagues in the process. To make matters worse, the trenches were half full of filthy water in some parts and they had to wade up to their waists to make headway. He was cold, wet and tired but the Passchendaele offensive had proved a particularly brutal and bloody one. An Irish regiment in the sector he had been helping to clear had been decimated, hundreds of them injured. Dying men lay in the soup-like morass of no man's land, waiting to be rescued. The faster he could ferry these poor souls to the aid post, the greater the chances of their survival.

He passed a small dugout reserved for two orderlies and turned the final corner into a communication trench leading to his destination. The dugout was unoccupied.

At the regimental aid post, the water in the trench was held back by a concrete dam forming the entrance. A sump had been dug in front of it to divert more water from the aid post itself. Two more orderlies within reached across and grabbed the handles of the stretcher as Will and Arup hoisted the back end to head height and pushed it forward. There were open doors on the entrance and a corrugated metal dome formed its roof. On top of that rested a concrete apron and a substantial number of sandbags of sufficient strength to resist all but a direct hit from falling shells. Even after a direct hit the expectation was that only part of the aid post would be damaged, leaving the other half to function normally.

Will and Arup stepped inside. The interior had a dry concrete floor with two trestle tables on which the stretcher they had brought in now lay. The regimental medical officer greeted them and bent over to examine the patient.

To the left, there were four tiers of three bunks, one on top of the other, any of which could be slid in or out on castors. A number of cupboards and cabinets in the corner stored the dressings, splints, gas masks, pain relief and other medical paraphernalia that could be needed at any moment. At the side of the room, adjacent to the MO's sleeping quarters where two orderlies could rest, stood a number of oxygen cylinders and blood transfusion bottles. One of the orderlies was attending to another casualty on the floor who was bleeding heavily from a bullet wound to his right side.

'I can't stop this bleeding, Dr Lamerton,' he said urgently, pressing a blood-soaked dressing hard against the wound.

'Press harder, then. Put your knee on it if you have to and give him another unit of blood.'

The doctor turned to address the newcomers. 'He's got a

bullet in his liver. Nightmare to stop the bleeding. But we can't operate here. Out of the question. Bryn and Sean, get that man out of here and over to the advance dressing station. Keep that pressure on.'

As the two orderlies lifted the man onto a wheeled stretcher and hotfooted it away down the communication trench, Dr Lamerton turned back to the soldier on the trestle that Will and Arup had brought. The whites of his eyes were glassy and rolled upwards, the pupils hugely dilated and fixed. The doctor put his stethoscope on his chest, listened for a few seconds and pulled the damp khaki-coloured blanket over the man's head.

'You've had a wasted journey, I'm afraid,' he said. 'But you did your best.'

'He looked OK when we found him,' said Arup. 'A bullet hole in his right side but not too much damage and good vital signs. We thought he was salvageable.'

'Always difficult to tell from the external wound. So much depends on the type of bullet and its weight and velocity,' said the doctor.

'And I suppose,' ventured Will cautiously, 'which internal structures it hits?'

'Precisely. Some of these bullets fired from modern rifles are travelling up to fifteen hundred yards per second. The extent of tissue damage is determined by the terminal ballistics. First the bullet crushes structures along its track. Then temporary cavitation causes shearing and compression forces, leading to the tearing of soft organs and the stretching of inelastic ones. Like the brain. As tissues recoil, hot gases dissipate and the softer organs collapse inwards. Any flying projectile can also transfer kinetic energy well beyond its own path, especially if it deforms and fragments after impact.

Slower-moving bullets can tumble and yaw as they plough a path through the body. Faster ones can ricochet off several bones inside the skeleton, causing huge internal damage before exiting from a completely different part of the body.'

Will had no idea for whom this grisly monologue was intended or whether the doctor was just expressing his own morbid thoughts out loud. But it certainly helped to explain why some of the wounded succumbed to what appeared to be trivial injuries more quickly than expected.

The three men looked down at the still lifeless body under the blanket.

'Hemorrhage is the most pressing problem in cases like these. You've very little chance if a major internal artery is hit. This fellow was simply unlucky.'

Will slumped down on one of the benches. Arup stood by the open doorway, looking up at one of several observation balloons and the palls of black smoke rising in the distance.

'It seems all you see is death and destruction. I had always imagined the life of a doctor would be about caring and healing,' said Will.

'Today, yes. Tomorrow, maybe. But there is more to my job than this. A regimental medical officer is in the most advanced position of all and sees more of the acute stuff. We are more likely than most to be able to save a life. And so we witness more loss of life. But it's not like this all the time. Sometimes we'll go for days, even weeks, with very little to do. It seems incredible to say that but it's true.'

Will was intrigued by this man who talked in such a blasé yet knowledgeable and informed way about the day-to-day life of an army surgeon. In Will's occasional surgical assistant role he, like other orderlies and nurses who had no formal training, helped with operations in emergency situations, but holding a retractor or applying a clamp on a bleeding artery was child's play compared to what this man was regularly doing.

'How do you spend your time on quiet days?'

'We're like private medical advisors to the men I suppose. Family doctors, in a way. We go along the line and get to know the men as individuals rather than mere numbers. We learn about their mental and physical attributes. Who is strong and hardy and who is of a nervous disposition and ready to crack. We can pick out the malingerers and the shirkers. Nip that in the bud and get them to pull themselves together. Sometimes it's just a case of housekeeping. Inspecting their feet or delousing them, that sort of thing. Why? Are you interested in a medical career yourself, young man?'

'I think I would like to do something like that,' said Will. 'If I could.'

'Be careful what you wish for. It's not for faint hearts.'

'He has the heart of a lion,' said Arup, turning. 'And the curiosity of a cat.'

Dr Lamerton studied Will and put a hand on his shoulder. 'Want me to show you around?'

'Yes, sir, if you have time. I'd be interested.'

Dr Lamerton showed them the cramped living quarters, which they could just make out in the flickering light of the acetylene lamp.

'We can let these rolled-up gasproof curtains down as soon as we hear a gas alarm. These here are spraying machines with bottles of anti-gas solution attached. The men carry these first-aid dressing packs in their tunics of course and once they are brought here we can give them morphine and hot drinks and keep them warm. Next task is to stop hemorrhages, apply splints if needed and dress wounds with antiseptics. We give tetanus antitoxin routinely and once we have ascertained the nature and extent of the injury we attach labels describing what we have seen so that triage elsewhere is expedited. But we don't operate here. We can't. The filthy conditions would just guarantee infection and be counterproductive.' The surgeon continued, 'Now, good thing we have the wheeled stretchers here as makes it easier to evacuate the injured and of course move on dead weight like this poor sod.'

He took the two handles at one end of the stretcher that Will and Arup had brought in and nodded at Will to grab the other end. Together they lifted the body onto the wheeled stretcher and slipped the other one out from beneath the corpse.

'You better get this one off and away in case we get busy, lads. Thank you.'

54

At the casualty clearing station, Grace and her nursing team had been struggling to resuscitate a number of soldiers suffering from the delayed effects of freshwater drowning. The waterlogged terrain of no man's land had turned into a lake. The muck clogging their lungs was hypotonic and causing the red blood cells in their circulation to expand and burst, which overloaded their system with cardiotoxic levels of potassium. The men who were not suffocating were therefore suffering fatal heart attacks. It was all hands to the pump, and the nurses performing manual cardio-pulmonary resuscitation time after time were exhausted. On top of this, the men they seemed to have saved yesterday were suffering relapses and dying.

Grace was sitting on the little stool at the entrance of the observation marquee, wondering why she had not seen Omelette for a day or two, when a local woman appeared carrying a young girl who could not have been more than eight years old. She was floppy in her mother's arms and one of her legs dangling down had been viciously ripped open by some kind of trauma.

'Help me,' beseeched the woman as she approached Grace. '*Aidez-moi, s'il vous plait.* This is my little girl, Dominique.'

'Come inside,' said Grace, standing and beckoning her in. 'Let me see.'

They laid the child down and exposed the leg. It was deeply gashed along the exterior, all the way from hip to knee and almost to the bone. There had been considerable blood loss and the little girl was rambling and semi-conscious.

'Jenny!' cried Grace. 'Jenny! Can you prep the op tent and put Major Morris on stand-by. We have an injured civilian needing blood and debridement.' It was an unwritten rule that the RAMC would provide emergency medical care to the local civilian population if it could. Much depended on how busy they were at any given time but for any native non-combatant living nearby there was precious little alternative.

As Jenny took the girl in her arms and carried her off to the next-door tent, Grace was able to explain in French to the frantic mother what they were planning to do. She took her over to the mess tent and sat her down with a cup of hot English tea before rushing off to help Jenny.

When she entered the op tent, scrubbed up and ready to assist, the young girl was already anaesthetised and Jenny and Major Morris, the principal surgeon for today, were ready to start.

Thank God for chloroform, thought Grace. What would a procedure like this have been like before it was discovered? And now, using the Carrel-Dakin method of treating wounds like these, a patient's full recovery promised to be a much more likely outcome. Alexis Carrel, an eminent American surgeon who had been serving with the French medical service since 1914, had trained an impressive cohort of colleagues in better techniques of debridement and repair. It meant cutting out all damaged tissue and either reconstructing what healthy tissue remained layer by layer or, in a deep and wide wound such as this, leaving it open to heal from the base. Henry Dakin, an English-American chemist, had at the same time perfected the use of sodium hypochlorite — a mild antiseptic made by bubbling chlorine gas through a solution of saline or sodium bicarbonate. It had taken centuries to recognise that bacterial contamination was the cause of so much post-operative infection and morbidity and that aseptic surgery — surgery performed under sterilised conditions — was the answer.

Jenny was irrigating the little girl's wound with it now and almost miraculously Grace could see the dead cells and debris floating to the surface. Grace used the suction to remove the contaminated fluid as the doctor trimmed and excised the dead, squishy blackened muscle.

Thirty minutes later, after the insertion of numerous deep sutures and irrigation with three litres of hypochlorite solution to thoroughly sterilise the wound, the surgeon left the surface of the wound open and downed tools, leaving the two nurses to pack the now superficial cavity and clear up.

Satisfied and pleased with how it was going, Grace and Jenny chatted cheerfully as they worked.

'This little one is going to be OK, Jenny.'

'I know. She's lucky. If she hadn't been living so close to the hospital she would never have got the latest treatment. Then again, she may not have sustained the injury in the first place. What was it, a shell or something?'

'No. Her mother said it had nothing to do with the fighting. She'd been playing on top of some rubble and slipped and fell about ten feet onto some rusty old farm machinery.'

'Just goes to show, doesn't it? We're all so focused on the war it's easy to forget that the usual routine accidents carry on happening as well.'

'I'm pleased for her, though. Such a sweet little girl. She'll live to fight another day.'

Jenny smiled at Grace's ironic remark behind her mask. 'Are you coming to the tutorial this afternoon?'

'I don't know about you, but I could really do with some catch-up sleep,' Grace said. 'Do we have any choice?'

'Probably not or Sister will be on the war-path again.'

Grace raised her eyebrows at Jenny's word choice. 'What's the tutorial on?'

'It's about the latest treatment of injuries to the face and jaw. They're the really hard ones, aren't they?' she said, shaking her head. 'So disfiguring, too.'

'Who is giving it?'

'A man called Gillies. Harold Gillies. Brilliant, apparently. Major Morris was telling me about him. Born in New Zealand and went to Cambridge. Won University blues for rowing and golf. Then he went to St Bartholomew's Hospital and became an ENT surgeon. He is now with the RAMC and, together with a French surgeon called something strange — Hippolyte Morestin? — they are having incredible success and literally changing the face of reconstructive surgery.'

'Well, we better go and listen to him then.'

'I suppose we should. Who needs sleep anyway?'

55

Dylan Parker had just been a little careless. A 22-year-old gunner in the Royal Field Artillery, he was well accustomed to firing the medium-calibre guns and howitzers deployed behind the frontline and confident in the handling of the horses that kept those weapons on the road and rapidly mobile.

He had only turned his back for a moment and had missed the signal from his brigade officer for the gun to be fired. The recoil of the 18-pounder on its two huge wheels smashed the rear end of the barrel against Dylan's left arm and broke it cleanly just above the wrist.

It was horribly painful and throbbing like hell. His hand hung down at a grotesque angle at the wrist and there was a sizeable ridge on the top of the forearm. The swelling was already considerable.

The x-ray at the CCS confirmed a displaced Colles' fracture of the radius and ulnar and while it was not a compound break — with an open wound vulnerable to infection — it was still going to require a manipulative reduction under anaesthetic to reset it, followed by a plaster of Paris cast.

That was the good news. The bad news was that all the orthopaedic surgeons, anaesthetists and other doctors were busy with much more serious cases and the chloroform and ether was being held back for them. That was why he was lying there now, ready to be treated by some unqualified fresh-faced stretcher bearer and his rather lovely-looking nursing sidekick.

Will, for his part, had been both surprised and delighted to have been given the trust and responsibility to get the job done himself.

'What's the problem?' Dr Lamerton had asked. 'You can do a Bier's block. One thing we should be grateful to the Germans for. Our orthopaedic man Major Morris tells me you've seen him do it several times. We'll all be tied up in the operating tent for hours and you can do it without general anaesthetic, too. The bugger is lucky to be offered any anaesthetic at all. And since it's his left arm and he is right-handed he can be back with his brigade by the morning.'

The RAMC doctors were always under pressure to restore as many casualties as possible back to the frontline quickly and many a soldier resented the doctors putting the needs of the military above their own health and well-being. But Will was in no position to argue.

Grace had prepared the trolley and the plaster and Will had rehearsed the procedure several times in his head.

A Bier's block. After August Bier's ingenious technique described less than ten years earlier at a surgeons' conference in Berlin, Will had learnt. A neat, safe and painless way to carry out short operative procedures on the lower arm or leg without putting the patient to sleep.

It was one of the few times that Grace and Will had ever found themselves working together as a team, especially on their own, and both of them relished this rare opportunity.

Grace gently placed a deflated tourniquet cuff around the top of Dylan's left arm and then applied a second one immediately below it.

Will guided a needle expertly into a vein on the back of the patient's hand and attached a twenty-millilitre syringe of 0.5% procaine to the end of it.

Together, they raised Dylan's arm above his head, and Grace wrapped a bandage tightly around the entirety of the arm below the cuffs to compress and empty the veins. Then, Will inflated the upper arm cuff to one hundred millimetres Hg above his patient's systolic blood pressure, to temporarily cut off the blood supply.

'Jesus, that's tight!' said Dylan, wincing a little.

'Don't worry, it's meant to be,' reassured Will, 'but it won't be uncomfortable for long.'

They allowed the arm to drop back to Dylan's side and removed the compression bandage. Will then slowly injected the entire contents of the syringe and waited for the local anaesthetic solution to do its job.

'It should take about twenty minutes for your arm to go completely numb,' Grace told Dylan. 'Then we can reset your broken bones back into their correct alignment.'

'Well, it can't work a minute too soon. It's been killing me and I'm dreading what this big guy's going to do to me, if truth be told.'

Five minutes later, he called them back over from the corner of the room where the two medicos had been having a private tête-à-tête.

'This tourniquet's beginning to really hurt now,' he said.

'Let's do something about that,' Will said. He pumped up the lower cuff, over the part of the upper arm that was now nearly numb, and released all the pressure in the upper cuff, which relieved the patient's discomfort immediately.

Fifteen minutes later, with no sensation in the arm reported by Dylan, Will pulled resolutely on his hand and wrist as Grace applied countertraction at the elbow, thereby separating and manipulating the broken and displaced bone ends back into their correct position and orientation.

As Will held the arm stable, Grace quickly and efficiently applied the plaster of Paris cast and they chatted cheerily for a few moments with their patient until it had completely set.

Will slowly and carefully deflated the second cuff so as not to release a large quantity of any remaining active local anaesthetic into the circulation, which he had been warned could potentially cause a cardiac arrythmia. Grace then put Dylan's arm in a sling and tied it around the back of his neck.

'Bloody good job!' said Dr Lamerton, who bulldozed in at that moment, taking a break between two of his own patients. 'Perfect alignment. Twenty degrees of palmar flexion, thirty degrees of ulnar deviation. We'll make an orthopod of you yet, Will. Give an honorary medical degree to that man! Now give your patient a cup of tea and get him the hell out of here and back to his unit. And Parker? Be a bit more bloody careful in future when you're firing shells at the enemy, would you? You could easily end up hurting someone.'

56

Detroit

John Gray leaned back in his upholstered leather swivel chair and put his feet on the desk in front of him. He scanned the front page of the *Detroit Inquirer*, curious to know what the latest developments were in the war in Europe. President Woodrow Wilson had previously boasted about being the man who had kept America out of the war and who'd maintained neutrality, but after the sinking of the British ocean liner *Lusitania* by a German U-boat in 1915, with the loss of 2000 lives including 128 Americans, public opinion had changed. Then, when the Zimmerman telegram revealed the threat of Germany forming an alliance with Mexico, Woodrow Wilson had finally asked Congress for a declaration of war with Germany and Congress had supported it. America had officially entered the war on the sixth of April 1917 and since then, and particularly because several of his good friends had sons serving on the battlefields or in the Navy, Gray had been following its prosecution with interest. As he read further, he learned that the Canadians and Australians had helped the British Third Army make rapid advances north of the Hindenburg Line at Vimy Ridge and at Arras in the same month that America declared war. Gray had no doubt his countrymen would achieve similar impressive results in due course. The black-and-white images of war printed on the first two pages of the *Inquirer* captured his imagination and intrigued him.

As a major shareholder in the Ford motor company based in Dearborn, Detroit, he was even more interested in this very nasty outbreak of flu which had started in March and had now resulted in over a thousand of the men working on the assembly line calling in sick and unable to work.

Henry Ford and Alexander Malcomson had put plenty of money into the company when they had founded it sixteen years previously, but they had gone through much of it early on and this level of absenteeism was a real financial worry. As he turned the pages, he realised that the flu was not limited to Michigan either. In San Quentin prison 500 of the 1900 prisoners had become ill; and in Camp Funston, a training camp for 20,000 recruits, and more than a dozen other army camps, thousands had been rendered ill and were bed-bound by the illness.

The company doctor had advised him and all the other members of the board that they should not visit any of the sick, even if just to show moral support. It was a very serious illness, he had warned. And highly contagious. Another shareholder, Albert Strelow, had already come down with it and it had almost killed him. And now the doctor himself had taken to his sickbed. Gray peered through the glass panels on his door to check the 'do not disturb' notice was in place and continued reading.

*

Étaples

In a large military camp at Étaples in northern France, Dr Thierry Lejeune slumped down on the angular wooden chair in his office and lit a Gauloises. He was exhausted. The influenza bug sweeping through the camp had overwhelmed his staff and resources. Every metre of floor space was occupied by sick soldiers.

He inhaled the thick aromatic smoke deeply, feeling its comforting warmth race through his airways and permeate even the smallest of the air sacs in his lungs. The first hit of nicotine would calm his fraying nerves. Maybe the heat of that smoke would kill off any germs he had already breathed in. Maybe it possessed some kind of protective element. Was it possible? At any rate, the cigarette made him feel better and was the only comfort available to him right now. He brought the dark tar-stained filter to his lips, took another drag and looked out of the window.

In the yard outside and around the farm next door roamed the ducks, geese and pigs whose faeces and dung was splattered everywhere and befouled the boots and uniforms of every war-fatigued soldier who had passed through during the last three years and been lucky enough to find a quiet place to sit. He had read somewhere that pigs and birds could also get their own types of influenza. Maybe they could even pass the germs between themselves, between the species. They could not pass it on to humans, however, he reasoned. He had never heard of that. Besides, he reassured himself, they looked in the prime of health with the poultry clucking and the pigs grunting happily. Nothing wrong there.

So, where the hell had this outbreak of influenza come

from? At least it was nothing too terrifying. Most of the soldiers and the civilians affected had a high temperature and aches and pains for a few days but almost all of them made a full recovery within a fortnight or so. But he still could not help but marvel at the spread of it. Almost everybody who came into contact with it succumbed to its consequences within forty-eight hours. Bizarrely, the doctor noted, unlike other infections which predominantly preyed on children and the elderly, it seemed to strike young, fit and healthy adults the hardest. Strange.

He stubbed out his Gauloises, tucked the blue-grey packet inside the top pocket of his white coat, and walked back to the ward full of coughing and spitting patients.

*

San Sebastián, Spain

Six hundred miles to the south-west and just over the border in Spain, spring was in the air and none of the townsfolk strolling by the sea on the promenade were wearing military uniform.

The tourist season had begun in February and the vibrant and quaint town of San Sebastián seemed a million miles from the bloody, relentless carnage taking place on the Western Front in its neighbouring country. Here, there was little talk of trench warfare, of bombs, mines, poison gas or mass slaughter. This was a thriving town in neutral territory where the days were sunny and bright and the nights inviting and romantic. The rest of Europe seemed a world apart.

But then, in March, many of the townspeople started to fall ill. Worse still, the illness seemed to spread like wildfire.

The town's officials were concerned for the victims, of course, but they were also worried that if word got around it would kill any hopes they had of a bumper tourist season. Señor Pedro González, who was the mayor's closest advisor and confidant, reasoned that they should confide in the local press agencies and put in a concerted effort to play down the influenza outbreak for all their sakes. The press were willing, to an extent, to comply, but the news got out anyway and San Sebastián soon became a place to be studiously avoided. The Spanish wire news service Agencia Fabra sent a cable to Reuters news service in London saying, 'A strange form of disease of epidemic character has appeared in Madrid.'

Within another two months, one third of Madrid and eight million people were bed-bound with the flu, including King Alfonso XIII himself, who was reported as being gravely ill. 'The Life of the King Hangs in the Balance', ran the headline in Madrid's *ABC* newspaper.

*

Picardy

Sergeant Martin Ellis of the 107th Ammunition Train, 32nd Division of the American Expeditionary Force, was chatting to his mates about the so-called 'three-day fever' that was sweeping through the ranks.

'There is nothing *three days* about it,' he said. 'It lasts at least a week. It hits you like a train and it chases the mercury right up to the top of the thermometer scale. You sweat, you shake, you shiver, your head splits wide open and every muscle and joint in your body feels like agony. I should know, I had it. Felt like I had the worst hangover for another couple of weeks after that.'

The other men listened apprehensively. It was not something they fancied happening to them and one or two of them surreptitiously sidled further away from their sergeant.

'I blame the 15th Cavalry. Soon as they got here, everyone started getting sick. We are worse off now than before the reinforcements came.'

'That's right,' said another. 'The British Army had to postpone a couple of big attacks they'd planned, I'm told. So it's affecting the war effort everywhere.'

'Might have come from Spain, others say,' mused the sergeant, 'but who knows? They're the only ones who don't censor their news reports at the moment, unlike us countries at war. Over there it doesn't have to be hushed up. I reckon they're the ones who will get the credit for it.'

'The Spanish flu. Has a certain ring to it,' said the private.

'Yeah. Let's blame the dagoes. It's not as if they've got any other fight going on, is it?'

57

Carantain

Grace woke on a mild summer morning wondering what the day might promise. It had been weeks since she'd had any time off and the current offensive was being fought further to the north near Armentières. The hospital was quiet and some of the other nurses had just returned from England to relieve those who had remained.

Exhausted by the care she had administered to the wounded and dying, she craved someone to tend to her for once. She missed her family at home and her father in particular, with whom she had the closest of bonds. She often thought of Henry, James and Rupert, all still in combat, flung around the globe in this world war.

She longed for someone to put their arms around her and hug her tight, to comfort and cherish her. But she sought the closeness and intimacy of something more, too. She had an energy and passion inside her that needed to be shared.

She knew there was only one man who could fulfil this for her.

Despite Will's tender years, he had awoken something within her and stirred her romantic imagination. There were times when his youthfulness was cute, but most of the time she had the impression of a man older than his years.

Today would be the first time in a while that Will and Grace would have a long time to themselves. They had snatched what moments they could while they waited for the right opportunity. Careful not to be seen by anyone else, they had occasionally stolen secret moments for a lingering kiss behind the ambulance or a longer private hug in the forest behind the camp. Grace had initially taken the lead. Will could kiss, that much was sure, but she had had to unbutton her tunic and guide his hand inside and onto her breast to move things on. He was a quick learner, however, and now his eagerness and hunger had become intense.

Neither of them could realistically have expected today to come about. A lull in the workload, the simultaneous granting of twenty-four hours of leave and a beautiful summer's day.

The FANY had even offered Grace one of their horses as a method of transport for her day off but then only because this particular mare, Boadicea, had recently been truculent and frisky to the point of being uncontrollable. Certainly, the horse was no use to the rest of the unit until she calmed down. If Grace could have a restraining influence on her, Sister Morgan had argued, then she was welcome to try. Had she known there would be two people riding double on the horse's back, Sister Morgan might have changed her mind, but ignorance was bliss and neither Grace nor Will would be likely to let on.

Grace had often ridden two-on-one with Charles on one of her father's Percheron mares or Belgian geldings to keep the horses fit, so a bigger, more muscular animal like this one was only a small challenge.

When Will first saw the horse, he was hesitant. It looked wild and angry.

'Medieval noblemen regularly rode like this with their ladies,' explained Grace. 'All we are doing is changing roles and positions.'

Steadying the horse under her expert control, she offered Will the stirrup and helped pull him up to take his place behind her. Boadicea clearly did not like this experience much and twisted and bucked at the effrontery of it. Grace soon had the measure of her, however, and with a squeeze of her thighs and a meaningful show of her riding crop they set off.

They rode westward at first, along meandering and deserted farm tracks, bypassing the heavily bombed villages of Cressy and Jonceau. Grace relished her accomplishment as a horse rider, and Will hung on to her with his arms around her waist, doing his best to synchronise his up-and-down motions of riding with hers.

Two kilometres further on, at the devastated little village of Carantain, they briefly dismounted to step over the rubble blocking their path. Here, they happily came across an intact bottle of local red wine in a splintered kitchen dresser lying in the street. Removing the cork with the point of Will's belt buckle they swigged it back as they picked their way through the debris. It was mellow and fruity and, unaccustomed as they were to such luxuries, they could feel it burn in the pit of their stomachs and flush their skin.

Mounting up again, they made their way to a copse at the top of the next hill before descending through a rich golden cornfield on the other side. There, finding a babbling brook at the bottom, they dismounted and took in the view. It seemed incredible that less than ten kilometres away, thousands of weary war-torn men faced each other over a pockmarked quagmire of grey sodden land, trying to kill each other. Here, the tall stalks of corn swayed and rustled in the breeze. The beech trees at the top of the hill behind them resembled a green crown above the sea of gold. Butterflies performed merry dances together, while rooks and blackbirds fluttered in the azure sky above. A crimson dragonfly skittered across the surface of the water and a bright blue kingfisher with its long beak and honey-coloured breast perched on a fallen log on the opposite bank.

They tethered their mount to the trunk of a nearby willow tree and sat on the bank to bask in the warm sunshine.

Grace, hot and flushed from her ride and her struggle with the temperamental horse, lay down in the grass, loosened her tunic and hitched up her skirt. Will stripped off his shirt, kicked off his boots and stretched out languidly beside her.

They had known each other for two years now, working together and helping each other to deal with the horrors and the senselessness of the destruction around them. They had witnessed so many atrocities together, taken serious risks and put their lives on the line on several occasions. They had worked tirelessly, never complaining or putting their own interests first. They had each consoled the other when fatigue and despondency descended. And they had laughed and talked together about everything and anything, whenever they found the opportunity.

Will had been longing for every minute that he could spend with Grace. He loved her face and her shape and the way she moved. Her intelligence and openness and bravery. He adored that smile and those green alluring eyes. Whenever he found himself most afraid, out there in no man's land between the trenches, he thought of Grace. He found that whenever he was in the greatest danger, he could picture her face and think of little else but seeing her again.

Grace, for her part, admired Will's strong physique and his easy relationship with those around him. And his sensitivity and reason. On more than one occasion she had watched him refuse to side with boorish and ignorant soldiers insulting Arup and she had been grateful only a few weeks ago when he had physically stepped in to rescue her from a much bigger man than him who, worse for drink, was moving in on her and talking lasciviously while she was trapped against a wall. That man had suffered a split lip and a dislocated shoulder as a result. She had never before seen any violence at all in Will and was secretly flattered that he had reserved it for her.

Typically, the very next day, in the absence of anyone else available, it had fallen upon Will and Grace to reduce the man's dislocation and patch up his lip. Will, never one to bear a grudge, had duly obliged. Grace, stretched out on the grass, smiled at the thought of it. While she had pulled back on the foolish man's collarbone to stabilise the shoulder girdle Will had skilfully performed the now familiar manoeuvre. He bent the arm to a right angle at the elbow and pulled it down hard to release the muscle spasm in the rotator cuff. He had then externally rotated the upper arm using the forearm as a lever, brought the elbow across the man's body to the midline and then finally internally rotated the humerus to pop the top of the bone back into the socket. 'Bloody hell,' the man had yelled as it clicked back into place. 'That ruddy hurt!' The pair of them giggled later, agreeing that they'd enjoyed the procedure all the more for the fact that they'd failed to offer the patient any anaesthetic.

Now, lying side by side at the edge of the water, they had never been closer, physically or emotionally. Intoxicated by their excitement and warmed by the sun on their skin and the wine inside them, they kissed. They kissed and they found they could not stop. Their bodies entwined and locked and they twisted and rolled as they explored each other urgently with their lips, hands and fingertips. They were still only half undressed when Will's body merged with Grace's and her pleasure was all the greater for Will's strong right hand in the small of her back and the other cradling her neck and shoulders. Her own hands were on his buttocks and waist as the two of them rocked and gyrated in harmony.

Grace was shocked and amazed by the strength of their passion. What greater contrast could there be? she wondered. The cacophonous hell of the battlefield, the constant risk of one's own death, the torn and broken bodies ripped apart by shells and shrapnel and then this tender, heaven-sent ecstasy of physical love and passion.

As Will lay with her, slowly moving inside her, a crescendo of something irresistible and powerful deep within his loins surprised and overwhelmed him. Driven on by some primeval power, over which he felt he had no control, he thrust deeper and harder, his body damp with sweat and his muscles taut and quivering. Grace, her eyes closed, and her full lips slightly parted, urgently sought out his mouth. Her breath now came in short, shallow gasps against his ear and she tilted her hips forward and held him ever more tightly within. And then, with a soft groan, Will permitted himself the final act, and while panting and tensing Grace surrendered to him.

They lay like that for several minutes, linking hands and kissing lips, cheeks, eyes and noses. They looked into each other's eyes and felt only longing. There was no awkwardness or embarrassment. No guilt or regret. It was as if this was the conclusion of something written, something inevitable. It was an intense release for both of them. They had become so close, so inseparable. From such different backgrounds, it was true, but in their spirit and in their nature, in their knowledge and understanding of the world and its people, so very alike and in tune. Now, as Grace lay half-naked beside him, she felt warm, fulfilled and elated. The sun beat down on her lily-white skin and rays of sunlight streamed through the trees, playing across the rocks in the river and dappling the reeds and grass. A zephyr of a breeze brought goosebumps to the soft flesh of her breasts and she heard nothing but their shallow breathing, the soft humming of the bees and the water as it rippled gently past them.

Will was stretched out beside her, his arm resting on her waist and a contented smile on his face.

'It's supposed to be clumsy, awkward and deeply unmemorable the first time,' said Grace. 'That's what everyone says, anyway.'

'So how deeply disappointing was it?'

'It wasn't at all, Will,' she said, giving him a playful slap. 'It was beautiful. And as for unmemorable – I will remember this for as long as I live.' She studied him. 'This is magical. It was meant to happen, I think. I trust you with all my heart and I'm glad I . . . I'm glad I did this first with you. But . . .'

'But what?' There was a pause and Grace looked suddenly serious.

'But . . . we are in the middle of a bloody war. Anything could happen to either of us at any time and we don't know what the future holds. Something, I don't know, something awful could happen. We could be posted somewhere else miles away from each other and never see each other again. It's all uncertain.'

'I know that, Grace. For me, that's what makes this so special. Who knows if we'll ever be able to recapture this moment? This might sound stupid, but if I died tomorrow, I'd feel at least I've lived. Because of this.'

She put her hand against his cheek and smiled. 'I feel the same.' She was pensive for a moment. 'So many young men, men about the same age as you, have not lived long enough to kiss a girl, let alone make love. It's such a waste.' Grace took him by the shoulder. 'You managed perfectly well before you met me, Will. And so did I before I met you. You make me feel good and you make me feel happy. With you, I can think, and I can laugh. You also make me feel valued. You're special to me. You know that. We wouldn't be here otherwise. But we still have a duty to perform. That's why we came here to the front, and we'll carry on.'

For a long while, they sat in silence. Later, as the light in the sky began to fade, they swam in a deep rock pool that they discovered at a bend in the stream and they let the whirlpools and eddies of the current massage and soothe them. Then they climbed the bank and went to rejoin Boadicea, waiting under the willow. 'I love these trees,' Grace said.

'You love every tree,' Will teased.

'I do. But there's something about a willow. Their sad-looking branches laden down with leaves tumbling to the ground like a curtain.'

'Standing here in the middle of it, it's like our own little boudoir. It's so quiet and private.'

'My father used to say they are sentient beings. Trees, I mean. He used to tell me they have a conscience. That they can communicate with one another and are aware of what goes on around them. I'm not sure about that, but he has thousands of trees on the estate at home and he taught me all their names and about their history.'

'What did he tell you about willows?'

'He said they originally came from China. They need lots of water, which is why you always find them next to lakes and waterways. In China, they are a symbol of immortality and rebirth. Elsewhere, they're associated with mysticism and superstition. In some places, with grief.'

'Is that why they're called weeping willows?'

'Maybe. They say that raindrops falling from its drooping branches look like tears. I suppose they do. Maybe they are crying because they don't live very long. This one might only last another ten years, I guess.'

'It might outlive us then, Grace.'

'Don't say that,' she said quickly. 'I want us to stay alive and as resilient as this tree is, well into our dotage. I wish we could survive as long as Old Tjikko.'

'Who the hell is old Tjikko?' Will asked.

'He is a Norwegian spruce. And he is nine and a half thousand years old. The oldest tree in the world, some say.'

'Well, I doubt if we will last that long,' said Will. 'But hopefully long enough to one day go and see it.'

'It would be nice to think so. And to spend more time at Bishop's Cleeve showing you all the trees we have there. My parents would certainly make you welcome again.'

'Even after today?' teased Will.

'Good point,' she laughed. 'Better to get captured by the Boche than ever let my mother find out how you ravished me.'

'Ravished you?' exclaimed Will, feigning hurt.

'Yes, now shut up, you silly boy,' she said, kissing him hard on the lips. 'And ravish me again.'

58

Jack was convalescing in a hospital in Hyde Park Gardens. He had suffered a concussion, a fracture dislocation of the hip, and taken several pieces of shrapnel in his shoulder when the shell had burst above them. Now he was on his feet again, moving slowly but steadily.

He had written a letter to Rhys Evans' wife, to tell her what a brave man her husband had been, and how he had saved Jack's life barely fifteen minutes before they were both hit. He had probably saved Jack's life twice, standing just in front of him and taking the brunt of the shrapnel that had showered down on them. When Jack woke up in the regimental aid post, Rhys's body had already been cleared away. 'Where's Rhys?' he asked the nurse. 'Is he all right?' Her look told him everything he needed to know.

When all this over, he wondered if he should travel to Wales and meet Rhys's wife. She might need a new husband to look after the two children, and, well — the decent thing would be to offer himself, whatever she looked like. He owed his life to the man. He could do that, if she wanted him to. He wondered what she looked like. And if Rhys would be pleased or horrified by the idea.

Though he supposed it didn't matter what Rhys thought. Rhys was dead. There was no God. No God could reward a man for saving another's life with a piece of steel through the heart. Everything was chaos. A man could do what he pleased — a man had to do what he pleased. Jack might be dead by next year, anyway, after he was sent back. He most likely would be dead. He could do what he liked in the meantime, as long as it didn't land him in prison or facing a court martial.

He had been making trouble with the matron on the ward.

'You are being overfamiliar with my staff,' she scolded him.

'Overfamiliar?'

'Paying them unnecessary compliments.'

'Who's to judge what's necessary? How do you know what's necessary? What the hell do you mean, necessary? Have you ever risked your life and watched your friends die? I'm alive and it's a miracle I am and your colleagues are kind and pretty and I tell them so. Who made you God, anyway?'

'Your language is atrocious,' she said, with pursed lips. 'I will give you one more chance before I report you for indecent behaviour. Try to be the gentleman you are clearly not.'

He had the urge to reach out and slap her behind as she left. The disciplinary might be worth it. He was getting angrier and angrier as he lay there thinking about everything. He wanted to let off steam, to scream and shout, to be bundled into a cell somewhere and punished for being alive when his good friend was dead.

He had never been a gentleman and never would be.

But he put on an act when Aunt Clara answered the door in Turnham Green, giving her his brightest smile, now missing a tooth that he'd woken up without.

'Oh, Jack,' she said. 'You look so changed.'

'I'm the same as ever, Aunt Clara,' he lied. 'Reliably unreliable. Now where's my lovely sister?'

She was jumping up and down behind Clara, trying to get past. 'Jack! Do you recognise me?'

He looked down. 'Is this really you?' he asked, then turned to Clara. 'Did you lose her one day after school, and bring this urchin back home by mistake?'

'Jack!' said Kitty. 'It's me!'

'My sister was much smaller, and much less squawky, and her hair was much lighter,' Jack went on. 'Now I don't doubt that this creature has some positive attributes, but she's— Ow!'

Kitty was kicking him in the shin now. 'You know it's me! You know it is!'

He reached down and picked her up so they were face to face. He screwed his eyes up while she thrashed her limbs around.

'Come to think of it,' he said, 'you do look a little familiar.'

Aunt Clara was shaking her head next to them. 'It's good to have you back, Jack, terrible influence on her though you are.'

It was a joyful reunion. Clara had queued from early in the morning to get hold of a chicken, which she roasted with potatoes. It was the best thing Jack had eaten since enlisting, so good it almost brought tears to his eyes.

'Did you kill any Germans?' Kitty asked. 'I hope you did.'

Clara smacked her sharply on the shoulder. 'Don't be so silly, girl. There's nothing good about killing, and it's not polite to ask Jack questions he might prefer not to answer.'

Jack carried on chewing. He remembered being so excited by explosives when he started. How many people had he helped kill that night on the Messines Ridge? Hundreds, thousands? That was no way to think. Whatever it took to stop the war for both sides was right. It couldn't go on forever and someone had to win. Might as well be the good ones. That's what they were, after all. Good.

'I, er . . .' He stopped.

'You needn't say anything, Jack,' said Clara.

'She's right,' he said eventually to Kitty. 'Nothing to be proud of about killing the poor sods on the other side.'

'Language,' said Clara.

He didn't mind being told to watch his language by her.

*

Trevor was back at his father's, where he'd lived since being discharged with a permanently weakened stomach and severe digestion issues two years ago. When he'd been hit by a machine-gun bullet, which caught him in the stomach and pierced his abdomen. He lost a considerable amount of blood but was rapidly evacuated to a casualty clearing station where he underwent a laparotomy under chloroform. The surgeon had to remove shrapnel and part of the stomach which had left it much smaller than it was originally. A part of the bowel had to be resected also, leaving Trevor with less intestine to absorb food and nutrients and the stomach not large enough to tolerate anything more than a small meal. Will had written to Jack and asked him to check on him. Jack was shocked by how thin and miserable he looked when he opened the door.

'Hello, mate,' he said.

'Jack! I had a letter from Will that said you were back in Blighty. Where did they get you?'

'My hip and my shoulders, mostly. Nasty wounds. It's taken me a while to get to the stage I can move my right leg without wanting to scream. There's still a fair bit of shrapnel in there, trying to come out. Itches something awful at night. But I'm lucky. I got a big bit that banged me on my helmet.

A couple of inches lower and I'd be dead. Chap next to me wasn't so lucky.'

Trevor winced. 'They got me on my first battle. Can you believe that? All those months and then I'm out there two minutes and it's all over.'

'There are lads out there who would love that.'

Trevor blew out and patted his stomach. 'It's not cushy, this. Half my stomach's gone. I can barely eat. Which I suppose is useful, considering how little food there is round here.' He looked behind him. 'Shall we go out?' He picked up his army greatcoat from behind him. 'At least I've got a warm coat now.' He stepped onto the street and the two of them turned right towards Hammersmith and the Dove pub on the river, which had been one of their favourites.

'So how have you been keeping yourself?' asked Jack.

'There's a little pension. Someone else does the bookie running now. A younger lad, with a bit more energy than I can muster up these days.'

'Is it all right in there?' Jack asked, looking back at where they'd come from.

Trevor blew through his lips again. 'It's better than the frontline. Conditions, anyway. I quite liked the company out there.'

'Will, too?'

'He's a decent chap. I'm sorry I used to tease him.'

'He's very teasable.'

Trevor grinned. 'I get the sense from his letters he's fallen in love with a nurse. I didn't have him down for that.'

'Yes, I've heard all about her from my aunt, though not a word from him!'

'Nah, he probably knew you'd rib him mercilessly.'

'I bloody well will! Where's a pen and paper?'

'Let him alone,' Trevor laughed. 'I never told you, Jack, but I wouldn't have made it back without him. Strong as an ox, your brother. Picked me up, threw me over his shoulder and somehow got me to the forward dressing station. Blood everywhere, and I was swearing at him the whole time because of the pain. But he didn't care a jot, despite the fact he could have got himself killed. Just got on with it. I haven't even had a chance to buy him a pint yet.'

Jack was used to Will getting all the praise and compliments from people. Especially in the past, from Clara, because his little brother had been such a good boy or done all his homework. But for some reason it jarred with him to hear his friend singing his brother's praises and becoming coy now about teasing him. It was too different from how it had been.

'What are we going to do now, Trevor?'

'You'll be heading out there again, won't you?'

'I guess so. I keep hoping it will end before I have to. But if I stay, well, what's here for me?'

'There'll be work for men. There will be fewer of us.'

'I suppose that's true. You know, you might even find a respectable job.'

'What's one of them? What do they look like?' Trevor was smiling now. Jack was too.

'We'll work something out,' Jack said. 'We'll find something to occupy us.'

59

Boston

Dr James Fogarty had convened the meeting hastily. It was urgent. The five doctors present in the large sparsely furnished office, the greatest experts in Boston in the field of infectious disease and epidemiology, all waited for confirmation of their worst fears.

Of the motley group of sailors who had docked at the Commonwealth Pier that August, a significant number had become sick with the same symptoms at the same time. On the twenty-eighth of August, eight of them were diagnosed with flu, and the next day a further fifty had become acutely ill. One week later, the sick toll had reached 119 and the disease had broken out among the civilian population as well. On the eighth of September people started to die: a merchant marine, a naval ranking and a civilian.

The Spanish flu they had heard so much about in the spring appeared to have returned. Only this time it had come back in a much deadlier form. One of the doctors present had adopted the original outbreak as the subject of a thesis and had been closely monitoring its evolution and development around the world. Originally, it had looked as if the spring epidemic had subsided and all but disappeared, but by the summer he and other medical epidemiologists had become aware of a further infectious outbreak laying waste to large populations of people throughout the Indian subcontinent and in Japan, China, parts of the Caribbean and whole areas of central and southern America. There was no doubt in his mind that this was now a pandemic and could sweep the entire world.

'I've been tracking it carefully,' he said. 'And my greatest fear has always been that it might land on our own doorstep one day.'

'How serious is it?' asked one of his colleagues.

'It's bad. About one in five suffer a fairly mild illness and have an uncomplicated recovery. The rest go one of two ways. Half become desperately ill very quickly. They can die within days, sometimes hours.'

He looked around the room to gauge the reaction.

'The others experience chills, fevers, a dry hacking cough and muscle pains for a few days. But then, and wholly untypically, the course of their disease takes a turn for the worse and they develop a pneumonia which either kills them or requires an extended period of recuperation. Many are left with a permanent respiratory handicap.'

'Jesus,' said Fogarty. 'We better start battening down the hatches.'

*

Fort Devens, Massachusetts

Three weeks later and thirty miles to the west of where Dr Fogarty had held his meeting in Boston, the hospital at Fort Devens in Massachusetts resembled a scene from the black death of the Middle Ages.

The flu had arrived a month earlier and almost overnight had devastated the 50,000-strong military contingent there. The doctors were familiar with pneumonia and had seen plenty of it during their medical careers. It was a common cause of death, particularly in the elderly, so much so that it was often referred to colloquially among themselves as 'the old man's friend'.

But the doctors had never seen pneumonia-like symptoms develop and kill so quickly. Neither had they seen it in pandemic form in younger people. Previously fit and athletic young men would be admitted to the ward only to develop that reddy-brown skin discoloration of blood poisoning and that spontaneous bruising under the skin of the face that was so severe it was impossible to distinguish a white man from a black man.

The medical staff had never in their entire lives seen anything like it. Not only did they feel therapeutically impotent to intervene, but they were scared.

They were now issuing death certificates by the dozen and pronouncing around 100 men as 'life extinct' every day.

Dr William C. Gorgas was the US surgeon general and the man who had eliminated yellow fever from Cuba. He knew a great deal about infectious disease and hastily dispatched a group of the nation's leading physicians to the camp to investigate. What they discovered shocked them. The hospital, designed to treat a maximum of 2000, was overflowing with four times that number. They had seen infectious disease associated with war and military activity many times before, such as dysentery, typhus and malaria. But nothing like this. Ever.

In the absence of sufficient nurses and doctors, they saw hundreds of men staggering in and searching for any floor space they could find on which to lie down.

Their lips and faces were blue, and they coughed up thick gobbets of purply-red phlegm from their lungs. The mortuary was stacked high with bodies and in the autopsy room the findings of the pathologist were horribly familiar each time. Blue bloated lungs with sopping wet foaming pleural surfaces. But very little 'consolidation', that typical hard solidification characteristic of ordinary pneumonia.

When the doctors recovered sufficiently to compile and send their report it was added to a stack of further reports coming in from hundreds of different military installations across America. In Ohio alone, at Camp Sherman, more than 13,000 men, about forty per cent of the total, had developed flu in the first two weeks of October, of whom 1101 died. The civilians were dropping like flies as well and thousands upon thousands were dying.

The disaster, like many before it, brought out the best as well as the worst in people. Many, with no medical or nursing qualifications but with hearts full of altruism, rallied around and volunteered to take the sick to hospital or provide food and clothing. Others worked as cooks, nursing assistants, or child-minders. Others, however, purely interested in self-preservation, hoarded supplies and locked themselves away from these modern-day lepers in the hope that the pandemic would kill everybody else but not themselves.

Hard decisions had to be made by the authorities. The Provost Marshal General of the US Army cancelled a draft call of 142,000 men destined to be sent to Europe to bolster the Allies' diminishing military forces. Health officials started a campaign banning coughing, sneezing and spitting in public.

Nurses wore white gauze masks for their own and others' protection but many people abused and shunned them for fear they might come near them and transmit the infection. Others swarmed around them in a desperate need for assistance and rescue.

Towns and villages closed schools, theatres, cinemas and hospitality venues. Cities resembled ghost towns and became as dead as the thousands of victims who had succumbed to the disease. The deserted streets and public places became a poignant urban symbol of this modern version of the black death that had indeed mutated and returned with a vengeance.

*

Nome, Alaska

On the hostile permafrost on the Seward Peninsula of Alaska lay a remote little village consisting of about eighty of the land's original inhabitants, the Inuit. Being some 100 miles by husky sledge from Nome, the nearest town on the coast, it was never easy to reach. For that reason, whenever the occasional visitor arrived it was regarded as a special occasion and they would be treated to the locals' famously warm and generous hospitality.

To any uninitiated outsiders, they seemed to have few luxuries to enjoy in their life and lived only a frugal existence. Yet their simple lives were full; their families tight-knit and content; and their feasts of reindeer meat, oily fish, blueberries in seal blubber and tea something to enjoy together and savour.

As far as they were concerned, they did not need the artificial pleasures and trappings of material wealth and modern civilisation. They had all they needed right there. They had the beauty and peace of the natural world all around them and they had their health.

What they did not have, however, was access to sophisticated medical care or even the tiniest shred of any immunity to a global viral pandemic. And although they were blissfully unaware of it, in early September of that year the latter was coming their way with the unstoppable speed and force of the worst winter blizzard they could ever have imagined. When the disease arrived, it would leave their community savagely decimated and almost all of them – men, women and children alike – buried in their final resting place deep beneath the icy tundra.

*

Upolu, Samoa

Puleleitte and his wife Teuila sat together on a smooth outcrop of volcanic rock and looked down at their children searching for seashells on the golden sands of the beach below them. It was a hot and humid twenty-nine degrees, but a gentle afternoon trade wind made the temperature feel more bearable and the palm trees sheltered them from the harsh rays of the sun. They smiled as their daughter Asoese shrieked with delight when she found a conch shell bigger than the one her brother Fetu had found five minutes earlier.

Their life on the tropical Polynesian island of Upolu was simple and uncomplicated and they had escaped the turmoil going on in other parts of the world as a result of war.

Four years previously, at the outbreak of war, the Samoan Expeditionary Force had arrived from New Zealand to capture German Samoa for the New Zealand government on behalf of King George V. While the Germans had officially refused to surrender, no resistance had been offered and the occupation had been achieved without a single shot being fired.

It had been New Zealand's first military action of the war and on the thirtieth of August in the capital, Apia, Commander Robert Logan had assumed responsibility as military administrator.

But other than that, the peaceful Pacific Islanders would not really have known there was a war on.

Teuila was now thinking about the meal she would prepare for the family that night. Faiai Eleni, fish in coconut cream with taro leaves, with Panikeke, sweet banana fritters, afterwards. Her food was always popular but it would be a nice change, she thought, to be able to enjoy some of the dishes that could not be concocted from local produce and which were imported by sea from New Zealand or Hawaii. She looked out across the glittering turquoise ocean to where the next ship would come from, bringing its rich cargo of culinary novelties.

As it happened, when the SS *Talune*, sailing out of Auckland, did arrive in Upolu a little while later, it brought with it a great deal more then was listed in the ship's manifest.

Several of the crew were incubating Spanish flu and Colonel Logan, despite the growing international awareness of the dangers of the current global pandemic, failed to subject the ship to any of the quarantine precautions that might have been prudent.

It was a pity that Puleleitte, standing on the dockside that day in his role as assistant harbourmaster, could not have lived up to his name. Puleleitte meant ruler who can foretell the future. If he had been a soothsayer of any note, he might have been able to predict the catastrophic events that would follow. As it was, the infected crew transmitted the Spanish flu to the unsuspecting islanders and it whirled and raged like a biblical viral maelstrom. Eight thousand people, one fifth of the entire island, would die as a result.

60

Héricourt

In the early part of 1918, the enemy position looked strong. The Germans had been stepping up their offensives all spring now they were not fighting the Russians on the Eastern Front, who had pulled out of the war when the Bolsheviks had overthrown the Tsar. At the same time, British troops had started to reduce on the Western Front, as the prime minister David Lloyd George, scared about an offensive mounted on home soil, kept forces back in Britain. This was a deeply unpopular policy among the soldiers, who had seen their brigades reduced to three battalions from four, and many of whom had now been separated from officers and privates with whom they had grown used to working, and with whom they had formed efficient relationships based on keeping each other alive. Now, at the end of the summer, the Germans were experiencing their own frustrations.

General Erich Ludendorff despaired of the prospect of his country having to surrender to the enemy. If his army had not been devastated by the flu that was sweeping across the world his July offensive might have succeeded in winning the war for Germany. This 'Flanders flu', as the Germans called it, had ruined everything. He was living in the forlorn hope that some divine intervention, some God-given miracle,

343

would come to the rescue. The flu, he imagined, would devastate the French Army to an even greater extent. Surely his men were fitter and stronger. They would fight longer and harder no matter what.

He had heard how the pandemic was devastating military camps in the USA, such as Camp Devens near Boston in Massachusetts and Camp Sherman in Ohio, where forty per cent of the camp came down with the disease. Was it possible that this would halt further recruitment of Allied soldiers and procurement of their armaments, especially from America, to allow Germany to consolidate its military position? In England, King George's Grand Fleet had not been able to put to sea for three weeks in May, with more than 10,000 men sick. Surely this was the Fatherland's divine opportunity to triumph. He had even written to Kaiser Wilhelm and received a most favourable and uplifting reply. But it was not to be. The pandemic flu of 1918 was a unique leveller.

Already, the illness had proven to the world that it was no respecter of nations, people, classes or religions. In May, even King George V himself had developed symptoms. It swept the globe, irrespective of whether countries were at war or not.

On the Western Front that year, thousands of soldiers already exhausted, malnourished, flea ridden and despondent struggled to show resistance to the pandemic's onward spread. The high command, informed by their medical staff, already knew that this flu killed nearly three per cent of its victims and was twenty-five times more virulent than ordinary seasonal flu. It had marched through the army ranks faster than the German Army had marched through Belgium.

It was not just the simple fact the soldiers in the armies of both sides were already sick from war. The way they worked and were billeted in such close proximity made transmission of the virus rampant. Military camps were particularly susceptible.

In one of them, a German hospital to the south east of Dunkirk, Jürgen Altmann was losing the will to live. And not just because he was nursing a fever of 103° and feeling as if there was a vice around his chest. He could hardly breathe without the hacking cough and its excruciating pain returning and it seemed as if the throbbing in his head might split it into two at any moment.

It was bad enough that his facial disfigurement had scarred him for life, emotionally as well as physically, but his promotion to command a phalanx of crack German storm troopers also accounted for nothing following the decisive defeats inflicted on them by the enemy.

Ludendorff was a fool. What had his objectives been in the great spring offensive? Did anyone really know? How many times had he changed his mind? How much did he expect Jürgen's storm troopers to achieve on their own, unsupported and undersupplied? Where were the tanks, fuel and food that he had been promised? Why were no re-inforcements brought in? He had all but lost them the bloody war.

He coughed and spat out a blood-flecked gobbet of phlegm into a kidney bowl. Maybe it did not matter now, he thought. His hatred of the enemy still knew no bounds, but his biggest enemy right now was the Flanders flu. As he'd lain there, hardly able to move, suffering the ignominy of needing a nurse to wash him and lift him onto a bedpan, he had seen over a dozen soldiers under his command in the same tent succumb to the disease.

He might not even live to see out the end of the war. His constitution was strong, however, and he had unfinished business to attend to before he was done. A fierce flame of unresolved hatred still burned deep within him, keeping him alive. Yet only by a thread.

All he knew was how to fight. On one front or another.

The nurse looked at him and saw the sallow skin and sunken eye sockets of a dying man.

In years to come, when she looked back, she would realise that this second, even more deadly wave of the pandemic that passed through the battlefields of France and elsewhere took some fifty million lives with it. The nine million servicemen who would die in combat during the conflict would be eclipsed in numbers by those who perished from the Spanish flu. She did not know it at the time, but this terrible virus was destined to claim more human lives in a similar timeframe than any other disease in the history of the world.

What she was realising, however, was that it was causing just as much devastation among the British, French and American ranks as it was here on the other side of that seven-hundred-kilometre stretch of parallel trenches which began in Switzerland and finished at the North Sea.

61

Will could not have missed hearing about the terrible illness interrupting operations and felling stalwart men in their thousands. Nobody could. But he hadn't imagined that it would have any implications for the work he was currently doing, nor for that matter the course of the war itself.

So, when Lieutenant Kelly, his RAMC commanding officer, took him to one side and asked him to go and join the American Expeditionary Force during the first week in October, he was staggered.

'But the work I do here, sir, is vital. You only have to look at the numbers of wounded men being brought in every day to see how badly I'm needed.'

'If you don't get over there soon, laddie, together with three of our nurses, we won't have any men left to fight at all.'

'Sir?'

'There are 16,000 of our lads apparently prostrate on their beds delirious with high fevers and incapable of taking part in any action. It's extremely serious and you're required there immediately.'

'But I'm a stretcher bearer, not a nurse. I know how to dress a wound and stop bleeding or put a splint on well enough but what good can I possibly do there?'

'They need extra stretcher bearers there too. As if they haven't got enough to do, they've got nurses running around trying to do the physical job themselves and their skills are better employed elsewhere.'

Will's mind was whirring. Despite the obvious dangers in staying put, he felt it his duty to remain at the frontline. He also relied heavily on the support and camaraderie of his friend Arup, with whom he had built an extraordinary rapport. Leaving Grace's side was also the last thing he wanted to do.

'Look, I haven't got time to argue with you. You've done a great job, young Will, I'll tell you that now, and we will miss you. But it's not negotiable. Its orders from above.'

Will nodded reluctantly.

'Mary, Alice and Beatrice are getting ready and I'll send Grace to join you in a week or two as well, as consolation. You work well together. God knows what else you do well together and it's probably best I don't. But good luck to you both. There's not much to put a smile on a man's face around here, that's for sure. And don't imagine no one's noticed either.'

Will was horrified to hear that their secret was out, and desperately tried not to blush. He resigned himself to packing his belongings and equipment and then went in search of Arup and Grace to say his farewells. Finding Arup carefully restocking a medical bag in the supplies tent he told him his sad news.

'I'll miss you, Arup. I don't think I would've got through this without you.'

'Nor me you, Sahib. You are an old head on young shoulders.'

'Grace should be joining me soon, but I wish you could come, too. We make a good team. But since you're under a different chain of command, I guess that's not possible.'

'There has been no better team since Everton won the football championship in 1914,' joked Arup. 'But you will win through all on your own. I have a feeling that whatever you choose to do in the future, young Will, you will be victorious.'

Arup offered his hand and Will shook it vigorously. Then he looked up at Arup, who had tears in his eyes, and gave him a manly hug.

'Take good care of yourself. Maybe I'll see you when all this is over.'

*

Will had been looking all over for Grace, but, try as he might, he could find no trace of her. He wanted desperately to explain that if he had anything to do with it, he would be staying. He was leaving against his wishes and he would miss her, and he worried the lieutenant's plans to send her on to join him soon might never happen. Will wanted to make arrangements so they could keep in touch. He wanted to tell her where he was going. But if she wasn't there, she wasn't there – she must be doing important work. But there was something useful he could do in the time it would take for the transport to be arranged.

Dear Major and Mrs Tustin-Pennington

I do hope you are both well and that James, Henry and Rupert are safe and flourishing, as well as Fitzwilliam and Amy back home with you. I also hope that the privations and rationing that are now necessary at home are not too tiresome to bear and that the maintenance of your beautiful estate is not too unmanageable.

Grace remains the force of nature you have always known her to be and she constantly earns respect from everyone with whom she works either on the ambulances or at the hospital. If anybody deserves a medal at the end of all this it will be her. Let me assure you she is in good health and never works in harm's way. For myself, I am carrying on as before doing what I can to bring our boys safely back from the battlefields, a grim and challenging task at times but an important one. I am protected by the combatants and the senior men, so you do not need to worry about either of us.

There is good news to share with you in that it looks increasingly as if the Germans' last throw of the dice has been unsuccessful and there is a real sense of optimism among the troops and HQ, who feel that the tide may finally be turning in our favour. On another note, there is worrying talk about a mysterious and highly contagious influenza bug that is sweeping across France and laying low, in quite a serious fashion, a significant number of fighting men and civilians.

Consequently, I have been seconded to travel westwards to a place near Tours to help in the hospital there. It seems they are inundated with the sick and are barely coping. I will miss Grace terribly, but I am hoping she can join me there soon.

I must confess that each day that might pass without her is a wasted day for me. She gives me hope and courage at all times, even on the bleakest of occasions and I must admit to you that I am besotted and will be in love with her for evermore.

It is with this in mind that I would crave to ask for your permission to marry her. I know I am not from a family of great social standing, nor do I have any financial means to speak of. Yet I am young and can work hard and earn well for many years to come. Most importantly I can devote myself to your daughter's happiness and welfare and would consider it an honour to do so. I am being presumptuous, I realise, but I cannot help myself. Why not wait until the conflagration is over? you might ask. I have asked myself the same question. Yet the course of war is uncertain, and our fates and outcomes are in the hands of God alone.

We cannot know how long it will be before we are repatriated, so I plan to make my proposal the next time we are granted leave together as a surprise. We know that we will be refused leave in England as circumstances here at the front are changing rapidly so if I can engineer it, I am hoping that a wedding might be arranged here in France. I realise that you would fervently wish to be there to give your daughter away on such a special day and that you might curse me for even suggesting anything other. Yet, I cannot staunch my impatience. Please forgive me.

I believe Grace feels the same way I do, and that postponement of our dreams would only make us restless and miserable. We have enjoyed much sadness and grief these last three years so the granting of your approval, should I be fortunate enough to receive it, would make everything I have believed in worthwhile and also make me the happiest of men.

Should I be mistaken about Grace's feelings then you know as well as I that she will simply turn me down flat. It is a risk of rejection I am willing to take, for the ultimate prize — if I am accepted — means more to me than life itself.

I pray that you will approve, and give me your blessing. If that is the case, I shall need your assistance with several items which our excellent Postal Service should be able to deliver. They are . . .

He looked for her again after he had left the letter to be posted. But there was no time for any further searching. A small sorry-looking cohort of nurses and medics had gathered together by the truck and were being ordered to climb in. Will, still fighting back his emotions, went to join them.

62

The Germans had been shelling the frontline with mustard gas that morning. Soldiers, waking up in their dugouts, had rubbed their eyes, wondering what the smoke was, and in doing so spread the burning surface all over their eyes.

Grace had been driving the ambulance all day. She had ferried ambulance after ambulance of blinded young men to the casualty clearing station, moaning in pain, terrified they would never be able to see again.

Not for the first time, she thought to herself how despicable gas was as a tool of war. The shells were bad enough, but gas, something that killed slowly, that crept towards the men, that lingered and sank into the places they tried to hide in, was terrifying. She shuddered at the thought.

'It's treatable, you know,' she called back to them. 'It might take a few days, maybe even a few weeks, but you'll see again.'

She hoped she was right.

When she dropped off the last load and collapsed against a wall, ready to cry, she saw Arup coming towards her.

'Arup, oh, I'm glad to see you,' she called.

'I am glad to see you too, young Grace. You seem distressed.'

'Mustard gas. About fifty young men in agony wondering if they'll ever see again.'

'It is a terrible thing, a cowardly way of war.'

'It's evil.'

'Yes. War is evil. And here we are, trying our best to do some good in it. We all have to cry sometimes.'

'Do you cry too, Arup?'

'Young Grace, you know my reputation is in tatters among my people. A soldier in the fearless Meerut who grew too timid to kill, who abandoned his sword. I don't know if I will ever be able to go home again. And now you want me to confess to crying? Like a woman?'

He was smiling at her, but she saw the pain behind his jokey manner.

'No one could doubt your courage, Arup.'

'You are kind, Grace. But the world is not kind. My people, who I love, are not kind about certain things. We are warriors. We have suffered and so we have had to become warriors. A man who will not fight, what use is he to his people? That's what they think. But this is a problem for another day. Now tell me, did Will manage to find you?'

'Will? No. Is he all right?'

'Oh, Grace, I have bad news to share.'

'No!'

'Not that! He is well.'

'Thank God.'

'But he has been moved by the general to just outside Tours. They have so many soldiers and support laid up by this flu. So many dying.'

Grace felt a stab of fear. Talk of this fearful virus was on everyone's lips around the hospital and the fatality rate was apparently dreadful. Plenty of fit young men like Will were losing their lives to it every day. Was there no end to the threats to the person she had come to love?

'That's . . . ah, well. I'm glad they'll have him to help.'

'They are going to move you there too, after a while. There

are more drivers due to arrive here and your skills as a nurse, much as your skills as a driver are exemplary, might be more useful right now.'

'I am happy to devote whichever of my exemplary skills are required, Arup.'

'An exemplary attitude, young Grace.'

'That, too. Make use of it as you will.'

'That is actually the main reason I'm here. I was sent to find you. We have a job to do.'

63

La Mairie, Saint-Aignan-sur-Cher

At the makeshift hospital in the former town hall at Saint-Aignan-sur-Cher, just outside Tours, Dr David Lamerton could hardly squeeze between the men lying in rows on the floor. He had been hastily transferred there two weeks previously to deal with the catastrophic situation. There must have been 400 at least in this one room, and they kept arriving. He was beyond exhaustion himself, but like his fellow medics he knew he would simply continue to work until he dropped.

All around him, men were coughing uncontrollably, their faces often mottled by frothy flecks of blood-stained phlegm, their respiration laboured and shallow. Others demonstrated that characteristic death rattle that occurs when the body is too weak to clear the airways of the copious secretions filling their lungs and windpipe. Suddenly the doctor felt claustrophobic and faint, overwhelmed by the unimaginable situation in which he found himself. He could hardly breathe, because the air inside the hall was so fetid and stale. Stepping outside for a moment, he leaned against a stone pillar and took in a deep breath of fresh air. Then he took a packet of Woodbine cigarettes from his top pocket and lit one. Inhaling deeply, he watched as an RAMC truck pulled up in front of the hospital. Three nurses emerged from it, one very young and the other two probably in their late fifties. Behind them stood the bright athletic lad he'd encountered a few times before.

'We are looking for a Dr Lamerton,' Beatrice, the most senior of the nurses, said as they approached.

'That'll be me,' said the doctor, blowing smoke away to the side of him.

'We've been sent over from Héricourt. I hope you were expecting us?'

'I'm expecting people from all over the place, to be fair. And there still won't be enough of you.'

'What can we do to help?'

'What can anyone do to help?' he replied. 'It's like a scene from Hades in there. From the underworld itself. I hope you're battle-hardened. Because what you will see in there is not for the squeamish.'

The nurses didn't quite know how to respond to this, but the doctor continued anyway.

'I'll have your things delivered to your sleeping quarters but if it's all right with you I'll give you some urgent tasks straight away.'

'What about Will, here? He's a stretcher bearer and has been helping out as a surgical assistant.'

'I know this. I've seen him work. Go and introduce yourself to Pierre – you'll find him in the mess. You two can go round the camp and help bring in anyone else who is sick. There'll be plenty of them. Some can maybe get here on foot with a bit of support. Others will need your stretcher for sure.'

Will was looking past the doctor into the building, plainly uncertain as to where any more patients could possibly be placed. Every square foot of space seemed to be occupied.

'Ideally, you'd want to separate these men and keep them as far apart as possible. But they are all suffering from the same virus and since you can't get the same virus twice, or a bigger dose of it, I don't suppose it matters. What does matter is that we get as many of the sick patients away from the ones who currently remain healthy.'

As he spoke, fifty or so men in the uniforms of their country filed towards the building in groups of a dozen or more, some doing their best to hold their comrades upright, others shuffling along under their own steam but pausing every few seconds to catch their breath.

Will nodded and promptly set off as the doctor dropped his cigarette on the ground and stubbed it out with his boot.

'Follow me,' he said to the nurses, then turned and strode in through the door.

The scene they found inside was shocking. All the cots were occupied and between them other men lay on the floor, packed together like sardines. Even the corridors and ante-rooms had been taken up with sick soldiers. Outside, they had seen some of the men with more moderate symptoms sitting patiently, waiting to be assessed, but inside most of the victims were in a terrible state. Their faces were grey-blue in colour and tilted upwards, head back and chin up, as if to steal as much oxygen as possible from the atmosphere and assist their struggling respiratory muscles. Their eyes were sunken and focused imploringly at the ceiling. All of them were coughing relentlessly and bringing up blood-stained mucus which they had neither the strength nor coordination to spit out.

Dr Lamerton bent down towards a patient who had just been brought in and who was lying on a stretcher in front of him. Placing the back of his hand against the patient's burning forehead he looked up at the nun who had come to assist with the triage.

'One hundred and four degrees, Doctor,' she said.

The poor man's breathing was extremely rapid and shallow. The skin of his sallow, gaunt face had turned a grey colour. It stretched across his cheekbones and had the appearance of shiny granite. His parched lips were pulled back in a grimace, exposing a row of irregularly shaped teeth resembling tombstones. Dried blood was caked between them.

Placing his stethoscope squarely on the man's chest, first at the front, then at the sides, and at the bases of the lungs at the back, the doctor listened intently. As usual at this moment he recalled the wisdom of his first medical tutor from when he was a student: 'What', the tutor would ask, 'is the most important component of a stethoscope? Is it the diaphragm vibrating on the patient's chest? The tubing transmitting the sounds? The fit of the earpieces?' The question always left new medical students floundering. 'Idiots!' he would yell theatrically, when they inevitably failed to find the correct answer. 'The most important part of a stethoscope is the part between your ears! It's the brain's interpretation of the sounds you are hearing that is most important of all!'

Dr Lamerton wondered what the erudite professor would have made of the circumstances his student now found himself in.

With this auscultatory advice in mind, the doctor continued. The diagnosis in this case, however, did not require a great deal of time or consideration. Fulminating bilateral pneumonia was difficult to confuse with anything else. Air entry into the lungs was almost nil. The lung was solid with consolidation. There was the unmistakable crepitus caused by fluid at the lung bases and the only other discernible sounds were the rales and bubbles of collections of liquids in the throat.

This man was not long for this world, and would soon be joining the pile of corpses hidden from public view in the tent hastily erected to act as a morgue behind the hospital.

The condition of the soldier next in line was similar except that in addition to the respiratory symptoms he had patches of dark mahogany on the skin of his face and torso, the pathognomonic signs of blood poisoning. At this advanced stage, it was as irreversible and fatal as pneumonia.

Standing up again and looking about him, the doctor took in the hellish scene and spied two nurses who were being tended to by their colleagues. They were still wearing the masks with which they'd been supplied, but which were clearly not up to the job.

His medical and nursing staff were falling victim to this modern plague just as quickly as the enlisted men. He had seen men killed in battle; he had seen thousands of men die from typhus fever or cholera. Yet never had he seen a disease as virulent and swiftly transmitted as this one. Some victims who had been perfectly healthy the day before were dying in as little as eighteen hours.

David Lamerton took the three newly arrived nurses, Alice, Mary and Beatrice, over to a quieter corner of the hall.

'Now you see what we're dealing with,' he said in a hushed tone.

They looked at him for guidance, with hope and expectation. Surely this was the doctor who was to be the saviour of all these men and rescue them from the jaws of death? There was bound to be a treatment of some sort that would get them through the worst and tide them over for the next few days. These were strong, sturdy young men after all who had withstood everything a determined enemy could throw at them over the last four long years.

Yet the look on the doctor's face said otherwise. Never had they seen a senior medical man look so distressed and disturbed.

'There is a pattern going on here, which you cannot fail to notice. Around twenty per cent of the victims of this disease have mild symptoms and recover without complications within a few days. They are the lucky ones. The rest have one of two horrifying types of illness. Some quickly become deathly ill and are unable to get enough oxygen into their bodies because their lungs fill with fluid and they drown in their own secretions.'

He looked at the group to gauge their reaction.

'They usually die within days, and sometimes even hours – delirious, with a high temperature, crying out for breath and lapsing into unconsciousness.'

The nurses were hanging on his every word, stunned by the awful description of the evolution of the disease and increasingly apprehensive about the risks to which they themselves were inevitably about to be exposed.

'And for some reason, contrary to all precedents for influenza, anyone exposed to it earlier in the year and who seemingly recovered from it without complications seems very much more vulnerable to its lethal effects.'

'But usually wouldn't we expect them to have developed a greater resistance to it?' asked Alice.

'Exactly. It's a profound paradox and we don't understand why it's happening. It's as if whatever they experienced in the spring has magnified their reaction to whatever this infection is now many times over.' He continued, 'And for the other half of the eighty per cent that don't recover quickly, it begins as a typical flu with a dry hacking cough, fever, chills and rigors. There's the expected sore throat, swollen glands, hyper-sensitive skin and aching muscles. Within four or five days, however, bacteria swarm into their damaged lungs and they develop a pneumonia severe enough to either kill them or which will at best lead to an extended period of convalescence. The major-generals don't like that,' he added bitterly. 'They expect to see these men back in their dugouts as soon as possible.'

Nobody really knew what to say. Alice eventually broke the silence with a question. 'Do we have oxygen, at least?'

'Oxygen!' mocked the doctor. 'I'm afraid all of Dr John Haldane's limited storage containers for weak concentrations of oxygen have long been used up. You can thank the Germans and their love of chlorine gas for that. And our Mr Haldane is currently impressing Lord Kitchener with his newfangled box respirator. Reduces gas levels, I'm told, but stops men breathing. Might pose a problem.'

The doctor's pessimism and despair was tangible. This was a man who was near his limit and another awkward moment passed in silence.

Will arrived to join them. 'We've brought all those needing stretchers to the door.' Not noticing the mood, he asked what he could do further to help.

Taking the initiative, Beatrice suggested they establish a protocol, define each other's roles and set up a chain of command to best manage the efficient triage of the patients. They would also liaise with the hospital staff and nuns already working there. At the mention of the word 'nuns' the doctor took his cue.

'Just like the nuns, one of the most important things you can do is give the men hope. You can give them comfort.

361

They don't want to know they are dying. They want a caring, sympathetic face, especially a woman's face, a face and a soothing voice that reminds them of their mother. Helping them to drink and tepid-sponging their brow to reduce their fever is one thing. But solace and care when they are looking into the abyss is greater than any medicine. Besides, we don't seem to have any medicine that makes a difference.'

'That's part of what we do, Doctor,' offered Mary, the youngest nurse. 'And we will do it to the best of our ability.'

'I know you will,' he said, 'and I thank you for it.' Glimpsing a figure moving about a few yards away, he added, 'Just keep that priest the hell away from me, would you?'

'Doctor?'

'What these men need is gentleness and warmth. The nuns give this in abundance. But here's this bloody man talking to these patients as if they are already dead. Asking them to confess their sins and reading them the last rites so everyone else can hear. It's almost as if he's saying they're dying because they were evil men, because they defied God, because they were sinners. Say your prayers and He may give you a shot at redemption, he tells them. After all these brave men have done and sacrificed. He scares the hell out of them with his warped mumbo-jumbo and leaves most of them sobbing and frightened. In this entire building he's the last man I'd want to see if I was at death's door.'

Will looked across at the man dressed in the long black cassock kneeling beside a motionless soldier and whispering into his ear. Whatever his motivation and personal beliefs, thought Will, at least he was here, brave enough to expose himself to the pandemic and attempt to support his flock in his own way. Dr Lamerton could provide more immediate and practical assistance to his patients, that much was obvious, but the doctor had clearly lost his own faith long ago. It occurred to Will that a little of both was needed in a purgatory such as this.

As if able to read Will's mind the beleaguered doctor stared at the ground and continued as if talking entirely to himself. 'Almighty God, that man told me this morning, is omniscient, omnipresent and omnipotent. I think he likes the sound of that. So, where the hell is this all-knowing all-powerful deity now? He certainly isn't bloody well here, is he?'

He looked up again and scanned the scenes in front of him.

'What kind of cruel God could oversee such carnage on the battlefield, with the loss of so many good and honest men, and then throw in a devastating pandemic like this one for good measure?'

It was another rhetorical question to which the doctor neither expected nor received any answer.

Tactfully, Beatrice drew her little team aside and exhorted them to get down to business. There was much to take care of, not the least being – as was obvious now – the desperate moods and mental well-being of their colleagues.

64

The artillery onslaught from the Germans had steadily intensified in their area over the last few days, with a greater focus
on hitting the communication trenches and aiming for the
headquarters behind the front and reserve lines. There were
more and more casualties among non-combatants, and both
Grace and Arup were worried. The barrage seemed to creep
closer every day, to the point where they wondered out loud
if it might even reach the casualty clearing station. Certainly,
the advanced dressing station they were heading to in the
ambulance, located in the crypt of a ruined church, was well
within reach of the shells.

'You don't think—' Grace stopped herself.

'What? Say what is on your mind,' said Arup.

'You don't think there's any way they can still win, can
break through?'

'I don't know, Grace. I don't know. I know they must be
suffering the same as us. The Americans are here now for
us, but who will arrive for them? They might win one or
two more battles but I don't think they will win overall.'

As they talked, they heard the dull thud of the cannons
in the distance. The soldiers grew to learn the different
noises the shells made, and which they needed to worry
about, and she had begun to get her ear in too. There was
the thud; then, if it was coming your way, the whizzing as it
came closer; the screaming as it arrived; and the bang, the

last thing you might ever hear, or the last thing you might ever hear with all your limbs attached.

She could see the earth lifting where the frontline was, as the shells found their target and sailed past, dangerously close to where they were.

'Let's hurry, Arup,' she said, and they jumped out of the vehicle.

It was a brutal sight in the crypt. Men too wounded to prioritise treating, dead or dying, while the medical officers and stretcher bearers tended to those with the best chance of pulling through.

Grace and Arup got to work.

They had loaded four men into the ambulance, and were ready to go. They would have to move quick. One man had an abdominal wound. Another man had lost both legs. Another's leg was badly mangled, and Grace knew from experience that this would require an amputation. Another's jaw had been blown away, a horrible wound. Arup sat in the back with the men and did his best to reassure them, while Grace put her foot to the floor and set off.

They had not gone far when a shell crashed down to the right of Grace's windscreen. 'Everyone OK?' she shouted.

'Not exactly, Grace, but no new damage,' called Arup.

But he was mistaken, and Grace realised this as the front of the vehicle listed and bumped against the ground. 'The shrapnel's taken out the front-right tyre!'

'There's a spare, don't worry, I'll change it.'

'I'll help.' It was nothing she hadn't done before. But the shells were still arriving and it was going to be very dangerous.

'You get in the back and look after the men,' called Arup. 'No point both of us risking our necks out there.'

Shells continued to sail in, and another one burst nearby
with a loud bang. The infantryman who had lost both of his
legs screamed. Before Grace had time to object, Arup had
swung open the back doors of the ambulance and was out
there in the open.

65

Although they had only just arrived at Saint-Aignan-sur-Cher and were tired from the journey, the team of nurses sent from Héricourt worked a full 24-hour shift, doing all they humanly could to alleviate the suffering and pain. This continued for the following days and nights, with the nurses only pausing to grab some water or a bite to eat when they could. They slept fitfully and sometimes had to be restrained from further work when lack of rest threatened to interfere with the safety of what they were doing.

Within five days, Will and Alice both experienced mild flu-like symptoms but were able to continue working. The other two nurses developed moderately severe symptoms and had no choice but to be confined to their beds for the duration. Beatrice, the eldest, suffered most, losing a stone and a half in weight and experiencing severe fatigue and breathlessness for several weeks afterwards. Both bravely resumed their normal duties within three weeks, however, as their services were required more than ever.

By that time, it had dawned on Will exactly why he, along with his team of carefully selected nursing staff, had been chosen for this new role. A conversation with another one of the doctors confirmed his suspicions.

The medical corps had noticed that the death curves were W-shaped. Three separate age groups were more susceptible to this flu virus than others. There were peaks for babies and children under five, for the elderly aged over seventy and also for the soldiers aged predominantly between twenty and forty. If you plotted a graph, the doctor explained to Will, of the number of people dying against their ages, the shape of the graph would resemble the letter W. It was clear that Will and the nurses had been specifically recruited for this job in the hope that they would resist the infection themselves and therefore better be able to serve continuously.

How they missed Grace. How he missed her himself, he thought, as he waited for her arrival. She was so hard-working and dependable. He was always more confident and capable when she was around, but more than that, he wanted to talk to her and embrace her. This separation only made him more aware of his growing love for her. On the other hand, he felt very protective towards her. This was a dangerous situation, more so perhaps than working near the battlefields themselves. A frontline of a different but equally menacing nature. Perhaps it was better that she had not yet been sent here. The truth was, Will was totally conflicted and could not decide what it was best to hope for.

*

A couple of weeks after arriving at this little village near Tours, Will found himself sitting, exhausted, in the mess tent refuelling with a welcome dish of cassoulet the French Army cook had skilfully concocted. There, he was handed a letter from a signalman drafted in to deliver mail. The postmark on it was a fortnight old and it was almost a miracle that it had reached him at all.

'Half of America's got it now,' announced the signalman to anyone who would listen. In truth, it was difficult not to hear it as the man was on something of a personal mission, shouting at the top of his voice and enjoying the platform. 'Half a million dead, they reckon!'

Everyone in the mess stared gloomily at him. 'It's killing Jerries too,' he continued. 'It's in Spain, Russia, China; across cities and tiny villages and faraway islands.'

Oblivious to the depressing effect he was having on his captive audience, the man clumsily ploughed on. He was clearly relishing being the uninvited centre of attention. A burly sergeant sitting at a trestle table near Will cleared his throat and interrupted. He looked like he could quite happily throttle this idiot with his bare hands.

'Well, a Victoria Cross for diplomacy and tact for you, mate,' he said menacingly. 'Why don't you keep your stupid bloody trap shut, Private? Can't you see what's been happening here!'

The signalman looked crestfallen but had the sense to remain silent.

'You got any good news for us?' asked Will, easing the tension in the air and removing his letter from its envelope at the same time.

'Well, possibly. For you, anyway. Hopefully right there in that letter of yours from home.'

It seemed a desperate attempt to make up for his crass insensitivity.

Will's heart leapt, hoping it would be from Grace or from her father, responding to his request for her hand in marriage. He had written to her but not heard back from her in two weeks. Sometimes he wondered if she had heard back from her father directly, ordering her not to be in touch with him. It was one thing professing a belief in equality between the classes in the abstract; it was another when a young man with nothing was requesting the hand of your daughter. Will had been so busy he had not had much time to obsess about this, and perhaps his letter to her had gone missing, along with the address she would need to write to him.

Now he hoped for news to allay his fears. But it was not good news for Will at all. Far from it. Kitty, his beloved little sister whose eighth birthday he had just missed, was seriously ill at home with the Spanish flu.

66

Grace was in the back, trying to calm the men, who had no good reason to be calm, caught as they were in the range of German cannons with their horrific injuries.

'Nearly done,' called Arup. 'Done. Let's go!'

And then she heard it, the shrieking of a shell coming in close.

The ambulance shook and was pelted with shrapnel. It took her a while to hear again in the aftermath of the huge bang of the explosion. The men were groaning.

'Arup!' she called. 'Arup!'

She flung herself out of the door and ran to the side, horrified to find her good friend lying on the ground, blood staining the front of his uniform.

'Arup, no,' she moaned. 'You poor man.'

She knelt quickly and checked his pulse. His eyes were shut and blood was soaking through his turban, and his right leg was twisted at an impossible angle. But there was still life there. His eyes opened.

'Grace,' he said. 'You must go. You will die if you do not go now. We will all die.'

'I'm not leaving without you,' she said.

'I don't think I am going to pull through.'

'You are, don't say that.'

Another whizbang exploded on the far side of the field.

'Go,' he said. 'You have a duty to those men. Go now, before it's too late. The barrage is passing. Perhaps I will be

OK. But Grace, I think it might be my time, whatever happens. Please get out of here.' He looked deep into her eyes. 'Go. Be happy. Love Will. I have loved you both.'

Quickly, she leaned over and kissed him on his forehead.

'I'm coming back for you after I've got these men to safety,' she said.

'Goodbye, Grace.'

She leapt up and into the driver's seat.

She heard the shrieking of a new shell coming in and ducked her head as it exploded, a piece of hot metal taking a chunk out of the windscreen with it.

She hit the ignition, put her foot down and drove, trying not to think about Arup lying there in the middle of this, trying to will herself on and obey his wishes. She was nearly through the gate and onto the road that led away from the field. She was almost through the gate and she heard it coming in, the screaming that turned into a bang. It lifted up the ambulance and rolled it entirely over and then once again. As it rolled, she thought of Will and their poor friend Arup and Charles and her father and all the men she had seen die and helped live, and then the ambulance was still and she no longer thought of anything at all.

PART FIVE

REMEDY AND REPARATION

1918

67

Kitty had been ill for days now, and Jack couldn't bear it. Memories were coming back that he thought he had buried for good: of his father pacing around in the kitchen, of an old woman coming into the house, followed by a younger one, followed by a doctor, and then the news of his mother dying. He was in the kitchen, pacing — in spite of the pain in his hip — just as his father had done. And then there was his friend Trevor, too, lying in his bed at his home around the corner. So many people were getting ill.

He wished Will were here. Will was good at this stuff.

He climbed the stairs again to Kitty's room, where Aunt Clara was bent over her, holding her hand and stroking her forehead.

'Any change?' he asked.

'She's burning up,' said Clara. 'But don't worry, Kitty, don't worry.' She reached down for a wet cloth and pressed it to her forehead. 'Your aunt Clara's here.'

Jack backed away and out into the corridor. He was useless here. Useless. He wished, not for the first time, that he was back in France or Flanders. He had been so glad to get out of there, but there was little for him to do that was useful here, and he couldn't help feeling guilty when he thought of all the men dying there, while the newspapers in the streets reported on trivialities, or focused obsessively on the bombing that was killing a tiny fraction of the people who died on the front every hour of the day.

He found himself walking down to the river, his hip grating with every step, which was all right — he wanted to feel a bit of pain. He was back in his uniform now, and the men and women he walked past nodded to him, a recognition perhaps of the wound stripe he now wore across the left forearm of his jacket.

*

That got him thinking about Rhys. He had written to Rhys's wife, and got permission to take the train to Swansea to visit her. He'd set off early and arrived in the afternoon. Rhys's wife — Bethan — had answered the door with a toddler clinging to her, a boy with the same blue eyes as Rhys looking out at him, and it had shocked him, as though he'd seen a ghost.

'He looks like his da, doesn't he?' she said, noticing the way Jack was staring.

'He does,' said Jack, and then he followed her along into the parlour, where little Edwyn pushed a wooden horse along the floor while she made them both a cup of tea.

Once they'd sat down, he noticed how beautiful she was. She had blonde hair and green eyes; there was something ethereal about her, though she had a loud laugh that brought her back to earth. He was surprised at how much she laughed — though he didn't think that was because she was happy about Rhys. It was a laughter that was close to crying, a nervous laughter, the kind of laughter he knew from the trenches.

The toddler grew tired and Bethan put him to bed.

He told her what a great soldier Rhys was, what a great man, how he owed him his life.

'There, there,' she said. 'Now don't you get upset or I'll start crying too.'

'I'm not crying,' he said, sitting upright.

'I know you're not, Jack. You're in safe company here, anyway. I appreciate you coming.'

She smiled at him and he looked at her and wondered if she would welcome him making a move. She was a young woman and he was a young man, and why shouldn't people in pain comfort each other?

He talked more about Rhys while he let that thought marinate. He told her about all the things Rhys had taught him, how useless he'd been at first, how little he'd known about mining, or — he paused — about women.

'Rhys taught you about women!'

'No, no, don't get me wrong — he wouldn't touch another woman, when I — he warned me — oh, I better shut up before I get myself in trouble.'

She was smiling at him now and he thought, maybe, yes.

And then she told him about their courtship and their wedding day and he saw Rhys's blue eyes looking at him out of his son's head and he thought, definitely, no.

And he started to apologise, for being alive, how it would be better if he had taken the brunt of the blast, with no one to miss him, and she came over to him then and put her arm around him and he looked into her eyes and their lips moved closer and it was definitely—

Edwyn started to scream from another room.

'Wait there,' she said. 'I won't be long.'

But he left. Those blue eyes looking at him. And now he had all the guilt and none of the pleasure.

He found himself walking up towards the hospital where Will had once worked. Perhaps he'd see a doctor there who knew Will and be able to ask him what was best for Kitty. There must be some medicine for this illness, the Spanish flu, as they were calling it. It was just a matter of knowing what to do. The doctor they'd had around probably didn't know what he was doing. Jack wandered around the perimeter of the hospital and it struck him for the first time just how serious this influenza outbreak had become.

Looking through the windows, he could see rows upon rows of beds lined up in the centre of the wards and all along the walls. Everyone inside was wearing gowns and masks. Ambulances were arriving all the time, discharging new cases — many of whom looked half dead already. The rest were coughing, spluttering and wheezing and barely able to talk.

One of the porters who had come out to ferry another patient inside was filling in some forms and Jack took the opportunity to approach him.

'Where is your mask?' said the porter, taking a good step back.

'Who do you think I am? The Scarlet Pimpernel?'

The porter didn't laugh.

'Sorry,' said Jack. 'I didn't know I needed one.'

'Keep your distance and say your piece.'

'My brother Will Burnett used to work here. As one of you lot. Two or three years ago. You might remember him?'

'Will? Yes, I remember him. Good lad. What of him?'

'It's our sister, Kitty. She's only eight and she's got this fever really bad. Can't seem to shake it, and we're worried sick about her.'

'What's Will doing about it then?'

'Will's in France fighting Jerry and looking after flu patients there. I really need to speak to one of your doctors. Do you know any?'

'I know plenty but none what'll give me the time of day.'

Jack felt disheartened. If the doctors wouldn't speak to one of their regular porters there seemed little chance of them speaking to him.

'You might try and find Dr Forrester though. I often used to see him talking to Will and explaining stuff and he seemed to have a soft spot for him. We all thought your brother fancied himself as a bit of a surgeon in his own right, tell you the truth. Wouldn't let him near me with a scalpel, mind. Yes, Dr Forrester. If anyone's got time to talk to you it will be him. But tie something round your face if you go in there, all right?'

Jack, with a hanky tied around his face, asked one of the cleaners for directions to the doctors' quarters. She looked at him funny but pointed him in the right direction. Climbing two flights of stairs and turning left down a wide, straight corridor he came to a door with a plaque saying 'Medical Secretaries' above it. Without knocking, Jack stepped inside and found four middle-aged women sitting at their desks behind typewriters with stacks of papers in trays either side of them and medical records piled high against the back walls. All had masks on, and two additional desks were vacant. One of them was speaking to a well-dressed gentleman of about sixty who wore bifocal spectacles and a stethoscope around his neck.

'Excuse me,' said Jack. 'Sorry for the intrusion. I'm looking for a Dr Forrester.'

The four secretaries looked up at the older man in unison.

'I'm Dr Forrester,' he said, smiling at Jack's appearance. 'How can I help you?'

* * *

The doctor said he would be round in an hour. Jack started to head home but couldn't bear the thought of becoming his father again, sitting in that kitchen, waiting for news that could destroy their family all over again. And where was his father, anyway? They'd sent the news about Kitty to his last known post but had received no word in return.

Instead of heading home, Jack went to sit by the river. And he sat there and prayed to the God he didn't believe in.

*

'It's so good of you to come,' said Clara to Dr Forrester after he explained why he was there, and had gone up to see Kitty. 'You were unexpected, but I can't tell you how grateful we are.'

'The young gentleman you sent put up a good case for it, that's for sure,' said Dr Forrester. 'Very persuasive, he was.'

'Well I do hope he was polite, sir. He was only worried about his sister.'

'With good reason, madam. With good reason. But I didn't do it just for him. If I paid a house call to everyone sick with flu right now I'd be visiting every other house in London. No. I did this for Will. I was most impressed with that lad and have high hopes that one day he might be doing this himself.'

'I hope so, too. I think he has the brains.'

'I agree, and I suspect an excellent mentor in yourself. So, let's hope he returns from the war safe and sound for all our sakes.'

'How do you find Kitty?'

'She is feverish and dehydrated, which you'd expect. The throat is red raw and she has an ear infection. But the good news is that her chest shows little sign of pneumonia.'

'Is there anything I can do for her?'

'You've done all the right things already. You can continue to strip her off and tepid-sponge her. Encourage regular sips of water and anything sweet and energy-giving that she will tolerate. I shall leave you these salicylic acid tablets – give her one every four hours to ease her throat and reduce her fever. I'll also give you these masks that found their way into my pockets at the hospital. Wear them. This is a particularly nasty infection that spreads rapidly and can kill otherwise young, fit and healthy people within a matter of days or even hours. It's already accounted for 150,000 souls in the country and shows little sign of abating.'

'Goodness, Doctor. We hadn't realised it was as bad as all that.'

'We haven't seen anything like it since the Middle Ages. Your nephew is fighting a war in France against a familiar enemy and we are fighting a different kind of war against an invisible one right here. We're going to need all our strength and resilience to overcome them both.'

Clara let him back down the narrow staircase and to the front door.

'I can't thank you enough, Dr Forrester. I'll be sure to tell Will.'

'You just tell him to look me up when he gets back. He's one of the keenest young men I've met.'

'Thank you again, Doctor.'

Dr Forrester smiled and adjusted his hat as he turned to leave. 'Don't worry too much about Kitty. She's an adorable wee creature. Unless I'm very much mistaken, she's over the worst and should make a full recovery.'

It was late when Jack got back to the house. He crept in through the front door, terrified he would find Clara sitting in the kitchen, looking at him with the worst news written on her face.

When he couldn't find her downstairs he climbed the stairs, slowly, heading towards the light coming from under Kitty's door.

He steeled himself, breathed in, and opened the door.

Clara, still by Kitty's bed, was supporting the girl's back while she sat up and took a sip of soup.

'Jack,' Kitty croaked.

'Don't tire yourself,' said Clara, glaring at Jack, a glare that couldn't help turn into a smile. 'You've got to keep your strength up to get better.'

Jack was over by the bed now and hugged them both in turn.

'You're getting better,' he said. 'Thank God. You're getting better.'

68

Écurie

Corporal Robbie Burnett was lying at the centre of the woods on the ground, waiting to die. The trees around him had been blasted into matchsticks. A German officer with a revolver was making his rounds of the other injured men from his battalion, shooting them in the head one by one. Which was all Smith's fault: hit in the thigh, but still feeling he had to aim his rifle and fire off pot shots. You couldn't blame the Germans for protecting themselves from sniping. You couldn't blame the young lads for losing their heads.

Still, Robbie was up for keeping his for a little bit longer, and he kept his eyes shut and stayed as still as he could, while blood ran into his eye from a cut in his forehead. That, he knew, was the least of his wounds. He had felt himself punched hard in the back when the shrapnel hit him, and there was a sharp pain in his chest, and he was finding it difficult to breathe.

It wasn't going to work. He opened his eyes and saw the German shoot Brown in the head. Brown had been dead for hours now. No, there was nothing for it. He reached down for his revolver.

'Halt!'

Not bloody likely. He lifted his revolver and tried to take

aim. The German did the same and they fired at the same time. Robbie felt a searing pain in the hand that wasn't holding the gun. He had missed the German completely, who paused for a second to look down at himself to make sure he hadn't been shot.

The German stepped forward quickly, taking Robbie by surprise. He had his revolver aimed squarely on Robbie. He pressed the trigger.

Nothing. He'd run out of bullets.

Robbie lifted his own revolver, which felt incredibly heavy, and he shot the German in the face.

He lay there for a long time, sometimes conscious, sometimes not. He thought of Will and Jack and Kitty. He thought of his wife. He wanted to know how they were. He wanted to talk to them.

And then he was on a stretcher in the back of a car, screaming as it went over the bumps in the road.

'Don't worry, we're nearly out of the rocky bit; it'll get easier,' called the young man who was driving the ambulance. Was he dreaming? Was he in heaven?

He was not in heaven. He was in agony. He looked up and, as he breathed, a small bubble of blood rose and fell against a hole on his chest.

His hand was pulsing. He seemed to have lost the tips of two of his fingers. They stung like hell.

My God, he was alive. He was still alive. But for how long? He tried to ask if he was dying but the ambulance was loud and he didn't have the energy and after a while he just closed his eyes and drifted away.

69

Héricourt

Will was becoming seriously worried about Grace, who now hadn't replied to three of his letters. He consoled himself by thinking that if anything had happened to her, Arup would have let him know.

At least he wasn't worried about Kitty anymore. Aunt Clara — and Jack! — had written to let him know about her recovery from the illness that they had feared would claim her life. Sadly, their mutual friend Trevor had not been so lucky. Already painfully thin, weak and malnourished as a result of his abdominal injuries, he had not found the strength to fight off the virus. He had died at home and alone at the same time Kitty was recovering. It had hit Jack hard. He was on his way back to France now, too, his medical board having deemed him sufficiently recovered for active service.

The work in the hospital kept him from thinking about Grace until his short breaks, or in those hours before he fell asleep, or when he woke up first thing in the morning, or in one of those fleeting moments in which no one was calling his name or looking like they needed him urgently.

Then, one morning, another letter arrived, short and to the point.

Dear Will,

I have to break some terrible news to you. Grace and Arup were badly injured by a shell hitting the ambulance. Arup didn't pull through. I'm so sorry to tell you this. Grace is alive — thank God, though she has a serious abdominal injury, and is rarely conscious. She is at the casualty clearing station behind Héricourt. You must go and see her if you can. It would be good for her to remember she has a very good reason to live.

Yours sincerely,

Jenny

Will found Dr Lamerton where he usually was, on his rounds between the hospital beds, wearing a mask and gown.

'Sir,' said Will. 'I hate to ask, but I must. I need to take a trip to the casualty clearing station in Héricourt immediately.'

'Whatever for? Absolutely not. You're needed here.'

'Please, sir. I'm worried sick. I can't think straight. It'll only be for a few days.'

Dr Lamerton looked up at him. 'What on earth's wrong?' he said, softening. 'What's happened?'

'Grace, sir. The nurse we were expecting to join us. She's been injured, sir. We were to be married, sir. I was waiting to hear from her fath—'

'For God's sake, go. You'll be no use to us here anyway. Go and come back as quickly as you can. You're a responsible lad and I know you will. You work as hard as anyone. Go and do what you need to, but promise me this.'

'What, sir?'

'Whatever happens to her — and if there is a God, let's hope he's ready to reveal himself — promise me you'll come straight back here and continue to work hard to keep these patients alive.'

'I promise, sir,' Will said. 'I promise with all my heart.'

Will found a lift with an ambulance that was heading there. The driver, an old Yorkshireman, tried to make conversation, but Will could barely respond. He was imagining the moment when Arup had died and Grace had been so badly injured – had it happened simultaneously? Had Grace watched their good friend die? What had happened to the patients they were carrying? Multiple possibilities played through his head, all of them vivid and real and tormenting.

'Try to think of the better outcomes,' said the driver.

'I'm trying,' said Will, tight-lipped.

'She sounds like a strong girl,' he said.

'She is,' said Will. 'She really is.'

She is. That present tense momentarily had the power to calm him. She is, she is, she is. He repeated it like a prayer as the ambulance made its painfully slow way towards her.

*

The sister led him to her bed. 'You got here just in time. We're moving her to the hospital at Le Tréport very soon.'

'Is she all right?' he asked.

'She's ah, well . . . here she is.'

She was so pale that Will almost didn't recognise her. Her eyes were closed and she was breathing shallowly. She had an intravenous drip in her left arm and there was a big sign above her bed saying 'Nil by Mouth'. Her blanket was pulled down to just below a swathe of gauze and cotton wool dressings wrapped around her midriff. A flexible rubber drain emerged from them, dripping pinkish fluid into a glass bottle attached to the side of her bed. Omelette lay purring at her feet.

'Is she going to . . .?' he said, turning to the nurse.

'Going to what?' came a weak voice behind him. 'What do you need me to do now? Can't I have a little rest?'

He turned to see Grace's eyes, half-closed and moistening, looking at him.

'Be careful,' said the nurse, as Will stepped forward, but she didn't need to warn him. Will knew the right care to take around the injured, and though he'd had the Spanish flu in mild form he did not know for certain he wasn't carrying the virus with him now. He stopped himself from his impulse to leap on top of her and shower her with kisses.

Instead, he kept his distance and smiled.

'You're here,' she said.

'You can have all the rest you need,' said Will. 'I'm here.'

'Can you stay?'

'For a little bit,' he said.

'Just a little bit?'

'I'm due back in a few days.'

'Good,' she said. 'They need you. Especially with me out of action. Will,' she said, 'I've something terrible to tell you. Poor Arup—'

'Shhh,' said Will. 'I know. Now's not the time. You're here and you're alive and you have to rest to get better.'

He stayed there for the next sixteen hours, looking at her from the same distance, wishing he was holding her hand. He watched her sleep and watched her wake, and was there for her to see whenever she opened her eyes.

*

Several days later, when Grace woke, Will was sitting there beside her and looking at her anxiously. Her eyes flickered open and his handsome face slowly came into focus.

'Will?'

'How are you feeling? You've slept on and off for days.'

'Let me see.' Her forehead creased into a frown. 'Not too bad. My head has stopped throbbing and my tummy doesn't feel like it's been ripped open by a scythe anymore. So, better, I think.'

'I'm glad to hear it. Your fever has settled and you've stopped crying out in your sleep. Your colour is improved as well.'

She turned to Will and tears sprang from her eyes. 'I couldn't save Arup, Will. I'm so sorry.'

'You did your best. You couldn't have done more. What happened?'

'There was a huge explosion under the ambulance which lifted it off the ground and turned it over. That's how I got hurt. Arup got hit when he was fixing a tyre from a previous blast. He didn't stand a chance. When I got to him, he was already nearly gone. He was suffering horrendous blood loss. He held my hand, Will, and looked at me. He knew he was dying and was so calm. He smiled, can you believe it? He smiled and said, Don't worry. He said that to me. Don't worry about me, he said, his God would look after him.'

Grace sobbed then, and winced because of the movement around her wound.

Will dried his own eyes. 'He was a very special man, Grace. A brave and fearless soldier of God. And a true friend. We shall never forget him.'

'I wish I could've done more, Will. I keep going over it. Maybe if I'd driven faster or taken a different route. Maybe if I'd waited until dark to be less of a target. Maybe those men in the back would still be alive if—'

'Grace, it wasn't your fault. If you had delayed leaving, those men in the back would've died anyway. You know that. Every minute that passes before they get to the hospital lowers their chances of survival. Arup was beyond help. And you yourself were badly hurt.'

'I wanted to bring him back with me, Will. To give him a decent burial and a service of some kind. He is so far from his country, his family and his unit. It seems so barbaric.'

'He was with his most recent family, Grace. You were there in person. I was there in spirit. He would have known that.' Will held Grace's hand more tightly and stroked the back of it with his thumb. 'How is your tummy?'

'The doctor removed a piece of metal and said I needed a bit of patching up. I don't remember much about it after the gauze and ether over my mouth but when I came around he said he thought I'd be proud of his sewing. Said it wasn't too bad for a man's handiwork.'

The doctor had given her some other news too, but she wasn't ready to share this with Will.

He had been brusque when he told her, perhaps thinking that on the scale of things this was a very minor issue. 'Impossible to say whether the ovary and fallopian tube on that side will ever work properly again.'

'Doctor, what?'

'You see, it's bruised and contused from the metal shard that pierced your lower stomach. I don't know; it might recover, it might not. You're very lucky anyway, you know. Lucky to be alive!'

'Yes,' she said meekly.

She was lucky, she knew. But the thought of not being able

to bear a child sent her into a tailspin. She was already dreaming of a family with Will, a man who would make such a caring and strong father. It would be criminal if he didn't get to become one. Which meant . . . she might have to give him up. He would stick by her, but— It would not be fair. She would have to give him up if the worst turned out to be true.

'When will I know, Doctor?' she asked.

'When you start, um, well, trying for a baby. You're not married, are you?'

'I'm not, no.'

'Well, quite some time, then.'

If Grace hadn't been so worried, she might have smiled to herself at that. 'But I can't get married to someone without knowing — it wouldn't be fair.'

'Young woman — there is little that is fair in this world, but you are a fine, decent, hard-working woman, and if you offer yourself honestly to someone, you do not need to worry about fairness.'

*

So, she vowed to be honest the next time Will came. But when she opened her eyes again and saw him sitting on the stool beside her, she noticed he looked world-weary and defeated. It was not really like him. His eyes were puffy and the lids red and sore-looking.

'Will?' she said. 'Are you all right?'

'I'm OK. You're the patient.'

She frowned. 'I know you better than that. Something's wrong.'

He sighed deeply. 'It's my father, Grace. He's been killed.'

Grace sat up, wincing with the pain, and put her arm around Will's shoulder. She was shocked and sorry for him.

'I'm so, so sorry, my love. When? How did you find out?'

'A letter from Clara. Last night. Died of wounds, she said. Don't know when or where. He was picked up with injuries and died in an advance dressing station.'

'Oh Will. Oh no.'

'It's . . . Perhaps it's for the best. I hate to say that, but . . . he hadn't been happy for a long time.'

Grace pulled him towards her and rested her head against his.

'He was lost, you see, when my mother died. After that, he was never the same man.'

Grace looked at him.

'Couldn't get over it. He was broken. There were times, when I was little, when I wondered why he was no longer the fun-loving, doting father he once was. I resented it. Felt angry. But now, with you in my life, Grace, I can understand it all properly for the first time. I really couldn't face living my life without you, you know . . .'

Grace immediately wanted to say, 'You won't have to.' But in view of what she needed to tell him, she held back.

'I loved him, Grace, but I lost him. I lost him a long time ago. Now, it's final.'

'He would never have stopped loving you. It's just that he couldn't show it. You'll be OK?'

'I don't know. This war makes you so hard. So numb. I don't feel much of anything except when I'm with you.' He pressed her hand.

Grace sighed now. 'I wish I didn't have to add more bad news, Will, but I do. The doctor, I didn't know how to tell you. He said . . . He said that I might never be able to bear children. The pelvic area was quite badly damaged on that side and he said it was only fair to warn me.'

'I know,' he said.

'You know?'

'Of course I know. I talk to the doctor all the time about you.'

'But—'

Will managed a small smile. 'You should be optimistic. You're young and they don't know for sure that you can't conceive.'

'Why didn't you bring it up?'

'You didn't mention it. I wasn't sure I was supposed to know. It felt, I don't know, like something you should talk about if you wanted to.'

'But Will — I was hoping . . . I know we've talked about the possibility of a life together, when all this ends. I can't expect you to marry me now that I'm scarred and barren and can never give you what it's your right to expect. I will completely understand if you want to reconsider.'

'Grace,' said Will. 'The only important thing is that you get better. We don't even know if we'll survive this war, for goodness' sake. Jerry has got a thousand different ways of trying to kill us, and if he doesn't manage it this wretched Spanish flu might do it for him. So we live for today. And we do it together. We've been through so much already, we can get through this.'

'But look at me,' she said, 'all pale and beaten up and unlovely.'

'Are you kidding?' said Will. 'I've never seen such a gorgeous-looking patient in my life.'

'Really? I hope that's ethical. But it's nice to hear anyway.'

She smiled at him and sent him an air kiss.

'Nature is a great healer. No one can know for sure whether you might conceive in the future or not. I know enough to know you've got two ovaries and two fallopian tubes, right? One is damaged but God designed you with a spare. One's all you need.'

Grace eyed him hopefully, and then she felt guilty for talking about her problems when he had just received such devastating news.

'Oh, Will, I love you. But your poor father. Your family. You poor thing.'

'We'll figure it out,' he said, squeezing her hand tightly again. 'I love you, too. And that makes me very fortunate.'

70

Le Tréport

The Spanish flu pandemic still raged in parts of Europe but mercifully it had marched onwards and away from Saint-Aignan and surrounding areas. There were many men still bed-bound in the hospital, but the virus appeared to be losing its virulence and these men were not quite as ill. A large cohort of relief nurses and doctors had also arrived from England to take over their care. Dr Lamerton had been transferred to a hospital near Amiens and Will had been granted some well-earned leave before being expected to return to the front. He felt blessed that he'd had only had a mild episode of flu, and that was several weeks ago. He was confident now there was no chance of him passing it on to anyone else.

He had been waiting patiently now outside the postal services depot near the quayside at Le Tréport for an hour. He had seen the beaten-up yellow Citroen van pull up at the back and discharge its boxes, but the disgruntled-looking officer had refused to open the front door. It was the third day in a row Will had been pestering him. It was still only six a.m. and the chill mist coming off the sea made him shiver. At least Grace was doing well since she had been transferred to the General Hospital and was recovering at a fast rate from her injury. He thanked God that she had survived and that now, two weeks on, she was sitting up in bed and putting on a cheerful face again.

He could not contemplate the war taking anyone else he loved away from him. Life without Grace would be unimaginable. Already he had lost Arup, his dear friend, in the same tragedy. He could not begin to think of the loss of his father, or Captain Daniels — or even of Charles, Grace's brother, though he had never met him. Nor could he dwell on the countless others he had befriended, worked alongside, and even owed his life to, now long gone and buried randomly somewhere in the battlegrounds of Flanders.

So what if she couldn't have children. It made no difference to him. It was Grace he loved, not some ephemeral dream of a family that might or might not come true.

The door in front of him finally swung open.

'Is this what you've been darkening my doorstep for these last three days?' growled the postmaster.

'Thank you. Thank you,' said Will, eagerly grabbing the brown envelope and large cardboard box from his spade-like hands.

He tore open the envelope and scrutinised the pages inside. There were two smaller envelopes within, a pink one with a bright red ribbon and a blue one addressed to Will. He peeled it open.

Dear Will

    It will be evident from the bulk of this delivery that I have granted you the permission you seek to ask for my daughter's hand in marriage. I would have sent you this weeks ago, but your subsequent letter arrived informing us of her injuries, which overtook all other consideration, and after that came your letters informing us of her progress through recuperation. All of which we are very grateful for. But now we should return to the main subject which you raised again in your last letter.

Whether she offers you her hand is another matter, of course! Pleasantries aside, I have no hesitation whatsoever in agreeing and Dorothy is just as thrilled and excited as I am. Having got to know you and having witnessed the devotion and love you afford to our daughter we know that you will love and look after her as any doting husband should. Furthermore, we are immensely proud of all you do in the course of your dangerous but vital work and you fool us not a jot in downplaying in your letters the risks and hazards that both of you face on a daily basis. We will be proud to welcome you into our family and we look forward with pleasure to uniting with yours. All is well here, although of course we miss you both terribly. Please find enclosed the items you requested. Dorothy was over the moon to be able to furnish you with the contents of the box and we wait with eager anticipation the evidence of the results.

Good luck with everything, stay safe and Godspeed for your safe return together in due course.

Yours affectionately,
Your future father-in-law,
Arthur

Will sealed the large envelope again, then used his thumb to prise open the lid of the box so he could peer inside. Looking up, he grinned from ear to ear, and with the two items under his arm he hurtled off towards the Trianon Hotel where the General Hospital Number 3 resided.

*

Grace was feeling better with every passing day. Her tummy was less painful, even when she moved from lying to sitting and back again, the gaping wound was already shallower and smaller, the drain bottle was dry and all her bodily functions were working. Even her undulating fever seemed to have permanently disappeared. The doctors and her fellow nurses had been wonderful, not just in putting her back together physically but keeping up her morale and never letting her believe for a moment that the outcome would be anything other than entirely satisfactory. They could never have guaranteed that, of course. She knew that. But their constant support and encouragement had been a major contribution in her recovery.

As she glanced around her room, she could not help thinking that things were looking up. She was on the mend and, not only that, she was lucky enough to be convalescing in what was normally a sea-facing deluxe room in a four-star holiday hotel.

The view over the Channel was spectacular, with all the fishing boats and merchant vessels ploughing across it this way and that, and from her bed she could also watch the rising sun in the morning and the to-ing and fro-ings of the townsfolk as they made their way around the harbour and the pretty little town. And it was all courtesy of the military and entirely free of charge. What more could a girl ask for? She looked down at the little beach by the harbour where fishermen were mending their nets and children were playing. The tide had receded and the children were slipping and sliding over the seaweed and barnacles that adorned the rocks.

The tide of the war seemed to have turned definitively, too. The great German offensive, beginning in March against the British, had been thwarted after four more last-ditch onslaughts and now the Allies were driving forward and German soldiers were surrendering in large numbers. What a price they had paid for it, she reflected.

When she thought of all those poor people she had seen, injured and dying, she could hardly feel sorry for herself lying here in this spectacular place.

Her reverie was interrupted by a smiling matron-in-chief.

'There is a young man here to see you, Grace. Terribly ugly. Unwashed. Dishevelled. Ill-spoken and very forward. You might like me to send him packing.'

Grace laughed. 'That sounds like Will,' she said, laughing gently but not so much that it would greatly contract her abdominal muscles. 'It's all right. I'll take pity on him. You can send him in.'

Will came in – rather sheepishly, she thought – and took a perch on the side of her bed. He had a box under one arm and an envelope in the other hand. 'Hello, Grace. How are you today?'

'Better for seeing you, Will.'

He leaned forward and kissed her. The matron behind him pretended to plump up the cushions on the chair in the corner.

'What's in the envelope?'

'Oh that. We'll come to that in a minute. I just wanted to ask you something.'

'Fire away.'

'Fire away?'

'Oh sorry, I probably shouldn't say that. There's been rather too much firing lately. What do you want to know?'

'I want to know, Grace, I want to know whether you will marry me?'

Grace opened her eyes wide and brought her face closer to Will's. 'Ow!' she cried wincing and holding her stomach. 'I beg your pardon?'

'I want to know whether you'll marry me?'

She smiled broadly at him and took his face in her hands as she had so often done before. 'Of course I will! I thought you'd never ask. It's about time you made a decent woman of me.'

She kissed him on the lips again and again.

'Well, don't mind me,' said Matron, feigning embarrassment. 'However, I do agree that yes is the right answer in the circumstances.'

Grace and Will stared at each other, scarcely able to believe what was happening and oblivious to everything else around them.

'It's a magical idea,' said Grace, 'but when will we ever get around to tying the knot? We are miles from home. I'm laid up in hospital and there's a war on. Besides, there are protocols and traditional niceties that need to be observed.'

'Quite right,' interjected the matron. 'It's a lovely proposal you've made there, young man, but it's not just about the two of you being united by the vows of marriage. You're bringing together two entire families and they will need to be involved. Not forgetting the customary authorisations.'

'Authorisations?' asked Grace.

'Of course.'

'What authorisations?'

'Well, your father's permission to start with, Grace. Imagine his and your mother's reaction if you just got married without them knowing. Eloping, if you will.'

'I'm sure they'd grant it,' Grace said.

'You also need to ask your commanding officer, young man. Don't you realise you need official permission to get married when on leave?'

'Do you?' asked Will, sounding surprised.

'Yes. You do. You also need all your documents authenticating your identity. And confirmed by your superior officer.'

Grace looked a little crestfallen and bowed her head.

'Damn! I wish I'd thought it all through first,' said Will sadly. Then he smiled. 'Luckily, I did.'

Grace looked up sharply.

'Take a look in the envelope.'

Grace pulled out several official-looking papers and a little pink envelope tied up with a ribbon.

'My birth certificate. Your birth certificate. And copies of Mother's and Father's as well. An Army-enlisted number and a note from Major Preston, the CO of your unit. And your passport.'

Will's passport, like all the others first issued in 1915, was just a simple piece of paper with a photograph and signature folded between two cardboard covers. Grace looked up and beckoned him over with outstretched arms for a kiss, an invitation he duly accepted. Then she opened the smaller pink envelope with the ribbon. She read it carefully, placed it on the blanket in front of her and sobbed with joy.

'From Mother and Father, giving us their blessing. Oh Will, how did you manage to engineer that?'

'I couldn't get over there just now, so I wrote to them. I explained how I felt and how I think you felt and asked them for permission to have your hand in marriage.'

'And they said yes. But they also wonder if I might want to wait until the war is over and someone more suitable turns up.'

Will looked horrified.

'They said that?'

'Of course they didn't, silly! I'm not going to embarrass you with all the nice things they said about you.'

The matron giggled. They had almost forgotten she was still in the room.

'I've got time.'

'I haven't! But while this is all so lovely, Will, we'll have to wait anyway. Who knows when we'll get home?'

'We can get married right here. Only if you want to, that is.'

'Here in France, you mean?'

'Here in Le Tréport. Here in this hospital. Well, just across the courtyard to be precise. In the Chapel of Sainte-Mère Église.'

Grace was dumbstruck but curious. 'When?'

'On Saturday at noon,' piped up the matron, suddenly smiling. 'I'm sorry to collude against you and pretend I was surprised by all this. It's all booked. It seems Will here has pulled a few strings.'

'How long have you known about this, Matron?'

'Oh, just a couple of days. Everyone is thrilled. It's been difficult keeping it a secret.'

Grace burst out laughing but immediately regretted it as a twinge of pain swept across her tummy. 'There still one little problem,' she said, looking at Will.

'Which is?'

'My passport. Obviously, I couldn't bring it with me. I was in no fit state. It's still lying in a holdall by my bunk bed at Héricourt.'

'Actually, it isn't,' said Will. 'I believe it will currently be halfway between there and here, safely tucked away inside Jenny Jenks's tunic.'

'She's on her way here?'

'Well, you're going to need a bridesmaid, aren't you? Who else?'

Grace started to cry tears of joy again. Then she had a sudden thought. 'But what will I wear? I've nothing but my ripped and blood-stained nurse's gown and these hospital pyjamas. I've hardly time to go shopping.'

'Just as well someone's done that for you then,' said Matron.

Grace shot her a puzzled glance.

'Look in the box,' said Will, handing it to her.

Gingerly, she opened the flaps of the box.

'Oh, my word!' she said taking out the traditional white bridal gown and stroking its silky texture. 'It's beautiful.'

'I'm sure you wouldn't expect anything else from your mother, would you? She told me it was her own wedding dress and that it should fit you perfectly.'

'That makes it even more special,' said Matron, flushed with happiness for both of them. After all, she had seen more than one patient die from wounds such as Grace's, when they had become chronically infected. 'I'll leave you two lovebirds alone now to spend some time together.'

'Thank you, Matron. I can't believe how lucky I am and how lovely you have all been.'

'You just concentrate on getting better. You're not out of the woods quite yet.' The matron turned and went to the door. 'Oh, and, by the way, congratulations.'

*

They stood together at the front of the little chapel with Jenny on Grace's left and the stand-in best man from the Black Watch regiment, who had been rapidly dragooned for the role, on Will's right.

The Royal Highlander, who had had his kneecap shot away at Passchendaele, had been languishing in the hospital corridor flirting with the nurses when Will had strolled along and asked for his assistance.

Standing there ramrod straight in his green tartan kilt and black headdress with its star of the Order of the Thistle emblazoned on the front he was clearly determined to play the part to the best of his ability. Prior to reaching the altar before the arrival of the bride, he had already checked and rechecked that the wedding ring was safely nestled in the bottom of his sporran, and he had surreptitiously removed the only other item within it – a treasured whisky flask – and shared some of its contents with the groom for Dutch courage.

When Grace had arrived and walked up the aisle, with Jenny beside her, the sight had taken Will's breath away.

The bodice of the beautiful white silk charmeuse dress accentuated Grace's slim waist and the full skirt flowed to the ground. The back of the gown was embellished with buttons to the waist and, further down, appliqués of butter-flies and birds in cream embroidery continued through to the train, which elegantly cascaded downwards and swept along the floor as Grace approached.

Grace herself had shed a little tear when she first put it on as when it was in the box she had not noticed the bird appliqués expertly stitched to the back. She had immediately thought of Charles. If he was to come back to this world as another creature it would be as a bird, he had often said to her. So, this, she told herself was no mere coincidence. Her parents might not be able to be here, but at least her brother was here in spirit.

The front of the dress, although plain, had a gentle sweet-heart neckline and long sleeves which flared at the wrist.

The simple net veil came down in front of Grace's face and dropped to the line of her bust. It was held at the crown of her head with a gold clasp comb and fell at the back in gentle sweeps, tapering to the same extent as the train itself.

On her feet she wore a pair of dainty cream-coloured Victorian ankle boots on a one-inch heel with lace at the sides and a generous bow at the top.

She looked like an angel, Will thought. A far cry from the tomboy she was forever describing herself as.

Will, for his part, looked smart and chipper in his recently pressed uniform, with his shoes brightly polished and his cap tucked neatly under his arm. He'd even had a tidy haircut, finished off with liberal quantities of some sort of pomade. The pair of them made a very handsome couple indeed.

The chaplain, Theodore Williams, had happily agreed to conduct the service. It was a pleasant change from ministering to the bitter complaints of recently crippled soldiers or to reading the last rites to those who would never reach home soil again. A vicar, formally from a quiet rural parish in Sturton by Stow, he was now a temporary chaplain, fourth class, in the 8th Battalion of the Lincolnshire Regiment. How he missed the traditional peaceful services of Sunday sermons; and the births, marriages and funerals which paid testament to the natural order of things and the omnipresent will of the Lord our God.

They were coming to the end of the ceremony now and Grace was finishing the last few words of her vows.

'From this day forward, for better or worse, for richer, for poorer, in sickness and in health, to love and to cherish, until death us do part.'

At that particular moment, nobody in the chapel could fail to miss the significance of those last five words. Every person there – the nurses, the soldier from the Black Watch, Will and Grace themselves and even the chaplain, who had and would again serve his time on the frontline – was fully aware that death could part them from each other at any given moment and in the blink of an eye.

'I now pronounce you man and wife,' Theodore Williams solemnly said before adding, with a warm smile, 'You may now kiss the bride.'

Will and Grace needed no second invitation and, much to the delight of the few nurses and other witnesses gathered there, Will lifted her veil, kissed her, picked her up and carried her down the aisle and out of the chapel as Jenny's confetti rained down over their heads.

Once outside, an accordionist requisitioned from a nearby café started up with a local tune at the same time as a photographer that Will had also arranged fired off a few snaps.

Grace looked down at the wonderful ring on the fourth finger of her left hand as it glinted in the sunlight of that bright autumn day and hugged Will ever more tightly. Until he had slipped it over her finger, she had not seen it before.

It boasted a bodacious and sparkling 0.35 carat diamond solitaire set in a floral cluster on top of a subtly ornate gold band. And it fitted perfectly.

'How on earth could you afford anything like this? It's so very beautiful,' Grace said.

'I had help, I must confess. I didn't ask for it. But I got it anyway.'

'What kind of help? I am intrigued.'

'Let's just say that I may be in your parents' debt for quite a few months after the war is over.'

'Oh, Will,' she said, laughing. 'What else could you possibly have arranged without me knowing?'

'Well, a honeymoon, for starters, if that's all right with you?'

'A honeymoon as well? I don't believe it!'

'I've got five more days of leave but you still have to come back here to have a fresh new dressing for your wound every day. So, we're not going far.'

'I am still grievously wounded, you know, and you'll have to be gentle with me.'

'I promise, Mrs Grace Burnett, to be the perfect gentleman.'

'I don't care about all that. Just be the perfect gentle man.'

'Oh, I will. But I think you're going to love our secluded little farmhouse on the clifftop overlooking the sea.'

'*Mais oui. Ça me fait beaucoup de plaisir!*'

'I couldn't agree more,' he said, without any idea whatsoever what it meant. He kissed her again.

71

We're winning.

Will didn't like to let this thought command too much of his attention, but it was infectious.

We're winning.

We're winning the war!

It was November and he was back at the front again, a married man, and every day he still saw awful casualties, but not slaughter on the scale he had seen — not on their side. The Germans seemed to have run out of steam. The Americans were here in increasing numbers, and the BEF had amassed a frightening amount of artillery guns and developed increasingly sophisticated ways of using them to punch through the depleted German forces and protect the Allied infantry who would follow up behind.

'Protect' meaning to limit the number of casualties rather than what 'protect' might mean in civilian life, of course. Shells still whistled through the air from all directions, and someone was usually just as at risk from the one that wasn't aimed accurately as the one that was.

He was treating increasing numbers of Germans as more and more surrendered as prisoners, and several of them were put to work as stretcher bearers alongside him. Will saw how nervous they were and tried to reassure them. Then he felt guilty: what if one of these men had fired the shells that killed Arup and wounded Grace? But, he thought, they were doing as they were ordered, same as the Tommies. As long as they could carry a body on a stretcher and go straight back for another afterwards, they were all right with Will. He would see to it that they worked as hard as everyone else, and if they did they would be treated kindly — by him, at least.

Now the end was in sight, the boys were getting jittery. How awful it would be to be killed just when it looked like Blighty was back in sight. Time passed slowly, and the guns kept firing in the distance.

Grace was well enough now to help out in the hospital at Le Tréport where she had recovered, and Will was hoping to get back there soon.

*

Grace was up and had started walking around the wards, looking for ways she could help out. One day she encountered a soldier lying at the end of a bay of several other battered-looking men. There was something familiar about him.

She stopped and looked closer.

He was lying back, staring at the ceiling, not seeming to notice her, and breathing shallowly.

Where might she have met this man? He was so familiar. Perhaps she had treated him before.

'Excuse me, sir,' she said.

He moved his head very slowly to focus on her.

'Yes?' he said, in a whisper.

'Are you OK? You don't recognise me, do you? I think I must have treated you in the past. You seem so familiar.'

'No,' he whispered. 'I don't remember you. What's your name?'

'Grace,' she said.

'I'm Robert,' he whispered.

'Good to meet you, Robert. Can I get you anything?'

'I want to write a letter,' he said, then he held up his hand, swaddled in bandages. 'I don't think I'll be doing that for a while myself. Don't suppose you'd write one for me, would you?'

'Of course,' she said. 'Give me an hour to finish my rounds and find a pen and paper, then I'll be back.'

*

There was much discussion about the German Navy, whose sailors had revolted and refused to follow orders. There was already an armistice with Austria, which had opened up a potential new front on the southern German border, and now it seemed impossible that the Germans, left alone, could prevail. All that seemed to remain now was the terms of their surrender.

Captain Couther, a medical officer at the casualty clearing station, was explaining this to Will. In the distance the pop of the guns continued.

'Good news,' said Will. 'It'll be even better if they stop firing shells at us.'

Both men looked around the tent, at all the injured bodies.

'Can't happen a minute too soon,' said Captain Couther.

*

Grace was not supposed to be straining herself, but she was feeling much better, and she was able to do some good here, dressing wounds and reassuring the men. She expected soon to receive her instructions to finally head home for further convalescence. She missed Omelette and knew she would never see her again. But she had been heartened to learn from Jenny that Dominique, the little girl whose leg they had patched up, had been more than happy to adopt her when she had returned with her mother to thank them for her treatment.

The afternoon had worn on until she remembered the man from before. She was so tired and she knew she really did need to sleep, but she didn't think this would take long.

She found him at the same corner of the ward, his eyes open as before, staring at the ceiling.

'I'm so sorry,' she said. 'I was so busy.'

'Don't worry,' he said, his voice still quiet but a shade now above a whisper. 'You have your work cut out for you here.'

'I do,' she smiled. 'But I got your pen and paper. Who are you writing to? A sweetheart back home?'

His eyes seemed to moisten slightly. 'No one like that,' he said. 'Not no more.'

'I'm sorry,' she said.

'*I'm* sorry,' he said. 'I've got a family, even if they don't have a mother. I've not been the best father to them.'

'Now, now. I'm sure that's not true. Is that who we're going to write to now?'

'It is.'

'Ready when you are.' She found a stool and pulled it to the side of the bed, where she took out the paper and balanced it on a clipboard that held his medical notes.

'OK,' he said. 'So: *Dear Clara.*'

She wrote down his words as they followed.

I am in a hospital on the French coast, with injuries that seem to be healing, though they have left me weak. When I am strong enough again

I will be moved, on the train, back to England, and I hope I may be stationed in London so that you and Kitty can come and visit.

The news, from what I hear of it, seems to suggest this may be all over soon, and I hope to God that is right. I am done with this now. I want to be a father again, to Kitty, and to Jack and Will, though they are too old now to need me—

'My God,' said Grace. She reached out and touched his arm to check it was there. She was looking intently at his face, seeing for the first time why it was she had thought she knew him. Then she pulled the letter off the top of the clipboard and looked at the notes below, which named the patient as Robert Burnett. 'My God!' she said. 'My God! I need to get a message sent — I'll be back in a minute!'

Robbie watched the pretty young nurse race away from him, wondering what on earth had just happened.

*

'It's happening,' said Couther to Will, 'it's about to happen.'

They had been up all night tending to a party of twelve soldiers who'd left the frontline and were marching back to billets ready for some rest when they were hit by a long-range German shell, fired over past the reserve line in the middle of the night. It was heart-breaking. A man lay there, sobbing at the death of his friends, with a mangled leg that would most likely need amputating. They had been so close to getting back to safety. So close.

Will hadn't heard a gun fire for a while now.

'Message for Will Burnett,' called the postman, and Will took the letter, delighted to see Grace's handwriting. He put

412

it in his pocket, deciding to save the treat for later, give himself something to look forward to after the misery of dealing with the shell.

'Cheer up,' said the postman. 'Haven't you heard? It's all but over. We won.'

'Go and tell that to the lads in there,' said Will, and he walked back in to deal with them.

*

The strange young nurse returned to Robbie's bed the next morning.

'I'm sorry I ran off yesterday,' she said.

'It's OK,' he said. 'Do you have time to finish the letter?'

'I do,' she said. 'I do. Though I should tell you first that you're supposed to be dead.'

'Oh, I know that, love. I've wished it a million times, and nearly seen it a number of times. I'm amazed I'm still here.'

'Your family will be too. You see, there was a bit of a mistake somewhere . . .'

*

The postman had been right. The news came down through the lines. No more shooting. War over. Not a shell had been fired since five o'clock that morning. There was still work to do in the tent, and it wasn't hard for Will to keep his elation in check as he helped Captain Couther with the work he was doing, and loaded bodies onto the field ambulances arriving to take them to the hospital.

What if something happened to Grace at this late stage? The Spanish flu was still rampaging through the whole of

Europe. She should have been safe enough where she was, but you never—

He tore open the envelope to find just a few sentences, scrawled in large letters.

Will! I think I have found your father. He is alive and here with me! Come as soon as you can. Love from Grace

*

He took the stairs slowly after the nurse showed him which way to go. Everywhere, people were laughing and joking, buoyed by the news that the war was finally over. He didn't know how to feel. Yes, he did. Scared. That there had been some mistake and the war was going to continue. He felt scared. Scared that the man in this room wouldn't be his father. Scared that it would be him, even more damaged, even more painful to look upon.

He paused outside the door, and when he did he heard a laugh he knew well. Grace's. 'That sounds so like Will,' she said.

Will took a step into the room and there, in the corner, was his father, sitting up and smiling, looking very pale and thin, but alive – and smiling?

He came forward. 'Father?'

Robbie's face fell. 'Son? You're – I barely recognise you. You're so big, so strong-looking.'

'It's me,' said Will. 'You all right? You look like you got banged up a bit.'

'Banged all over this damn country, son. I'm amazed I'm here to tell the tale. Grace told me I was reported dead. I'm so sorry, Will. I'm so sorry.'

'Don't be sorry, Father, it's wonderful news. I can't believe you're alive. But I never got used to the idea that you weren't . . .' Will's voice trailed off and he dabbed his eyes.

He came over and sat on the edge of the bed. His heart thumped and his hands shook. Suddenly, and quite unexpectedly, Robbie reached out and grabbed his wrist.

'I had no idea, you see. I lost my identity tag when I was injured. It seems it was attributed to some other poor fellow who was unable to deny it.'

The two men looked at each other, and then they were silent.

Will wanted to ask, 'Are you feeling better? Do you want to live?' but he couldn't.

Grace stepped in to fill the awkward space in the conversation.

'Your father was telling me about you as a child, Will. Apparently, you fed the ducks with a very fair-minded technique.'

'I don't remember,' said Will, looking up at his father.

'No?' he said. 'I remember the last time we walked out with your mother. Down to Strand-on-the-Green. You counted the ducks and tore the bread into equal-sized pieces. Oh, it was funny.'

He was smiling. It was a smile that contained a lot of pain, but there was happiness in there too.

'Oh, Dad,' said Will. 'I'm so glad you're here. I'm so glad we found you.'

72

In London, the news filtered through over the course of the morning and it was not until the afternoon that the ceasefire reached the papers. Now the streets were thronging with people; soldiers in uniform were mobbed by gangs of women; everyone was outside and happy and joyful. Crowds of people were leaving Turnham Green to head into town and celebrate in the public squares and outside Buckingham Palace.

Clara was outside with Kitty, trying to believe everything was as good as it seemed. What a time they'd had with the post recently. First Will informing Clara that he was going to ask for Grace's hand in marriage. Then the shattering letter about Robbie's death that arrived only a day before Will wrote to tell them about Grace's injuries. Then the gradual good news about Grace's recovery, which allowed a ray of sunshine into her grief about her brother. And then the equally shattering news that Robbie was alive after all! A mix-up over a mistaken identity or some such. He was on his way back any day now to recuperate further in a hospital in London. His letter to her had glimpses of the boy she had grown up with: amazed by life, hungry for news, keen to see what was going to happen.

'Are they really coming home then, Clara?' asked Kitty.

'They really are.'

'And everyone will live here again?'

'I'm not sure about that, Kitty, but you'll certainly get to see everyone a lot more.'

Clara thought that Jack would have other plans now, which she wasn't sure she wanted to know about. And Will would want to live with Grace. But Robbie, hopefully Robbie would return and be a father to his daughter while she was still a child. Those boys were children no longer.

Next door, Jim and Sally Wilson were standing on their doorstep. Sally had persuaded Jim into his uniform but he looked uncomfortable wearing it. Someone let off a firework in the distance and Clara watched him flinch and look wildly around him before his wife calmed him.

'Thank you, Jim,' she called out. 'Thank you for what you did out there.'

He looked at her and tried to smile. Sally led him back inside.

Was this what Robbie would be like now? she wondered. Robbie, with his three wound stripes and his medal awarded for bravery? She hoped not.

And what of Jack? What harm lay beneath the slick charm of his presentation? Time would tell.

Will, she worried less about. Though was that fair? Didn't he have as much right to be affected by this as the other men in the family? After all, he was the youngest. He had Grace though, thankfully. She would look after him, and he would look after her.

There was much to worry about but for now it was time to put this aside and celebrate.

'What do you say we go into town?' said Clara to Kitty. 'Join in the fun?'

'Can we, Aunt Clara? Can we?'

Clara leaned down and picked her up and hugged her to

her chest, though of course Kitty was far too old for this and let her know about it by scrunching up her eyes and looking at her indignantly. 'Come on,' Clara said. 'Let's go and join in.'

73

Six weeks after the Armistice was declared, the London train pulled into the station at Cheltenham. The atmosphere was noticeably different from the last time Will and Grace had made this journey. Gone were the blackout blinds on the train windows and so were the Ministry of Defence signs. Decorations hung from the rafters of the platforms and sparkling Christmas trees in wooden planters adorned the walkways, surrounded by poinsettias, snowy chrysanthemums, white freesias and festive tulips. Even the guard had a joke and a smile to share as he held the carriage door open for Grace to descend.

Dorothy and Arthur were already there on the platform, and Dorothy raced up to both of them and hugged them for what seemed like an eternity. When she finally released them, she saw Arthur had tears in his eyes to match hers.

'I'm not usually given to such public displays of sentiment,' he said, 'but I thought on this occasion I might make an exception.'

'It's wonderful to see you, sir,' said Will. 'And you too, Mrs Tustin-Pennington.'

'My name is Arthur, Will. And from now on, given you're our son-in-law, we will just be Arthur and Dorothy.'

Grace was crying now, too. 'Come on. Let's get home,' she said. 'We've got so much to tell you.'

As they approached Bishop's Cleeve, Amy ran out to meet them, wearing what was obviously one of her latest fashion creations — a dress with a noticeably shorter, fuller skirt — but Grace barely had time to examine it before she was enveloped in her sister's breathless embrace.

'It's so good to see you, Grace. We've all been so worried about you. Both of you. And your injury. And your wedding! I want to hear everything about it, with nothing left out, and then I'll tell you all about my new fashion business and what every girl about town will be wearing next spring.'

Grace looked at Will over Amy's shoulder and winked at him. Ladies' contemporary fashion might be her sister's raison d'être but it was way down the list of her own priorities. She and her sister were poles apart in terms of personality and passions, but they were still very fond of one another.

'Hey!' yelled Fitzwilliam behind them as he came down the stone steps. 'Where have you been for the last two years? How very rude of you to avoid us for so long.'

'I've missed you too, Fitzy. How have you been?'

'I'm OK. Still a bit short of puff but I probably always will be. Can still beat Amy in a foot race though. But that's not saying much.'

'I'd like to see you try,' said Amy.

'I've never seen you run at all, come to think of it. So, I wouldn't have to try.'

Grace was laughing now and gave Fitzy a hug.

'Let's go in,' she said. 'I want to hear all the news from both of you and what's been going on at Bishop's Cleeve.'

*

Dorothy had spent the last few days making sure that the Christmas lunch would be a feast to remember. Despite widespread rationing and the limited choice of produce available, it was surprising what could be obtained locally in return for turkeys, geese or mutton from the estate. She was determined that these two heroes returning victoriously from the war would want for nothing. Arthur had spent his time constructively, popping downstairs to his wine cellar, and now one empty bottle of Dom Perignon and one of a vintage Château Lafite-Rothschild stood in the middle of the immaculately laid table.

Amy had not been able to contain her excitement about the emerging haute couture and was regaling them about the trip to the fashion houses of Paris and Milan she was planning for the spring.

'We've already seen shorter, fuller skirts supported by petticoats and hoops. Now it's all about rayon or silk dance dresses and day dresses — with long narrow sleeves, bright colours and sashes with big pockets and contrasting buttons. You'd look great in a super-skinny jazz suit, Will, they're all the rage for young men getting back into civvy life in good physical shape. But plenty of colour, Grace. Forget the drab grey conservative attire of the past. It's all going to be about blues, greens, browns and burgundy in the winter and pink, lavender, white and light blue to cheer the spirits in the spring and summer.'

Everyone around the table listened patiently, mesmerised not so much by the content of what Amy was saying but more by her passion and enthusiasm.

Grace smiled along with the rest of them and found it quite lovely to hear about these frivolous things that had been so far from her mind these past few years. Yet, she could not help thinking about the contrast of this environment to the reality of so many ordinary people who had sacrificed so much and had been left with so little. Fashion had had no place in her life or many women's for so long.

She thought of the so-called 'slumber suits' or onesies some women had worn in London in case of Zeppelin or aircraft raids. She thought of the reports of people who had been found in the aftermath of bombing raids with whatever clothes they had been wearing physically blasted from their bodies. It was less than six months ago that the last of the fifty-one airship raids on the British Isles had dropped its wretched bombs.

'I know what you're thinking, Grace,' said Amy, who had noticed her frown. 'This is no time for dressing up and making merry. But it is, don't you see? People are tired of war and privations. There is always a time for fashion. Aren't many military uniforms tailored to make statements of some kind?'

A memory surprised Grace, of Viscount Xavier Moreau, the debonair French cavalry officer who had proudly worn the ridiculously ostentatious bright red-and-blue ensemble of his cavalry unit and who had died in her care.

'Of course, the war will have made a difference. There will be calmer, simpler styles now. Rather shapeless shift dresses that slip over the head with minimal fuss or fastenings. There is a dressmaker in London called Elspeth Phelps and she's written about this. War has made women think about life, she says. Clothes will be simpler, more functional and practical. But even in the bleakest of times, women — well, women like me, at any rate — will always want to look good. Bombing raids or not.'

'Heaven forbid you'd ever be whisked off to hospital in anything but your Sunday best.'

'It's true, Grace. One fashion editor recently wrote an

article raving about her new black silk pyjamas. She said she almost hoped there would be a Zep scare just so people could see her in them. She didn't want anyone to be killed, though.'

'Well, that's decent of her,' said Arthur. 'How very thoughtful.'

'Daddy, I'm just saying. People need to be cheered up. Fancy clothes help.'

'She's right in a way, Father,' said Grace. 'Traditional values and roles have changed a lot in the war. Plainer and shabbier clothes will be popular, even with the aristocracy.'

'I've only really seen Grace in one beautiful dress,' said Will. 'Her wedding dress. Your wedding dress too, Dorothy. I wish you could have been there. She looked magnificent in it.'

'I'm so glad it fitted. And that it arrived,' said Dorothy, smiling.

'So, tell us about the wedding,' said Amy.

'All in good time,' said Will. 'What about you, Fitzwilliam? What have you been up to?'

There was the sound of scraping knives and forks on plates.

'Not enough. I tried the medical a second time when conscription came in. But my heart still wasn't strong enough.'

'Your emotional heart is strong, Fitzy,' said Arthur. 'And your spirit is even stronger. And you will serve your country one day, I have no doubt. But using your brain rather than armaments, I imagine. That's just as important.'

'It might be more important,' said Will, looking at Arthur. 'Good leaders and tacticians win wars and save the lives of countless able-bodied soldiers and civilians, no matter how brave and heavily armed they are.'

'And others use their brains to avoid wars in the first

place,' said Arthur, 'and I think one day you'll be doing what I'm trying to do now. Lobbying parliament to make sure all of this never happens again.'

'I'll do my best, Father.'

'I know you will.'

Grace peered out of the window at the formal gardens, the sweeping grounds and the forest of trees beyond them. How she had missed this peaceful place these past four years.

'What of the estate, Father, and what about the two of you?' she asked.

'We are fine. We've been fine. Just worried sick about all of you,' said Arthur. 'After losing Charles, well, we went into a bit of a decline.' He sipped his champagne.

'Dear Charles,' said Grace. 'What a void he's left. I'm so glad you agreed with my thoughts about his grave.'

'The place where he lies sounds blessed,' said Dorothy. 'You said it is beautiful and serene, so why disturb it?'

Grace had found it again, as she'd promised him she would – the majestic oak with his initials carved on it, and at the foot of the grave a sturdy little sapling stretching eagerly towards the heavens. Will had held her hand as she'd shed a tear and stood there considering the offer that had come to move him to the military cemetery at Chapelle Blanchette. It was only a stone's throw from where he already was. But it seemed peaceful and private there, under the tree, and when she looked up its branches reached to the sky. The sky he'd so loved.

'That's right. I really thought it was best to leave him.'

'We agree,' said Arthur. 'Your mother and I feel that if it was us, it is what we would want and what Charles would choose for himself. With your guidance, Grace, we can even visit, as soon as we get the chance.'

'Of course.'

A long pause followed, as they chewed and sipped, during which time Arthur reflected on how much less of an inveterate worrier his wife had become. Paradoxically, the crushing blow of losing Charles had shifted other worries and foibles onto a more rational plane for her. She'd still worried about the other children, of course, and would until they were finally safe home, but as for the small and inconsequential things – they were no longer a source of constant angst.

'As for the estate, it's a little run down. We haven't had the manpower, but hopefully now we can rebuild.'

'We lost poor Douglas, unfortunately. Tuberculosis.'

Will frowned. Yet another fatal infection. It seemed to have become the bane of his life. Surely, with the considerable medical advances made during the war, prospects to prevent or cure such diseases should be just around the corner?

Arthur continued. 'And we've no horses, of course. The Army took the lot. But we can start again.'

'The loss of so many horses broke my heart,' said Grace. 'Eight million, they say, if you include the donkeys and mules used by both sides. They lost seven thousand at Verdun in a single day, especially Clydesdale horses. I saw so many carcasses. I even called in to a veterinary hospital once up near Cambrai. Some had been shot, some gassed, some were just exhausted or ill. They managed to save about a quarter of them, though only to return them to duty.'

Indeed, they had been deemed so precious that if a soldier's horse was killed or died, he was instructed to cut off one of its hooves to show his commanding officer – to prove he hadn't just been separated from his horse, which might then

425

be useful to the enemy. One horse died for every soldier killed throughout the war.

'Let's build our stock again then and make them the best-looked-after horses in England,' said Arthur.

'I hope you can, Father, that would make me so happy.'

'What of your other sons?' asked Will.

'Rupert is still away at sea,' said Arthur, 'and then there's all sorts of shenanigans going on, even after the Armistice. The U-boats were still sinking our ships a few days before it and, had it not been for the German mutiny in Kiel, they'd have launched that final suicide attack on our Navy that had been ordered in October. Their fleet is currently interned at Scapa Flow and I'm not betting on that little caper ending well, either. I just hope Rupert doesn't get caught up in it.'

'And James is well,' said Dorothy, 'and is returning with his unit from Serbia next month. Henry is busy dealing with prisoners of war in Belgium but has been promised leave in March. Thank God they are both unharmed,' she said with a mixture of pride and relief.

'And you, Mother?'

'Looking after your father. It's a full-time job these days,' she teased, holding her fork aloft with a piece of potato. 'We've looked after each other, to be fair, with Amy and Fitzy by our side. It's very exhausting to feel so helpless. To think of the little things I used to worry about! Your return has given us a new lease of life.'

'Your family have done you proud, Arthur. Every one of them. And I feel honoured to be a part of it now,' said Will.

'And we are as proud of you as we are of Grace. But you are stationed back in England now, I believe. What are your plans?'

'The RAMC have offered me an apprenticeship at the Queen Mary Convalescent Auxiliary Hospital. In Roehampton.'

'I've not heard of it.'

'I think you'll approve, sir, because of your own artificial leg. Two hundred years ago, it was a stately home. In 1915, it was bought by a shipping magnate of Ellerman's Wilson Line who placed it at the government's disposal for the war effort. They billeted soldiers there. But during the war around a quarter of a million men had suffered total or partial limb amputations as a result of their wounds. A certain lady called Mrs Holford had come across a soldier who'd lost both arms that year and was so moved by his predicament she vowed to start a hospital where those unfortunate enough to lose a limb could be fitted with the best possible artificial limbs that human science could devise.'

'She must've had help.'

'She did. With VIP supporters to fundraise and Queen Mary herself as patron she opened the hospital within five months and last year 11,000 patients were treated there.'

'Maybe I should go there myself,' said Arthur, patting his metal leg. 'Get an upgrade over this rusty old contraption.'

'Why not? I can't wait to start, Arthur. It's become known as the human repair factory. Men are not only taught to walk again but to take on many other aspects of civilian life such as carpentry skills and playing billiards.'

'There are 900 beds there now, Father, and a waiting list of more than 4000 patients,' added Grace. 'And guess what?'

'What?'

'I'm going to be working there too. With the QAIMNS. I applied for a job there and one of the matrons I'd worked under in Flanders put in a good word for me, and with so much work to be done I was accepted.'

'That's astonishing,' said Dorothy.

'I was the most astonished, believe me. The sister I'm talking about was the most fearsome and formidable person I've ever worked with. Sister MacCailein. We used to call her the whispering witch. And then she goes and surprises me.'

'You must've won her over,' said Dorothy. 'And anyway, they would be mad not to have you.'

'Better still, we found some married accommodation locally which, although cramped and sparsely furnished, is clean and private with a lovely view over Richmond Park.'

'And with Kitty and Clara, as well as my father, only two short bus rides away, we can visit them any time we like.'

'That's wonderful news. I'm very pleased for both of you. So will you now be pursuing that medical career we talked about, Will?'

'I'm certainly going to try, sir. But, realistically, there are many hurdles to overcome as you know.'

'And I want to help you jump them.'

'I'm already embarrassed enough to be in your debt for Grace's beautiful wedding ring. I can't and I won't ask any more of you.'

'We'll see about that. What you're going to be doing next will serve you in very good stead. It's an excellent stepping stone towards your future career. Which field of medicine interests you most?' asked Arthur. The fire crackled in the grate.

'There's a question,' replied Will, fleetingly thinking about his own mother's death from childbed fever and the vast numbers of soldiers who had died from gas gangrene or sepsis. 'I don't know if it would be in the field of infection, in the study of germs and contagion, or in orthopaedics, reconstructive surgery, anaesthetics or even psychiatry.

Because when I think of my friend,' he shook his head, 'when I think of my friend Captain Daniels whose shell shock . . .'

'Will?' interrupted Grace, sensing his distress.

Will paused for a moment and collected himself.

'I've got this chance at the convalescent hospital and I'm going to give it my all.'

'Whichever path you choose to follow, Will, I have no doubt you'll make a damn good fist of it. You're still young but you've already achieved so much.'

'Thank you, Arthur. I'll certainly give it my best shot.'

He had never forgotten the pompous and arrogant medically trained major who had sentenced Captain Daniels to death and who had cruelly held off telling Will that Daniels had already been executed as Will was trying to make a case for him.

'First, though, I'll have to overcome a certain prejudice within medical circles when it comes to admitting people like me into medical training.'

'But, as Grace said,' chimed in Dorothy, 'times are changing and the barriers to social mobility are crumbling.'

'And in my opinion,' said Arthur, 'after everything you've been through and the hard-earned experience you have already gained, you must already know ten times more than those quacks and charlatans in Wimpole and Harley Street.'

Will grinned. 'Unfortunately, it would appear that practical experience still takes a back seat to academic qualifications.'

'Well, let's make sure you get those qualifications. I know a few people at the Worshipful Society of Apothecaries and I daresay the Tustin-Pennington name and a select cohort of my grandee friends could ruffle a few feathers at the General Medical Council as well.' Arthur lifted his glass and held it in front of him. 'Time to toast the newlyweds, I think,' he said. 'To Will and Grace. Here's to a lifetime of living, loving and laughing together.'

'Wait,' said Grace. 'Since we are all here, I have one other bit of news.'

'What's that?' said Dorothy.

They all placed down their cutlery and glasses, sensing the importance.

'I'm expecting a baby. In the summer.'

Everyone around the table except Will looked dumbstruck.

'Well, you didn't waste any time,' said Amy.

Grace was overwhelmed by the excitement and joy around the lunch table as Arthur promptly popped open another bottle of Dom Perignon. At first, Dorothy was overcome with happiness. She knew Grace had been warned that her fertility might have been affected by her abdominal surgery in France, and had harboured the fear that she might have to rely on Amy and her sons' future wives to provide her with the grandchildren she craved to have.

Now, Dorothy, whose capacity to worry about things had been only slightly reduced, began to fret about whether her daughter would be able to safely carry the pregnancy to term.

Fitzwilliam was thrilled to think he would soon be an uncle, and Amy was still trying to get over the fact that her tomboy sister was married and pregnant and shortly going to be a mother.

As they sat again after the hugging and fussing, they pressed Grace to reveal more about her experiences in the war. There was so much to tell, and Grace was not sure where to start. There were plenty of servicemen and women who, like Robbie after his traumatic bereavement, could not bring themselves to talk about their loss.

For many, the horror and hell was too awful to relate. It was still raw, and distressing to remember. Many would likely suffer nightmares and harrowing flashbacks for the rest of their days. But Grace had had the benefit of Will, with whom she could share her emotions. And vice versa. They had supported each other, imploring one another to share the day's distressing events, and had cried on each other's shoulders. It had been a regular catharsis, a necessary outlet for the immense anger and sadness that arose from relentlessly witnessing the pitiful consequences of modern warfare. Their companionship and love had kept them sane. Grace was not ready to tell the rest of the family any gory details, especially not with Amy and her mother there, so she began by telling them about her first few days in Belgium and the role of the cavalry and the horses. She described the ebb and flow of the war and the characters she came across and, as she did, Will found himself drifting off into private reminiscences of his own.

He looked around the room. As the flickering lights of the roaring fire played across their faces, he could not help thinking about how lucky they were. Just a few short months ago, the outcome of the war and all their futures remained wholly uncertain and precarious. Now the war was over and a period of peace, optimism and renaissance beckoned. Kitty had survived the terrible influenza pandemic, which still raged in some of the remote parts of the world but at least showed signs of finally abating. The soothsayers and religious fanatics who had claimed it was some kind of divine retribution from God had been proved wrong. So had some of the soldiers of both armies who had feared at first that it must have been a new and terrible form of biological warfare.

Grace was expecting a baby and his father Robbie had

somehow survived and had miraculously rediscovered something of his appetite for life. He was back from the dead in more ways than one. Soon he'd be demobilised and sent back home. Even more encouragingly, he said he could hardly wait. Jack, although still slightly handicapped by his stiff shoulder and hip, was otherwise well and there were encouraging signs that he might be becoming more responsible, more concerned with planning for his future. He was currently earning a few extra bob over in France helping the engineers with the clear-up and would soon be back in Blighty. Yes, Will thought, many things were looking up.

Yet he could not help looking back at these past years and reflecting on the dreadful cost of it all.

Twenty-five million people had lost their lives as a result of hostilities and millions more had lost their homes and livelihoods. Twice as many looked likely to have perished from the Spanish flu – 200,000 in Britain alone – including Jack's best mate Trevor and several of Grace's nursing friends.

His dear friend Arup, who had proved to be one of the bravest men there, who had been constantly discriminated against because of the colour of his skin or accused of cowardice because he would not carry a gun and 'fight', had died trying to save the lives of others. At the same time, Grace had been so badly injured, and before that her older brother Charles had made the ultimate sacrifice, shot down in his biplane over northern France.

Captain Jacob Daniels was one of the most courageous and honourable men that Will would ever have the privilege of knowing. He had saved Will's life, as well as many others, had served his country faithfully in many different theatres of war and been twice decorated for it – and he had been shot by firing squad for desertion. His only crime, Will knew, had been to become a victim of shell shock, which the Army — either through ignorance or design — had continually failed to recognise. It caused Will acute pain to think of it. Thousands of other men were wallowing in sanatoriums even now across the country with similar symptoms and would never fully recover or even receive a military pension because of them. Tens of thousands had been left crippled or maimed through injury and some of them hideously disfigured, blinded or scarred with no future prospects of employment or marriage.

Here at home, inflation was running out of control. The value of the pound had fallen by sixty per cent. Abroad, drastic political, social and cultural change was occurring with the issue of Home Rule in Ireland growing and with the Russian Revolution.

Sometimes it surprised Will that there was anyone left alive at all. International boundaries were still being disputed all over Europe and whole populations and ethnic groups were being uprooted, dispossessed and displaced. The Allies' latest concern was that Germany might be overrun by communists while at the same time the terms of the Armistice were still being bitterly disputed.

'Will?' interrupted Grace. 'Are you still with us?'

'I'm sorry, I was miles away.'

'What were you thinking about?'

Will looked around the table at their expectant and optimistic faces. It was the first time they had gathered here together for two long years. The decorations on the ten-foot-high Christmas tree in the corner of the room sparkled in the fire-light. A stack of carefully wrapped presents was piled high beneath it. It did not seem appropriate right now to share his rather dismal and gloomy thoughts.

'I was thinking about the future,' he lied. 'What good might come from the war.'

'I'd like to hear that. I need to, I think,' said Grace.

'Me too,' said Arthur.

Will paused a moment to collect his thoughts.

'You know yourselves about the risks that so many men and women took and the sacrifices they made. The heroism and courage. The patriotism and comradeship. It's inspiring. I think the ordinary man — of the lower ranks, if you like — who gave everything to their country will win a newfound respect. And better individual rights and pensions, I hope. I also hope that the independence for India which my friend Arup and his compatriots fought so hard for is quickly granted.'

He smiled and turned to Grace.

'And now that women have shown what they can do, and do so well, they should be given the vote and command the equality they so richly deserve.'

'I hadn't thought of that,' said Arthur, 'but it is difficult to disagree with you.'

Arthur stood up, went over to the sideboard and picked up a half-full bottle of Napoleon brandy.

'I was also thinking about how, with every war, comes the development of more devastating weaponry and the capacity to maim and kill men in even greater numbers. But it also brings about vastly improved medical treatments and techniques. At the beginning of the war, most men died of infection. At the end most survived it. For the first time, this was a war where more men died of their injuries than from disease. We had blood transfusions for the first time, mobile X-ray units, we carried out surgery nearer to the frontline and had much better organisation.

But there is far more that we can do, and I want to be involved in that future.'

'I do believe you and Grace together could achieve almost anything,' said Dorothy.

'Well, I'll drink to that,' added Grace, taking the brandy bottle from her father's hand and pouring a generous two fingers of the golden liquid into his and Will's glasses.

'A toast,' she said, picking up her own modest glass of mineral water. 'To the future Dr William Burnett.'

The two men smiled, raised their glasses and chinked them together.

'To Dr William Burnett,' came the chorus around them.

74

Picardy

Jürgen Altmann had taken a seat next to the train carriage window for a good reason. He had become increasingly conscious of the ugly deformity disfiguring the left side of his face, and he wanted to hide it. He looked at his own reflection in the glass with despair. The two livid scars continued to contract and were pulling his lower lip even further downwards towards his chin, into a hideous snarling grimace. When people looked at him, he saw the brief but poorly disguised reaction of horror in their eyes. He had become a circus freak.

It had been a humiliation to have been superficially wounded and captured during the last throes of the futile final offensive of the war. He had found himself in an Allied hospital in Boulogne after having only just gone back to the fight after recovering in the German hospital from the Spanish flu. Thank God he was now homeward bound. In the Allied hospital he'd bitterly resented being labelled a prisoner of war and imprisoned in his dormitory ward along with so many of his comrades. If he could call them that. What lily-livered spineless chicken hearts they all were. Laughing and joking, full of joie de vivre, and fraternising with the doctors and nurses and even the patients in the other wards who recently had been fighting against them. Where was their shame?

For a strong leader of men like him it was nothing but a reprehensible demonstration of resignation and submissiveness. He'd looked around with utter disgust and the strongest sense of betrayal at their happy faces and excited body language, their delight at their country's defeat. How could they react like this to such a humbling and ignominious loss of face?

A loss of face. What a bitter irony, he thought. The excruciating stabs of pain he suffered behind the scar tissue constantly reminded him of the sacrifice he had personally made for the cause.

The scars were horrible. Two jagged, zigzag, sinewy cords of flesh: one running from the corner of his mouth to halfway up his cheek and the other cleaving his lower lip and tugging it southwards towards his chin, exposing the lower teeth on that side. The injury had cut through the muscles around the circumference of his mouth, making it impossible to fully purse his lips, so he constantly had to dab the saliva that would collect and dribble away. If only he had seen one of his own doctors immediately after the injury. Even a relatively young and inexperienced doctor in the German Army should have been able to clean and tidy up the wound straightaway and stitch it up neatly. The result would have been a tidier, thin line and because of the rich blood supply in that area he'd have a fully healed and functioning lower lip.

But he had not been able to present himself for immediate treatment after the trauma. Fleeing the scene of his attempted rape of the young British nurse when the shell exploded was one thing, but abandoning the men under his command who were being slaughtered in the very same trench in which he had hidden was quite another. He had waited, delayed, and bided his time as the fighting raged around him. He had kept his head down, stayed quiet and licked his wounds. It was a full three days later, having aimlessly wandered about to kill more time and ensure that none of his men had survived to testify to his disappearance, that he staggered into the military hospital behind his own lines and related his made-up story of heroism. He did not know that would be the first of several hospital stays.

The wound was nasty, the German doctor had said. Very ragged and torn. Not a clean, tidy laceration at all. Furthermore, the edges were contused and swollen. Possibly infected. It would be difficult and potentially dangerous to suture them without removing and debriding some of the dead tissue first. Regrettably, this would necessitate extending and widening the gap, resulting in less scarring but greater visible stretching of the facial skin and lips as it healed. The missing and broken teeth were the least of his problems.

At the time, he had cursed his bad luck. He had always considered himself classically good-looking, and this was a blow with which he would find it difficult to come to terms.

As the scar tissue shrank and contracted the visible disfigurement was becoming even more obvious and it was hurtful when people he turned to talk to recoiled in surprise. Worse still, just recently, the scar tissue had started to bubble up and expand as if it had a life of its own and was growing. In a way it was, the English doctors had told him, when he'd been in the Allied hospital. They had explained to him that he was developing something called keloid scarring, a well-documented inflammatory reaction where an overexuberant healing process resulted in further unsightly and irregular lumps and knurls. What glee and satisfaction it must have given them to have to tell him that, he imagined.

And no, they had said, there was no therapeutic treatment available to remedy the condition, only soothing creams and ointments to prevent the skin drying out and cracking.

But Jürgen Altmann could not be soothed. Certainly not by any mere balm or unguent. His mind was as lacerated and damaged as his face and within it the seeds of bitterness, resentment and hatred were growing like a malignant tumour.

Through the train window, he looked out east towards his motherland and across the ravaged landscape that he and his comrades had so very recently come within an ace of conquering. 'Celebrate your victory: it will be short lived,' he muttered. 'Germany will soon rise up stronger than ever and crush you.'

The horizon was dark and beyond it in Russia a monumental revolution had taken place. Another revolution would now take place in Germany, he promised himself. To overthrow the Kaiser and replace him with a stronger leader. Those pathetic politicians Erzberger and Von Hindenburg had capitulated to Foch and turned over their entire arsenal. How would his loyal fellow compatriots in Alsace-Lorraine feel now, living with the indignity of Allied forces occupying their homeland along the banks of the Rhine? Those weak and cowardly negotiators responsible for agreeing to such terms should be hunted down and shot. He had a mind to do it himself.

They needed strong and powerful leaders. Leaders who could mobilise his countrymen left starving at the hands of the British naval blockade. To resist the humiliation of defeat, the dismantling of the once mighty German Army, the surrendering of the merchant and naval fleet, and the undoubtedly unfair terms of the Armistice. Leaders who would rebuild and regenerate his country and ultimately wreak vengeance on a weak, gloating and complacent foe. He looked again through the window and in the failing light watched the soldiers he could see tidying a bloodied field in the distance.

They might well be content to think that the hostilities of the last four years were finally over. For Jürgen Altmann, they were only just beginning.

*

There were times when Jack sometimes regretted the decisions he made. This was definitely one of them. The financial inducement of an extra two and sixpence a day over and above his Army salary had seemed like a good idea at the time, and since he still had a few months to go before demobilisation he thought he may as well cash in. What a mistake. He would gladly pay the money back to Lord Kitchener himself if only he could get out of it. But with a diminishing number of volunteers for the job and the task in hand nowhere near finished, he was just going to have to get on with it.

It was gruesome, dangerous and distasteful work but as his CO frequently pointed out, someone had to do it.

It would not be so bad were it not for all the oddballs and misfits with whom he found himself working. Many of them had nothing to go back home for and others seemed simply too broken and despondent to even question what they were doing. Jack was desperate now to get back to Blighty and have a blast. Thank God for the little local bistro he had found. Chez Maxime. Cosy. Warm. Well stocked with ale and frequented by the occasional unattached female. The perfect spot to while away the hours and drown your sorrows after a hard day's toil on the fields of Flanders.

'So how was your day?' he asked the soldier sitting across from him, Tyler, who had earlier introduced himself as a Corps burial officer for the 2nd Canadian Division.

'Much like any other lately,' he said. 'Bloody miserable. Horribly macabre. And totally ghoulish. How about yours?'

'Oh, you know. Just another day at the office. A couple of crates of unexploded poison-gas shells A few boxes of live grenades, a stack of Lee-Enfield rifles, and no shortage of assorted ammunition belts for good measure.'

'Well, happy days,' said Tyler, ironically lifting his glass tankard of *bier* and chinking it against Jack's. 'Cheers.'

'I don't know how you do it, mate,' said Jack. 'For every bit of ordnance we come across or dig up and expose, you find a body. I'm not sure which is worse. The risk of getting blown to hell or having a smell of decomposing flesh in your nostrils for the rest of your life.'

'It's got to be done though, Jack. There are half a million dead and missing on the battlefields out there and each of them has a right to a decent burial. They all have a mother or a father or a brother or sister. Or a wife and children back home. They can't just be left to rot. The families need closure. If we identify a dead soldier it gives them the certainty of the death. It kills any forlorn hope they might have of their loved one being alive. And hope can be a torment. We can give them comfort that their loved one's remains will be treated with dignity and interred in a sacred, cherished place of remembrance. Families can visit the graves and pay their respects.'

'It's the least we can do, I suppose,' said Jack.

'As far as the military are concerned, it's just pragmatic. They need to account for the missing men and maintain morale. As far as the people back home are concerned, it's a basic human need and part of the grieving process.'

Jack would have preferred to talk about the waitress but he sensed his companion needed to share something, so he carried on. 'It's funny the way people are, isn't it? Standing over the grave where a relative is buried and saying a prayer for them is somehow better than saying one not knowing where they are. As if being physically near to their corpse makes a difference.'

'There might not be much of that relative there, either. We give them this idea that the man they saw off at the station to go and fight for his country months before is lying there under the ground intact, unviolated and sovereign. But it's not like that. I wish it was.'

'What do you mean?'

'A lot of the time I have to pick up the remains of what was once a fine brave man with a shovel. A little pile of bones and maggots which I have to carry over to a common burial place. We find bodies lying submerged in water at the bottom of shell holes and mine craters like the ones you guys created, Jack, but when you touch them they are just a white slimy mess of chalky stuff that falls apart when you move it. I have to search about with my hands trying to find the identification disc or some other physical clue as to who they might be.'

Jack winced. 'You have to do that with your bare hands?'

'Oh no. They are very accommodating with kit,' he laughed sardonically. 'My squad of thirty-two men are supplied with two pairs of rubber gloves, two shovels, stakes to mark out where the bodies are found, canvas and rope to tie up the remains, stretchers, cresol — which is a strong disinfectant — and wire cutters.'

'That's nice of them.'

'We get a small white bag in which to tie any personal effects we might find and if there's an identity disc we securely tie it to the neck of the bag.'

'What do you look for, exactly? Apart from the disc?'

'If the body is relatively well preserved, in an intact uniform, we might look in the pockets and find a pay book, letter or photograph. There might be something personal such as an engraved watch, a ring, a cigarette case or compass. Today we reckon we will be able to trace someone we found by their boots. It was up in the wood between Sainte-Marguerite and Missy. So, this soldier was wearing a pair of boots made by National Co-op Society Ltd Roundwood 1913. We know which regiment was fighting in that sector and we know where he got his boots. That and the engraving on the buttons on his tunic should help us to discover who the poor blighter was.'

'Right,' said Jack.

'The worst time for me, Jack, was before the Graves Registration Commission was set up.'

'When was that?'

'1915. Before that, each division was responsible for clearing the battlefield themselves and burying their own men. Can you imagine? You go into battle, you fight, you risk your life and then at the end of the day and during the night you go back into no man's land to retrieve the comrades you fought alongside. Damn it, some of them were their friends or relatives. Brothers and cousins. The effect on the men was devastating. And then they are expected to go back over the top and fight all over again after witnessing that carnage.'

'How did it change?'

'It got better organised, at least. I was with the Canadian Corps at Vimy Ridge in — what was it? — April last year, and by then a group of us Corps burial officers had been appointed, tasked purely with the job of retrieval and burial. It made it easier for the others. Burying and salvage parties, we were officially known as to the top brass.'

'Body snatchers and cold meat specialists to everyone else.'

'Precisely. We got quite good at it. An experienced CBO could locate a body almost totally buried underground. We learned what the clues were and what to look for.'

'Clues?'

'A rifle sticking out of the ground bearing a helmet, say. Partial remains or equipment on the surface or protruding from the earth. Rat holes. Rats would often bring small bones to the surface to chew on there. Then we look at any grass. Grass turns a vivid blue-green colour and develops broader leaves if there is a body underneath. Any collections of water turn a greenish black or grey colour.'

'God, it must be awful.'

'Yes. It is awful. It's the most ghastly job I can imagine. So depressing for the men. It makes the hardest of them sick on a regular basis. There are so many bodies. It makes us all so nervous and sleepless. Men become irritable and irrational. They get insubordinate and rowdy. It's a release, I suppose. Some drink themselves to oblivion whenever they get the opportunity, and I don't blame them.' Tyler took another few gulps of his beer and replaced the glass on the table again. 'So far I've resisted that.'

'It wouldn't be the end of the world, Tyler. People would understand. But tell me, why do you do it? After three years, surely you've done your bit and could stand back?'

Tyler paused and looked at Jack with a level gaze. 'My brother is out there somewhere. Gabriel.'

'Jesus. I'm sorry, Tyler, I had no idea.'

'Why would you? He is . . . missing. I don't know whether I want to find him or not so, you know . . . I have him in my memory. In my memory he is alive and well, still. In reality . . . who knows?'

Jack caught the waitress's attention and signalled for two more beers and two rums. He briefly thought of his father, Robbie, who had been missing and then dead and then came back to life again. It crossed his mind that he could so easily be lying out there somewhere next to Gabriel. Or Rhys. Or even dead in the ground at home, like poor Trevor. Any of those men could instead be his father, or Will, or him.

'I hope you find peace, Tyler. Whether you find Gabriel or not.'

Two local French girls strolled in arm in arm through the doors of the Bistro Chez Maxime at that moment and walked up to the bar. Normally, Jack would have gone straight over to them and offered to buy them a drink. But, uncharacteristically, he had not even noticed them come in.

'Drink that rum, Tyler boy. I think you bloody need it.'

*

Jack carefully placed the forty-five kg unexploded shell on the pile with all the others. The white star emblem on the outer casing told him exactly what it contained. A very nasty combination of chlorine and phosgene gas. He knew all too well that the bloody thing was lethal, so he handled it gingerly. As he did with all the other bits of ordnance he had been clearing from the fields of Flanders and loading into the wooden crates for removal and safe disposal. Much of it was just lying on the surface and in plain sight but huge quantities still lay buried underground, beneath the soft loam where their trajectories had randomly taken them or in the trenches or dugouts which had collapsed or simply been bulldozed over.

German and Allied artillery had peppered a wide area and enormous swathes of countryside either side of a 450-mile stretch of trenches extending from Switzerland to the North Sea. Jack suspected there must be an enormous tonnage of high explosives and weaponry that would never be recovered and would rise to the surface many years later. It was hazardous and painstaking work, but important because every shell that was missed could be accidentally disturbed and claim innocent lives in the future.

He stood up straight and arched his back to relieve the ache in his muscles born out of the constant bending and lifting. His shoulder and hip ached like hell as well, but the Army doctors had passed him as fit for duty and he was certainly not prepared to let anyone regard him as disabled. He knew there were thousands of men much worse off than himself. There were also others, like his friend Rhys, who had paid the ultimate price and lost their lives. Who was he to complain?

He looked across at another group of soldiers from a different regiment who were working solemnly just fifty yards away. They were one of several exhumation parties charged with the macabre job of finding bodies, identifying them and respectfully transferring them to the sites earmarked to become military memorial cemeteries. He wondered if his new Canadian friend Tyler was among the working party.

His attention was interrupted by a female voice behind him with a distinctly chirpy French accent. Spinning around, he was delighted to see a slim, attractive young woman in a navy-blue dress and a bright red beret set at a jaunty slanted angle on the top of her lovely blonde head. She is cute, he thought. She was carrying a tray with several cups of café au lait and biscuits, which she had brought for the troops. Jack strolled over to her at once.

'*Pour vous*,' she said, smiling.

'Why thank you, mademoiselle,' answered Jack, grinning and then taking the tray from her and setting it down on the wooden crate. He knew his French was terrible, so he did not attempt any. He did not want her to think him foolish or clumsy. 'We should go over there, miss, it's too dangerous here.'

'*Dangereux*?'

'*Oui*. Yes. Very. These bombs are live. Unexploded. *Comprenez*?'

'Ah, *oui*. *Merci*. This is the farm of my father. It is good that you make it safer.'

'It's your family's farm? Do you live here with your husband?' It never took Jack long to cut to the chase.

'*Non, monsieur*, my husband was killed at the beginning of the war.'

Jack's interest perked up further. Not only a young, slim, attractive woman but a woman who had also been widowed these past four years. He studied the distant farmhouse and its broken roof and walls.

'You can't have been living here throughout the war, though?'

'Brest.'

'Breast?' Jack had a one-track mind, and he was aware of it.

'I have just returned from staying with my sister in Brest. It's a city. In Brittany on the coast Atlantique.'

'Ah! Well, I hope we can make your farmland worth coming home for.'

'We are, how you say, *très reconnaissant*. Er, grateful, for all you do. My father, though, he is upset a little. He must give up some land for a big cemetery. So he cannot farm there. But I tell him I think it is OK. Those poor men. They must rest in peace and we owe them so much.'

'We do. We do,' said Jack, looking at her alluring figure. 'What's your name?'

'Amandine. Amandine LeClair. *Et vous*?'

'*Je m'appelle* Jack.'

'Jacques! My husband. His name also was Jacques. Bizarre, *non*?'

'Yes. Quite a coincidence.' Jack could not help thinking about whether he could take Jacques' place in more than just name.

'You must be tired, and your men.'

'They have only just started work,' Jack lied. 'But I've been here all day. What I wouldn't do for a lovely glass of red wine.'

'But I have some, if you'd like?' offered Sylvie. 'In the farmhouse. I also have some bread and camembert. Would you like to join me?'

Jack briefly pretended to consider the welfare of his mates, who he fully intended not to invite along.

'I wouldn't want to put you to any trouble,' Jack lied again.

'*Pas du tout*. Come on. I open a bottle to say thank you.'

She turned, and Jack followed behind her. Her hips swayed tantalisingly as she walked.

When they'd almost arrived at the farmhouse, Jack looked up. The blood-red sun was setting in the west and for the first time in a long while he felt optimistic about the future and glad that the war to end all wars was finally over.

THE END

Author's note

The events described in this book are a reflection of historical fact. Death in childbirth was all too common at the beginning of the last century and, in the absence of antibiotics, infection was rampant and often lethal.

The Great War inflicted terrible injuries on millions of soldiers, more of whom died from the medical complications of their wounds than from the trauma itself. Nurses and surgeons did their level best but aseptic surgery, pain relief and anaesthesia were primitive and risky.

Men and women aged as young as fourteen or fifteen and barely old enough to have left school enlisted in the Army or medical services to help with the war effort, blissfully unaware of the horrors that awaited them.

The life expectancy of a stretcher bearer in 1916 was six weeks. RAMC officers carried arms but could only use them in self-defence. RAMC stretcher bearers were not armed. They were just as brutally exposed to the risks of battle as the fighting troops, and nearly 7000 of them became casualties. Twenty-two million servicemen lost their lives, many of them slaughtered on the killing fields of France, an unreturned army of brave soldiers who sacrificed their lives for their country.

Some were wounded repeatedly but patched up again and again in order to rejoin the fight in the trenches. Some three thousand were convicted by court martial of desertion and given the death sentence. Hundreds suffering shell shock or madness were put in front of a wall and shot by firing squad.

Thousands who considered themselves lucky to have survived the conflict perished within months as a result of the devasting Spanish flu pandemic of 1918, which killed twice as many people as the war itself.

It was supposed to be the war to end all wars. Yet it was not. It merely sowed the seeds of a lasting bitterness and resentment which culminated in an even greater conflagration just over two decades later.

There was no real victor as such. No conqueror in the accepted sense. Except perhaps one. One conqueror of a sort. It was love.

It was love of country that drove men to sacrifice their lives. It was the love of their brothers in arms that gave them the courage to bravely fight together. And when all seemed lost, and their very souls were bereft of hope and pity, it was love of family back home that gave them a reason to carry on.

For Grace and for Will, teenage heroes in their own right, it was the intense physical and emotional passion of the very first taste of love that kept them sane and alive.

Frontline is their story.

Acknowledgements

Fighting a pandemic is like fighting a world war on many different fronts. First comes the threat, then comes the onslaught – closely followed by death and destruction and desperate, life-saving resistance. One country after another is dragged into the affair and the consequences of the crisis bring out both the worst and the best in people.

Whilst commenting daily in the media throughout 2020 and 2021 on the Covid-19 situation, it struck me how many parallels there are between the two types of conflict and how much civilisation and survival depend on the humanity, courage, altruism and professionalism of people working on the frontline. So, firstly, I would like to acknowledge the astonishing and selfless work of everyone involved in health and social care both here in the UK and throughout the world in giving me the inspiration to write my debut novel, *Frontline*, set during the time of World War I and the Spanish flu of 1918 when both tragic events occurred simultaneously.

I was also inspired by my grandfather, William Jones, who fought on the Western Front with the Queen's Westminster Rifles, where he was wounded and returned to the battlefield three times. I am in awe of him and his entire generation, many of whom made the ultimate sacrifice and never returned home.

I would like to thank my literary agent, Kerr MacRae, for suggesting the idea of a series of novels to me in the first place and for his intelligent guidance and support from the outset. For me, writing *Frontline* has proved a great antidote to the relentless and sometimes harrowing focus on public health messaging during the Covid-19 pandemic and I have learnt a huge amount during its creation.

I have been constantly bolstered by the encouragement and enthusiasm of my editorial team at Welbeck and would especially like to thank Luke Brown, Angela Meyer, Jon Elek, James Horobin, Rosa Schierenberg, Alexandra Allden, Nico Poilblanc, Rob Cox, Maddie Dunne Kirby, Angie Willocks, Carrie-Ann Pitt, Sophie Leeds, Annabel Robinson and Sam Matthews.

I would like to thank my wife, Dee, for forgiving me my preoccupation with the book and also my mother Noreen for her enduring wisdom, experience and support.

My thanks to Kim Chapman, my hard-working and long-suffering agent and PA for juggling my diary, and to Rob Cremin, India Achilles and Jane Manley for their much appreciated behind-the-scenes assistance.

I have drawn on various sources of research for historical detail but would especially like to critically praise Gina Kolata's excellent book *Flu: The Story of the Great Influenza Pandemic of 1918 and the Search for the Virus That Caused It* (Macmillan, 1999), *True World War I Stories* (Robinson, 1999) and Charles Horton's *Stretcher-Bearer: Fighting for Life in the Trenches*, edited by Dale le Vack (Lion, 2013).

WELBECK

PUBLISHING GROUP

Love books? Join the club.

Sign up and choose your preferred genres to receive tailored news, deals, extracts, author interviews and more about your next favourite read.

From heart-racing thrillers to award-winning historical fiction, through to must-read music tomes, beautiful picture books and delightful gift ideas, Welbeck is proud to publish titles that suit every taste.

bit.ly/welbeckpublishing

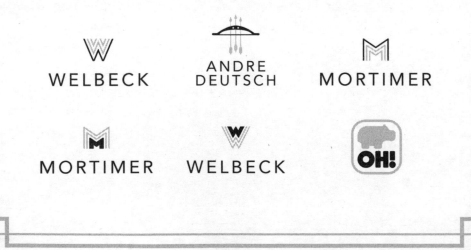